MEDEA

MEDEA

ROSIE
HEWLETT

bantam

TRANSWORLD PUBLISHERS
Penguin Random House, One Embassy Gardens, 8 Viaduct Gardens, London SW11 7BW
www.penguin.co.uk

Transworld is part of the Penguin Random House group of companies
whose addresses can be found at global.penguinrandomhouse.com

Penguin
Random House
UK

First published in Great Britain in 2024 by Bantam
an imprint of Transworld Publishers

A CIP catalogue record for this book
is available from the British Library.

ISBNs
9781787637290 (cased)
9781787637306 (tpb)

Typeset in 10.5/17 pt Fournier Std by Falcon Oast Graphic Art Ltd
Printed and bound by Clays Ltd, Elcograf S.p.A.

The authorized representative in the EEA is Penguin Random House Ireland,
Morrison Chambers, 32 Nassau Street, Dublin D02 YH68.

Penguin Random House is committed to a sustainable
future for our business, our readers and our planet. This book is
made from Forest Stewardship Council® certified paper.

MIX
Paper | Supporting
responsible forestry
FSC
www.fsc.org
FSC® C018179

1

For all the women who have ever been
called 'too much' or 'not enough'.

When I was a child, I turned my brother into a pig.

I found it amusing, at the time, to watch his bones break and hear the fleshy popping as his muscles and tendons transformed. I giggled when he screamed, as his nose smeared into a snout and a little curly tail sprouted from his swollen, pink behind.

Nobody else laughed.

The slaves wailed when they saw what I'd done; some even fled the palace, never to return. Others fell to their knees, muttering desperate prayers, their implorations shivering on their twisted lips.

When my parents found out, my mother shed tears whilst my father struck my face. A predictable response from both.

'Why did you do this?' he asked.

'Because I can,' I replied.

Apparently, that was the wrong answer.

Though truthful, this was not the only reason for my actions. Apsyrtus was cruel. He tormented my little sister and me, and though I can endure his nastiness, Chalciope is made of softer matter. A harsh word can cut her like a blade, embedding itself beneath her skin and taking root there. She is not built to withstand cruelty. She is like fresh snow, pure and delicate, letting the tiniest speck of dirt stain her. Whilst I am the frozen ground beneath, hard, unyielding.

So, I transformed Apsyrtus into a swine because he acted like one. I believed it a fair sentence and I've always believed in pun-ishment – my father made sure of that. My justice was easy enough to execute, just a simple concoction I peppered over his morning porridge. To Apsyrtus' credit, he somehow sensed my deceit at the second mouthful, attempting to spit out the 'poison'. He was too late, of course. My magic had sunk its teeth into him the moment it passed his.

Nobody else saw the justice in my actions because, to them, Apsyrtus' behaviour was not something to be corrected. He was just 'being a boy' and, apparently, that meant it was in his nature to be cruel. Though that justification has never made sense to me.

After the incident, my father locked me in my chamber, placing two guards on watch outside. At first, I found it quite amusing that my father, Aeetes, the formidable King of Colchis, was afraid of his little, quiet Medea. It was not until later that I discovered this absence of freedom was far from entertaining.

When night fell that day, my father came to my room and told me to undo the spell.

'I do not know how.'

It was the truth, but he beat me like a liar, like I had a secret inside me he was trying to crack from my body. I can still remember the sound of his breathing, those heavy, uneven gasps as he swung his arm back, ready for another blow. They were the same kind of ragged breaths I could hear shuddering through the walls when he was alone with my mother.

Unlike my mother, I never cried when my father hurt me. I think he found this irritating, which is probably why he did it so often. But I've always found tears to be entirely useless. I told this to Chalciope once, when she was sobbing over a dead bird we'd found in the court-yard. She stared at me with wet, sparkling eyes.

'Sometimes you say things that scare me, Medea,' was all she replied.

'Everything scares you,' I said, poking the bird's lifeless body with a stick and prising open its wound. Chalciope screamed for me to stop, but I ignored her and dug the stick in deeper. I wanted to see what was inside.

When my father finally relented and accepted that I did not know how to fix my brother, he turned to other means. A last resort.

My aunt.

I found this a curious turn of events, as I had never met my aunt before.

In Colchis, she was more myth than woman, with a rich tapestry of rumours woven tightly around her name: *Circe*.

I had heard my father banished her years ago; for what, nobody seemed to know. Though this did not stop Pheme, the Goddess of Rumours, from spreading her incendiary touch throughout the land, igniting the legend of my aunt.

There was another name they called her, too, a word the slaves whispered behind cupped hands in their native Colchian tongue. *Witch.* I did not know what it meant as a child, but it was spoken with such venom, I could only assume it was something fascinatingly terrible.

In my head, Circe was some kind of evil monster. Like a winged Fury, hideous and ruthless. I pictured her flying across the land, exacting her cold judgement on unsuspecting mortals. I was deeply captivated by her, or rather, by the potential of who she could be. I suppose you could say she was something of an obsession of mine. My mother did always say I could get fixated on things.

Circe arrived two days after Apsyrtus' transformation, in the dead of night. I can still remember the thrill of fear it sparked within me, when I woke to a dark figure towering over my bed, painted in silvery, moon-cast shadows.

She must've sensed my fear, for Circe pulled back her cloak immediately, revealing a pair of eyes the same shade as my father's, brilliantly golden, and a softly curved smile. Though it was her hair I noted first, cascading into glossy sheets around her shoulders. I had never seen hair so pale and radiant, like sunlight shattered across the clearest water.

I took a moment to soak in her appearance, realizing as I did so that she was undoubtedly the most beautiful thing I had ever seen.

Behind Circe, my father's presence was like a stain against my chamber walls. I remember he wore a face of cold composure that night, trying to mask the fear I had exposed only days before.

'Hello, Medea.' Her voice was strong and commanding, yet lit by a warmth I was immediately drawn to. 'Do you know who I am?'

'A witch.'

The word made my father visibly stiffen as he monitored the silent hallways. But, to my delight, Circe laughed at my response. The sound was sweet and smoky, like burnt honey.

'I prefer the term "sorceress".' Circe's eyes glowed with a bright mischievousness.

'Sorceress.' I repeated the word slowly, drawing out each satisfying drop of sibilance.

'You may leave us now, Aeetes,' Circe instructed my father without looking at him.

A flash of dread cut across his stony mask. 'You cannot—'

'I will take it from here.' Her tone was soft, yet there was an undeniable edge to her words, like a blade wrapped in silken sheets. 'Goodbye, brother.'

My father stared at us, his face twitching as he fought to hold his composure. The King of Colchis was not used to taking orders.

In the silence, I was certain I could hear Apsyrtus' distant squealing from where he was hidden in a makeshift pen within the depths of the palace.

'Well . . . I shall be outside . . . for when I am needed.' My father lifted his chin defiantly, his ego more bruised than my entire body.

'You will not be.' Circe winked at me.

My eyes followed my father out of the room, my mouth hanging slightly open. Never, in all my life, had I seen him obey anyone's command before, let alone a woman's.

'So, Medea, how long have you been studying magic for?' Circe asked once we were alone, sitting down on my bed and folding her long, slender hands neatly into her lap.

'Magic?'

'Why, yes, Medea. How else do you think you turned your brother into a pig?'

I paused. I had not considered the 'how'; all I knew was that I could, so I did.

'I . . . I just mixed some things together . . . plants and roots. That was all.'

Circe leant in close, her warm scent filling my nostrils. '*That* was magic, Medea. Tell me, how old are you?'

'This will be my eighth winter.'

'That is a very advanced spell for your age.' A spark caught in her eyes as she added, 'And, did you know, it is one of my favourites?'

I let her words settle inside me. 'But what is . . . "magic"?'

Circe smiled with a slow, languid curl of her lips. 'Magic is a gift from the goddess Hecate. She is the one who blessed you with this ability.'

'She did?'

'She did. She has chosen you, Medea, and that makes you very special indeed. Do you realize that?'

I twisted my hands nervously in my lap. 'Everyone says there's something wrong with me—'

'People often do not like what they do not understand,' Circe smoothly interrupted. 'But I do not think you should let other people's ignorance get in the way of your own potential . . . do you?'

I felt a smile twitch at my lips as I shook my head.

Her eyes fell to the bruise already blossoming along my jaw. My father usually took care only to hurt me in places that could be covered, but his fury had got the better of him. I still remember the look in Circe's eyes, the quiet rage followed by an eerie stillness that seemed to seep into every inch of her body.

After what felt like a small eternity, she finally spoke again, her voice filled with a warm intensity. 'I am here now, Medea. You are not alone any more.'

From that moment, I was completely hooked.

I had often questioned my father's claim to his divine parentage, his assertions that he was the child of the Sun God, Helios. But seeing Circe, I was now certain she must be descended from the divine, for no mortal could create such perfection.

I had never met a woman like her. She was not weak like my mother, nor sensitive like Chalciope, nor cynical like the slave girls. Circe possessed an effortless, unapologetic confidence I believed only men could exude. Though, unlike my father, she executed it with a quiet self-assuredness. She was utterly captivating.

She was everything I had never realized I wanted to be, until that exact moment. I wanted to climb inside her smile and wear her skin as my own, to harbour that power, radiate the confidence, master her poise. It felt as if I had been stumbling in the dark my entire life, and

Helios' light had suddenly fallen across my path, allowing me finally to know exactly where I was going, who I was meant to be . . .

I suppose that is what made her abandonment all the more painful.

'Can you do nothing right, Medea?' My brother's scornful voice splinters my thoughts, pulling me back from the edges of my memories. I find I spend most of my time lingering in the past, thinking of Circe.

Her absence is a tangible emptiness inside me.

I readjust my focus on the loom, my eyes running over the tangled mess of threads. There is so much potential suspended between these strands and yet, beneath my fingers, it is just a muddle of knots, a mess my mother will have to unpick and amend, weaving over my mistakes as if they had never happened.

'It's embarrassing,' Apsyrtus continues, plucking at one of the threads.

Often, I wish Circe had never reversed my spell. He was far more pleasant as a swine.

Behind Apsyrtus, my sister hovers in the doorway like a flickering shadow. Our eyes meet and a nervous smile twitches at her lips.

'Father has summoned you.' My brother towers over me obnoxiously. He smells musty, like horses and dried sweat.

'I was just thinking about the time I turned you into a pig, brother,' I say, letting his scathing gaze burn into me, yet feeling nothing. 'That was . . . how long ago now? Nine winters, I think. Do you remember?'

His eyes flash with a dark shame that quickly thickens to anger. He reminds me so much of my father when he is angry, when that same ugliness knots across his face, carving deep lines into his forehead. I believe rage ages people beyond their years, which is why Apsyrtus looks so weathered despite only being two winters older than I.

He strikes my face with an open palm. I hear Chalciope yelp softly as the pain sparks along my nose, making my eyes water. I hold myself still for a moment, letting the sting settle as a familiar feeling stirs in my veins. *Your magic*, Circe's voice glows inside my mind, *listen to it, Medea.*

I smile at the ground.

'You are forbidden to speak of your *curse*.' Apsyrtus spits the word with such venom.

'I know. Father has made that clear enough.' I lock my gaze into his. 'But I simply cannot stop thinking about how adorable your little curly tail was.'

'*Medea*,' Chalciope gasps.

She is still afraid of the power Apsyrtus boasts, for she has not yet realized how hollow it is. But I am not so naive. I can see through my brother's act; I can sense the weakness pulsating beneath the authority he so desperately clings to. I have exposed it before. I could expose it again.

'Be careful, sister. You do not have our bitch of an aunt to protect you any more.' These words hit harder than his slap and he smiles at the pain flashing across my face, leaning in closer. 'When I am king, I will have you banished for ever, and I will have all witches like you hunted down and killed. I will wipe the stain of magic from Colchis' reputation.'

Foolish brother; he does not realize his banishment would be a gift, not a punishment. I have spent my whole life longing to escape this prison. As for hunting down other witches, I have only ever known of Circe and myself harbouring such abilities. Though I would love to see my brother incite Hecate's fury. She is a mysterious, feared goddess, perhaps because of the ominous domains she rules over – magic, darkness and ghosts.

I have no doubt her punishment would be swift and severe.

'Do you know what you are, sister?' Apsyrtus continues, his hand stroking my head with mock affection. 'You are a disease. You will infect everything you touch and make it rot from the inside out. And do you know what we do to infections? We *cut* them out.' As he speaks, he rips out a few strands of hair, his smile widening as I wince.

'Apsyrtus,' Chalciope whimpers.

'*Chalciope.*' He mimics her whine. Then, he straightens himself up, letting my strands of hair fall from his fingers. 'Go and see Father.'

'As you wish, brother.' I rise slowly and walk from the room, catching Chalciope's gaze in the doorway. Her eyes widen as I approach.

If someone saw us together, they would not think us sisters. Chalciope is short and petite, with hair like spun gold and delicate features that look as if you could shatter them with a single flick of your finger. Whilst I have always thought myself harsher, uglier. If we were flowers, I would be one with spikes and knots, designed to protect and repel, whilst Chalciope would be the kind that draws everyone in with its sweetness, wishing to be adored.

'Stay back, sister,' Apsyrtus hisses at her. 'You do not know what evil the witch is capable of.'

I sometimes wonder if my brother would have become such a cruel man if I hadn't done what I did to him. He was always a bully, of course, but perhaps he would have grown out of that. He could have softened with age, like fruit slowly ripening in the sun. My magic scarred him, not visibly, but deep inside, leaving the stain of distrust and humiliation upon him. A dangerous combination for any young man. But, despite this, I believe there would have always been too much of my father in him. My hand merely accelerated the inevitable.

After all, violence breeds violence. Circe taught me that. She taught me everything I know.

2

When we were younger, my father made us watch him beat his slaves.

He filed us into his throne room and delivered speeches about 'the consequences of our actions', his words filling the room with empty ideals of duty and honour. Apsyrtus' eyes would gleam with purpose as he listened, whilst Chalciope would sniffle nervously, unable to look at the slave quivering on the floor. I would stand motionless, awaiting the inevitable.

He beat the slaves with his fists, or sometimes with a whip, if he did not wish to bruise his knuckles. The whip was always the worst.

Even now I still hear their screams, each unique cadence of pain permanently etched into my memory.

Chalciope would close her eyes, weeping quietly as she grabbed my hand, as if squeezing my fingers could somehow make it all better. Even the 'fearless' Apsyrtus would have to glance away eventually. But I did not. I forced myself to witness every inch of their agony, to let it carve through me, hollowing me out until I could taste the acidic shock of their suffering in my mouth.

To look away felt as if I were somehow denying their pain, and I did not want to give my father the satisfaction of making me cower and flinch like the others. I knew he fed off weakness.

Circe once told me my father's cruelty came from a place of deep insecurity. I found this fascinating at the time. My father ruled one of the most successful, wealthiest kingdoms in all the world, and was a direct descendant of the Gods. What did he possibly have to be insecure about? Circe had smiled at my disbelief.

'The child of a famed god, born completely ordinary. Can you imagine how humiliating that must be? That will always be Aeetes' greatest shame.'

In that moment, it made sense – his cruelty, his anger. Yet, despite my father's flaws, it was I who was seen as the monster. I was the one kept at arm's length by all those around me, shut out by the world.

Even Circe turned away from me in the end.

I have often wondered if there is a monster inside me, cloaked in the skin of a young, quiet girl. Perhaps everyone can see it pacing restlessly beneath the surface, and that is why they keep their distance.

Maybe that is why I did not look away when my father beat the slaves, because the monster inside me wanted to watch, wanted to enjoy it.

My sandals clatter against the brightly patterned floors as I walk to my father's throne room.

It is a long space that yawns out towards the entrance of the palace, adorned with grandiose decorations that reek of desperation. A decor that suits its king.

To my right, at the centre of the space, a large circular hearth glows lazily, framed by four pillars. The slaves beside it flinch and withdraw, as they so often do when I enter a room.

Directly in front of the hearth, on a raised dais, my father sits. His gilded throne is framed with crimson drapery that hangs from flanking pillars like bleeding wounds.

My father is an ugly man. His face sharp and angular, nose slightly hooked. He has the same golden hair and eyes as all the Sun God's children do. I did not inherit this divine colouring, not that I care. My dark features are of little consequence to me. Besides, I find it fitting that I was born to look as different as I feel from my family. Admittedly, though, when I first met Circe, I longed to possess her golden beauty; I wanted to be just like her, to absorb every inch of her. To mirror every breath, echo every heartbeat.

'Father,' I say in greeting. The word feels hollow in my mouth.

'Medea.' My father nods slowly. He rarely speaks directly to me like this. 'Phrixus, this is my elder daughter.'

Beside my father's throne stands a man I have never seen before. He is tall and narrow, with awkwardly long limbs. His face is thin and drawn together tightly in a look of permanent worry. His eyes, a deep brown, shift to mine and I see a sadness in them that nearly takes my breath away.

I hold the stranger's gaze for longer than I know I should, captivated by the grief he carries so visibly.

Darkness calls to darkness, another of Circe's wisdoms.

'You think she can . . . do it?' he asks my father.

I note how different Greek sounds on his lips, the vowels soft and smooth. Hearing it now, I can understand why my father has so often scolded me for 'butchering' his native tongue. My Greek has always been encumbered by the harsh, familiar edges of the Colchian dialect I have grown up around, burdening me with an accent my father has tried to curb in me since infancy.

Glancing back to the king, I note the inner conflict darkening his eyes. Is he marrying me off to this man? He has always claimed I am not 'fit' for marriage, but could his mind have changed? At seventeen winters, I have believed myself too old to be desirable now.

A sharp thrill pierces my stomach. This melancholic stranger could be my path out of Colchis.

'She can do it. She has been trained by the witch Circe herself,' my father says, distaste edging his words.

Circe. It has been so long since anyone has dared utter her name within these walls.

'Your sister?'

There is a slight pause before he huffs, 'Indeed.'

'Then it is true what they say about Colchis' magic ... Perhaps Circe can offer us her aid herself?'

'My sister no longer resides here.' My father's voice is stern. 'And she will not be returning.'

I watch the vein in his neck pulse, thick and slow. My gaze then drifts down to where his hands grip the arms of his throne, his tendons like rope protruding beneath his mottled flesh.

'Princess,' Phrixus gasps. His eyes catch mine and I smile, but then I taste blood in my mouth and quickly cover my face. 'Your nose ... Are you all right?'

'For Zeus's sake, make yourself presentable, girl.' I wipe my bloodied nose with the heel of my hand, burning quietly under the weight of my father's glare.

'It is nothing,' I mutter, flicking my gaze between them. 'Why did you summon me here?'

A tense silence swallows the room. Outside, I can hear the birds singing their morning calls as the balmy air rolls in around us, making the fire shiver and spit. I slide my tongue along the back of my teeth, tasting the metallic residue of blood. It seems Apsyrtus hit me harder than I realized.

Beside my father, Phrixus glances nervously around the room, the firelight carving out the hollows of his cheeks and eyes, making him appear more skeleton than man. What have those eyes seen that make them cradle such anguish?

'Phrixus has bestowed upon me a gift.' My father finally speaks, his voice slitting the tension like a knife through flesh. 'It is a gift from the Gods themselves, one that must be protected at all costs.'

'That will not be a problem. Colchis has the finest army in all the world, finer than any in Greece,' Apsyrtus booms as he storms into the room. I feel my insides hardening as he regards my bloodied nose with a smirk. 'Wipe your face, sister.'

Our father looks conflicted as he replies, 'We need more than mortal men to protect this gift. We need Medea's . . . *abilities*.'

I blink slowly, registering his words.

'Father, that cannot be! You said yourself her magic is a curse. We should be punishing her sickness, not encouraging it!'

'Sometimes we must appeal to the darkness to protect the light,' Phrixus says under his breath, catching us by surprise. His eyes briefly touch mine and I feel something uncoiling in the pit of my stomach, making a warmth press hotly against my cheeks.

'What in Hades' name is that supposed to mean?'

'It means your sister may be our only option, Prince Apsyrtus.'

'I will do it,' I say, holding Phrixus' gaze with a sudden intensity. 'Whatever it is you ask of me, I will do it . . . But—'

'But?' My father bites down on the word.

'I want to see the gift I am protecting.'

His face darkens, eyes shifting to Phrixus as a silent discussion passes between them.

'Very well.'

3

Circe did not reverse my spell on Apsyrtus without payment.

She made my father promise that she could stay and tutor me in the ways of magic. My father agreed, for he had no other choice, unless he wanted a pig for an heir. Of course, he loathed the decision he had been forced to make. But for me, it was the greatest gift I have ever been given.

During her time as my tutor, Circe did not reside in Colchis. She usually stayed until Selene's cycle was complete, and then would disappear for an agonizing length of time. The days between her visits were an empty void, like the barren winters Demeter inflicted on the world when she was separated from her beloved Persephone. Only my winter was internal, a coldness that spread through my entire body, freezing over my insides. When Circe returned, it was like Helios had finally risen, thawing the ice that had set into my bones.

Her lessons were primarily theory-based rather than practical, as that was the simplest way to keep my father's temper at bay. He could stomach me studying magic but refused to let us conjure spells on his land.

So, Circe focused on breaking down the properties of each spell, explaining which plants and incantations could summon which effect. We would spend endless hours strolling through the forests, draped in their lazy shade, whilst Circe would tell me about each flower, plant and shrub we came across. She knew every single one, without ever even hesitating.

Usually, I would slip off my sandals so I could wiggle my toes into the soil and feel the power humming within.

'Nature is magic, Medea, and magic is nature. It is the rawest essence of our world, a power infused by the divine when they created it. It sings through Gaia's veins, but only few can hear it, only those Hecate allows. Listen.' I would close my eyes as Circe spoke, focusing on that tug of magic beckoning me forwards.

After a time, Circe stopped telling me things and started asking instead. I used to love when she tested me like this, even more so when I impressed her with the correct answer.

'And this is?' She would point to a plant at random, an eyebrow arched in challenge.

'Asphodel.'

'And what spell could you conjure with it?'

'If burnt correctly under a full moon, you can summon a connection to speak with the dead.'

'Very good, Medea.' That smile would crack across her beautiful face, filling me with pride.

When I grew a little older, Circe found new ways to challenge me.

It began during my tenth summer when, as usual, we were out in the forest making our routine sacrifice to Hecate beneath the waxing moon. The goddess preferred her offerings at night, so Circe said.

I had been the one to slit the sheep's throat, and I remember the way its blood glowed an eerie silver in the moonlight, coating my palms and wrists.

'I want to play a game.' Circe was kneeling opposite me, a small fire crackling between us. I watched the flames burn in her eyes, melting their golden glow to a warm ochre. 'I have laid before you a selection of flowers, one of which grows in the mountains, sprung from the blood of Prometheus.'

Prometheus. His name seemed to hush the forest around us; even the incessant chorus of cicadas fell silent. Prometheus was the infamous Titan punished by Zeus for gifting humans with fire. Upon Colchis' jagged mountain range, Prometheus remains chained for eternity, his insides pecked out each day by bloodthirsty birds, only to grow back overnight so his torment may begin again anew. They still say that, to this day, you can hear his screams ringing between the peaks.

I stared at the flowers laid out before me, wondering which could spawn from the blood of a divine immortal, a *Titan*.

Circe continued, 'This flower, when prepared correctly, can create an ointment that will grant you the ability to repel fire. I want you to show me how.'

My eyes snapped back to my aunt. 'But . . . I have not learnt that spell yet. You have not taught me.'

'And who taught you the transformation spell you used on Apsyrtus?'

She had a point; she always did.

'I—'

'You followed your instincts, your *gift*. Hecate called to you, and you answered. That is how a true sorceress masters her craft.' I am not sure if it is just in my memory, but I swear the fire burnt brighter, as if fuelled by her words. 'Do so now, Medea. Trust your instincts. Believe in yourself, as I do.'

Her encouragement blazed inside me, hotter than the flames, bolstering my resolve. And so, I set to work. I reached for the flowers laid before me, taking each one in my hand and turning it carefully between my fingertips. I kept my eyes closed, for it did not matter what the flowers looked like but rather how they *felt*, how they whispered against my skin, rallying the magic that paced eagerly in my blood. I imagined I could hear them calling to me, bright little voices – *Pick me! Pick me!* Each one held magical properties; that was evident enough from the tug I felt in my veins. But only one would cast the spell Circe had asked of me.

One flower held my interest. Its petals were soft and creamy, its magic rippling like a sigh beneath my touch. Though this was not what caught my attention, but rather the thick undercurrent of power I sensed beneath. I focused my mind on it, opening my magic to that pulsing current. A violent vision suddenly burst before my eyes – I saw a colossal bird swooping to attack, blood dripping from its razor-sharp beak, its shriek piercing through me.

I flinched, dropping the flower.

'That one,' I told Circe, snapping my eyes open. The flower had long, curved petals like a crocus and a stem that ended in thick, fleshy roots. 'That is the one.'

'That flower?' Circe had been watching me over the flames, her expression entirely impassive. 'Are you certain?'

My magic flared inside me, hot and urgent. 'It is not the flower. It is the root. That is where its power lies.'

'If that is your decision, then prepare the spell.' She motioned to the sheep lying cold and still beside us. 'All you need is blood from a sacrificial beast and soil of the earth. Then the spell will be complete . . . *if* you have chosen correctly.'

Circe passed me a shallow bronze bowl and I placed the flower's root inside, stripping it open with my fingernails. It oozed a thick, black sap that mingled with the blood already staining my hands. The humming in my veins intensified as I scooped dirt into the bowl and began binding the ingredients together between my palms.

'There,' I announced proudly when I was done. 'Well? Was I correct?'

'You must find out.' Circe nodded to the flames and a wisp of fear shivered through me.

'What?'

'Place your hand in the fire.' She said it so calmly, as if she were merely asking me to take a stroll with her.

My hands tightened around the bowl, my certainty in my decision waning with every sinister pop of the flames. 'But what if I am wrong?'

'It is called trial and error, Medea. How else do you think I learnt?'

I remember I was afraid; the feeling was sharp as a blade inside me. Yet more terrifying than the fire was the prospect of letting Circe down.

I would have rather burnt my flesh to the bone than disappoint my aunt.

So, I coated my hand with the salve I had created and offered up a prayer to Hecate. The gritty texture seeped into my skin instantaneously, leaving a cool buzzing sensation in its wake.

The flames hissed and spat at me, like a frothing hound eager to be let loose. Through the curling smoke, Circe's golden eyes watched me, calmly assessing.

A moment passed, then another. Finally, her face softened as she whispered, 'You do not have to—'

With that, I plunged my hand into the fire.

The flames instantly dipped away, obediently bowing beneath my touch. I wiggled my fingers and watched, mesmerized, as the sparks tickled lightly against my skin.

'You trusted your instinct, Medea. Well done.' Circe smiled at me, and to this day I can see that pride shining in her eyes, beautifully bright.

I had been right, as Circe had known I would be.

From that day, I learnt to trust my instincts, my magic, daring to push myself further. With Circe by my side, I felt invincible. She was an excellent teacher, always so diligent and patient. She made every effort to impart all she knew of magic. Well, nearly all . . .

'Dark magic is too dangerous, Medea.' She would dismiss me, as she always did when I brought up the subject, begging to know more. 'Besides, even if you wanted to, you cannot tap into that kind of power. Have you not realized that it does not call to you like the magic of the earth does? Hecate lets us access earth magic as a gift. But to wield dark magic, we must give something in return.'

'Give what?'

'Something we can never take back,' was all she would reply, until I eventually let the subject go, tucking it away in my mind like a forbidden trinket.

For two more glorious summers Circe continued to visit and then, one day, she simply stopped.

Just like that.

'But why would she leave me?' I asked my father when he told me my aunt would not be returning.

'Why?' he scoffed. 'Circe is a selfish creature. She probably grew bored of you. Do you not think she has better things to do than your silly lessons?'

His words pierced my heart, cruel and cold. He knew exactly how to hurt me, even without his fists. But I would not believe him, I *refused*. I knew Circe would return; she would not leave me like that, she could not. So, I waited for her.

And waited . . .

And five summers on, here I am. Still waiting.

*

My father leads us from the throne room, instructing his guards not to follow.

I expect him to take us to his treasury, where he keeps his most precious items, gifts from distant kings eager to gain his favour. But, to my surprise, he walks us behind the palace to the stables.

The sickly-sweet stench of manure hangs in the air as my father leads us inside. Sunlight seeps through the cracks in the walls, spilling golden strips across the muck-stained floor. From the stalls either side of us, shadows shift and sigh gently.

It seems Helios' glow is impossibly bright today, illuminating the far end of the stable with a strange intensity. As we draw closer, however, I realize this burning light is coming from another source hidden within the furthest pen. Four armed guards stand watch outside, shielding their eyes from the harsh glare.

I glance questioningly at my father.

'Stay calm,' he instructs, before heading inside.

I follow him without hesitation.

For a moment, the brilliant light overwhelms me, obliterating all my senses. It is like plunging into ice-cold water, my body temporarily paralysed by shock.

I shield my eyes with my hands and, gradually, detail begins to return to the world. I can make out the corners of the room and the large formation that stands at the centre of it. A creature with a coat so golden and radiant it emits a light of its own.

Beside me, I hear Apsyrtus mutter a prayer to the Gods as I strain my eyes to get a better look at this magnificent beast. It is the size of a horse, horned and hoofed, with a tightly coiled coat. It could be a ram, though on its back two brilliant, feathered wings are tucked neatly away.

The creature's head slowly sways to look at us and its blazing eyes burn into mine as if they were reaching into my soul. I wonder if it is afraid of what it sees there.

Instinctively, I reach out a hand and feel the air pulsing with the intoxicating whisper of divine power. I can almost taste its richness coating my tongue ...

'That's enough.' My father grabs my arm, steering me away.

'What was that?' I breathe, dark splotches blooming across my vision as my eyes adjust to the shadowy stables outside.

'A gift from the Gods,' Phrixus says. 'They instructed me to bring the creature here, to sacrifice to Apollo in his sacred grove.'

'Its fleece possesses great power,' my father murmurs to Apsyrtus, throwing his arm around his shoulder. I pretend not to listen as he continues quietly, 'The Gods told Phrixus whoever harbours it will have untold glory. Do you know what that means, my boy? The owner of that fleece will be undefeatable. Once word gets out, many will wish to obtain it for themselves. It is our duty to protect the fleece, whatever the cost.'

My father's actions make sense to me now. He does not wish to protect the fleece to appease the Gods, but rather so he can hoard its promised power for himself.

The thought of him as undefeatable makes my blood turn cold.

'I will give my life to the cause!' Apsyrtus announces, his face flushed with purpose.

I wonder if my father believes this act of valour, or can he see the emptiness within it? Apsyrtus will lose interest in this creature as soon as a pretty girl catches his eye, or someone looks at him the wrong way. His interests are always self-facing. This ram will not hold his focus for long.

'Medea.' My father turns to me. 'You must create a spell so great, so powerful, that no man can surpass it. Do you understand?'

'Yes, Father.'

'Are you sure she is up to it?' Phrixus mutters, his face turned slightly away.

'I am up to it,' I interject. 'How much time do I have?'

'Until Helios next rises.'

'Then you should move out of my way. For I have work to do.'

4

'I do not understand.' Chalciope pouts at me, a small crease appearing between her fair brows. 'I thought you were banned from doing magic.'

She is flitting around the palace kitchen, periodically peering over my shoulder as I work. We both know our parents have forbidden her to be alone with me but, as usual, she doesn't leave, and I do not ask her to.

'Apparently that rule is void in certain situations,' I say.

A small fire is lit, over which I am burning the flowers and herbs I instructed my father's guards to fetch me.

I would have gathered them myself, but I am no longer allowed beyond the palace walls save for public ceremonies where my attendance is mandatory for my father to uphold his illusion of a united, obedient family. But those events sometimes feel more oppressive than my marble prison, with the people's eyes watching, assessing, judging . . .

Did you hear what she did to her brother?

'Because of a ram?' Chalciope prompts, tugging my attention back to her.

'It is not just a ram, it is a gift from the Gods,' I say as I burn the flowers, watching their violet petals glow gold and crimson. A thin stream of smoke curls upwards and Chalciope leans away just a fraction.

Once they are burnt, I transfer the remnants into a small bowl along with the blood of a snake I carefully gutted before Chalciope arrived. I rub the ashy concoction between my fingertips, feeling the power of the flames mingle with that of the flowers. It sings through my body, coaxing my magic to life so it begins to stir in my veins, causing my mind to fizz.

How I have missed this feeling. It revives me, grounds me, like a voyager taking their first step on land after months lost at sea.

'But why bring the ram here?'

'Because the Gods said so.'

'But why do we have to keep it hidden?'

'Because Father said so.'

'But—'

'*Chalciope.*' Her name escapes me as a frustrated rush of air, making her flinch. Sometimes I forget how afraid of me she is. I meet her wide eyes and feel something in me soften. 'I have to get this potion done before sunrise, or else . . .'

'Or else what?' she asks nervously when I trail off.

To be honest, I do not know. What greater punishment is there than the imprisonment and loathing I already endure? I suppose my father could kill me, though I doubt such punishment would be worth the divine wrath my death would invoke. The Gods who rule our world may be deeply flawed, but they are very particular about murdering within bloodlines. They have peculiar morals.

'Is it safe?' Chalciope leans over the pot, wrinkling her nose.

'Yes, it is safe.'

'How do you know what to do?'

'I just do . . . It's difficult to explain.'

'Can you try?'

It's the first time in a long while we've been alone together and

25

able to talk freely, without the oppressive eyes of our family dissecting every word we share.

I used to love being Chalciope's sister, before my parents made me feel unworthy of the title. I loved the way she looked up at me with those giant, curious eyes and asked endless lisping questions. Whatever answer I gave, she would believe. I could spin nonsense in the air, and she would still gaze at me as if I were the Oracle of Delphi herself.

She never looks at me like that any more, with that unreserved adoration. Now her eyes are always tinged with a slight fear, a fear that has been impressed upon her by the others. They have tainted her, taking a piece of her away from me for ever. And I hate my family for that.

And yet, despite this, Chalciope continues to steal these moments alone with me, even though she knows she risks our father's wrath. Though I would never allow that. I would rather endure the full force of his fury than let him lay a single finger on her.

'Please?' she prompts, leaning in closer so that her golden hair falls across my shoulders, tickling my skin.

'I suppose it's like asking you to explain how you breathe. It's just something your body knows how to do.' Chalciope considers this for a moment, chewing her lip thoughtfully. 'The plants, they have magic inside them; I just have to coax it out ... The best way to do that is with the elements: fire, water, earth, air.' I nod to the fire, and it crackles as if in agreement. 'Once the magic is extracted, I can infuse it with my own and bend it to my will ... It is all a science. That's what Circe says, anyway.'

'There's magic in plants?'

'There's magic in all of nature.' I motion vaguely with my hand and Chalciope gives an uneasy glance around us, as if magical demons skulk in the corners of the room. 'Magic is nothing to be afraid of.'

'Then why does Father fear it?'

'Because it is a power he cannot command.'

'*Chalciope.*' Our mother's voice makes us both jolt. She is standing in the doorway to the kitchen, her glassy eyes fixed on my sister. 'You should not be in here.'

'I was just—'

'Out. Now.'

Chalciope bows her head in submission, slipping silently from the room. My mother watches her go with an empty glare, as if she is trying to be angry but cannot muster the energy to feel it. She then turns to leave without registering my existence.

'The magic is Father's bidding,' I tell her. I'm not sure why.

She tilts her head slightly to the side, so I can see the delicate curve of her nose and lips. I notice her hands are gripping the folds of her gown, making the thin fabric ripple. The silence drags itself around us.

Please, a small voice aches inside me, *say something. Anything.*

'Princess?' Phrixus appears behind her, puncturing the tense stillness.

My mother instinctively cowers and quickly retreats, her head bowed low.

'I did not mean to intrude.' He watches my mother leave, wringing his hands behind his back. His voice is delicate and strained. I find it incredibly endearing. 'Your father sent me to see if you are ready?'

'I am,' I say, tipping the contents of the bubbling pot into a small vial tied to a cord. A faint charred smell wafts upwards and makes Phrixus lean forwards curiously.

'What is the spell?'

'An old favourite.' I loop the cord around my neck, letting the potion rest warmly against my chest.

27

Unsure of what to say, Phrixus fidgets awkwardly, as if groping the air for the right response. He then picks up one of the flowers discarded on the table, twirling it between his thumb and forefinger.

'An ingredient,' I tell him as he regards the flower's little violet faces crowded together. 'For my spell.'

'Your magic – can it work without these ingredients?'

I'm surprised by his curiosity. Nobody ever asks about my magic, save for Chalciope. 'No, not really. It is like art, I suppose. An artist cannot create without his tools.'

'And Hecate – you require her involvement as well?'

'Yes. The goddess allows the connection between my magic and the magic of the earth. Without her, none of this would be possible.'

'Has the goddess ever made herself known to you?'

'Not yet.' I brush away the familiar press of disappointment, refocusing my attention on the flower still in Phrixus' hand. 'They're called *heliotropes*, named after my grandfather. They say there was a nymph who was madly in love with Helios, but when he left her for another lover, she could not bear the heartbreak. So, she wasted away and eventually transformed into this flower. That is why they always grow to face the sun, for it is the spirit of the nymph looking to her lost lover.'

Phrixus twirls the flower slowly as he considers my words. 'That is a sad story.'

'It's not all bad. Now these flowers have the power of transformation within them. I suppose you could say in her death she became more powerful.' His eyes touch mine then flit away.

'Your Greek is very good,' he comments, perhaps to change the subject.

'Colchis is a land of trade; it suits the people here to speak many dialects. But my father made sure his children shared his native tongue. He still thinks himself Greek, even though he has not stepped foot in his homeland since he was a young man.'

Phrixus considers this, his eyes finding mine again. 'He has built quite the kingdom here. Admittedly, it is not what I had expected.'

'What did you imagine to find here, wild savages?' His eyes pop at that, and I cannot help but smile. 'We have all heard the rumours you Greeks spread about us; the people here laugh at them.'

'I meant no offence, Princess . . .'

'I am not offended.' I shrug, taking a measured step closer to him. 'May I ask you something now?'

Phrixus immediately tenses. He reminds me of a skittish creature, constantly poised to flee. 'I suppose so.'

'I see a sadness in you. Where does it come from?'

My question catches him off guard, cracking open his composure and causing a streak of pain to slice across his face. He collects himself, coughing as if to clear the rise of emotion in his throat.

'I will not say a word to anyone,' I add. Something in his face softens at that and for the first time he meets my gaze without seeming like he wants to look away.

When he finally speaks, his voice is thick in his throat. 'We had to flee our home, my sister and me. Our stepmother wanted us dead, and she was going to stop at nothing until she succeeded. Through the mercy of the Gods, we were aided in our escape. They sent the golden ram and instructed we come here, to Colchis. They said it is what the Fates had decreed and . . . well, you know, you cannot disagree with the Fates.' He smiles sombrely. 'But our journey – it was . . . challenging.'

'What happened to her?' I prompt as he glances away, and I study the sadness glistening in his eyes.

'I could not save her.' His words are just a breath caught in his throat. He pauses to gather himself. 'I tried to. I tried to reach for her, but I could not ... She had always protected me, always been there for me, and when she needed me most, I failed her. But I *tried*. Gods, I tried ...' He trails off as the tears begin to spill down his cheeks. He covers his face with his hands as a sob rips through him.

For a moment I watch him cry, captivated by the rawness of his emotion. I have only ever seen men express their sadness through anger and violence. It is fascinating to see it take a softer, delicate form.

Carefully, as if trying not to frighten off a wild animal, I take a step forwards and gently peel his hands from his face. His palms feel wet and warm against mine. He is surprised by my touch, though he does not pull away, as I thought he might.

'It is OK to feel lost,' I tell him. 'I have felt lost my whole life.'

He looks as if he is about to say something, but then his eyes settle into mine and he falls silent, letting his pain ache between us for a quiet moment. I cannot remember the last time somebody looked at me like this. Like they could trust me with their words, their vulnerability. It fills my chest with an overflowing warmth.

In the silence I find myself thinking of his sister and feel a stab of jealousy piercing my gut. How wonderful it must be to have been loved so deeply that your loss could cause utter torment, that your death would be capable of ripping someone apart with grief.

Would anyone care if I died?

Perhaps Chalciope would, though her sadness may be tinged with relief. I imagine Apsyrtus would laugh as he joyously danced on my grave. But what about if *he* died – how, then, would I feel? I probe inside my mind for some kind of visceral response, yet all I am met with is emptiness.

As I gaze up at Phrixus' red, swollen eyes, I toy with the urge to brush away his tears. But he suddenly withdraws his hand from mine, as if stung by wherever his quiet thoughts had taken him. I remain still, staring at the empty space between my fingers where our hands had intertwined.

'I apologize, Princess,' he mumbles, rubbing his eyes. 'It is not proper. I . . . We, um . . .' He coughs nervously. 'We should go. The others are waiting.'

'We should,' I agree, remaining perfectly still.

'Yes, well . . . I can escort you . . . if . . . if you would like . . .'

'Do you always have difficulty with your words?'

'I do.' He laughs at that, the sound smoothing the worried creases in his face. 'But it seems intensified around you.'

'Why?'

'I am not sure.' His eyes hold mine for a moment and I can feel something tugging in my chest. 'To be truthful, I have never met anyone like you, Princess.'

'Are you afraid of me?'

'Afraid?' He seems surprised by the suggestion. 'Should I be?'

'No. Never.'

'Well, I shall take your word for it.' His hands slowly stop twitching as his eyes soften.

Take me away from here. Please. The silent plea screams inside my head, so loud and intense I feel as if it might crack me in two. *Please.* The desperation rings through me and then, suddenly, in the echo of that despair, an idea sparks in my mind. A plan.

My smile widens.

'You're right. We should go.' I nod, drawing a breath as my plan settles inside me. 'But I must speak with my father first.'

I find the king in his throne room.

He stands beside the circular hearth at the centre of the space.

The weather is mild outside, yet the hearth burns continuously in respect to the goddess Hestia and as a mark of our united household. A hollow symbol.

The palace seems quiet and yet I know the slaves are close by. They are experts at being invisible, existing in the shadows. They are somehow able to subsist at the edges of our lives, whilst simultaneously serving at the centre of it. They facilitate our very existence without ever really existing themselves.

My father nods as I approach him. The firelight throws flickering shadows across his face, distorting his features in hideous ways, as if revealing glimpses of what lurks within.

'Are you prepared?' he asks as I stand opposite him.

'Yes.'

Seeing him like this, fire reflected in his golden eyes, reminds me of that night with Circe, when I willingly cast my hand into the flames for her.

'I never liked your aunt; I have made no secret of that,' my father says, as if somehow reading my thoughts. His gaze loosens into a memory as he continues, 'I have always found her to be an untrustworthy woman. That is evident enough from her little vanishing act, is it not? How long has it been now since she last visited you?' I know better than to answer, so I wait for him to go on. 'There has always been something wrong with her. I have sensed it ever since we were children. Something vile and malevolent.'

'Your words may offend Hecate,' is all I can think to reply.

'I have no qualms with the goddess's power. I respect her, as I respect all the Gods. It is *because* I respect them so deeply that I have tried to stifle your abilities, Medea. A power like that should only reside with the Gods, not mortal girls. It is unnatural.' He pauses then, his eyes finding mine across the flames. When he continues, his tone relaxes. 'But now I wonder . . . perhaps all these years I should have been guiding your hand, not binding it.'

His words stun me into silence. It is the closest my father has ever got to admitting he was wrong.

But I am not looking for reconciliation, and this weak attempt will not sway me from my purpose.

I clear my throat before speaking. 'Father, I have prepared a spell that will protect the Golden Fleece and ensure no mortal ever lays their hands on it . . . but I have one condition.'

'Condition?' he repeats, the word slow and heavy in his mouth.

'I wish you to give me to Phrixus. As his wife.'

A wisp of surprise catches in my father's face, then hardens to cold amusement. I know what he is thinking. He believes me a silly, infatuated girl, struck by Eros' sweet, burning arrow of love.

'He is a prince, from a well-respected family. He would be a suitable match and ally for Colchis,' I continue steadily. 'He intends to return to his land and overthrow his treacherous stepmother; he says the Gods promised to aid him once he delivered the fleece here safely. He will be a king.'

Though I believe I could easily come to love Phrixus one day, it is not affection that drives my decision. I am not blind to my limits as a woman. The only way I can safely leave this land is under the guardianship of another man, with the approval of my father. To try to flee any other way would be a death sentence, for one of us at least.

Marriage is my only way out of this prison.

'Very well.' My father nods slowly. 'Once your spell is done, I will announce the union.'

'Do I have your word?' A slash of irritation cuts across his face at the question, but he settles it quickly and nods.

'You have my word.'

5

The ram is silent as it dies. Stoic.

When my father went to cut its throat, the creature lifted its head willingly, as if it knew this was the fate it must abide. It is supposedly a good omen when sacrificial animals die easily. But something about the ram's compliance makes its death feel more unsettling than if it had screeched and thrashed. At least then it would have fought for its life, fought for a chance.

I watch as the blood pools into the bronze bowl Phrixus holds beneath its neck. Some spills over, dripping thickly down the altar and forming crimson rivulets that creep across the floor.

Despite the ram's magnificent, shining fleece, it still bleeds red like the rest of us.

Heavy darkness swathes the cave we are gathered in. It is an ancient darkness, the kind that feels as if it was forged long ago from the remnants of shadows cast when only chaos and emptiness existed. Before the primordial Gods came and teased out those tendrils of disorder and tied each one to a meaning, a purpose.

At the far end of the cave there is a pool of water stretching around a gathering of rocks. These stones are cloaked in thick greenery and form a raised platform on top of which a man-made altar stands. Here, a near-constant pillar of light reaches down from above, soaking the altar in an ethereal glow.

This place is known as the Grove of Apollo, a sacred sanctuary tucked away in the heart of the Colchian mountains and a place I have never been allowed to step foot in before.

'Phrixus, if you will.' My father stretches out his hands.

As Phrixus passes him the bowl, I find I cannot stop staring at the slash gaping across the ram's neck, the wound grinning at me like a wet, toothless mouth. As its life ebbs away, the creature's golden radiance seems to retreat with it, dulling to a gentle glow.

'Mighty Apollo, we offer this sacrifice to you,' my father continues as he pours the collected blood over the small fire. It crackles and hisses, choking out great wafts of smoke that billow upwards, filling the lofty cave. The smell of burnt blood sticks in my throat.

As my father continues his appeal to Apollo, I wonder if I am supposed to feel something, some shift in atmosphere that tells me the Olympian is listening. But I feel nothing. My father's words just bounce off the gloomy cave walls, hollow.

If it were not for my gifts from Hecate, I would wonder if the Gods existed or if they were just another of mankind's weapons, wielded to instil fear and obedience.

'Princess, we must skin the creature now,' Phrixus tells me quietly, his brown eyes swallowed by the darkness. 'You would perhaps prefer to wait outside? It is not a sight for ladies' eyes.'

His concern makes me smile and I consider telling him that I would prefer to watch. Yet I know I cannot, for I have work to do.

'I shall prepare my spell,' I say.

'Do not fail,' Apsyrtus spits as I exit through the mouth of the cave.

This grove is a place many have heard of, but few know its true location. It is a secret passed down between Colchian kings, so they say. If anyone ever tried to discover its whereabouts, they would have great difficulty, for only a specific, hidden pathway carved into the side of the mountain can guarantee safe passage. Even the entrance to the cave itself is hard to locate, just a narrow crack splintering the rock. Nobody would assume a beautiful, divine grove lay hidden within.

Outside the entrance, a small lip of rock juts outwards. The view is breathtaking, a rolling valley that ripples like the soft curves of Gaia's belly. Beyond, I can see Colchis sprawling in the distance, a shimmering mirage on the horizon.

I remove my veil, the one I am required to wear whenever I am outside. I then draw in a deep lungful of air, so rich and pure compared to the stagnancy inside the palace. It has been too long since I felt able to breathe this freely.

The mountain range stands silent and watchful. I close my eyes and listen. I want to know if the rumours are true. If you can truly hear the screams of Prometheus suffering his eternal torture amongst these peaks. I focus on the low whistle of the wind tugging at my hair, remembering the vision that startled me when I touched the flower sprung from Prometheus' blood. That razor-sharp beak, bloodied and hideous . . .

'Princess Medea, is it time?'

I turn to find my father's most trusted guard standing beside me, as still as the rock surrounding us.

'Amyntas.' I nod to him. 'Why am I not surprised you were the one to volunteer?'

'It is my duty to serve my king,' he replies stoically.

Amyntas has served my father for as long as I can remember. When I was younger, I used to think of him as his shadow, always lurking two steps behind. He was a soldier in his youth, elevated through the ranks by his skill and dedication, until he was selected to be one of the king's personal guards. 'The ultimate honour,' he had called it. But the glory of battle must taunt him as he wastes his days shackled to my father, watching him eat, sleep, even piss. The king's paranoia really knows no bounds.

Perhaps that is why Amyntas is here now: he wants to inject the thrill of battle into his life again. I cannot blame him. I would take any opportunity I could to escape that palatial prison.

'Has the king told you what this will entail?'

'Magic,' he says, without any hint of the disgust I am so familiar with. 'To enhance my ability to protect the sacred fleece.'

'Good. Shall we begin?'

'Yes, Princess.' He does not hesitate. They always said he was the bravest of my father's men.

'Drink this.' I remove the potion from around my neck, handing him the vial.

He sucks in a slight breath, his weathered face hardening. He's trying to mask his fear, but I can feel it tightening the air around us. For a heavy moment, I think he's going to refuse.

'For my king. For Colchis,' he says, before swallowing the potion.

I smile.

'Now, remove your breastplate.' He regards me warily but complies, averting his eyes as he unbuckles the leather straps and strips it away. I do not think I have ever seen him without his armour before, and I take a moment to regard his broad, muscled chest beneath his tunic.

I place my palms over his heart. 'What are you doing?'

'Waiting.'

'For what?'

'To feel the magic inside you.'

He stiffens at that but says nothing.

I draw in a slow breath, closing my eyes. The air is thin up here and so cold it stills my lungs.

Hecate . . . I call to you, Goddess . . .

For a long moment I feel nothing, just the quickening of his heart-beat. A sense of doubt wriggles into my mind. Did I do the spell correctly, or has my magic faded after so many years of disuse? What if Hecate has turned from me after neglecting her for so long? My father sacrificed to her this morning, as I advised he must, but perhaps a single bull was not enough . . .

Wait . . . *there*. Something flickers in Amyntas' chest, a gentle buzz-ing. I press a little harder with my hands and I feel a warmth begin to glow beneath my fingertips, as if I am coaxing a fire to life within the depths of his body.

'Can you feel that?' I breathe, my voice catching with excitement.

'I am not sure . . .'

I can sense the potion igniting inside him now and I lock myself on to it. Invisible sparks shoot up my arms, making my skin tingle and ache. A sharp tang cuts into my nose; it is the smell of wet earth and warm fires, salty waves, and swollen clouds before a thunderstorm. It is the smell of the earth, the smell of magic.

I steady my excitement, taking another slow breath and clearing my mind.

Magic must come with discipline. Circe's voice comes to me. *Otherwise, there will only be chaos.*

With a measured breath, I lean in close and whisper against his chest, '*Drakon*.'

Despite all his bravery, Amyntas still screams like my brother did.

He falls heavily to the floor and begins to writhe around as if he were possessed by the madness of Dionysus. His choked cries of pain are amplified by the mountains, as if they were sharing his hurt, crying out alongside him. Or perhaps they are the distant cries of Prometheus, mingling with his own.

'What is going on?' my father demands, appearing beside me. His robes are stained with the ram's blood.

'The spell is working,' I reply.

Apsyrtus retreats near the mouth of the cave, raw fear cut across his face. I wonder if he can still remember the feeling of being transformed. I wonder if it still haunts him.

'We must help him.' Phrixus, now considerably paler than before, steps forwards to where Amyntas writhes on the floor.

My father blocks his path. 'It must be done.'

Phrixus opens his mouth to argue, but our attention is caught by the sound of cracking bones and wet, snapping muscles as Amyntas' body begins to transform. His blood-curdling cries intensify, making even my father wince, though there is something else in his face, too – curiosity, perhaps even wonder.

'Father, this is wrong!' Apsyrtus yells as he withdraws further into the cave.

Amyntas begins to swell to an enormous size, so large his skin starts turning purple and red, looking as if he might burst. His face contorts with terrified pain. Then he collapses to the ground and begins to elongate, as if his body were being rolled out. His belly stretches, his spine snaps and begins protruding out of his back, forming a long, flicking tail. His fingers and toes splinter into large talons and his skin tears and hardens into dark, glistening scales. All the while he is growing larger and larger.

It is a hideous, magnificent sight and I cannot help but feel a thrill tremble through me as I witness the extent of my power.

Thank you, Hecate. Thank you, Goddess.

Amyntas' face extends next, hundreds of razor-sharp teeth cutting through his gums, crowding his mouth as his tongue stretches. His pained cries morph into a low rumble that erupts into a spine-chilling hiss.

He turns his face to us then, his fearful human eyes replaced by fiery amber irises, with dark, sinister slits of obsidian at the centre. His previous terror has vanished now and the beast stares down at us calmly, a forked tongue flicking outwards.

There is a tense pause, then two scale-covered bones break out from his back, as if he were growing two additional spines. They arch upwards into the air, stretching out a thin canvas of skin, like sails catching in a strong wind. It takes a moment for these strange limbs to take form as they quiver and flap.

'Wings,' my father breathes.

I stare up in awe, watching the sunlight filter through them, illuminating the veins sparking across the stretch of leathery skin. The talons at their apex glint as the dragon flaps his wings, stirring up a menacing wind. He then steps a heavy, taloned foot towards us, making the ground tremble and causing the men to recoil instinctively backwards.

Only I do not move.

'What has she done?' Apsyrtus shouts.

'Zeus protect us,' Phrixus whispers.

'You do not need the Gods' protection any more,' I say, turning to face them. I can feel the creature stirring behind me like a monstrous shadow. 'You have a dragon for that . . . The fleece is safe now.'

'Safe? What about the rest of Colchis, you mad witch?' Apsyrtus hisses from where he hides. 'You've just created a beast capable of destroying our entire kingdom!'

'He is no threat to us.'

'Are you sure?' My father cannot take his eyes off the dragon.

'Yes. Amyntas still lives on within the creature, or at least an essence of him does. And he is loyal to us, to you.' I look to my father, watching an ugly smile slash across his face.

I choose not to disclose that though Amyntas is loyal to my father, I am the dragon's sole master, as I am its creator. He answers to me and me alone.

'He is magnificent,' my father says, and I feel a rush of warmth spread through me as his hand closes over my shoulder. 'Well done, my daughter.'

6

That night, we celebrate.

Or, rather, the men celebrate. It is not 'appropriate' for women to join in the festivities. But I do not mind; I am satisfied enough enjoying the glow of my success, relishing the effect it is having on those around me. The mood in the palace is lighter than I have ever known it to be, the suffocating tension finally lifting, like poison bled from a wound.

My father's delight is infectious; even the slaves seem in a brighter mood. It is almost peculiar to see him so joyful, but how could he not be? The Golden Fleece now hangs safely in the Grove of Apollo, protected by a dragon that will secure him a legacy which will live on for generations.

'History will sing of the Dragon King!' I hear his voice bellow.

I smile to myself, sipping idly at the wine my father had a slave deliver to my chamber. An unusually warm gesture from him.

I wonder what Circe would think if she saw what I have achieved today. It is by far the most ambitious spell I have ever attempted. I hope she would be proud. All I ever wanted to do was prove myself worthy of her, her time, her love.

'Medea?' a voice whispers from my doorway.

'Chalciope, come in quickly; someone might see you.'

'Do not worry, sister. The guards are far too drunk to care.' She grins as she walks in and sits beside me on my bed. 'I just had to ask you, is it true . . . about the *dragon*?' I watch her eyes widen as I nod, waiting for the fear to seep in. 'Medea! How in Gaia's name did you do that? You are a wonder!'

'You think so?' I feel my lips twitch.

'I have always thought so.' She reaches out and squeezes my hand. 'I have never seen Father like this. He's acting like he's just conquered all of Greece.'

'I cannot remember the last time I heard him laugh.' I stare at her small, slender hand resting in mine.

'He has quite an ugly laugh, doesn't he?' She smirks. 'I didn't even know Father could make such sounds.' Chalciope mimics his throaty cackle, contorting her face into comical expressions.

I feel a laugh rise in my throat, but quickly swallow it down. 'Shh, someone will hear you.'

'OK, *OK*!' She falls back into her usual melodic giggles.

'Father even sent me this.' I hand her my cup of wine and nod for her to take a sip. She gulps down a mouthful, wincing at the sour taste. A little dribble slips down her chin and makes an unexpected snort escape me.

'Why do they drink that?' she exclaims, then we break into more laughter.

When our amusement subsides, we sit quietly for a moment, her hand still resting in mine. Such a simple thing, and yet I cannot remember the last time my family touched me like this, with love instead of loathing.

My eyes drift to Chalciope's face, soaking in her beautiful, golden features. I reach out to stroke her hair, waiting for her to flinch and recoil away from me. But she simply smiles, letting my fingers run through her shimmering curls. They are a darker hue than Circe's, rich and honeyed and delightfully soft.

We are both the granddaughters of Helios, yet I believe his light has infused us in different ways. Chalciope is a delicate sunbeam, the kind that lightly touches your face on a mild spring morning, gently warming your cheeks. Whilst I would be the shadows cast by that sunbeam, dark and twisting. But . . . perhaps I could be the light also. Have I not done something good for my family today, for Colchis?

'It's nice to see Father happy,' she says. 'Maybe things will be different now.'

'They will be different,' I reply gently.

'How do you know?'

'Because I am leaving Colchis.'

'Leaving?' A flash of panic sparks in her eyes. 'Why?'

'I am marrying Phrixus.' I cannot stop the small smile from curling at my lips.

'You are?' she gasps, her hand tightening around mine as she forces herself to mirror my smile. She has always been terrible at hiding her emotions. 'That is *wonderful* news, sister. I am so happy for you. But . . . I must admit, I will miss you terribly.'

'I will miss you, too.' I feel the sharp edge of guilt cut through my happiness. Though my father does not lay his hands on Chalciope as he does with me, I still loathe the thought of leaving her here with him. 'Once we are settled, I will send for you. I promise I—'

'You really are stupid, aren't you?' Apsyrtus' voice slices into our tender moment. I look up to see him leaning in the doorway, swirling a cup of wine. From the looseness in his gaze, I can tell he is drunk.

'Go back to the celebrations, brother.'

'You really think you're going to marry Phrixus?' He lets out a nasty laugh, rolling his head back against the wall. 'How pathetic.'

'Yes.' I raise my chin defiantly. 'Father gave me his word.'

'His word?' Another laugh. Beside me, I feel Chalciope stiffening,

44

withdrawing her hand from mine. 'Medea, Medea, you walk around here acting as if you are so above everyone else. But you really are just a stupid little girl, aren't you?' He knocks back a mouthful of wine.

'I know you hate me for what I did to you, Apsyrtus, but—'

'Do not!' he snaps, staggering forwards a little and catching himself on the wall with an outstretched hand. His golden hair tumbles over his face, crimson robes dishevelled. 'Listen here, Medea. Father giving his word to you means *nothing*. You know why? Because you are just a girl. And kings do not make deals with girls . . . let alone witches.'

'You forget a marriage would be beneficial to Father as well.' I rise slowly as he draws closer, positioning myself in front of Chalciope.

'More beneficial than having a witch at his command?' Apsyrtus' grin darkens. 'Do you really think Father will ever let you leave Colchis, now he knows what power he can wield through you? Oh, Medea, you truly are a fool. You created that dragon to try to bribe your way out of Colchis, but you have just locked the door to your own prison.'

His words settle heavily inside me, making my confidence shift and give way to a wave of cold doubt.

'And do you think Phrixus would even *want* to marry you?' Apsyrtus continues. He knows his cruelty has pierced through my conviction and now he twists that dagger in deeper. 'Firstly, you are clearly *far* too old to be anyone's wife. Who wants worn, shrivelled-up goods?' He motions to me with a flick of his hand. 'But even if you weren't too old, Phrixus would still never want you. Not now he's seen what you really are, what you are capable of. He is *disgusted* by your magic, by the very thought of you. He told me himself.'

'That is not true.'

'No? Well, if you are so sure, why not go and ask him yourself?' He beckons to the doorway with a jerk of his head. 'Whilst you're at it, you can ask our father about *his word*.'

'Fine.' I lift my chin. 'I will.'

Apsyrtus' eyebrows quirk slightly, as if he were not expecting me to agree so easily. 'Lead the way, dear sister.'

I storm through the palace, my siblings following in my determined wake. I can hear Apsyrtus' sandals clattering as he staggers behind me, attempting to keep up with my sharp strides.

As I walk into my father's entertaining quarters, I am hit with the heavy aroma of cooked meats, woven with the distinctive, acrid smell of sweat. It's the kind of odour that clings unpleasantly to your skin. The men, my father's guests, are reclining on plush loungers, displaying their fat, sagging bodies as if they believe themselves pure works of art. Food is piled high at the centre of the room and slaves flit around, refilling plates and cups.

Around the men, beautiful women dance seductively, their bodies flowing as freely as the wine, their skirts rippling on the evening breeze.

'Father.' My voice cuts across the drunken commotion and the king's gaze fixes on me, a flash of irritation visible on his ugly face.

'There she is . . . The little witch! The dragon summoner!' someone shouts, and the room erupts into a cheer as the men raise their cups, pouring the contents on to the floor in an offering to the Gods.

For a moment, I am stunned by their praise, feeling a strange lightness unfurl inside my chest. I glance around at their elated faces, searching for the fear or repulsion lurking behind their eyes. I see none.

The only person not rejoicing is Phrixus, who sits beside my father with his eyes set on the ground. In his hands is a still full cup of wine.

'Father, Medea has a question for you,' Apsyrtus announces, focusing my attention back on the task at hand.

'Daughter, can you not see we are celebrating?' My father's tone seems amicable, yet I can sense the anger lurking beneath his empty warmth. I have crossed a dangerous line stepping into this room un-invited. 'This can wait for a more appropriate time.'

'No, it cannot,' I say, daring another step towards him.

'Let the dragon summoner speak!' one of the guests booms, his words sluggish in his mouth. 'She has earned it, surely?'

My father manages to remain composed as he waves a flippant hand, feigning disinterest. 'Go on, then. What is it, girl?'

'I want you to honour our agreement.' My voice is calm and clear. I realize in this moment that the music has entirely stopped. 'I want you to announce it right now, to everyone here.'

'Ah, yes.' He flicks his gaze to Apsyrtus, and they share an amused look. He then rises to address the room. 'My daughter is correct. Tonight is indeed a night for celebration, so what more suitable time is there for me to announce my marriage offer to Phrixus?'

A cheer erupts across the room as Phrixus' head jolts upwards. There is a strange tightness around his eyes, as if he is fearful of what my father is going to say next. I long to soothe those worried lines from his face.

'Marriage?' he asks with that familiar anxious edge to his voice.

'You have blessed me with a great gift, the greatest gift Colchis has ever known.' My father reaches out a hand and guides him to his feet, placing an arm around Phrixus' thin shoulders. 'It is only proper that I should return the favour.'

'That is very kind, but—'

'Prince Phrixus, it is my honour to give you my beautiful, obedient daughter as your wife.' My father throws his hand out towards me, and I feel a swell of relief blossom in my chest. My eyes shift to Phrixus and I let a smile shine from my face as I step forwards.

Here is my future, my freedom, standing right before me.

Here is my chance for a better life.

'Chalciope!'

The smile freezes at my lips. *Chalciope?*

'Come on, come forwards, dear,' my father encourages. 'She is incredibly beautiful, is she not?'

I spin round to see my sister cowering in the doorway, gripping the folds of her pale gown. As she gingerly walks forwards her eyes search for mine, but I cannot bear to look at her.

When she is close enough, my father grabs her by the arm and steers her next to Phrixus. I watch them share a shy look with one another, causing Chalciope's cheeks to stain a girlish shade of red.

For a moment, I'm not sure if I can breathe.

I'm not sure I want to.

'Do they not look the perfect couple?' Apsyrtus raises his cup aloft. 'To my little sister, the blushing bride!'

'*NO!*' The word slices through me like a strangled scream, stripping all warmth and merriness from the room. Around me the torches gutter, some of the flames extinguishing completely. 'You gave me your *word*!'

'Silence, Medea. You are making a fool of yourself,' my father hisses, offering an apologetic smile to his guests.

'Phrixus, please.' I turn to him, desperate to rekindle the connection we shared mere hours ago. 'Do not let him do this. Do not leave me here.'

I step towards him, but he recoils backwards, pulling Chalciope with him.

'Please,' he gasps, positioning himself protectively in front of my sister. 'It is not her fault. Do not hurt her.'

'Hurt her?' I breathe. 'You believe I would *hurt* her?'

'I do not know what you are capable of, Princess. Not after what I saw today,' he murmurs, his eyes stained with that familiar look. He lowers his gaze to the floor.

'Is that really what you think?' My voice is choked, knotting itself around useless emotions. I wait for him to respond, but he just continues staring at the ground. He cannot even look me in the eye. Pain thickens to anger inside my veins, roaring in my ears. '*LOOK AT ME!*'

I surge forwards to grab his face, causing everyone in the room to reel backwards in fear, even my father. Somewhere in the commotion, I think I hear Chalciope scream.

'Guards!' my father bellows. 'Restrain her! Now!'

Just as I reach Phrixus I feel brusque hands wrapping around my arms and waist. I let out a furious screech as I am wrenched backwards.

'Is this how you treat your *dragon summoner*?' I snarl at my onlookers.

They remain silent, their faces a wall of cold hostility, exposing the fear that had always lurked beneath those hollow masks of admiration. It was a lie, all of it. They do not respect me. They never did. They never will. All they care about is what success they can carve from me to feed their fat egos.

'Do not hurt her!' Chalciope wails.

She is crying now, but Phrixus is muttering something soft and comforting in her ear. He moves to hold her hand and I feel my body go quiet as I stare at their intertwined fingers, fitting so perfectly together ...

'Get her out of my sight,' my father snarls as the guards haul me away.

Something inside me snaps. I feel it shattering as my fury surges upwards, setting my veins alight, scorching my blood. I begin to thrash against my jailers, kicking and screaming.

'You cannot keep me here for ever!' The words rip from my throat, clawing at the walls as I am dragged back to my chamber, my prison.

But these are not mere words. They are a vow, a promise forged in the fiery depths of my hatred.

I will escape this prison. Even if it means burning it down from the inside.

ONE YEAR
LATER

7

It is a humid summer's day when they arrive.

The heat makes the palace feel stagnant, airless. I am sitting in the sliver of shade in the courtyard, wishing I could peel the clammy warmth from my skin. Everywhere I look, brightly coloured statues smile outwards, their faces frozen in perpetual, mocking glee, though their eyes remain blank. Dead.

I see my mother walking past with a gaggle of personal slaves in her wake. They seem excited about something, their voices mirroring the hum of bees in the flowerbeds. I try to catch my mother's eye but, as usual, she ignores my very existence. Despite my father's new-found interest in my magic, my mother has remained her usual aloof self.

Shortly after, another rush of slaves runs past, their sandals slapping eagerly against the stone floors. Their voices stumble together, so I can only catch the word 'ship'.

More men seeking the Golden Fleece, it seems. Though I do not know why this would evoke such excitement within the palace. It is not as though these are the first challengers; many have come before.

It was shortly after Chalciope and Phrixus left when the first men came in search of the Golden Fleece. Rumour of its divine powers had spread quickly overseas; soon all of Greece was abuzz with news of the magical King Aeetes, his Golden Fleece and the distant, 'savage' lands of Colchis.

My father had welcomed the hopeful heroes with open arms and a cunning smile, giving the same insufferable performance each time. He assures the voyagers that the fleece is theirs if only they can succeed in his simple trials. The men accept all too willingly, hungry for the opportunity to prove their *kleos*, their glory. Though what these men fail to realize is that they are not trials at all, but death sentences. Death sentences that have been set in place utilizing the magic my father once loathed and now cannot seem to get enough of.

As expected, none have survived. The Golden Fleece remains in its grove, untouched.

I cannot help but wonder if their blood is on my hands. Sometimes I imagine I can feel it, the weight of their lives piling on top of me, growing heavier with each hopeful arrival. Suffocating.

But I try not to think on it too much, for those are the types of thoughts that feed off your every waking hour and prey on your sanity, if allowed free rein. So, I keep mine on a tight leash that I loosen only on occasion when I feel compelled to do so, like picking at a painful scab.

I sigh, tilting my head back and closing my eyes, feeling the sunlight glow red behind my lids. Sometimes I like to imagine what it would feel like simply to burn away, to evaporate like water and become nothingness.

'Medea.' A coldness touches my face as my father's broad frame blocks the light.

I readjust my gaze and see that he is dressed in his finest robes, a deep, crushed crimson with gold detailing along the edges. His wrists and fingers drip with glittering jewels, matching the layered pendants jangling against his chest.

'You must come with me,' he says. His voice sounds strained with a panicked excitement.

'Where are we going?' I eye the guards' swords behind him.

'To greet our visitors.' He takes my elbow and guides me to my feet. 'We must make a show of strength to the people, to show we are not afraid of these so-called *Argonauts*.'

'Argonauts?' The word is foreign to me.

'A band of heroes who have come to seek the fleece. The finest men Greece has to offer,' he says as he steers me through the courtyard. Behind us, the guards clatter like a metallic wake. 'I had heard word they were coming. Some say Herakles is amongst them. Imagine that, imagine if I defeat the famed son of Zeus himself.'

He laughs and the sound makes a familiar hatred stir inside me as I stumble to keep up with his urgent strides.

'We will greet them on the palace steps,' my father continues. 'We will show the people that Colchis has nothing to fear . . . Think of the stories, Medea. Think of the glory when the greatest of Greece's heroes fall at our feet.'

The slaves have gathered by the entryway, peering curiously round the large vine-wrapped columns dominating the front of the palace. When they see my father they scatter nervously, vanishing into the shadows.

'There are a lot of them,' my mother says, her eyes brushing briefly over me. As always, she looks unnerved by my presence.

'Good. Follow behind me. Look presentable. Medea, pull your veil down. Where's Apsyrtus? Apsyrtus! Ah, there you are!'

'What is all this fuss for, Father? Who are these foreigners?' My brother appears beside us, slapping away a slave who fusses with his robes.

'The Prince of Iolcus and his little band of heroes. Argonauts, they call themselves. But they will soon be just a memory; a story people tell to celebrate Colchis' might.' My father barks out another sharp laugh.

'Argonauts?' Apsyrtus picks at his fingernails, seemingly bored.

'Named after the ship they sailed here on, the *Argo*. Supposedly the largest ever built, not that that will be of much use to them here,' my father says as he flicks an invisible speck of dust off his robes. 'Come, stand beside me, son. Let us greet these fools.'

They stride out together, shoulder to shoulder. Apsyrtus is dressed so similarly to my father, it is as if he walks beside his own hideous reflection.

I glance to my mother beside me, but her face is vacant, her gaze loosely focused ahead. Standing this close to her I can see how tired her eyes look. She is so thin these days, her features drained of all colour and character. The corners of her mouth are creased with the memory of a smile, one I have not seen for many winters.

She catches me watching her and quickly pulls her veil down. I sigh, mirroring her movements, letting the silver material ripple over my face like water.

Once shielded, we follow the men outside.

I blink as the burning light momentarily blinds me. I can feel the heat of the steps beneath my sandals, baking in the sun. The air is heavy and sweat immediately gathers at the nape of my neck, slipping down my spine.

As my eyes adjust to the brightness, I see that the long entryway leading from the palace walls to the foot of the steps is now full of people. When they see my father an obedient cheer ripples out, though their faces are quick to turn away, their attention drawn elsewhere. I crane my neck to try to catch sight of what they are looking at.

The Argonauts.

They are easy to locate in the crowd, for they walk with such purpose, cutting cleanly through the masses, the people moving out of their way like waves receding under Poseidon's command.

My father leans over to mutter something to Apsyrtus and my brother's ears twitch as he smiles. They are enjoying this: the attention, the excitement crackling in the air. My father is not afraid of the Argonauts' fame, for the greater the hero, the greater his victory against them. He cannot wait to feed his own legend with their lives.

The audience peels backwards as the heroes finally reach the edge of the crowd. There are so many of them, near forty at least. They pool at the base of the palace steps, a wall of muscle and might, glinting dangerously in the sunlight.

I see a woman standing tall amongst them with a bow slung over her shoulder. She looks calm and confident, with dark auburn hair that is plaited tightly at her temples and flows down her back. A small smile curls at her lips, eyebrow quirked as she surveys the palace, as if she is amused by it.

I did not even know a woman could be a hero.

'Greetings, Argonauts,' my father's voice rings out. 'May I ask who is the leader amongst you?'

'I am, King Aeetes.' A man steps forwards, the sunlight catching his breastplate, setting him ablaze. 'My name is Jason, son of Aeson, and the rightful heir to the throne of Iolcus.'

I feel my breath catch in my throat.

Jason.

He is the most handsome being I have ever seen, as if the Goddess of Beauty had carved the prince herself. I cannot tear my gaze away from his flawless features, the chiselled sharpness of his bone structure balanced by the softness of his eyes and lips. He is not the tallest nor broadest of his men, and yet his presence effortlessly commands the crowd. The people are captivated by him. Even the sunlight seems to tilt in Jason's direction, as if the world were drawn to him. The honeyed rays catch in his golden curls as he sweeps his hair backwards with a casual, strong hand.

The Prince of Iolcus takes a moment before continuing, 'My men and I have travelled here on the greatest ship ever built, the *Argo*. On our journey, we have faced great hardships and even greater losses. But now we have reached your famed lands and we will take what is destined for us. The Golden Fleece. We do not come as your enemies but . . .' He offers a confident smile. 'We will not be leaving your shores without it.'

His eyes lift to where I stand and I feel something strike deep inside me, piercing through my chest. My breath hitches in my throat as a strange warmth blossoms from the invisible impact, smouldering throughout my body.

Despite my veil, I can feel Jason's eyes locking on to mine with a dazzling intensity. Those cerulean eyes are so penetrating it feels like he is staring deep inside me, touching the edges of my soul. The world dims around us, as if Jason had cast a mighty shadow across it, throwing everything into meaningless darkness except him and me.

His smile seems to soften, and the strangest sensation overwhelms me. It is the feeling of familiarity, as if I know this man, as if I have always known him. Yet how can that be possible when I've never seen him before in my life? But perhaps this awareness is not from my past at all. What if it is the future beckoning to me? It is as if time has creased and allowed a glimpse into the threads the Fates have spun for me.

'Jason of Iolcus.' My father's voice splinters the moment, pulling Jason's attention away. As soon as his eyes release me, I feel a little foolish at the intensity of the effect he had on me with a simple glance. My cheeks feel unbearably hot beneath the thin material of my veil. 'I welcome you to Colchis with open arms. We are honoured to have you and your crew as our esteemed guests. I assure you the fleece will be yours to take.' A wisp of surprise ripples amongst Jason's men.

'I have heard praise of your power and might, King Aeetes, but your kindness is a true gift worth celebrating,' Jason says, bowing his head graciously.

My father mirrors his movement. 'Indeed, the fleece will be yours to take, so long as you can succeed in three trials.'

'Trials?' His smile remains perfectly in place.

'You did not expect me merely to hand the fleece over, did you?' My father laughs theatrically, throwing his gaze across the crowd. I feel the hatred curdling inside me as I watch his familiar performance. 'Surely a man of your excellence knows that a reward must be earned, yes?'

'Naturally.' Jason's tone is easy, light, despite my father's jibing. 'So, tell me, what are these trials you speak of?'

'So eager, young Jason,' my father tuts, shaking his head. 'You have had a long and difficult journey; your men looked famished. I propose you come inside, let us fill you with Colchis' finest food and wine, and then we can discuss what you seek.'

Jason turns to his men. 'Well, what do you say?'

They cheer in response and clash their swords to their shields. The sound electrifies the air, like a bolt of Zeus's lightning, and is amplified by the crowd breaking out into applause as the heroes ascend the palace steps.

'Come, come! Welcome, Argonauts! Welcome, heroes!' my father booms with open arms.

As Jason draws nearer, it feels as if all the air has been sucked out of the world with the casual cut of his strides. His beauty is even more devastating up close. Surely he must be a god, for no mortal could possess such utter perfection.

My mother bows her head as the prince passes by, yet I remain still, staring unflinchingly.

'Princess.' He nods to me as he passes. His voice seeps into my mind like rain into the earth, enriching the dirt so that beautiful things may grow.

There is a slight amusement touching his eyes, and yet his gaze is still piercing. I do not look away. I do not want to.

I open my mouth to say something but my father interrupts, throwing a possessive arm around Jason as he steers him into the palace and says, 'This way, Jason, this way!'

As I watch him walk away, I hear my mother hiss, 'Compose yourself, Medea.'

I ignore her, distracted by the rush of adrenaline knotting inside me, laced with a dizzy breathlessness I have never felt before. But there's something else there, too, something clear and sharp cutting through the commotion.

Silently, I follow the men inside, my eyes firmly set on Jason.

8

I wait in my chamber as my father entertains his new guests.

Their merriment reverberates through the palace walls and I find myself trying to locate Jason amongst the rising clamour, desperate to carve his voice out for myself so I can seize it like a lifeline.

I pace in my room, treading and re-treading the same twelve steps from wall to wall, forcing myself to control my breathing, focus my mind. But I cannot. Thoughts of Jason have plagued my entire body. He is like a devastatingly delicious sickness, one that is devouring me whole.

Is this what men always sing about? Is this that infamous feeling of Eros' fateful arrow burying itself into my heart?

No. I am not foolish enough to believe those fantasies. Ideals such as love at first sight only exist in worlds spun by dreamy-eyed bards.

I turn to retrace my steps once again but feel my pulse leap through my body when I see Chalciope standing in the doorway. My heart constricts, the breath catching in my throat.

Sister ...

I take an instinctive step towards her, but lucidity soon sharpens my vision as I realize it is not my sister at all. Of course it is not. My sister is worlds away, living happily with her sweet, devoted husband.

My chest aches with a pain I refuse to acknowledge.

'Hello, Mother.'

'Your father wanted me to make sure you are presentable,' she says, stepping into the room, hands tightly clasped together. Her voice is clipped, as if she has cut around each word, trimming all the emotion so only the sharp syllables remain.

'Presentable?'

'The prince has asked to see you.'

'Jason?'

She does not reply, but instead takes a few measured steps towards me. Her eyes still will not meet mine.

Sometimes I wonder if my mother died years ago, and the woman who now listlessly slips through these hallways is just a ghost, a memory of the Queen of Colchis who once laughed and danced and sang. I wish I knew that version of her.

Was this my fault? Did having a witch for a daughter do this to her? Or is this what happens when you are married to a man like my father? Has his darkness slowly sapped away her light, leaving her this cold husk of a woman, a body without a soul?

Perhaps we are both to blame.

'Turn around, let me fix your hair,' she instructs, and I silently obey.

I hear her inhale before she begins to sweep her slender fingers through my ebony locks. She is hesitant at first, but then begins to tug aggressively at the knots, snapping through the tendrils with little care, making my eyes water. But I do not mind the pain; it is worth it just to feel her touch.

I cannot remember the last time she touched me.

'Your magic has turned your father into a monster, I hope you realize that.'

'He was always a monster,' I reply, turning to face her.

She stares at me wordlessly and I can see the misery weighing in her eyes, eroding her from the inside. My gaze dips to the bruise along her jaw, one she has tried to cover with powder, just as I have done before. You'd think our shared suffering would bond us, but it has only ever driven us further apart.

She swallows and readjusts herself, her emotions closing off like that veil being drawn across her face once again. She turns my head back with her hands and continues untangling my hair.

I sigh, closing my eyes, letting myself be lulled by the sweep of her fingers tickling against my scalp and neck. I feel like a child again, sitting on my bed, my little legs swinging idly back and forth as Chalciope giggles beside me.

'My hair is not as agreeable as Chalciope's.'

'Nobody's hair is as agreeable as hers.'

'I miss her.' This admittance feels as if I am reaching my arms across that dark, gaping void between us, willing my mother to take my hand.

I want to say more. I want to tell her just how much I miss Chalciope and how painful it is to do so. I want to know if her absence has carved the same hole inside her chest.

I never even got to say goodbye.

'We all miss her,' my mother replies dismissively, though I can sense a change in her touch, her fingers softening as she begins to slip heavy, jewelled pins into my curls.

'Even Apsyrtus?' I ask, letting my silent accusation fill the space between us.

'*Do not* speak ill of your brother. You have no right,' she snaps. I want to turn to look at her, but she holds my scalp with surprising firmness. 'He is the way he is now because of *you*.'

Her hands fall away then and I hear her draw in a careful breath. I remain staring at the featureless wall in front of me, tracing the ugliness of Apsyrtus' sneer in my mind.

'He still has nightmares. About what you did,' she whispers, so quietly I'm not sure at first if I imagined it.

'I . . . did not know,' is all I can think to reply.

'Of course you did not. He is too proud to tell anyone.' She pauses. 'I wake most nights to his screams. I do what I can to soothe him, but I know it is not enough. There is nothing I can do to protect him from the poison *you* planted in his mind.'

I turn then but find her expression is eerily empty, vacant. I can only see the ghost of a long-suppressed emotion catching in the tightness of her jaw.

'You did not only break his body that day, Medea, you broke his *soul*. And for what? For your own amusement?'

'I never meant—'

'I am done,' she cuts me off, her eyes drifting absently over my hair. 'Go and see your father now.'

'Mother, I—'

'Go and see your father.' She keeps her gaze focused on the wall ahead, refusing to look at me.

I say nothing as I walk away, leaving her alone in my chamber.

A guard escorts me to my father's private chamber. It is a room I have never been in before.

It does not have the grand opulence of his throne room, as it isn't frequented by visitors. I am told it is where the king meets with advisers, where important decisions are made.

The understated space is dominated by a bronze table with three rounded legs carved in the shape of clawed bird's feet. The rectangular surface is strewn with various stacks of parchment and wax tablets, lit by quivering oil lamps. Around us, the walls drip with the crimson drapery the king favours.

'Medea, there you are. Come.' My father beckons me inside.

I force myself to keep my eyes set on him as I enter, though I can immediately sense Jason beside me. His presence is like the rich taste of thunder in the air before a storm – electrifying.

'Jason wanted to meet you,' he continues, and I can hear a slight smugness curling in his voice. It makes my skin crawl.

I draw in a careful breath. I do not have to look at Jason to know his eyes are on me; his piercing stare on my exposed face feels unbearably intimate.

'Jason has heard of your . . . *abilities*, daughter.'

So, that is why I am here. My father is showing off his prize weapon. Like sharpening a sword in front of your enemy, before driving it into their heart.

'Princess.' Jason's voice slips over my skin like a summer-kissed breeze, making the hairs on my arms stand on end.

I nod in his direction as he bows deeply. Halfway through rising, he takes my hand, his gaze lifting to mine as his lips brush my skin.

In that one movement, I feel the world slow to a sluggish pulse, as if time itself had been staggered by the touch of his lips. He lingers for longer than we both know he should, the softness of his mouth turning my insides molten. Heat pools through every inch of me and I imagine my body melting away beneath those lips, dripping between his fingers.

'Is it true, Princess Medea, what they say of your powers?' he asks as he finally straightens up, the question grounding me back in reality.

'That depends on what they say.' I hold his eyes with mine, savouring the way they slightly crinkle as he smiles. They are the colour of a summer sky, bright and endless. Full of infinite possibilities.

'They say you are a thing of wonder,' he says, and I become aware how loud my heart is beating. Can Jason hear it, too? Can my father? Gods, I hope not. 'Did you learn under your aunt?'

'She did.' My father speaks for me, placing a firm hand on my shoulder. I notice then just how ugly the Greek language sounds on his tongue compared to the rounded richness of Jason's accent. 'But then Circe got herself exiled to that pathetic little island, Aeaea. She always was a troublemaker, you know. So now I oversee all of Medea's magic. I guide her.'

My mind snaps into focus.

Exiled?

'I had heard news of Circe's exile,' Jason says. 'A shame for her powers to be wasted in such a way.'

My father makes a non-committal noise, his eyes shifting to me as he realizes his mistake. He had never planned on telling me this. He would have had me continuing to believe that Circe had *chosen* to leave me, that I had done something to drive her away. But that was all a lie. She has been *exiled*, kept from me against her will . . .

Circe did not abandon me.

And my father *knew* that.

The heat beneath my skin shifts from those embers of desire to flames of white-hot fury.

'It is truly a marvel, to harness the powers of Hecate,' Jason continues, though I can barely hear him over my rising rage. 'I know there are many in Greece who would be fascinated to meet Medea, to see her talents. Kings, queens, scholars—'

'Colchis' borders are open. If they wish to meet the princess, there is nothing stopping them,' my father replies tightly.

'Just a suggestion.' Jason smiles, then regards his empty cup with a flourish. 'I don't suppose you have more of this wine, Aeetes? It is truly delightful.'

'Of course.' My father saunters over to the elaborately decorated jug on the far table. 'You know, they say Colchian wine is the finest in all the world. Dionysus has truly blessed our vineyards.'

As soon as he turns away, Jason leans in and whispers to me, 'It seems wrong to keep your powers locked away like this.' His words are hot against the nape of my neck, causing a shiver to ripple down my spine. I feel that shiver resonating inwards, caressing my anger, letting it settle in my veins. 'I would never neglect a gift so ... *beautiful.*' My toes curl at the word.

He pulls away and smiles as my father walks back to us, seemingly oblivious. Jason accepts his refilled cup with a gracious nod, his behaviour so calm and collected I almost wonder if I imagined the whole encounter. Yet, I can still feel the remnants of his breath prickling along my neck.

I silently pray my face is not as flushed as it feels.

'So, Jason.' My father swirls his cup idly in his hand. 'Tell me, why is it you seek my fleece?'

'I was tasked by my uncle.' Jason takes a slow sip of wine. I watch the liquid touch his lips and slip down his throat with a strange ache of envy.

'And why would he ask such a thing of you?'

'It is our agreement. If I hand over the fleece, Pelias swore Iolcus' throne is mine to take.'

'He would just hand his kingship over?' My father quirks a brow.

'I am Iolcus' rightful heir.' I see a muscle ticking in Jason's jaw, though his expression remains calm. 'I intend to honour my father's life and take back what my uncle stole.'

'And you truly believe Pelias will honour his word? A man who killed his own brother to be king?' My father tilts his head, a knowing glint in his eye.

'I suppose we shall see when I return with the fleece.' Jason holds

67

his gaze, offering another of his easy smiles. 'But everyone knows I am the king Iolcus needs, the one the people deserve.'

My father gives a sharp, dismissive chuckle at that. 'I must admit, Jason, I am surprised your uncle let you grow to such a fine age. He must have known you would be a threat to his title.'

'In truth, he believed me dead until recently. He thought I died in the prison cell he locked my family away in.' Jason takes another sip of wine, though his eyes darken slightly, a cloud passing over that summer sky. 'But my clever mother managed to smuggle me out of the city. I was only a child at the time . . . She and my brother were not so fortunate.'

'Your uncle killed them?' The question escapes me in a shocked breath. Beside me, I feel my father stiffen, as if he had forgotten I was here.

'They died of sickness under his imprisonment, so I am told.' Jason's eyes are gentle as they hold mine. He then shifts his focus to my father, and I see something igniting in those eyes. 'And so, I seek the fleece so I may avenge their deaths and take what is rightfully mine.'

'A noble cause.' The king nods, his smile greasy with condescension.

'The Gods seem to think so.' Jason lets his unspoken threat hang in the air for a moment. Beside me, my father remains impassive. 'So, these trials I must face tomorrow . . . I am assuming they are no ordinary tests?'

'Come now, Jason. You seem to be a man who enjoys a challenge, yes?'

'Of course. I accept your challenges readily, King Aeetes. I only ask, respectfully, that you will let us leave this land without conflict when I succeed.'

'Such confidence.' My father flashes me a sideways look I try to ignore. 'Of course, my boy. *If* you obtain the Golden Fleece, you may leave Colchis freely. You have my word.'

Your word means nothing.

'You honour me with your graciousness. Thank you.' Jason grips my father's forearm, a quiet tension coiling tighter between them despite their amicable words. 'Now, I must go and check my men have not bled you dry of your fine wine. Time at sea has made them quite the animals.'

'Ha! I shall send the slaves to fetch more of whatever they desire. Tonight is about celebrating our esteemed guests!'

'Thank you, King Aeetes . . . Princess.' He bows his head to me, his eyes sparkling with unspoken words.

Once Jason disappears, I loosen a sigh, feeling as if I can finally breathe again. Beside me, my father paces to the table to refill his wine.

'What a fool,' he sniggers, gesturing vaguely to where Jason had been standing. 'Such arrogance. He really thinks himself capable, thinks the Gods are on his side. A fool indeed.'

'He will die tomorrow.' The realization settles heavily inside me, like a stone dropping into the pit of my stomach.

'Of course he will.' My father barks out a harsh laugh. 'No one can match my power.'

'*Your* power?' The question slips out before I can stop myself, followed by a wave of sickening regret.

My father stills, as if his whole body has drawn inwards. When he speaks, his voice is lethally quiet. 'What did you say?'

'Nothing.'

I make a move towards the door, but he catches my wrist and wrenches me round to face him. I can see the familiar anger twisting his face, the violence written in his golden, hateful eyes. I knew it would not be long before I saw it again.

'Say it, girl,' he hisses, his words flecked with spit, dashing across my cheeks. 'Go on. Say it to me.'

I hold his gaze but remain silent, feeling a coldness close over me, numbing my insides. Preparing for what is to follow.

He strikes my face. I feel the pain slice through my cheekbone, the jewels from his rings cutting my flesh. I touch a hand to my face and stare at the blood smeared across my fingertips, a violent shade of red against the paleness of my skin.

'It is *mine*, do you understand that, Medea?' His voice is ragged. I can feel the rage pacing inside him, waiting to strike again. 'You are mine. Your powers are mine. You are *nothing* without me. Do you understand that?'

I stare at him, letting my gaze cut a thousand silent insults in the air between us.

'I said, *do you understand*?'

'Why did you not tell me?' I whisper, my voice trembling with a quiet ferocity. 'That Circe was exiled? That she was trapped on an island?'

'Because it was of no importance.'

'But all this time—'

He raises his fist again and I flinch. It's a minor movement, but it's enough. I watch a hideous, satisfied smile crawl across my father's face. It is so rare he elicits such a reaction from me, and I can tell he relishes it, relishes my fear.

I hate myself for allowing him that gratification, for exposing such weakness before him.

My father reaches out and I do not recoil this time. But, instead of hurting me, he simply runs a finger over where he struck me before, smearing the blood across my cheek.

'Such a mess.' He clicks his tongue. 'Not that you were much to look at in the first place. Go on, get out of my sight.'

'Yes, Father.'

9

I walk back to my chamber alone.

My father did not bother to summon a guard to escort me, too distracted by his own impending glory, perhaps.

My face throbs, but the pain is numbed by an anger I can barely contain, as those words repeat over and over again . . .

You are mine . . .

Your powers are mine . . .

You are nothing *without me . . .*

And yet, embedded within that fury, I can sense an idea unfurling, like a boat battling against the storm of my rage. For the longest time I had felt myself lost within that tempest, not knowing how to get out. But now, my father has unwittingly carved out a destination through those treacherous waters, filling my sails with hope. *Aeaea.*

I feel my plan solidifying inside me. A plan for freedom . . . and revenge.

My face stings as I smile to myself.

'Are you all right?'

I almost stumble as the voice catches me off guard. Glancing up, I see the female Argonaut standing before me. I have heard my father's guards refer to her as 'the huntress', though I do not know what type of prey she hunts.

Her hair is the colour of dark, sun-baked terracotta, tangling down

71

her back in carefree waves. She is tanned and muscular, her skin flecked with small, bone-white scars, no doubt each one woven with a fascinating story. The story of a woman who has actually *lived*.

She is undeniably beautiful, but her beauty is like that of nature – wild, carefree, uninhibited.

My eyes then shift to her clothes. A wolf pelt is shrugged around her shoulders, underneath which she wears a light tunic that barely covers her toned figure, leaving her arms and legs bare. I could never imagine wearing such a thing in private, let alone in the company of others.

'Medea, isn't it?' she asks, glowing with a self-assuredness I have only seen one other woman possess.

'Do you realize you are addressing the Princess of Colchis?' My voice is as sharp as the blades in her leather belt, my defensiveness flaring up. 'You should not be wandering the palace alone. What do you think you are doing?'

She shrugs. 'Just looking around. I had heard a lot of stories about this place, and I must say I'm a little disappointed. I haven't seen a single dead body strung up in a tree.' Her tone is serious, but her face is lit with amusement. 'That's what they say, you know – that you hang your dead from the trees.'

'And do you always believe everything you are told?'

Her grin widens at that as she slips her gaze up and down me. Her eyes then narrow to my throbbing cheek, which has no doubt begun to swell around the gash. I feel a warm trickle of blood but do not move to wipe it away.

'What happened there?'

'I fell.'

She folds her toned arms, arching an eyebrow. 'Does the ground hit you often?'

'What does it matter to you?'

'Perhaps I'm curious.'

'Perhaps you shouldn't be.'

She snorts. 'Are you always so uptight?'

'Stop asking me questions.'

'Would you like to ask me some instead?' A confident humour prowls in her eyes.

I consider her invitation for a moment, eyeing the empty hallways, weighing up the time slipping between us.

'You are one of them? An Argonaut?' She nods. 'How?'

'I proved myself, like everyone else.' The huntress shrugs again, as if it were not a remarkable feat.

'But you are a woman?'

'Very observant, Princess.'

I choose to ignore her insolence. 'How did you prove yourself?'

'I fought the others ... and won,' she adds with a grin. 'I am Atalanta, by the way.'

I regard her once more, my gaze tripping over her sculpted muscles.

'Are you Jason's lover?' The abruptness of this question makes her laugh, the sound warm and inviting.

'Gods, no. I don't believe Jason could be in love with anyone other than himself.'

'What makes you say that?'

'What makes you care?' she counters.

I feel a rush of heat stain my cheeks, my eyes flickering to the floor as my reactive shyness quickly hardens into something else.

'He will die tomorrow,' I tell her.

'I would not worry, Princess. The man has many talents. He is favoured by the Gods.'

'Not against this, not against my magic.' I hold her stare, feeling the air shift and tighten around us as my words click into place. Her smile hardens as she considers the threat I'm posing. 'Only I can save him.'

'You? Save him? Now, why would *you* do something like that?' She scans the shadowy, empty passageway, her eyes focused and alert. The eyes of a huntress.

'I have my reasons,' I say carefully. When I speak again, my voice is just a whisper. 'Tell Jason I will come to his chamber tonight and I will give him the spell that will ensure his victory tomorrow.'

'But why—'

There is an eruption of laughter near by as drunken figures appear down the corridor.

'Atalanta, there you are!' one of the Argonauts bellows, his words splitting open the tension between us.

'Just tell Jason I will be there tonight. Will you?'

I do not wait for her to reply before hurrying away, melting into the night's comforting embrace.

10

My palms sweat as I slip through the darkness.

The guest wing of the palace is crawling with guards tonight; they clatter down the hallways, patrolling the same worn routes they always do. But I have spent my life evading these men; I have memorized their patterns, know all their blind spots. Besides, their attention is not on me tonight. They are focused on the Argonauts, my father's 'esteemed guests'. So, it is easy enough for me to slink to Jason's door undetected.

I know which room is his, for I know my father will have put him in our grandest guest chamber. He wants to impress, after all. He always does.

As I approach, I reaffirm my grip on the small *pyxis*, the cylindrical container, clasped between my damp hands. The spell inside feels warm and alive. I prepared it as soon as I returned to my chamber, using the stash of ingredients hidden beneath my bed. I have been collecting these ingredients ever since I was allowed to practise my magic again. Though I could only ever steal small morsels at a time, for my father now monitors every step of my magic process.

I always intended to use them in spells to aid my escape, but I had not believed an opportunity would arise so soon. I had not dared hope.

It is a gift, this spell, one that will save Jason's life. I pray he accepts it and believes my intentions are true. I pray, too, that he does not recoil from my willingness to betray my own flesh and blood.

My mind drifts to the story of Scylla, a girl who betrayed her father for love. She stole his sacred lock of hair, the one that harboured his gift of invincibility, and gave the lock to his sworn enemy, King Minos. But instead of returning her affections, Minos was disgusted by her betrayal and punished Scylla for her actions. He tied the girl to his ship and dragged her to her death.

I wonder how it feels, to drown. To have the salty waves beat your body and invade every inch of you. To be dragged under by clawing currents and sent to a watery, worthless grave. Laid to rest in Poseidon's bed, your body swollen and decaying.

It is a cruel end, to be a soul lost for ever amongst the anonymous waves.

'You must be the witch.'

A voice rumbles from the shadows, making me jump. I realize I am standing outside Jason's door, directly in front of a towering figure. I stiffen but do not step back.

He shifts into the light, the torches fringing the passageway illuminating his giant, muscular body. His skin is a deep, dark brown which emphasizes the paleness of his olive-green eyes. His hair is the colour of fresh earth and hangs messily down to his broad, hulking shoulders. Along his right cheek his skin puckers into a pale, Y-shaped scar.

I have never seen a man so large, yet his intimidating size is offset by the disarming grin spun around his thick lips.

'Are you going to put a spell on us, little witch?' That smile broadens, eyes sparking.

'Meleager.' Atalanta materializes as if out of thin air. 'Stop trying to frighten the girl.'

Meleager. I know of him. Even across Poseidon's mighty seas we have heard of Greece's beloved Prince of Calydon. Breaker of bones and hearts, so they say.

'He does not frighten me,' I interject, to which Meleager rumbles a thunderous laugh.

'I like her,' he says to Atalanta. 'She reminds me of you.'

The huntress regards me, that scepticism still weighing in her eyes. She is like a waterfall, equal parts beautiful and strong, serene and dangerous.

'You came,' is all she says, leaning back against the wall, her hair coiled over her shoulder. In the torchlight I can see little gold cuffs winking in the plaits at her temple.

'Did you talk to Jason?'

She nods, her expression unreadable. 'He's inside.'

As I go to move past her, she slams a hand against the wall, blocking my path. I stare at her sleek, bronzed arm inches from my face. The huntress leans in, lowering her head so her grey eyes are level with mine. She is so close I can smell the earthy richness of her skin; the scent reminds me of the forest after a downpour.

'We will be right here, Princess,' she purrs in my ear. 'Remember that.'

A warning. Understandable. I have given her no reason to trust me, yet.

I hold her gaze, trying to decipher what is written within it. There is something more than distrust here. Curiosity, perhaps? She claimed she'd heard many stories about Colchis. I wonder what she has heard of me.

Finally, Atalanta slinks backwards and jerks her chin towards the door. 'Go on.'

I hold her eyes for a beat longer before heading inside.

When I enter, Jason is standing over the hearth with his back to me. The firelight soaks the space in a warm, inviting glow, yet I can only feel the whispering chill of the tension coiling round my body.

'Medea,' he says softly, turning.

My name has always been an ugly sound to me, a stain on other people's tongues, hissed, shouted, uttered in fear. But around Jason's lips, it sounds . . . beautiful. *Medea.* The way the vowels roll so fluidly, like a gentle sigh. I want him to say it again and again; I want him to shout it at the top of his lungs for all of Colchis to hear.

'Jason.'

His eyes are so dazzling they remind me of the Dog Star, Sirius, the brightest in all the night sky. As I stare into those eyes, I feel as if I am standing on the edge of a precipice, a sheer drop yawning below me. I cannot see what lies beyond, but I know with a chilling certainty that I want to take this blind leap. I must.

'Do you know why I am here?'

'Yes.'

The firelight shivers in anticipation, its shadows carving along Jason's throat, accentuating the sharpness of his jaw. I wonder, vaguely, what it must be like to possess such beauty, to have the world melt at your touch.

'The Gods have spoken to me,' he says. 'They have told me I will not succeed without your help.'

The Gods? His words make my thoughts stumble over themselves.

He moves towards me then and I instinctively stiffen. It is just a slight tightening of my muscles but enough for Jason to notice and halt in his tracks.

'Are you afraid to be alone with me?' His voice is a smooth caress. 'I can assure you I would never let any harm come to you, Princess.'

'I am not afraid,' I reply levelly, stepping closer. The movement causes his eyes to narrow, a slash of concern cutting across his face.

'What happened?'

He closes the distance between us in two long strides, and I feel a cold retort hardening in my throat. *Nothing happened, I have always been this way.* But then, to my surprise, his hand cups my face and I feel his thumb gently probe the cut along my cheekbone.

'Nothing.' The word is just a breath against his warm palm.

'Who did this to you?' A quiet rage underpins the question. 'Your father? I will make him suffer if he has hurt you, Medea.'

'It is nothing.'

I turn my face away and he drops his hand, keeping his eyes on mine. The tension in the room feels palpable, as if the air is charged by some strange energy burning between us. I hope Jason can feel it, too.

'Is it truly nothing?' he asks, his hand reaching out to graze mine. Perhaps there is something in my eyes that makes him add, 'Are you sure you want to do this? If you need a moment—'

'Your first task will seem simple,' I say, pulling away from his touch and striding over to the fire. There is no time for doubt, not now. If I'm going to shatter my world, I need both hands firmly on the weapon to deliver that final blow.

Jason's eyes follow my movements, a question tugging so clearly in his gaze that it makes me ask, 'What?'

'Do you not wish to know more about me before offering your aid? To see if you believe my intentions are true?' He tilts his head, a smile tucked away at the corner of his lips.

'Are not all men's intentions the same: valour and glory and all the rest of it?' I shrug and that smile of his curls wider. Gods, that *smile.* It is beautifully disarming yet somehow dangerous. 'Your intentions are of no consequence to me. I will help you if you help me.'

'Do you always speak your mind so freely?'

'Should I not?'

'Some would say so.' He nods, moving to lean against the bed with his large hands braced along the frame. I try not to let my eyes linger on the way the shadows accentuate the corded muscles of his arms.

'And what do you say?' My throat feels thick and dry all at once.

'I like the way your mind speaks. In truth, I find you rather remarkable, Princess.'

I turn back to the fire and bite down on my smile. *Focus, Medea, focus.*

Clearing my throat, I say into the flames, 'For the first task, my father will make you plough a field with two oxen. It seems a simple challenge, but I assure you it is not.' I consider my next words, remembering the way Phrixus' eyes had darkened when he witnessed the true extent of my powers. 'I spelled the oxen so that they are no ordinary creatures ... They breathe fire.'

'Fire?' A flicker of surprise catches somewhere between Jason's smile and eyes. 'Well, that does complicate things, doesn't it?'

A silence follows and I can see his thoughts turning in the way his eyes skim around the room. He is considering his tactics, hunting for a solution he will never find.

Not without me.

Believe in yourself, as I do. I have been replaying these words over and over in my mind. Words from a night many moons ago, when I taught myself this very spell and Circe taught me her most important lesson of all.

Trust your instincts.

'I can help with the fire. I can make your skin repel it.' I reaffirm my grip on the *pyxis* as Jason regards it.

'Repel fire?'

I nod. 'It is a drug called *prometheon*. It is made from the root of a flower that grows in the mountains. They say the flowers first sprouted from Prometheus' divine blood, after the flesh-eating birds ripped apart his body.'

Jason draws in a slight breath as he folds his arms. 'Forgive me for asking, Princess, but how can I be sure you are telling the truth?'

'You cannot,' I say simply. 'Not until I show you.'

I remove the lid from the container and scoop out a small amount of the thick, gritty contents. I then smear the paste across my right hand, uttering a prayer to Hecate. The balm absorbs into my skin, as it did before. But this time I do not hesitate when I place my hand into the flames.

'*Medea . . .*' My name is a breath caught in Jason's throat.

The fire bows beneath my fingertips, its heat reduced to a muted tickle against the magic buzzing over my skin. I watch Jason's reaction, waiting for the disgust, the repulsion, to unravel his handsome features.

'Do you see?' I ask, glancing back to the flames, watching them dip and dance around my hand. Within the embers, I see Phrixus' revolted fear glowing back at me.

But when I look to Jason his eyes are shining.

'Incredible,' he says, and I feel the word ignite inside me.

Incredible.

I withdraw my hand and hold it out to him. He steps forwards and takes it in his, running his hand over my unharmed skin, tracing circles in my palm that tease up to my fingertips.

'It does not even feel warm,' he murmurs.

'I will enable you to obtain the fleece, Jason. I can assure you of that.' I tug my hand from his. 'But in return I ask one thing from you.'

'Name it. Anything.'

'You will take me with you when you leave.' His eyes spark but his face remains calm, open. 'You will grant me safe passage to Aeaea. Can you do that?'

'Aeaea. To Circe.' He nods slowly as he comprehends my plan. 'I shall take you there, Medea. I swear to you. But I must ask . . . with a gift such as yours, why do you need my aid?'

A gift. That is how he sees my magic. Not a curse or a disease, but a gift.

'I have barely stepped foot beyond the palace walls my whole life,' I admit, turning my face to the shadows. 'There are only so many spells I can prepare without knowing what awaits me beyond Colchis. You are a proficient voyager; you know of the dangers beyond our shores. I have power but I need your experience to get to Aeaea.'

'You will have it.' Jason nods, his eyes brushing up and down me in a way that makes my pulse strike against my skin.

Focus.

'You must swear it. Swear you will take me to Aeaea.'

'I swear it, Medea. You have my word.' His voice is so strong, so reassuring. And yet . . . I know where a man's word has got me before.

'How do I know I can trust you?'

'I could ask you the same thing. For all I know, this could be one of Aeetes' elaborate tricks,' Jason counters, though his voice is gentle rather than accusing. 'How can I trust you are willing to betray your loved ones?'

'Because they are not my loved ones,' I say impassively. 'They are my family by blood, nothing else.'

Jason considers that for a moment. If he is disturbed by my betrayal, he does not show it.

'I suppose we will just have to take this leap of faith together, won't we? Are you willing, Medea?'

'I am willing.'

He smiles, that beautiful, dangerous smile. Sweetness and sin rolled together. 'Shall we begin, then?'

I nod and turn to set down the *pyxis*. As I move, I can feel his eyes on me, making me hyper-aware of every action, every breath. A sudden nervousness weaves its way around my mind, causing me to fumble the potion.

'Are these the clothes you will be wearing tomorrow?' I ask, pointing to the breastplate and tunic strewn at the side of the room. He nods and I make quick work of smearing the balm across the garments, repeating the same prayer to invoke Hecate.

Goddess, I call to you . . . lend me your power . . .

Once done, I turn back to Jason.

'Your robe.' I nod to him, my voice dry from the tangle of nerves in my throat. 'You must remove it.'

He raises an eyebrow. 'That's very forward of you, Princess.'

'Any part left uncovered will be vulnerable to the fire.'

'Well, we don't want that, do we? I'm quite fond of all my parts,' he jests, I assume in an attempt to soothe my uneasiness.

But any attempt is thwarted as Jason nonchalantly unhooks the clasp of his robe, letting the material ripple to the floor and pool around his feet. That one movement seems to suck all the air from the room, choking the breath from my lungs.

I stiffen at the sight of his naked body glowing golden in the firelight. He seems so at ease bared before me like this, proud almost, and why should he not be? Jason is flawless, like a statue to which an artist has devoted painstaking hours to ensure its absolute perfection.

My eyes roam across his chiselled chest, and the tuft of golden curls gathered at the centre. They then drop to the compact muscles knotted over his stomach, tracing lower still to his hips carving into a V shape, reaching down towards . . .

'Are you enjoying the view?' Jason asks, his tone warmly teasing. I immediately snap my eyes back to his, cheeks aflame. 'It is all right, Princess. Take all the time you need.'

Trying to ignore the amusement in his eyes, I scoop the paste into my hands and draw in a steadying breath. *Focus, control.* Circe had called these disciplines the 'pillars of magic'. I remind myself of that as I place my palms on his bare chest, flicking my gaze up to meet his. Jason's eyes are now intense, any hints of humour vanishing beneath my touch. I quickly glance away, focusing my attention on his body as I rub the paste into his skin.

I murmur my invocation to Hecate as the tang of magic pierces through my nose, sharp and rich. I then begin to feel it buzzing beneath my fingertips, sparking against Jason's skin. I hear him gasp a little, his eyes widening as he feels the magic course through him.

'Is that OK?' I peer up at him.

'Yes.' He trembles, though not in fear.

He is warm and strong beneath my touch, like marble wrapped in silk. As I move my hands over his body, I feel something new and unfamiliar unfolding deep inside my own, a dormant piece of me stirring awake. My pulse begins to throb through every inch of my being, as if my very core were melting. It is an entirely new sensation, one that is both pleasurable and torturous all at once.

'Are you all right?' Jason asks, his voice breathless.

I nod, the words lodged in my throat.

Time seems to stumble and slow around us as my hands work every inch of his body. I move to his broad back, along his arms, down to his legs. His breath hitches when I touch certain places, making my heartbeat quicken and the aching in my core swell, as if my body were calling for something, needing more . . .

I want Jason to touch me.

I do not care how. He could strike me like my father, and I would feel nothing but pleasure for his skin against mine. I want to dig my fingers into his flesh, to drag him towards me and taste that smile spun so easily around his lips.

I hold his gaze as I move to stand in front of him once again, running my hands over his muscular stomach. I then reach my hand between his legs, the only part of him I have not yet touched. I watch the surprise flash in his eyes at my forwardness. Those eyes then roll back as a look of pleasure ripples across his face, filling me with a startling satisfaction.

When he speaks, his voice is ragged. 'You're going to have to stop that.'

I snatch my hand away, stung by his words.

'I am sorry,' I murmur, lowering my eyes.

'No, no, it's fine. It's just . . .' He smiles, tilting my face up to his with gentle fingers. 'I am not sure you realize what your touch is doing to me . . . or what it makes me want to do to you.'

'You can do whatever you want to me,' I breathe. 'Anything at all.'

He leans in, his hand lingering under my chin. 'What do *you* want me to do to you, Medea?'

I do not know. How can I shape this desire into anything coherent? How could I possibly limit this feeling to the stifling confines of language?

So instead of using my words, I do the only thing I can think of.

I kiss him.

My eagerness makes me clumsy and awkward, my teeth clattering against his. But Jason responds perfectly, wrapping his arms around my waist to pull me smoothly into him. He deepens the kiss, crushing his mouth against mine with a sudden urgency that leaves me breathless.

I can taste his hunger. It is a hunger unlike any I have ever experienced, but I can feel it spreading through me, its roots burrowing deep.

'I've wanted you since the moment I saw you on those steps,' Jason whispers against my lips.

He *wants* me. *Me.* The feeling is intoxicating, as if I am drunk on his touch, his desire.

Suddenly, Jason hoists me around and lowers me on to the bed, his large body towering over mine. I feel the adrenaline glow beneath my skin, sparking and popping inside me like a raging fire.

'Is this OK?' he murmurs against my neck.

'Yes.' I gulp down the word.

His mouth explores my skin, trailing his way down my neck, along my collarbone, tasting me with such sweet reverence. I lock my hands into his golden curls as I feel his own slip between the folds of my gown, brushing against my inner thighs, teasing that unbearably sensitive stretch of flesh. A sudden nervousness rises inside me at this brazen intimacy, but the feeling is pierced by a sharp bolt of pleasure as Jason nips at my earlobe, making me gasp out loud.

I can feel Jason smile against my neck as his free hand pulls at my shoulder fastenings.

He *wants* me.

But why would someone like him want someone like me? He who is beloved by all around him, even the Gods. What interest would a celebrated hero have in a loathed witch? Perhaps he has no interest at all. Perhaps he is toying with me, manipulating my weak emotions.

You are a disease.

You will destroy everything you touch.

Darkness calls to darkness.

Violence breeds violence.

No, *no*. He wants me. He said so.

But it is too late. My thoughts have sparked a silent panic, letting it mutate inside me. For a moment I feel as if I cannot breathe, as if my skin is crawling off my bones. My mind then rolls out of my body, spilling into the air, watching from above. I see myself beneath Jason, watching him move against my body as my face stares out blank, emotionless. As if I am dead.

The vision darkens and I see my father over me, his hand on my throat, fist slamming against my face.

I cannot breathe.

'Wait!' I gasp out the word, sitting bolt upright.

Jason draws backwards so he is now kneeling between my legs. He inclines his head towards me, his golden hair flopping over his eyes.

'What's wrong?' he asks gently. 'I am sorry if I—'

'The second trial,' I interrupt him. 'I have not told you about the second trial.'

'Right,' he says as I pull my gown back over my shoulder.

'For the second task, my father will ask you to sow the teeth of a dragon,' I say. Jason sits on the edge of the bed. The small space between us feels cavernous, as if my words are echoing into the expanse.

'A dragon?'

'Yes. Dragon teeth possess powerful magic. When they touch the earth, soldiers will rise from the ground. Though they are not of this world. They are the corpses of men who died some time ago.'

Jason's face gathers in thought as he turns to pull on his robes.

'Can they be killed?'

'They must die by one another's hand. They are designed to slay whoever makes the first move against them. When they appear, make sure you are hidden from view and throw a stone amongst them. They have the bodies of men but not the minds. They will be confused as to who made the first blow and will attack one another until none are left standing.'

'So, I am not to fight them?' He walks over to the fireplace, plucking a grape from the low table situated beside it. I can still taste his disappointment in me like a sourness in the air.

'If you strike one down, two more will rise up. It will be an endless battle you cannot win.'

He tilts his head, considering my words. He then pops the grape in his mouth, and I hear it burst wetly against his teeth before he asks, 'And what of the third task?'

'For the third task you will need me there. I will handle everything.'

'But what is—'

'Just trust me.' I kneel on the edge of the bed, and he turns his face to mine, a resolution settling in his eyes. 'Tonight, you must make a sacrifice to Hecate beneath the full moon, to ensure you are in her favour. Can you do that?'

'Of course.' He must read something in my face, for his own softens as he comes to sit beside me. 'Medea, I cannot thank you enough for your help and I am deeply sorry if I overstepped ... I did not intend to act so rashly. It's just that you have this peculiar effect on me.' He gives a slight laugh, shaking his head. 'I do not wish you to think less of me.'

'Less of you?' I stare at him, my mind groping for the right words to explain. But how can I explain something I do not understand myself? Perhaps it is this palace. This prison. Perhaps I cannot allow myself to be happy in a place that has only ever fed me misery. 'It is not your fault.'

'Medea.' His gaze skims the harsh angles of my face, his eyes soft enough to sink my teeth into. 'You are so beautiful.'

Beautiful. The word sings through my veins.

'Nobody has ever said that to me before,' I admit.

'That is because the people of Colchis are fools. All of them. They do not see what a prize they have before them.' I feel my heart swell as he brushes a careful thumb over my swollen cheek. 'I will take you away from this place, Medea. You have my word. I will give you your freedom.'

'Thank you.'

'You do not have to be sad any more.'

Sad. It seems a trivial word. What even is sadness? I know the shape of it, the familiar cold edges, like a trinket you have played with over and over in your hands, keeping close to your heart. But it is a feeling no different from the others. Anger, loneliness, pain – they all end up tasting the same in your mouth. Bitter. Empty.

'I have felt more in these few minutes than I have ever felt in my entire life,' I confess. My eyes flicker to his, waiting to see the judgement in his eyes.

But he only smiles at me, a warm, understanding smile. His hand closes around mine, and I feel, perhaps for the first time, that he is truly seeing me, seeing the dark parts as well as the light. I wait for him to pull away from it, but he remains still, his hand resting over mine. I turn my palm upwards so our fingers intertwine, fitting so perfectly together, as if they always belonged there.

In the small windows high up behind Jason's head, I see Selene's gleaming face watching over us, her delicate moonlight soaking the room in a silvery glow.

'You must go and make your sacrifice to Hecate, before dawn awakens,' I say, reluctantly pulling away from his touch. 'And I must return to my chamber before the slaves notice I am gone.'

Jason rises as he watches me move towards the door.

'Medea.' His voice halts me, and I turn my face to him. 'Thank you.'

'Do not thank me, not yet. Not until we succeed.'

'We will succeed, Medea.' He steps forwards, smiling. 'How can we not, when the Gods are on our side?'

11

I am dressed in crimson.

The colour drips from my body in flowing folds, so dark it looks almost black in certain lights. It is the colour of death, I think to myself. A colour my father chose for me to wear when he told me I would attend Jason's trials today. My presence is never normally permitted, but Jason knows of my abilities, so my father has no reason to hide his deadly secret. Instead, he wants to brandish me by his side as a weapon.

I sit in my chamber, staring at the wall, waiting to be summoned.

In the stillness I find my mind wandering, as it so often does, to Chalciope. What would my sister say if she were here? Would she understand my betrayal, support it even? Or would she think me mad for trusting my life to a man I have just met?

'And are you?' The words ripple from behind me, soft and rich.

I spin so fast I nearly topple over, my heart swelling at the familiar voice. 'Circe?'

My chamber stares back at me, its emptiness mocking my excitement. My hands clench at my sides as I glance around. The shadows seem to have thickened, gathering in heavy folds that swallow the watery morning light.

'Am I what?' I prompt the sinister silence.

'Mad?' That voice comes again, seemingly from all around. Hearing it now, I realize it's a deeper, smokier voice than my aunt's. The sound of it seems to beckon the shadows closer.

'Who are you?'

'I think you already know that.'

She appears then, as if her words breathed life into the darkness, moulding it to the form of a woman. No, not a woman . . . a *goddess*.

Hecate.

Her skin is as pale as moonlight and seems to glow with the same soft radiance. Though that luminosity does nothing to dissuade the darkness, which wraps itself around her like a cloak, smoky tendrils coiling over her limbs, caressing her skin.

She is beautiful, but it is an unnerving, ethereal kind of beauty, her features severe yet stunning. High cheekbones, so sharp they look as if they could cut flesh. A narrow nose pointed over a small, plump mouth. A jaw that looks carved from the coldest marble. I imagine if I touched her, she would feel like ice beneath my fingers.

My eyes settle on hers and I note how black they are, how depthless.

'Goddess.' I bow, feeling her power vibrating in the air. It makes my magic stir chaotically in my veins, like a hound tugging towards its true master.

'Rise, Medea.' Her voice sounds as if others are woven within it. She tilts her head, her hair flowing over her shoulders. It is pitch black, just like mine.

Atop her head it looks as if silver spikes protrude from her skull, forming a sinister crown. At her sides she holds two torches, yet her hands remain clasped in front of her. As I look closer, I see faces staring out from her left and right. They are mirror images of herself, glowing like umbral spirits, rippling and refracting with each movement. The harder I stare at them, the more they seem to blur from view.

'So, you know who I am?' Her voice is neither warm nor cold, but some liminal, shadowy space between.

'Yes.'

'I thought you might have forgotten.' Those depthless eyes narrow, and the darkness seems to pulse. 'Since you pray so rarely to me these days.'

'My father forbade me to do so for many winters,' I say carefully. 'I hope I have not offended you, my Goddess.'

Her face seems to roll to the side then, spluttering and fading like a flame as the head to the left slips to the forefront, sharpening into clarity. Her features remain the same, yet there is something different about these eyes; they seem to spark brighter. Her face loosens into a smile as she turns her neck, as if stretching out an ache.

'Offended?' she chuckles, her voice lighter now, curling with amusement. 'If I were offended, Medea, you would certainly know about it. I wouldn't let you cast your little spells, for a start.'

'You can do that?' I ask as I watch her stroll across the room, picking up random trinkets and turning them over in her hands. With a new face at the forefront, her whole demeanour seems to have transformed; she appears more relaxed and playful, younger somehow.

'Of course I can. Your magic only works because I allow it.' She shrugs, picking up a small pot and sniffing it. 'What's this?'

'It is charcoal ... Women put it on their eyes.'

'Why?'

'It is considered beautiful, I suppose.'

'Humans are so peculiar.' She places it down and continues to float around the space, the faithful shadows trailing behind her, toying with her gown.

To her left and right those faces keep watch, their edges dancing and distorting like wisps of smoke. I can feel their eyes on me even though I cannot clearly see where they look.

'May I ask why you are here, Goddess?'

'Why should I not be?' She quirks an eyebrow, a distinctively human reaction, which makes it seem all the more disturbing upon her immortal face.

'You have never made yourself known to me before . . .'

'Ah, yes, but that is because you were so incredibly *dull* before.' *Dull?* I try to swallow the insult as the word clangs through me. 'Except for that time you turned your brother into a pig. Now, *that* was amusing.'

'And what makes me interesting now?' I force my tone to remain neutral.

'Because now, Medea, you have a decision to make.' She turns back to me and, as she does so, her face slips away again, letting the quieter, composed version shift back into position. The smoothness of this transition is somewhat unnerving; it is as if I am talking to two separate goddesses altogether. 'You are at a crossroads. Whatever decision you make will send you towards a future you cannot turn back from.'

I knew Hecate was the Goddess of Crossroads, amongst other domains, but I had always believed this to be quite literal. Not the figurative ones that mortals encounter in their lives when faced with a decision. In truth, I did not think we had much control over such matters, due to the indisputable power of the Fates.

'Surely the Gods have already decided my path for me?' I say as I watch Hecate float around me, realizing I have not moved an inch since her arrival. My feet feel rooted to the floor, perhaps by fear. Or perhaps it is Hecate holding me in place by some invisible power.

'There are many, many mortals in this world, Medea. The Fates cannot decide every single detail for each one.'

'They cannot?'

'For the important mortals, the Fates will dictate every knot and thread, yes. They will ensure they are bound to the future your world requires of them. For other, less significant lives, they can be . . . more vague. They set their beginning and end but allow the middle to be woven by the individual.'

'I never knew that.'

'Of course you didn't. Because all mortals want to believe themselves important, that their existence has purpose. But the reality is, so few lives hold any kind of meaning. Most humans are insufferably dull, are they not? It is only a select few who truly matter, of which *you* were not supposed to be one. Though I changed that.' The other, impish face flickers to the front as she adds, 'The Fates were not pleased when I gifted you with magic. It wasn't part of their little plan.'

'But why did you?' It is a question I have wondered my whole life.

The smirking face takes centre stage, eyes glowing mischievously as she says, 'Boredom, I suppose. Immortality can be so tedious at times. I wanted to see what would happen if I gave a mortal a drop of my power. No other god has tried such a thing before.'

'You gifted me this power out of *boredom*?' I cannot help the irritation seeping into my voice.

Hecate's third face snaps to the front, eyes simmering with a deadly rage. Behind her, the darkness seems to rear up in response.

'*You question my actions?*' Her voice swells around us, making the entire room tremble. I stiffen instinctively, my body locking with pure, raw fear. But she pulls herself back, stretching and cracking her neck again as if restraining herself causes her physical pain. That furious face melts back to her side, letting the calm Hecate settle once again. 'I am not here to justify my decisions, Medea.'

'Are you here to tell me which path I must choose?' I ask carefully, not wanting to trigger that ferocious side of her again.

'Where would be the fun in that?' she asks with a slight grin, and I seem to have lost track of which version I am speaking with. Talking to Hecate feels like slowly descending into madness. 'The choice is yours to make . . . although I know Hera and Athena will disagree with that.'

'What do you mean?'

'Come now, you must have felt it. That horribly sweet pain . . . right here.' She smiles slowly, tapping the space where her heart would be if the Gods possessed such a burden. 'Those goddesses are very meddlesome. They will do whatever it takes to ensure their darling Jason succeeds. And they *love* to take the credit for a mortal's success.'

'I don't know what you're talking about.'

Her lips curl knowingly. 'We can pretend love has nothing to do with your actions, if you like.'

Love. The word causes heat to rise into my cheeks.

'I am only concerned with my freedom,' I counter, unable to curb my defensiveness. 'And my decision on the matter has already been made.'

'Then why are you questioning yourself?'

'I am not.' I cannot. For I know I have already taken that leap and all I can do now is let myself free-fall and hope the landing will not destroy me.

'And what if I told you that you are choosing the wrong path?'

My body stills as I stare at her, icy claws of uncertainty scraping away my resolve. She holds my gaze, her expression entirely unreadable.

When I speak, my voice is a whisper. 'I am?'

'Perhaps, perhaps not.' She shrugs with irritating vagueness. 'But once you choose your path, you cannot turn from it. You must follow it to its end.'

'But which path is the right one?'

'You know, I find it quite amusing,' she continues, as if I had not spoken. 'All this fuss over such a useless little object.'

'You mean ... the fleece?'

She cocks her head towards me, amusement flickering across her face like the wild shadows that dance between flames. 'Come now, you must have realized? The fleece is entirely *useless*, Medea.'

I think back to the day I saw the ram, that intoxicating power it radiated. 'But ... the creature ...'

'The ram was powerful, yes. But its powers died with it.' She gives a dismissive wave of her hand. 'Next time you touch the fleece, you will understand.'

'But ... the Gods demanded it be sacrificed.'

'I know.' She laughs, the sound so sharp it seems to slice the shadows around her. 'We have quite the sense of humour, do we not? Come, Medea, do you really think we would allow mortals undefeatable glory? Such a thing is far too dangerous for your foolish kind.'

'But—'

A knock splinters the moment, followed by a gruff voice. 'Princess, it is time.'

I spin to the doorway to see a guard lingering outside. When I turn back, the darkness has vanished and Hecate along with it. Shy sunlight begins to filter back into the room, which appears entirely unchanged. There is no sign Hecate was ever even here. All that remains of the goddess is the question she lodged in my mind.

What if I am choosing the wrong path?

We ride out to the farming fields beyond the city.

We are a magnificent sight, a glittering wave of bronzed might surging through the gathered crowds. I ride in a chariot beside my father, flanked by Jason and Apsyrtus in their own chariots. Behind us, the Argonauts and a selection of my father's finest soldiers ride in smaller, far less luxurious carts.

I try my best not to allow any part of my body to touch my father as we jostle over the uneven road. Thankfully, he seems to ignore my presence, though every now and then I feel his eyes flicker in my direction. My face remains a veneer of calm under my veil, masking the storm that swells beneath.

Farmers stop and stare as we pass, shielding their tired eyes from the glaring sun. Their children tangle around their feet, shrieking and waving excitedly.

I see one little girl with dark, wild hair fighting her brothers, using sticks for swords. She is a ferocious creature as she darts between them, her 'sword' cracking loudly against theirs. As they stop to watch us pass, I see Atalanta waving at her.

The girl breaks into a run beside their cart, pointing to the Argonauts and then to the huntress. She calls to her in the common Colchian tongue, 'Are you one of them?'

Atalanta must understand the nature of the girl's question, for she points to herself and says, 'Argonaut!'

'Argonaut! Argonaut!' the girl choruses, tripping over the syllables.

The child slows at the edge of her father's field and watches us ride on, wonder spilling across her face as the horizon opens out before her.

I realize I am smiling slightly as I watch the girl dwindle into the distance.

We finally stop at an open field, no different from all the others. The yawning pasture is framed by the Colchian mountains in the distance, like stoic giants keeping watch. As we dismount, I hold my head low, carefully avoiding the Argonauts, who now scan the area.

'Does Aeetes want Jason to plant some crops?' Meleager sniggers.

'Are the Colchians really so low on labourers?' another smirks.

Their amusement makes a slight irritation prickle at my temples. Do they not realize what is at stake here?

I want to snap at them, though I know my anger is misplaced. It is the conversation with Hecate that has left me so on edge. How many winters have I longed to meet the goddess, only to have our first encounter be infuriatingly vague and fleeting? It felt like she was merely toying with me. But, then again, what else did I expect from a god?

Boredom. That was why she had given me this gift – this curse – that has permeated every corner of my life, carving me apart from everyone else. Not because I was special, nor destined for some higher purpose, but because she was simply *bored*.

It feels so meaningless now.

Hecate's revelation about the fleece has been weighing inside me as well. Could it really be as useless as she claims? Since leaving my chamber this morning, I have wrestled over whether I should tell Jason, warn him that his efforts may be in vain. But, if he no longer wants the fleece, he will no longer need my help, and I cannot lose this chance of freedom.

I watch Jason now, smiling out across the field with a quiet confidence. As if sensing my presence, his eyes swivel to mine, meeting them easily despite my veil.

This is the right path.

It must be.

I turn away, bowing my head as I move to stand behind my father and brother. Apsyrtus smiles at me, though the curl of his lips is more like a sneer. He is dressed in his battle gear, perhaps as a silent warning to the Argonauts. The plume of his helmet bristles in the wind, the jawline engraved with a ram's horns, curling back towards his cheekbones and framing those cold, golden eyes. I ignore him and turn my attention to my father, who strolls over to place an authoritative hand on Jason's shoulder.

'So, my boy,' he booms, commanding the attention of the crowd. 'Are you ready for your first task?'

'I am.' Jason smiles easily, as if he were accepting something as casual as an invitation to dinner.

'To obtain the Golden Fleece, Jason, you must first . . .' He pauses for effect, and I am grateful for my veil masking my eye-roll. 'Plough this field.'

A confused murmur ripples amongst the Argonauts as my father's smile darkens.

'Has the old man lost it?' I hear Atalanta mutter to the tall, willowy man beside her.

'All is not as it seems,' he murmurs back, his voice warm and fluid, like sunlight dancing through water. I notice he does not carry a weapon at his side, but rather a lyre on his back. He must be Orpheus, the famed musician. I had heard rumours he was amongst Jason's crew.

In the distance, I see the two oxen grazing. They are as I remember them from when my father brought me here several moons ago, after he told me of his desire to create new 'trials'. It seemed the dragon was no longer enough for him, and he believed his idea of disguising a deadly twist within a simple task was some stroke of genius. I, however, thought it sounded idiotic and somewhat sickening. He is like a predator toying with his food.

Still, I obeyed his command to enchant the beasts. For what other choice did I have?

'There are two conditions,' my father continues. 'Firstly, you must use those oxen, and secondly, you must complete your task alone.'

A knowing look touches Jason's face. 'Those are the only conditions?'

'Indeed. And, once the field is ploughed, all you must do is plant this.' He gives Jason a small leather pouch, closing his hand around it and patting it firmly. 'Those are your first two trials.'

'Well . . .' Jason casts his gaze across his audience, his eyes careful not to meet mine. 'What do we think, men?'

The Argonauts roar, thumping their fists against their chests as Jason picks up the plough and strides towards the oxen. I watch my father share a smirk with Apsyrtus and mutter something in his ear that makes him laugh. My hands itch with anger as I glower at them, their arrogant sniggers dragging over every nerve in my body.

Soon those sneers will be wiped clean from their faces.

I turn my attention to the Argonauts and catch Atalanta frowning at me quizzically. I give the faintest nod in response, my veil quivering. *Trust me.*

She swivels her focus back to Jason, who is now close to the oxen, preparing the halter of the plough. The creatures seem oblivious to him, stooping their heads to graze. They do not appear threatening in the slightest, and yet I can feel their power thrumming in the air, reflecting in my father's eager eyes as he licks his lips.

No, not their power.

My power.

The ox closer to Jason swings its head around with a flash of hostility, flaring its nostrils and pawing at the dry earth. Jason remains calm, moving nearer to the creature with a hand outstretched. His mouth is moving, though I cannot make out what he is saying.

A rush of brilliant fire suddenly flares from the ox's nostrils, scorching Jason's skin. I am the only person not to flinch; even my father steps back a little.

I hear the shouts of the Argonauts as they move to draw their weapons, Atalanta already with her bow in hand. But, after a moment, they lower them, for they believe they are too late. Jason's body has been engulfed by the flames and now the other ox has joined in the attack, spewing streams of unnatural fire that swallow him whole.

Even from this distance, I can feel the heat of their fire stroking my cheeks. But that warmth turns cold as a whisper of doubt slithers into my mind . . . *What if my spell did not work?*

Disbelief weighs heavily in the air as the Argonauts watch their brilliant hero burn before them. I glance to my father, hating the smugness written across his face. But, as I watch him, I feel a deep satisfaction bloom inside me when his expression disperses into shock.

Gasps punctuate the silence, followed by loud cheers, and a sweet relief swells inside me as I watch Jason emerge unscathed from the flames, fastening the plough on to the oxen's backs. The creatures continue to hurl their fiery breath, but the flames dip and dance around Jason's body, just as they did last night with my hand. Right before I ran those hands all over him . . .

Rough fingers rip me from those thoughts, tugging at my arm. I stare up into my father's furious face as he shakes me hard, making my head rattle. In the haze of his anger, he can only make out one word, coated with spit and desperation: '*How?*'

'I do not know,' I say calmly, holding his gaze.

His grip tightens, fingernails digging into my flesh. His lips twitch as if he is about to say more, but then he simply releases me, storming back to watch as Jason ploughs the field. He gives us a jovial wave as the Argonauts erupt into more cheers. Beside me, the Colchian soldiers look on, stunned into silence.

Nobody has ever succeeded in this trial before.

'He must have the aid of the Gods,' one of them fearfully concludes.

As Jason completes his task, a tension begins to thicken amongst his audience. The Colchian soldiers can sense their king's agitation and they begin to shift, fingers inching closer to their weapons. I look to the Argonauts, who are now twirling their own weapons and winking playfully at the soldiers, goading them.

There is a storm brewing on the horizon.

Once the field is ploughed, Jason releases the oxen and slaps their hinds, sending them bolting off into the distance with flames curling angrily from their nostrils. He then opens the pouch my father has given him and holds up the item within. A singular, milky-white tooth, long and curved, the same size and sharpness as a large dagger.

The tooth of a dragon.

My dragon.

Jason places the tooth into the earth and unceremoniously scoops a handful of soil over it. Once done, he pauses for a moment, regarding the ground before him, his hand twitching over the hilt of his sword. I feel a sudden rush of panic hiss in my mind. *Do* not *fight them*, I silently plead. *Do as I told you, Jason.*

After a painfully long moment, he smiles to himself, a smile I somehow believe is reserved only for me, one that says, *Do not worry, Princess, I will heed your commands.* He then paces quickly to the discarded plough and crouches behind it. I try to stifle my sigh of relief.

'Is he . . . *hiding?*' one of the Argonauts smirks. 'Why is he—'

His words are cut short by the sound of the earth cracking and splintering. A hush falls over us as we watch little mounds of dirt sprouting around where the tooth has been buried. I hear a gasp as a hand shoots up from the earth, the fingers wriggling and writhing. The Argonauts' own hands move to their weapons in response, readying to fight. A second later, a dozen more reach upwards from the ground.

Men begin to claw themselves out of the earth, like grotesque budding flowers. But these are no mortal men. Their bodies are rotten, their skin grey and sagging, peeling back from their visible bones. Their jaws hang slack, so their teeth are permanently bared, and their pale eyeballs are barely fixed to their sunken sockets.

'How can such a thing be possible?' someone whispers.

It is a hideous, fascinating sight, though I cannot take credit for this spectacle. All dragon teeth are bound with this strange power. When their discarded teeth touch the earth, the corpses of those buried there will become animated by their power. All my father had to do in preparation was bury a small army in this field.

I do not wish to think where he got those bodies from.

'May Hades protect their souls,' another person murmurs.

The undead soldiers begin to stagger to their feet, reaching for the weapons sheathed in their rusted, ragged armour. They glance around themselves with hollow, rotten eyes, searching for whoever dared wake them from their eternal slumber.

In that moment, Jason peers round the cart and hurls a stone at the corpses, ducking back immediately behind his hiding spot.

He is doing exactly as I told him.

The stone smashes against one of the soldier's faces, knocking his decayed jaw clean off. The jawless one lets out an inhuman screech that makes the hair on my arms rise. He then lifts his sword, cutting down the soldier closest to him in wild fury. This sets off a frenzied attack as the undead soldiers begin to clash together, a mash of metal and bone.

As I predicted, it does not take long for the soldiers to kill one another, considering they were barely alive to begin with, strung together by dragon magic and rotten flesh. Their bodies fall to a crumpled heap on the ground, withering quickly to dust.

Now, only two corpses remain. They each deliver a fatal blow to the other's head, striking and falling in unison, as they both yield, once again, to the hand of death.

After a brief silence, Jason reappears from behind the cart and approaches his audience with a humble shrug. Everyone's eyes shift to the king, who is staring at Jason with that thick vein pulsing in his throat. Apsyrtus looks as if he is about to say something, but my father shoots out a hand to silence him. He then swallows, slowly arranging his features into a smile so forced it looks as if it might crack his face in two.

'Well, well, well, Jason.' His voice sounds smooth, but there's an undeniable edge to it. 'Congratulations.'

'Thank you.' Jason bows graciously.

'What possessed you to throw that rock? A smart move.' He tries his best to sound nonchalant.

'Intuition, I guess.' Jason gives an easy smile. 'Now, what of the third task?'

The king stiffens as his lips twitch into a grimace. He is panicking, for he had not prepared for this, had not thought it even possible for someone to overcome these trials. This means he is going to stall Jason, buy himself time to plan his next move.

'So eager!' His forced laugh sounds rough in his throat. 'It is far too humid right now for such strenuous tasks, do you not agree? I propose we return to the palace for refreshments, and I shall tell you of your final task there. What do you say?'

'How gracious of you.'

You cannot stall for ever. The thought flickers darkly in my mind.

Your fate is coming for you, Father. As slowly and surely as death's final breath.

It is coming for all of you.

12

There are no celebrations when we return to the palace.

The previous night's jovial atmosphere has evaporated in the warm, thick air, exposing the hostility that beats beneath. It is a slow, heavy pulse, like the heartbeat of a predator stalking its prey, waiting to strike.

When we reach the palace, my father dismounts and hisses in my ear, 'Inside, now.'

He does not even look at Jason as he storms up the palace steps, his robes billowing behind him. The king's cordial act is finally cracking, allowing his true nature to seep through.

With my father gone, I partially lift my veil. Jason's eyes slip into mine so easily, as if his gaze had always belonged there. He does not smile, but there is a softness in his face that makes my insides feel as if they are being slowly prised open, letting the emotions I experienced the previous night surge upwards.

As the men buzz around us, Jason moves to stand beside me. He bends down, pretending to inspect the horse attached to his chariot.

'Are you OK?' he murmurs, just loud enough for me to hear.

'Yes,' I whisper.

He stands up, brushing his hand against mine as he does so. There is so much danger in such a small gesture, so much that could be exposed. Hot shivers ripple along my body, pooling in my stomach as my mind dips to the night before ... The way Jason's naked body glowed in the firelight ... The feel of his lips on mine ...

'The third task?' he murmurs.

'Trust me,' I say, forcing away those heated memories.

I turn and head towards the palace. Behind me, I can feel Jason's eyes on my back. He does not like being unprepared; he wants to know what lies ahead. I understand, but I have got him this far – should he not trust my plan by now?

The smell of wine sours the air as I walk into my father's throne room. He is standing with his back to me, staring into the hazy shadows draped across the floor. Despite the lofty expanse of the room, it feels horribly stifling.

My father tilts his head back, draining the cup of wine in his hand. The silence paces around us as I wait for him to say something. From somewhere in the depths of the palace I can hear the delicate patter of sandals as the slaves scuttle about their business.

When my father finally speaks, his voice is quieter than I expected. 'How did he do it?'

He turns his face to the side, so I can see the sharp angles of his profile, the hooked curve of his nose and weakness of his chin.

'I do not know.'

'Do not lie to me, Medea.' He throws his cup across the room, narrowly missing where I stand. The clatter of bronze upon stone sounds magnified against the gathered hush.

'He must have had the aid of the Gods,' I say, watching a slave peel themselves from the shadows to retrieve the cup, then melt away. 'They say he is favoured by both Hera and Athena.'

'But *I* have the fleece. I am supposed to be *undefeatable*.'

He turns then and grabs my throat, ripping off my veil. I hold his glare as the blood swells in my temples. He squeezes tighter and I can feel my pulse thumping against his fingertips. A darkness begins to crawl across my vision, but I force my eyes to remain locked on his.

After a moment he releases me, making a disgusted noise at the back of his throat, as if I am not even worth the energy it takes to hurt me.

'He will not get past the dragon,' I say, my voice raspy.

'How can you know that?' he spits with a wild panic in his eyes. 'If he truly has the aid of the Gods, what can we do to stop him?'

'I know of a spell, a poison made from hemlock, infused with my own magic. If Jason somehow, by some divine intervention, does evade the dragon, I will curse the fleece so that all those who touch it will immediately fall dead.'

'Immediately?' His eyes glow, a nervous tongue darting over his lips.

'Yes.' I give a slow nod, knowing I must tread carefully with my next words. 'Let me go with him to Apollo's Grove and I will ensure he does not come back alive.'

'You cannot trust her!' Apsyrtus' voice fills the room, snatching my father's attention away. I inhale a frustrated breath through my nose, turning to see my brother striding forwards, his figure etched by the sunlight slanting through the columns. 'Her only poisons are the lies she drips in your ear, Father.'

'What else do you propose?' Our father stalks to his throne and sits down heavily. 'If Jason is aided by the Gods, what can we do to stop their will?'

'We have a finer army than any Greece has to offer.' Apsyrtus pushes past me to stand before the king. 'I say we put an end to this now. Let us see how heroic those Argonauts are when faced with a real army.'

'That is madness and you know it, brother.' I step forwards so I am side by side with him. 'Father, do not let Apsyrtus' arrogance blind you. These Argonauts are heroes famed for their countless victories in battle.'

'It is all talk. Pretty words spun to an empty melody. They prob-ably pay that singer of theirs to make up grand tales to spread fear into their enemies' hearts.' Apsyrtus laughs dismissively. 'That Jason is a spineless mutt.'

I swallow the anger thickening in my throat, trying to feign non-chalance as I say, 'It would be unwise to underestimate the man.'

'I think Medea's problem is she cannot decide if she wants to kill the foreigner or fuck him,' Apsyrtus snarls, eyes narrowing on me.

'What?' I almost choke on the word.

'I've seen the way you look at him. You're like a bitch in heat.'

'You have lost your mind—'

'*Enough.*' Our father's voice silences the room.

He stares at me then, the panic in his eyes settling into something darker. His face draws together as he considers his options, his fingers tapping sinisterly against his throne like a heartbeat. *Tap. Tap. Tap.* I hold his gaze, trying to suppress the dread rising inside me like a ter-rible wave. Has he seen through my lies? Has Apsyrtus exposed me?

Have I just ended Jason's life?

Have I ended my own?

Tap. Tap. Tap.

The seconds drag by, painfully slow.

Tap. Tap. Tap.

'You are confident in this spell?' he finally asks, leaning back in his throne.

I quietly exhale, fighting to keep my expression impassive, burying the relief blossoming inside me.

'Yes.'

'But, Father—'

'Silence, Apsyrtus,' he snaps, holding out a firm hand. 'Medea, the fate of Colchis rests on this. You cannot fail, do you understand?'

'Yes, Father.'

He nods slowly. 'You will both go with Jason to the grove.'

'Both?' I blurt.

'Is that a problem?' He raises a brow, challenging me to press him further.

'What of you, Father?' Apsyrtus steps forwards, pulling his attention away. 'It will show weakness if you do not—'

'*Silence*,' he snarls, his fingers turning to claws against the arms of his throne. 'Go. Make sure he dies.'

'I will, my King.' Apsyrtus bows dramatically, whilst I merely nod beside him.

I try to keep my steps steady as we walk out of the palace, my mind stumbling chaotically with a rush of panic. Outside, dark, swollen clouds have rolled their way across the sky, fattened by the heat and charged tension in the air.

Below, Jason and his men wait at the foot of the palace steps, surrounded by a wall of my father's soldiers. The atmosphere is palpable as the Argonauts taunt the men with lewd comments and cracking knuckles, their weapons glinting. I see Meleager twirling his spear, making it appear like liquid metal in the air. My father's soldiers do not react; they remain fused to the ground like motionless grey statues.

'Come, sister,' Apsyrtus grins. 'It is time for the final trial.'

13

We set off towards the mountain where the Grove of Apollo lies. Above us, the sky is hazy and heavy with the promise of rain.

Apsyrtus and I ride out in front, flanked by a selection of my father's soldiers.

'If you are planning anything, Medea, know that you will fail,' Apsyrtus had snarled at me as we set off. I kept silent and, mercifully, so does he for the remainder of the journey.

Jason and his men follow in carts a little further back, keeping a healthy distance between us. Distrust is thick in the air. I can feel the soldiers stealing glances my way, their faces stern. They do not understand why their king is not with us.

When we arrive at the foot of the mountain, the Colchian soldiers pull back.

'Why are they stopping?' Jason asks.

'Only those given permission by the king are allowed to visit the Grove of Apollo,' Apsyrtus says as he dismounts from his chariot. 'Your men are to remain here.'

I can see the wariness tightening around Jason's eyes. I do not blame him – what man would willingly leave his men and follow the enemy into the ominous unknown? I stare at him from beneath my veil, hoping my words from earlier are resonating within him. *Trust me . . .*

'If you are afraid, Jason, we can turn back,' my brother offers, a dark grin cutting across his face. 'There is no shame in acknowledging your limits. Although, I'll admit, I did not believe you a defeatist; you seemed more—'

My brother is so busy taunting, he does not notice me approach behind him. In a fluid motion I cover his nasty little mouth with a strip of material torn from my gown, soaked in a mixture I prepared earlier.

'May Hypnos take you,' I whisper in his ear as Apsyrtus thrashes against me, whirling round and breaking free.

'What in Zeus's name do you think you are . . .' His words grow sluggish in his mouth. He takes a step towards me then staggers, falling to the ground with a mighty thud.

'A sleeping drug made from poppy juice,' I explain to Jason, who stares at Apsyrtus slumped at his feet. 'He will be fine. At most, he will wake with a slight headache.'

I hear the threatening sing of unsheathing swords as my father's men dismount from their cart.

'What have you done to the prince?' one of them barks at me.

Before he can advance, Meleager has knocked him to the ground. The other Argonauts follow suit, making quick work of my father's men. They disarm them as if they were plucking toys from children, forcing them into submission.

'Do not kill them,' Jason orders. 'To do so would be an act of war against Aeetes.'

'Jason, we must go now. We do not have much time,' I say.

'Keep watch over them. If the prince awakens, *do not* harm him,' he commands the others before turning to me. 'Lead the way, Princess.'

'You will go alone with the witch?' one of his men interrupts, the question heavy with unspoken accusations.

'I will.' Jason nods. I can feel the weight of his trust in his words, and I cradle it inside me like a gift.

'This way.'

He follows close behind me as we pick our way up the harsh mountain. The climb is not far, but the route is unrelentingly steep. Before long, I feel my breath grow ragged, my lungs aching in my chest. Beside me, Jason seems unfazed by the challenge, for his is a body hardened by the elements, whilst mine is accustomed to the quiet prison within which it has rotted.

After a while, the path tapers to a narrow strip carved into the mountainside, like a thin vein exposed along the rock. We scale it one at a time, stepping carefully across the loose stones. Beside us, the cliff falls away sharply, disappearing into a bed of damp, grey haze.

Jason walks behind, reaching out his hand to steady me. I do not need his help, but I take the offer, anyway, enjoying his skin against mine and the comforting feel of his concern.

As we near the mouth of Apollo's Grove, the path widens out once again. I feel Jason draw close beside me, his arm brushing against mine.

'We are close,' I say, but the words are immediately swallowed by a bone-shuddering screech splitting open the sky.

Jason unsheathes his sword and moves to stand in front of me. His instinct to protect me makes a warmth glow inside my stomach. But, of course, I am not the one who needs protecting.

'That is no ordinary creature,' he says, eyes scanning the misty sky. The fog is close to us now, so close we can barely see a few feet ahead. I can tell this lack of visibility is making him uneasy, his sword held aloft to the unknown danger. He then glances to me and offers a tight smile. 'Perhaps it is time you tell me what the third task is, Princess?'

I walk forwards, nudging past Jason's blade. 'The fleece is protected by a dragon.'

A muscle in his jaw ticks, the only sign that he could be afraid. 'And how do we kill it?'

'You do not need to. The dragon is under my power. I can control it.'

'Are you certain?'

The truth is I have not visited Amyntas since the day I transformed him. I have only heard word from quaking men who returned from their quest, the blood of their comrades splattered across their armour. But, even from afar, the beast has obeyed my bidding. He has not taken flight and disappeared to another land, nor wreaked havoc in Colchis as my brother feared he might. The dragon has remained on the mountain and defended the fleece, as I have commanded him to do.

Trust your instincts. Circe's voice shimmers in my head, bolstering my resolve.

'I am certain,' I say.

As we come to the lip jutting out in front of the mouth of the cave, the air finally clears. Around us, jagged mountaintops pierce through the mist, their sharp tips like teeth sinking into the clouds. Jason moves to step forwards.

'Wait,' I order, and he stills beside me.

'What is it?'

At that moment, a spine-chilling hiss rips through the gathered stillness. The ground beneath us shudders, as if the mountain itself were trembling in fear. The shaking underfoot intensifies, making loose rocks begin to vibrate and tumble away over the cliffside.

I glance to Jason and see something flash across his strong features: fear perhaps. But he quickly channels it into focused adrenaline, his sword readied in his hands.

The hissing intensifies as giant claws close around the side of the mountain, sending cracks sparking like bolts of lightning. An enormous, scaled head then materializes through the mist, forked tongue slashing outwards as if tasting our fear staining the air.

I feel Jason tense beside me as the dragon steps forwards, proudly unfurling his wings. He dwarfs us completely, his body a glittering wall of obsidian scales, as impenetrable as the mountain itself.

He is terrifying.

He is magnificent.

He is mine.

Without hesitating, I walk forwards. In response, the giant creature lifts his head and lets out another screech. A blaze of fire rips from his throat, igniting the air and soaking the mountainside in crimson and smoke.

I take another step, feeling the warmth of his flames singeing my skin. The dragon then lowers his head, his blistering amber eyes locking on to mine. I stare into the black slits of his pupils, wondering what remnants of Amyntas exist within those depths. Does he recognize me? Is he angry for what I did to him?

The dragon moves forwards, teeth bared, burnt embers whispering from his nostrils. His foot slams down beside me and I can see the beautifully intricate detail of each glittering scale, alongside the talons worn down from his time spent climbing the harsh mountain range. His forked tongue darts out again, so close I can feel the sharpness cut through the air, inches from my skin.

He is truly glorious.

'Medea!' Jason calls from somewhere behind me.

I hold my hand up, locking my eyes on to the dragon's fiery gaze.

'Sleep,' I say, the word sounding gentle against the dragon's hideous hissing. 'I command you to sleep.'

Amyntas swells above me, readying to strike. He begins to beat his wings, whipping up the mist around us so it nearly knocks me down.

But I hold my ground.

'I am Medea, Sorceress of Colchis, your creator, and I command you to *SLEEP*!'

Amyntas bares his teeth again as he lowers his head. His front fangs are the size of a full-grown man, and I can see my outline reflected in their deadly glint. He then widens his mouth as if to swallow me whole, the rancid stench of death wafting from his cavernous throat.

He gives a mighty roar, the sound reverberating through my whole body, making every bone rattle inside me as if I may crumble to dust.

Still, I do not yield.

'*Sleep*.' The word is laced with a low, animalistic snarl. It is a voice I do not recognize.

There is a long pause as if Amyntas is debating how best to devour me, considering which limb to start with, which stretch of skin to peel off first. But then he lets out a deep, smoky huff that seems to rumble from his very depths. He rests his head heavily on the ground as his body collapses, making the mountain shudder beneath the sheer weight of him.

He lets out another, gentle hiss before falling quickly into a deep slumber.

'Rest now,' I command, placing a hand on his scales. They feel rough and surprisingly cold beneath my touch.

I turn back to Jason, suddenly fearful of his reaction. He looks at a loss for words, shaking his head slowly as if finding it difficult to process his thoughts.

'Medea . . . you are truly incredible,' he finally whispers.

I smile and reach out my hand to him. 'Are you ready to claim what is yours?'

14

As I lead Jason into the Grove of Apollo, I am acutely aware of his hand in mine, the strength and warmth of his calloused palms. But I force my mind to focus on the task in front of us.

The inconspicuous cave opening leads to a thin passageway, the space constricted by jagged rocks like blades embedded into the walls.

That ancient darkness greets us again and I feel Jason stiffening, his hand clammy in mine.

'I have never been fond of confined spaces,' he admits. The shadows are so heavy they seem to absorb every word, every sound. 'It reminds me too much of my childhood, of that prison cell my uncle left us to rot inside after he murdered my father and stole my birthright . . .' He trails off, voice thick. 'I have hated small, dark spaces ever since.'

Perhaps it is the anonymity of the darkness that allows him to admit such a vulnerability. Or . . . perhaps he truly trusts me.

'It is just a little further,' I assure him.

We head deeper inside to where the tunnel opens out. I feel Jason's hand relax in mine as he sees the light at the far end of the cave, illuminating the altar and the spindly tree atop the rock formation.

I lead Jason towards the tree, finding a path across the rocks. He is silent as he follows and when I steal a glance at his face, I can see his wonder glowing through the gloom.

Delicate sunlight filters from above, but it is the fleece that brightens the space. Even now the ram is dead, the tight, golden curls still emit a buttery glow of their own. It glints in Jason's hair, reflecting off his breastplate and sending sparks of light dancing across the walls. Beside him, I stand half draped in shadow, watching his eyes widen as he studies the fleece before us, hanging on the lowest branch of the tree.

His hands glimmer as he reaches for it. But before Jason can touch even a single hair, I grab the fleece myself. As I dig my fingernails into its coarse curls, I realize I can no longer feel that intoxicating power, the one I sensed in the presence of the ram . . . I feel nothing at all as I turn the fleece over in my hands.

Next time you touch the fleece, you will understand.

I glance up at Jason, studying his expectant eyes. Should I tell him? Admit that the purpose of his entire, perilous journey is as useless as any old pelt? But what if he turns against me, believing I had deceived him? Our alliance is so new and delicate, I cannot risk shattering it now.

Besides, I only promised Jason the fleece. I never promised him its rumoured glory.

'I have honoured my end of our bargain,' I say, my voice low and steady. 'Now you must assure me you will honour yours.'

His voice is warm as he says, 'Princess, I am your humble servant. Now and always.'

'You will take me to Aeaea.' It is not a question.

'Of course. I will take you wherever you wish to go. Wherever calls to you, Princess. Wherever you feel you belong.' His gaze roams across my face as if trying to anticipate a response to an unspoken question. I lean closer, wishing to stoke whatever I can see burning in his eyes, but not daring to imagine what he might be implying.

118

We can pretend love has nothing to do with your actions. Hecate's words jolt through me again, sharp and urgent. But I force them away.

This is not for love; this is for *freedom*.

And I will go to Aeaea, for that is where I am meant to be. With Circe.

That is where I belong.

I hold out the fleece for him, its golden glow illuminating our faces. I keep my voice steady as I say, 'I am putting my life in your hands, Prince of Iolcus.'

Jason's eyes narrow as he steps forwards and reaches out, but, instead of taking the fleece, he closes his hands around my cheeks. A small gasp escapes me as he tilts my face up to his.

He leans in and kisses me then and I feel myself go rigid with the shock of this sudden intimacy, as if my body were closing in on itself. But his touch is so gentle, so loving, it begins to prize open those shields, invading inside, until I soften beneath his fingers, letting him mould my body against his.

His hands slip down my neck as our kiss deepens and I feel hot shivers shooting from his touch, sinking down into my core.

When he finally pulls away, I move to drape the fleece around his broad shoulders.

'Thank you.' Jason smiles, his eyes holding mine. 'You truly are in-credible, Medea. I mean that.'

As we make our way back, my body fizzes from the adrenaline of his kiss, making me feel faintly giddy. Though it is Jason's words I replay over and over in my mind, the sound of them somehow even more pleasurable than the feel of his lips against mine – *you truly are incredible*.

Incredible.

*

'Friends,' Jason calls to the Argonauts once we have finally descended the mountain. Their eyes widen as they regard the fleece, yet none are more stunned than my father's men, who murmur quiet pleas to the Gods. 'Let us take a moment to pray to the mighty Apollo and give thanks to him for allowing us safe passage to his sacred grove.'

My stomach tightens as I glance around our group. 'Where is my brother?'

'The little prince scrambled away with his tail between his legs,' Meleager tells me, visibly irritated by the fact. 'Do not worry, we sent two of ours after him. He won't get far.'

'How could you let that happen?' It is the closest I have ever heard Jason to being annoyed.

'Well, *someone* said we couldn't hurt the prince,' Meleager counters. 'It would've been much easier to contain him if we could have bruised him a little.'

'We must go.' I turn to Jason, a sharp panic crawling up my spine. 'Before Apsyrtus warns my father.'

At that moment, Atalanta appears beside us, her breathing ragged.

'Aeetes' men are positioned to the west; they're blocking the path to the *Argo*,' she reports. The others must have sent her to scout the area, knowing she is the fastest amongst them on foot. 'It looks like there's fighting on board the ship. Aeetes' men are trying to overrun it. Our men are holding, for now.'

Icy dread closes over me. *He knew.* My father knew I was going to betray him. And I know, with a certainty as cold as death, that he will not let Jason leave with the fleece. Or with me.

'Finally, we can have some fun!' Meleager booms, twirling his spear eagerly in his hands. 'This visit was far too civil for my liking.'

'Where is Aeetes?' Jason asks Atalanta.

'He's heading up the army blocking our passage.'

'Let's show those Colchian bastards who the real victors are!' a golden-haired Argonaut booms, smashing a fist against his breast-plate. The man beside him mimics the movement, and I realize they are completely identical.

'We have to find another way to the *Argo*,' I say to Jason, squeezing his hand tighter. 'My father will kill you all before he lets you pass.'

'Princess, your help has been truly invaluable.' He smiles down at me. 'But now you must let us handle things. I will reason with Aeetes.'

'He will not listen to you.'

'He gave me his word.'

'His word means nothing,' I press again, trying to curb the panic from my voice. 'The Colchian army is fierce.'

'We are fiercer,' Meleager cuts me off with a shrug.

'Medea is right.' I am surprised to hear the melodic voice of Orpheus beside me, his words so fluid it almost sounds like he's singing them. I turn to regard his solemn, angular face as he continues, 'Aeetes is not a king known for his morality. If there is another route to the *Argo*, perhaps we should consider it.'

'I will not cower from battle,' Jason replies, his eyes blazing brighter than I have ever seen them. 'I would rather risk my life than flee without honour. We are *nothing* without our honour.'

I see a glimpse of him then, the boy who witnessed his father's death, who was locked inside a prison cell at such a tender age, left to die in the darkness. A boy who managed to escape, at the cost of his mother and brother, who had to grow up in secrecy, without a family, a homeland, with nothing but the thought of bringing justice, bringing honour, to his lost loved ones. Those loved ones he never even got the chance to truly know.

'Besides,' Jason continues with a smile, 'I have the fleece now, and are not all those who possess it promised undefeated glory?'

A cheer breaks out amongst the Argonauts as Hecate's smirking voice fills my mind. *All this fuss over such a useless little object.* I silently curse myself for not warning Jason sooner. But what use would there be in telling him now? It would only risk knocking his resolve, and Jason needs to believe his victory is achievable if we are to stand a chance against my father's formidable army.

'You will be safe by my side. I will never let anything happen to you,' Jason murmurs to me, reaching out to gently tuck away a strand of my hair. 'Will you trust me, Medea? As I trusted you?'

I hold his gaze, feeling the unease tug inside me as I nod. 'I will.'

15

Snaking down from the Colchian mountains is the river Phasis, named after the god who supposedly guards its sparkling waters. This river leads directly to the sea, and it is there that the *Argo* awaits us.

A stretch of rolling fields separates us from the Phasis: flat, open grasslands that would have taken no time to cross, if it had not been for my father's army in our path.

As we march across the fields, the sky splits open with a thunderous clap and heavy sheets of rain begin to fall. The downpour is thick and hot, like blood spilling from a wound. It softens the earth, making the ground loosen and shift underfoot.

We left the Colchian soldiers tied up and disarmed at the base of the mountain, unharmed except for their sorely bruised egos. Jason made the decision to travel on foot; he claimed arriving in my brother's chariot would look too hostile. As if he truly believes avoiding bloodshed is an option.

I can sense the excitable tension within the Argonauts, their determination cutting through the air as we trudge towards the *Argo*. Towards victory. Yet all I can feel inside me is a heavy, leaden dread. Jason believes my father will honour his word, yet I know he will never let Jason take what he believes to be his.

In the distance, I can see the river swathed in hazy folds of mist. To our left looms the city, the palace rearing its ugly head in the distance.

My home. My prison. In this moment, I know with a chilling certainty that I will die before I step foot within those walls again.

Then I see them, or rather I *feel* them first, the weight of their sinister, violent presence. The Colchian army.

They dominate the ground before us, yawning outwards like a terrible, deathly shadow, standing in stiff formation. Sombre statues of war. The rain thrumming against their gleaming helmets and breastplates.

A shiver passes through me as I feel the promise of death whispering in the air around us. There are *hundreds* of them. I glance to the Argonauts beside me. They are a mere fraction of their size.

'This just got interesting,' Meleager murmurs, eyeing the soldiers with a playful grin.

'How many do you think you could take?' Atalanta challenges.

'More than you, huntress.' He winks.

'Do you want to bet on that?'

It seems they are impervious to fear. Or just foolhardy. Perhaps a little of both.

Someone shouts something and the army shifts and pulls back with a harsh clatter, revealing a thin pathway. I feel the fear coiling inside me, like a creature ready to strike. But when I see my father riding through the cleared path, my fear hardens into something else, something cold and deadly. Unyielding.

He dismounts his chariot and walks towards us, stopping in the vacant land between the two armies. The seconds pulse by slowly as he awaits his opponent.

Jason strolls towards the king with a cool confidence, the Golden Fleece glowing triumphantly around his shoulders. I do not know if he is feigning this nonchalance or if he is genuinely unfazed by the hostile wall of death before him. He must truly believe the fleece's promise of glory.

'King Aeetes.' Jason's voice cuts cleanly through the downpour. 'I stand before you as your humble guest. When I first came to your prosperous lands, I told you I would not leave until I obtained the Golden Fleece. I was true to my word and now I hope you will be true to yours. I have acquired the fleece and thus ensured safe passage for me and my men.'

The king does not reply. His attention is not even on Jason, but rather beyond him – on *me*. There is such untold violence written in his glare, I do not dare think what he would do to me if we were alone.

But I refuse to give him the satisfaction of my fear, so I raise my chin a little higher and hold his gaze with equal intensity. I want my father to see the hate in my eyes as I betray him.

When the king does not reply, Jason continues, 'I am grateful for your hospitality, Aeetes. I hope you understand this is far bigger than both of us. It is my destiny to claim this fleece; it is the will of the Fates.'

'Was it the will of the Fates for you to fuck my daughter?' my father asks with lethal composure. I can only see the back of Jason's head, but I sense him stiffening at his words, surprised by their vulgarity. When the king speaks again, he lifts his voice to address me directly. 'You are pathetic, daughter. You get thrown a scrap of attention and you spread your legs like a begging whore.'

I feel my cheeks burn hotly but I do not break away from his glare.

Jason says something, his voice so low I cannot catch it. My father barks out a strangled laugh in response. 'I will speak about my property however I like ... unless you wish to steal her also?'

'With your blessing.' Jason keeps his voice level, trying to cling to any scrap of civility between them. 'I wish to take Medea as my bride.'

The collective shock is like a palpable spark in the air. I swear even the stone-faced soldiers draw in a breath.

Bride? The word clangs through me, though any sense of excitement is immediately doused by the icy dread sluicing my veins. I feel my magic stirring faintly, protectively.

A long silence follows, the sound of the rain seeming to intensify within the eerie stillness. My clothes are soaked through, clinging heavily to my skin as I look to my father, waiting for the impending explosion.

The storm seems almost mocking, imitating the swelling tension beneath it.

Suddenly, he lets out a laugh. It is heavy and strained in his throat, sounding like stones being scraped across marble. It makes my skin crawl over my bones.

'You think I would let you simply leave with what is rightfully mine?'

'You gave me your word we would have safe passage if I succeeded in your trials,' Jason counters calmly.

'You did not succeed, you fool. You *cheated*!' my father hisses. 'You used *my* daughter's witchcraft to cheat your way to victory. I knew from the moment I laid eyes on you that you were a spineless thief.'

'You never said—'

'You speak of the Gods' will, but their greatness is a stain upon your tongue. The Gods entrusted *me* with protecting the fleece from common thieves like you.' He steps closer to Jason then, his robes heavy and damp. He is the only man here not dressed for battle. 'You will never leave this land with the fleece, nor my daughter. They are mine and mine alone. But . . .' He pauses, surveying his army. 'I am a generous man, perhaps too generous. Despite the disrespect you have shown me, I will offer you a chance to redeem yourself . . . Hand over what is mine and you and your men may leave Colchis unharmed. You have my word.'

'Just as you gave me your word last night?'

My father ignores the jibe, instead turning to beckon to me, his voice eerily calm as he says, 'Medea, come here. Come, daughter.'

A beat passes. Then I walk forwards, each step feeling harder to take than the last, weighed down by the sea of eyes tied to my skin. Everyone is watching, even the rigid Colchian soldiers.

I stop beside Jason; his face is turned to me, but I keep my focus locked on my father. Around us, rain continues to pummel the ground like angry, relentless fists. Within those hissing droplets I hear Circe's voice whispering, *Violence breeds violence.*

'Bring me the fleece, daughter,' my father orders, his voice uncomfortably soft. He reaches out his hand and I stare at his palm, imagining each line is a remnant of his violence, his cruelty. How many times have I been hurt by those hands? How many times has my skin turned black and blue beneath those fingers?

Staring at him now, I wonder why I ever let such a pathetic man hurt me. This man, who stands before us in his kingly robes with absolutely no intention of fighting his own battle. This man, who will let others die in his name without giving their sacrifice a single thought. This man, who will return home and beat his defenceless wife and slaves instead of his own enemy.

'Well, daughter?'

I continue holding my father's glare as I reach out and take Jason's hand, lacing his fingers in mine.

As fury slices open my father's face, I let a small smile lift my lips.

'You listen here, you wretched little bitch.' He storms towards me then, but Jason moves in front, his hand hovering over his sword. Around us, I feel the soldiers and Argonauts bracing themselves, readying for the inevitable.

'Your battle is not with Medea.'

'So, it *is* a battle you wish for, Jason?' My father raises a challenging brow.

'You forget who now possesses the fleece. Its glory belongs to me. You do not want to fight me for you know you cannot win.'

'You *stole* it; it does not belong to you. Its powers can only be passed on when given willingly, you fool,' he spits, his bloodshot eyes bulging.

'Phrixus claimed no such condition to its power,' I interject.

'And what would you know of it, stupid girl?'

'Your insults are growing tedious, Aeetes,' Jason replies. He then turns to me with a smile and says, 'Shall we go home now, Princess?'

Whilst Jason is angled towards me, my father lunges forwards, a dagger winking from the folds of his robes. A warning scream rises in my throat, but before I can even make a sound something long and dark carves through the air, slicing through the narrow space between Jason and me and knocking the king backwards.

I blink, taking a moment to register Meleager's spear protruding from my father's shoulder. He is now sprawled across the muddied ground, howling in pain. Jason glances down at the dagger discarded beside the fallen king, his face paling as he turns back to Meleager, who unsheathes his sword.

'That's enough foreplay,' Meleager bellows. 'Let us finish this.'

'Stay close,' Jason instructs, swooping his arm around my shoulders as we run back towards the line of Argonauts.

Time seems to slow as the Colchian soldiers surge forwards, as if Chronos were toying with the seconds, making them stumble around us. I glance back to see the soldiers raising their swords aloft, illuminated by sinister flashes of white light as Zeus's thunder splits open the sky above.

My senses are heightened, magnified by the fear sparking through

128

my veins. I can feel every drop of rain on my skin, every thud of my heart deafening my ears. Then, all at once, time snaps back into place just as the soldiers and Argonauts collide.

Bodies clash like wild tidal currents smashing together, their metallic waves pushing forwards. The armies' collision rips through the air with a cacophony of noise I can barely process. Amidst the chaos the world seems to lose all detail, as if the edges have blurred together, a mash of mud and metal and bodies and blood.

I focus on Jason's arm around my shoulder, the strength and warmth of him as he guides me back behind the Argonauts' advance. But then that reassuring weight vanishes, and I am being knocked to the side as Jason swivels to block an attack, unsheathing his sword. Fear numbs me as I watch him slice his blade upwards with devastating force, cutting down his first opponent easily, then pivoting to parry the advance of a second.

'Retrieve the princess!' I hear someone shout, as three Colchian soldiers begin to rush towards me.

'Jason!' I call to him, but he is already surrounded.

I feel my magic sparking as the three soldiers advance and I curse myself for using all my sleeping potion on my brother. If only I had another spell prepared, something, anything . . .

'Get behind me,' a calm voice utters in my ear, making me flinch.

I turn to see Atalanta beside me, looking cool and composed, so at odds with the madness around us. She draws back her bow, letting three arrows simultaneously sing through the air like swift kisses of death. She does not miss. Each one strikes directly in the soldiers' narrow helmet slits, killing them instantly.

She shoulders me behind her, nocking another arrow.

Within Atalanta's reassuring shadow, I watch the battle unfolding before us. The Colchians are meticulous in their attack. They move as if they are one living, breathing beast, as only men who have trained together for many winters can. They are using unified techniques that have been drilled into them, tried-and-tested methods that have won against countless opponents before.

But the Argonauts are no ordinary foe.

They are a law unto themselves, each fighter entirely unique and unpredictable. As I watch them, I can finally see why they are such famed, formidable fighters. Whilst the Colchian soldiers wield their weapons, the Argonauts *become* them. They are death incarnate, cutting through the masses with such wild passion that they make the bloodshed seem like some kind of divine awakening.

The Colchians are too clean, too predictable, whereas the Argonauts are messy and capricious. They do not fight because it is their duty to their king; they fight because they were born to do it, because it is in their very blood.

The battle is brutal, but I cannot turn away.

It is hard to make out individuals through the downpour, but I manage to pinpoint Meleager. He is like a hurricane, barrelling through the soldiers with chaotic power. He retrieves his spear and hurls it through the mass, impaling two opponents. I hear their screams as they fall to the ground, knowing they will not rise again. When I look back to Meleager he has a sword in either hand, swooping the blades upwards and simultaneously slicing open his attackers' bodies. Soldiers swarm him but the Prince of Calydon seems unfazed, cutting each man down with deft precision. Their bodies fall at his feet one after the other and he steps over them with little regard.

Next to Meleager I see Orpheus. He is as fluid as the rain, slipping between the enemies with deft ease. He fells his opponents quickly and cleanly, without any of Meleager's theatrics. His face is grim, mouth set in a thin line. I can tell he does not enjoy the bloodshed, but he knows it is necessary. He pivots and spins with the grace of a dancer, making the act of killing seem unnervingly beautiful.

I can locate Jason easily. Amongst the violent confusion, the Golden Fleece glows, a blazing beacon that lures the attackers inwards. But the Argonauts have positioned themselves around their leader, forming an impenetrable barrier.

'Push forwards!' I hear Jason bellow as he starts to move through the path the Argonauts are carving for him. 'To the *Argo*!'

'Come, we need to go,' Atalanta tells me.

I nod, but before I can take a step forwards, I feel fierce arms wrap around my waist, forcing the air from my lungs as I am hauled backwards. I scramble viciously to break free, but the grip is like iron clamped around me.

Atalanta draws her bow as another attacker lunges from behind, kicking her down. She roars into the ground as she retrieves her sword, throwing herself at the soldier with terrifying fury.

'ATALANTA!' I cry out to her, but she is being swarmed by soldiers now and the sound of my desperation is immediately swallowed up by the battle. 'JASON!'

The soldier hauls me away as I thrash and kick, a chilling panic choking through my body. I glimpse the Argonauts in the distance, working their way towards the river Phasis. Jason is now in the lead, his face glowing golden.

Do not leave me.

I try to turn back to look for Atalanta, but my attacker holds me firm, forcing my head forwards as he drags me to a line of trees fringing the battlefield. Here, the soldier throws me down, my knees slamming against the warm, wet earth. Large fingers lock into my hair, now wrenching my head backwards.

'Well done.' I hear a familiar voice as I feel the bite of a blade poised against my throat.

From the shadows gathered beneath the undergrowth, my father emerges. He clutches his arm, which is bleeding profusely, staining his robes. His face looks dangerously pale, his lips pulled back into a grimace as he walks forwards.

'Did you really think I would let you leave, daughter?' he asks, voice raspy.

A slash of lightning cuts behind me, illuminating the whites of his eyes, the glint of his blood-etched teeth. The way he stares at me, the way he licks his lips as he regards the blade at my throat.

I know he is going to kill me.

'Well? Nothing to say for yourself?'

'I did what I had to,' I reply breathlessly.

'Is that so?' His smirk is strained. Where he clutches his shoulder, I can see the blood seeping between his fingers. 'So, you believed you *had to* betray your own family?'

'You gave me no choice.'

Behind us, the storm is punctuated by the sound of the battle raging, screams of the dying underpinning the clash of metal. I can only pray they are not Jason's.

'Whatever is the matter, daughter?' He tilts his head to one side. 'Are you surprised your darling future husband has left you behind in the dirt?'

I remain silent, feeling the coldness of the blade against my skin as I swallow.

'Tell me, child, do you *love* him?' he mocks. 'You do, don't you? And you will give Jason everything because of it. Every inch of you, every shred of your pathetic soul … but, trust me, it will never be enough for him. *You* will never be enough, Medea.'

He steps closer, his eyes scanning down my body as if inspecting a creature before its slaughter, checking the flesh is fit for him. I see his jaw flexing as he suppresses the pain from his shoulder; his pallid skin has an unhealthy sheen of sweat.

'Go on, then,' I spit, leaning into the bite of the blade. I feel it pull away from me before it can pierce my skin.

'What? No spells? No tricks?' His grin darkens. 'I am almost disappointed. I expected more from you, daughter.'

If only I had a spell to command fire rather than repel it. To harm rather than heal.

Circe taught me powerful spells, but they all take time and patience and she never strayed far into the violent side of magic. The darker side. I know it exists; I have *felt* it pacing inside me like a restless creature. Circe always warned me such things were not worth the risk . . . but, right now, I want nothing more than to embrace the vilest, most destructive parts of my power.

'*Some doors opened can never be closed again,*' she told me once.

Well, I want to rip that door down. Consequences be damned.

I just wish I knew how.

My father grabs the dagger then, whilst the soldier holds me in place. He runs the smooth side of the blade along my throat, as if tracing the curve of his own smile there. 'I could kill you right now. I could slit your throat. The Gods will know you are deserving after your betrayal. But . . .' He draws the dagger back and inspects it in his hand. 'Why would I kill my most valued weapon? That would be a foolish move, would it not? No, no, I plan to keep you nice and safe. Locked securely away where nobody can lay their filthy hands on you ever again.'

'I'd prefer death.'

He smiles at me beneath lowered brows. 'What you *prefer* is of no interest to me. As my property, you will do as I please.'

Something whistles past my head then, followed by a wet *thud*. I turn to see the soldier behind me crumpling to my feet, an arrow sticking out of his throat, the only visible part of flesh where his helmet and armour meet. I stare at the ribbons of blood spurting from the wound.

A moment later, Atalanta appears, striding through the rain like one of the Furies themselves. Her eyes blaze, face covered in blood I hope is not hers. Her bow is drawn, the fletching quivering against her crimson-streaked cheek.

'Get away from her,' she orders my father, her arrow trained on him.

'And here is Jason's other whore,' he sneers at her, baring his teeth. 'Tell me, did Jason let a woman come aboard to keep his men entertained? I assume they get quite restless out at sea. Do they take turns like gentlemen, or do they all have a go at once?'

'I said, get away from her,' Atalanta repeats. She nods to his shoulder. 'Meleager missed your heart. I will not.'

My father's smile hardens with a flinch of fear.

'Guards!' he shouts.

'Your guards are all lying face down in the dirt, fighting for their last breath. Did you really think they stood a chance against us? Fleece or not, your army is no match,' she scorns, before flicking her eyes to mine. 'Get behind me.' I obey without hesitation. 'I do not want to kill you, Aeetes, because I really do not want a price on my head for killing a king. So, I am going to count to five and I want you to lower the dagger, turn around and walk back to your ugly little palace. Do you understand?'

'I do not follow orders from women.'

She ignores his sneer, pulling the bow taut so that the string creaks threateningly. 'One ...'

'Father, do as she says,' I order quietly.

'Two ... Three ...'

134

His eyes dart between us, indignation flaring in his face as he grips the dagger tighter with his good hand, coating the hilt in his blood.

'Four . . .'

He hurls the dagger at Atalanta with surprising force given his wounded state. But the huntress catches it smoothly, inches from her face, whilst simultaneously letting her arrow fly. A strange noise rips from my throat as I watch the arrow cut towards my father, though I am not sure if I am terrified of her missing or hitting.

Perhaps both.

The arrow lodges in his shoulder, in the exact same spot Meleager had hit, embedding itself into the fresh, gaping wound. It is too accurate to be a mistake.

'We have to go, *now*.' Atalanta grabs my arm as I watch my father collapse in agony, pressing his head to the ground as if in supplication.

I feel as if I should say something, some final, cutting remark. But as I stare at my father writhing pathetically on the ground, my mind feels utterly blank, empty.

I wordlessly turn to Atalanta and allow her to tug me away, back towards the battlefield.

'We must be quick,' she says as we break into a run, the ground wet with mud and blood. 'Take this.' She passes me a dagger. 'Do you know how to use it?'

Before I can respond, a shadow surges towards us. Atalanta pivots, narrowly dodging a crashing sword. She then shifts her weight backwards, forcing the attacker away with a kick to his chest. The man staggers from the impact, giving Atalanta time to grab her sword and drive it into his gut.

She turns to look at me, her blade still embedded in the man's entrails. 'Stay close.'

We push forwards and I can tell Atalanta wants to move faster, but

135

she steadies her pace so I can keep up. Her feet are so swift and elegant, it is as if she were gliding over the muddied earth. Meanwhile, I stagger behind her, tripping over the broken bodies strewn in the Argonauts' wake. Ahead of us, they have broken the Colchian army's formation and are seeping into their lines, forcing their opponents back towards the river.

I feel a fragile flicker of hope strike inside me.

'Are you OK?' Jason asks when we reach the others. He is barely recognizable, caked in bloodied dirt, his hair limp and stuck to his face from the rain and sweat.

'Medea? Is everything OK?' he presses when I do not answer, his eyes wild and alert. I simply nod, too breathless to speak. I have not run like that since I was a child.

Jason turns to the others and begins shouting, 'Push, men! Push!'

I follow him as the Argonauts cut a path towards the sandy riverbank. Some of my father's soldiers have begun to scatter and flee, their duty dissolving into wild panic as they watch death approach them.

'We're close,' I hear Atalanta murmur, grunting as she drives her sword into another body hurling towards us. I only nod in response, readjusting my grip on the dagger she gave me. It feels cold and heavy in my hands.

The mist has started to lift now, allowing me to finally glimpse it – the *Argo*.

I have never seen a ship so large. It is like a colossal, imposing monster made up of dark wood and rippling sails. It creaks and groans restlessly, eager to be out on the open sea, cutting through the waves.

On deck, I can see men running to and fro, preparing the ship for launch. Below them, bodies bob in the hazy water, an indication that my father's attack on the *Argo* was as unsuccessful as his blockade.

'Move! Move! Carry the wounded!' Jason barks.

Small wooden boats await us on shore and the men clamber inside. Aboard the *Argo*, the rest of the crew have begun firing down on our enemies, covering our escape. I can barely see their arrows amongst the chaos, but I hear the whistle and thud as they land every target, thinning the already depleted Colchian army.

'Here, little witch.' Meleager nods to me, his large hand guiding me into an awaiting rowing boat. Numbly, I take a seat as Jason climbs in beside me.

'Keep your head down,' he instructs as the others begin to heave at the oars, guiding us towards the *Argo*. 'Medea? Did you hear me?'

I nod stiffly and Jason's eyes drop to Atalanta's dagger trembling between my hands. He gently relieves me of the weapon and sheathes it in his belt.

'It's nearly over,' he whispers. 'Just hold on.'

When we reach the base of the *Argo* the giant hull moans as if in greeting. The men scale the rigging, moving like quick, nimble lizards. I follow their lead, the knotted rope rough beneath my trembling palms. My damp gown clings to my body, dragging me downwards as I hoist myself up and up. I let out a yelp as my footing slips, but Jason is there to steady me with a strong arm.

Once aboard, I gulp down a shivery breath of relief. Above us, another flash of lightning carves open the sky. I glance upwards, realizing how numb I am. I cannot feel the rain any more, nor the chill in the air.

'Perfect sailing weather, Argus,' someone says.

'This ship can stand any weather,' a short, barrel-chested man snaps back. His voice sounds like rusty swords clashing.

I brush my hand against Jason's and he turns to me, as if seeing me for the first time since the fighting began. He looks exhausted, his soft face hardened by the remnants of violence.

'Are you all right, my Princess?'

'Yes,' I say quietly as Jason leans in to brush a kiss at my temple.

'See? I told you you'd always be safe beside me. With the fleece in my possession, nothing can stop us.'

Behind him, I catch Atalanta rolling her eyes.

The *Argo* stirs to life around us as the men – those who can still stand – take up position on the oars and begin to ease us forwards. A handful of others continue firing arrows at the soldiers on the river-bank, though it seems my father's men have begun to retreat.

As I glance around the deck, I have a creeping feeling that something is wrong.

That's when I sense it. The figure pressing in behind me.

'Hello, sister.' His voice crawls from the shadows. 'Going somewhere?'

16

'You look surprised, sister. Did you really expect me to miss all the fun?'

His sword glints in the storm's restless shadows, his helmet and breastplate making him appear taller and mightier than he truly is. Through the slits of his helmet I see his golden, hateful eyes glowing. The eyes of my father.

Around us, the Argonauts have pulled their weapons on him, forming a wide circle. Above, the clouds begin to recede, as if the Gods were clearing the skies to get a better view of the events unfolding.

'Are both Aeetes' children looking to escape Colchis?' Jason folds his arms as he approaches my brother. The bloodied dirt etching his body appears far more fearsome than Apsyrtus' freshly polished, untouched armour. I hope Jason can smell the reek of desperation on him, that poisonous desire to intimidate others in an attempt to hide his own cowardly heart.

'I would never abandon Colchis.' Apsyrtus' words are laced with a dark growl as his eyes cut to me.

'So, you snuck aboard my ship for what purpose? To single-handedly take on my men?' Jason cocks his head to one side. 'I have heard that you think highly of yourself, Apsyrtus, but surely you are not so deluded by your own arrogance to think *this* a smart plan?'

'After I woke up from my sister's *little spell*, I knew what events were about to unfold. I planned to wait here for your arrival. It was quite easy to slip aboard amongst the disorder of your crew.'

'Skulking in the shadows whilst your own men laid down their lives?' Jason arches a brow. Beneath his helmet, I can see Apsyrtus scowling. 'Still, I do not see the logic in your plan.'

'I am not here to fight,' he says as he removes his helmet and tucks it under his arm. 'I am here to trade.'

Jason grips the Golden Fleece a little tighter at his shoulder, yet it is not the fleece my brother is looking at.

No. I feel the word settle like a stone in my stomach.

'And what exactly do you have to trade with? You are on my ship, surrounded by my men . . . so what could you possibly have to offer me?' I watch the smile trace lazily across Jason's lips and feel my own lips twitch at his cool confidence.

'Turn around, thief, and perhaps you will see.'

I watch Jason as he turns, seeing that smile harden at his lips, his eyes slightly widening. I then follow his gaze to the shadows gathering in the distance, where the river's mouth opens out into the sea. No, not shadows . . . but ships.

The Colchian fleet . . .

My father had prepared for this.

He had not only positioned an army, but a fleet as well. That was why he sent me away with Jason, so he could ready his blockade. The king has been one step ahead this whole time.

The *Argo* may be the greatest ship ever built, but what use is that if we are trapped on this river? Even the Argonauts, for all their might and skill, seem to acknowledge this. I watch their faces darken as they survey the devastation that awaits us.

Any hope of freedom withers inside me – we have lost.

'So, Jason, are you still interested in that deal?' Apsyrtus' voice drips with venomous amusement.

I feel anger burn through my fear as I turn back to my brother. If only I had the spell prepared so I could turn him back into that grovelling swine. My magic stirs inside me, but it is useless to me now, like a bow without arrows.

Beside me, Jason seems to have stilled, as if his body has closed inwards on itself. His smile remains fixed at his lips, yet his eyes are distant and quiet.

'I am not giving you the fleece.' Jason's voice is steady as he meets Apsyrtus' glare.

'I do not want the fleece.' My brother's eyes are on me. 'I want to take my darling sister home.'

My heartbeat stumbles but before I can speak, Jason asks, 'Why?'

'Because she belongs to us,' Apsyrtus says, his gaze still weighing on me. I can see the promise of violence in those eyes, can *feel* it, like a cold caress against my soul.

'What of the fleece?' Jason presses, ignoring the glare I throw at him.

'I never cared about that damn fleece,' my brother scoffs, brushing his fingers over the plume of his helmet. 'That fleece is a curse. Ever since it came into our lives it has only weakened our father. It is all he thinks about, all he cares about. I am quite certain it has driven the man insane – why else would he have been encouraging her *disease*? Take the damn thing and rid Colchis of its poison . . .' He motions to me, whetting his smile. 'All I care about, dear sister, is taking you home, so I may teach you an important lesson about the consequences of your actions . . . You know how strongly father believes in punishment.'

'I will die before I go with you,' I spit at him, taking a step forwards.

'You will all die if you do not.' He looks towards the awaiting fleet. 'One signal from me and the onslaught will begin.'

'But *you* will die before they reach us,' Jason warns.

'I may not be able to take you all on, but I guarantee I could hold you off for long enough.' My brother shrugs. 'Besides, we have the best archers in the world aboard those ships. They will not miss their mark.'

'I find that hard to believe,' Atalanta mutters, eyeing the threat.

'Let us just kill the bastard now!' Meleager steps forwards as my brother holds up a hand.

'Easy there, Prince of Calydon. My men are watching. Get too close and they will have no choice but to attack. Is that really what you want? Or would you rather hand over the witch and leave this land with the fleece and your lives?' My brother turns back to Jason. 'Tell me, is her life really worth the lives of your entire crew? I am told you are a smart man. Time to prove if that is true.'

Jason's eyes flicker to mine and a cold voice crawls inside my head. *He is going to hand you over.* The breath stills in my lungs as the voice digs its claws in deeper. *He has used you. His word meant nothing.*

You foolish girl.

'Hand her over!' one of the Argonauts yells from behind, his outburst inviting more voices to join in, so eager to seal my fate.

'She betrayed her own – how can we trust her?'

'She is not worth our lives, Jason.'

'Rid us of the witch now before it is too late.'

'Go on, Jason.'

I guided these men to victory, and *this* is how they repay my aid? A cold anger rises inside me, its thick fingers locking around my spine.

'*Enough!*' Jason snaps with uncharacteristic ferocity, throwing a hand up to halt his men.

A deathly silence yawns around us, punctuated only by the churning waters below. In the distance, my father's fleet silently watches and waits, a dark stain against the tauntingly endless horizon.

I meet Jason's gaze and I sense his decision before he even speaks.

No, I silently plead, my eyes burning in their sockets. *Please. Do not do this.*

'Please.' The word escapes me as a cracked, broken breath. Beside me, I am faintly aware of Apsyrtus sniggering.

'All right,' Jason says, and I feel the word spear through my heart. For a moment, I am certain I cannot breathe, cannot even think. Disbelief blinds my senses so I can only stare dumbly at Jason, though he now refuses to look at me.

'Wise choice, Jason,' my brother drawls, smiling so wide I can see each of his sharp, crooked teeth.

'I will hand over the princess,' Jason continues, each word like another twist of that dagger in my heart. 'But may I have a moment alone with her . . . so I may say my farewells?'

Apsyrtus rolls his eyes. 'Make it quick.'

Jason grabs my hand and pulls me to the helm of the *Argo*. I numbly follow, still unable fully to comprehend what is unfolding before me. As I stumble behind him, I catch Atalanta's gaze and feel her pity brush over me. It makes me feel sick.

'Please.' I finally manage to find my voice again as Jason stops and turns to face me. 'Do not do this, Jason, please. He will kill me.'

'We must do this.' His voice is detached, distant, yet his eyes are focused intensely on mine.

'After everything I did for you,' I bite out, feeling the anger cut through my shock. 'You said I could trust you, you said—'

'Shh, Princess.' He kisses my forehead and then pulls me into an embrace, yet I can barely feel him. Where his touch once elicited a spark of life, now only emptiness ricochets through me.

His left arm tightens around me, but I remain rigid beneath him, feeling the hurt fury clot inside me. Jason then presses his lips to my ear and murmurs in a low, firm voice, 'Aim for his throat.'

As he says this, I feel his other hand press something cold and firm into my palms.

I know what it is immediately.

'What?' I breathe, trying to grasp his meaning as my fingers close around the dagger's hilt. It is the same one he took from me mere moments ago.

Jason ignores my question as he guides my hand into the folds of my skirts, concealing the weapon before he pulls away. His eyes hold mine, his dark intent hardening between us.

Aim for his throat.

Before I can process his words, Jason steers me around by the elbow and walks me back to where Apsyrtus waits.

Surely, he does not mean . . .

The ground feels unsteady beneath my feet, the air dizzyingly light as we close the distance to my brother.

'You must promise no harm will come to her.' Jason's voice sounds warped, as if I am submerged beneath the waves.

'She is not your concern any more.' Apsyrtus grabs my arm and hauls me towards him. 'Hello, sister.'

'Apsyrtus.' His name catches in my throat. 'Do not do this.'

'I must,' he hisses back.

The words clatter through me. *I must.*

Of course he must, for if he were to return empty-handed to our father . . . would he beat him like he beat me? Has Apsyrtus ever been beaten by him? I have never seen him do it, but that does not mean it has not happened. Apsyrtus' skin was often dappled with bruises, but I always assumed it was from his training, from being a young, reckless boy.

The realization settles heavily inside me. Do we share the same wounds? Do the same demons haunt us? My mind flickers to what my mother said about Apsyrtus' nightmares ...

Or am I his demon, the face that keeps him up at night, wrenching him from his dreams?

Am I his monster, as my father is my own?

'Do I have your word you will let us pass freely?' I am faintly aware of Jason's voice.

'Take me to my fleet. Once I am aboard my ship, I will inform the men to let you pass.' Apsyrtus pulls me closer to him. I feel the hardness of his armour digging against me, my eyes catching on his neck, that exposed strip of flesh. I watch the ball in his throat bob as he talks, his pulse thumping in a thick, snaking vein.

'Do I have your word?' Jason repeats, his eyes focused.

'I swear it on the Gods.'

I shift my eyes to Jason, a silent plea aching from the very depths of me. *Do not make me do this.* His eyes are heavy as he meets mine. He knows he has left me with a hideous choice – either end my own life or my brother's.

'I am sure Father will be delighted to see you.' Apsyrtus tugs one of my dark curls idly. 'No doubt he is already anxiously awaiting our return.'

As I drag my gaze from Jason and stare up at my brother, a wild, animalistic hatred sparks in his eyes. I wonder, then, if he ever truly came back from the beast I turned him into.

'Is it my fault that you are like this?' I whisper.

I see something catch in those eyes, a flicker of something beautifully vulnerable, something human. But it vanishes almost as quickly as it appears. He then opens his mouth to deliver whatever sharp, dismissive retort he has loaded.

But I do not give him the chance.

I plunge the dagger into his throat. Just as Jason told me to.

Apsyrtus' eyes bulge as he stares down incredulously at me. His hand closes over mine, trembling fingers trying to pull the dagger out, but I hold firm. He chokes out a gargled cry, blood dribbling down his lips and pulsing from his throat.

He staggers forwards, then falls heavily. I fall with him, our hands still intertwined around the blade, until we are kneeling together on the floor. His eyes slowly lift to meet mine and I watch his shock give way to fear, as the realization settles over him. He is dying.

I feel the cold shadow of death fall across us. Apsyrtus opens his mouth to say something, but all that escapes is a wet choking sound and another spurt of blood. It coats our hands, thick and warm against my cold skin.

He looks so afraid.

I remain silent as I watch the light drain from his eyes. After a moment, his face grows slack and I brush a blond curl from his forehead, thinking how much younger he looks when his features are soft like this.

A shudder ripples through me, as if I can feel his soul ebbing away gently to that place beyond. I feel his hands go limp and fall away at his sides, his head slumping forwards against mine so that our foreheads are touching.

The world goes still.

Quiet.

Empty.

'Medea.'

I look up at Jason and feel a coldness rattle through me, trapping itself between my bones and taking root there. I shiver despite the warmth in the air.

'He is dead,' is all I can think to say. Jason rests a hand on my shoulder.

'I know.' He nods, his voice like a warm embrace. 'Medea, we must act quickly. The fleet is approaching.'

I pull the knife back and a fresh wave of blood spills over my hands as Apsyrtus slumps forwards. The weight of his body nearly knocks me over, but Jason is there to hoist him up.

'Strip him of his armour.' He barks the order. To whom, I do not know.

'His armour?' My voice sounds strangely vacant, distant. As if it were not my voice at all. 'Why?'

'Because we still need to get out of here alive.'

'This will never work.'

The Argonaut, who I now know to be called Telamon, glares out from my brother's helmet. The armour fits him perfectly, the armour that is still warm from the life that had just been held within it.

'It will have to work,' Jason says.

I stand beside him, staring at the blood smeared across my brother's breastplate. Telamon follows my gaze and tries to wipe it away with his hand but ends up spreading it into dark circles.

The other Argonauts are back rowing, their strains and huffs falling into strange harmony with the shushing of the waves as we glide towards my father's fleet.

Towards death or freedom. Time will tell.

I watch the ships approaching, but in my mind all I can see is Apsyrtus slumped in the storeroom beneath the ship, growing colder by the minute. But that is no longer my brother, not any more. It is just a body, just flesh and bone.

I push the thought away as I feel Telamon grab my arm, acting the part of the cruel, entitled prince. The fleece is draped across his shoulders, its golden light illuminating the paleness of my skin.

I stare down at my hands, now clean, yet the blood has crusted beneath my fingernails like crimson crescent moons.

When I blink, I can see the fear in Apsyrtus' eyes, burning beneath my closed lids. I had believed nothing could be worse than that arrogant sneer he always wore. But the sight of him so afraid, so helpless ...

He deserved it, I silently remind myself. *He brought this upon himself.*

'Colchians!' Jason's voice rings out when we are close enough to the ship leading the fleet. 'I have made a deal with your prince. He will return with Medea and the fleece, if you will grant us free passage from Colchis.'

'Prince Apsyrtus, is this true?' a voice calls back.

'It is true,' Telamon bellows, his voice muffled by the helmet obscuring his face. He has mimicked the sharp tilt of my brother's accent, edged with an arrogant snarl. 'Clear the way.'

A tense pause. Then a bark of orders echoes across the fleet as the ships begin to groan to life and peel backwards, like waves parting for Poseidon himself.

'This cannot actually be working,' I hear Meleager mutter behind me. 'Did they not see the witch slit his throat?'

'Let us thank the Gods for giving Colchians bad eyesight,' Atalanta whispers back.

The *Argo* begins to crawl forwards through the gap the Colchian ships have carved for us. A path to the open sea beyond.

I feel my heartbeat quicken as we pass through the heavy wall of ships. Hostile eyes scrutinize us, hundreds of drawn arrows trained on each Argonaut, ready to fire if we make one wrong move.

Sweat pools at my neck, slipping down my spine. Above, the storm has receded, the clouds curling backwards towards Colchis. Ahead, the sky is clear and glassy, the bright stretch of blue beckoning us forwards.

The seconds seem endless as we creep towards that horizon, freedom so close I can taste it . . . yet it is strangely acidic in my mouth.

As we draw up to the final vessel in the formation, the Colchian soldiers prepare a bridge to place between the ships. I look to Jason, waiting for his next move as the plank of wood lowers towards us.

Any minute now they will uncover our ruse.

Any second now those arrows will be released.

But freedom is so close . . .

'NOW!' Jason bellows.

The Argonauts grab their shields and Telamon throws his own over me, obscuring my view so I can only just catch a glimpse of Jason and the others hauling something over the deck. I see an arm, a leg, a head.

My brother's head.

It cannot be.

I push past Telamon's shield, rushing towards the edge of the *Argo*. Below, I watch the cruel waves toying with my brother, tossing his limbs back and forth like children playing with a new toy.

My brother's body.

No. *Pieces* of his body. Severed and scattered into the sea.

'MEDEA!' Atalanta crashes into me, throwing her shield over us as a dark wave of arrows lifts into the sky, blotting out the sun.

They rain down on the ship in a storm of flint and fury. All around us I can hear the arrows landing with a sickening *thud*, thundering on Atalanta's shield. She hisses as one of the arrows slices her exposed shoulder.

149

Behind us, the Colchian fleet falls into disarray as soldiers begin jumping into the sea, desperate to retrieve the pieces of their fallen prince.

'On the oars! *Now!*' Jason barks.

There is a rush of movement, and then we are suddenly gaining momentum, propelling forwards as arrows continue to rain from above. The *Argo* moves with incredible speed, and the men raise a cheer as we watch my father's ships dwindle behind us.

The Colchian fleet does not pursue us. The men are too busy scrambling in the water, searching for Apsyrtus' body.

The pieces of it.

I remain silent as I peer out beyond Atalanta's shield, watching my brother's remnants being dragged under and spat out by the waves, knocking this way and that.

After a long while, when the fleet has melted beyond the horizon, I feel a heavy arm close around my shoulders. 'You are all right, Medea. You are safe.'

Jason.

'You cut him into pieces?' I whisper.

He leans in and places a kiss on my temple. 'We did what we had to do to survive, Medea. We both did.'

17

The Gods are angry with us.

No one has dared utter these words aloud, but it is a certainty that hardens with each swell and crash of the merciless waves.

The storm has followed us from Colchis, intensifying its hold like a hand tightening around our throats. It is an unearthly storm; unlike anything the Argonauts have seen, so they claim. Colossal waves dwarf the *Argo*, standing tall as mountains, tossing us this way and that. They are like giant, mythical beasts battling around us, each one eager for the chance to swallow us within its treacherous, watery jaws.

Any other ship would have been ripped apart by now, its crew lost beneath the raging waters. Thankfully, the *Argo* is no ordinary vessel. I have heard the men uttering that Athena herself, Goddess of Wisdom and War, aided Argus in its construction.

'The ship will hold,' the ship-maker repeatedly shouts over the howling winds. 'She can stand any storm.'

But this is not just a storm; it is a warning. We have angered the Gods and they want it to be known.

Despite this, Jason pushes onwards, forcing his men to row through the night, through exhaustion and hunger.

'Aeetes' fleets will already be after us,' he warns. 'We must put distance between ourselves and Colchis.'

Even those wounded from battle are expected to hold their positions and I watch as the Argonauts drain every ounce of strength they have left. Some of them pass out from sheer exhaustion, though they return to their gruelling task as soon as consciousness finds them again.

Jason advised I take refuge below deck where it is safer, but as soon as I saw the blood-stained floors, I knew I could not stay there. I would rather take my chances up top than sit alone in the dark beside my brother's drying blood. So instead, I tuck myself away at the stern, focusing on not emptying my stomach with every violent surge and sway of the ship.

Other than the helmsman, Tiphys, the only Argonaut not to take up an oar is Orpheus. Instead, he plays his lyre beside me, his melodies slicing cleanly through the storm by some Gods-given gift.

At first, I had wondered why Orpheus did not use his energy to row with the others, for I had seen him in battle and knew he had the strength for it. But, as I listened, I realized – his music is the heartbeat of the *Argo*. It rallies the men, lifting their spirits when their bodies are broken, filling us with light when we are swallowed by the midnight sea. Even I can feel it, the power of his melodies. I find myself focusing on every note, each pluck of his strings and gentle lyric from his lips. I let it steady my nerves, drown out my fears. It becomes my lifeline; one I cling to desperately. Though I know Orpheus' music, for all its divine beauty, cannot save us from this ordeal.

After a while, time begins to lose all meaning, the hours unravelling in the chaos of the tempest. We could have been rowing for days or weeks; I cannot tell. I think of Sisyphus' eternal punishment in the Underworld, forced to repeatedly roll a giant boulder up a hill, only to have it roll back down each and every time he nears its crest.

Such is how this voyage feels, a perpetual losing battle with no end in sight. I know the crew can feel it, too; I can sense their motivation fracturing beneath the weight of their hopelessness. Though they will never admit defeat. They are too proud, too stubborn.

But a storm sent by the Gods is not a battle meant to be won.

'We must find land,' I tell Jason when I can bear it no longer. I need to shout to stop the vicious winds from stealing my voice. 'I fear this storm is Hecate's doing; she is angered because we have not thanked her for her aid.'

'We are still too close.' He strains against his oar as he replies, gritting out the words. 'We must go further.'

'This storm will not relent unless we appease her, Jason. Look around you – even the *Argo* cannot battle these conditions for much longer.'

He slows his pace then, my words puncturing through his haze of determination. His eyes, bruised with exhaustion, regard his men, as if seeing them properly for the first time since setting sail. I watch the decision battle across his pallid, weathered face.

'Medea is right,' he finally announces, echoed by groans of relief. 'We must find land. We must appease Hecate.'

The dagger is heavy in my hand.

I do not like how familiar it feels, nor the way it moulds so easily into my palm, as if it always belonged there. Staring down at the blade, I watch it wink at me conspiratorially in the firelight: *Hello again, remember me?*

Before me, the Argonauts wait expectantly, etched by the fire they have built. They do not rush me, but I can feel their impatience tightening in the air. They are hungry and tired and not in the mood for my hesitancy.

We have taken refuge on a small island. Though 'island' is probably too grand a term for this tiny stretch of desolate land. It is obvious why it is uninhabited, for everything about this place feels unwelcoming, from the steep, jutting rocks to the sharp, nasty little shrubs that cling to them. But we did not mind; the steady ground beneath our feet was all that we longed for.

I turn to stare down at the boar beside me. It was Atalanta who caught the beast, so I am told, though some of the Argonauts have tried to contest this fact. Meleager has been quick to silence their scepticism.

I squint up at the sun piercing through the heavy, sullen clouds. It feels wrong to sacrifice to Hecate not beneath moonlight, as I know she prefers. But Jason said we could not delay.

My focus drops back to the boar, watching its snout quiver with fear. My eyes then dip to its throat, that thick strip of flesh. I step closer, my sudden movement making the creature reel backwards, screeching loudly. The sound of its panic rips through me, reviving the nausea that had gripped me at sea.

'I've got it,' Meleager says, holding the thrashing creature down and forcing its head upwards. 'Do it now. Go on. Make the sacrifice.'

His commands rattle in my chest, stumbling over my heartbeat as I stare at that exposed throat waiting for my blade. Something tugs inside me, heavy, sharp. Or is that Meleager tugging me?

'Do it now! Now!'

'Go on!'

'Hurry!'

In my mind I hear the furious shouts of the Argonauts as they encouraged Jason to hand me back to my brother, back to my prison and perhaps my death. They were so quick to dispose of me after all I had given them.

154

The feeling inside me intensifies, fuelled by the memory of their injustice. It is as if someone is pulling me forwards. Around me, the shadows press in. Closer, closer . . .

Come closer.

'Medea, it's OK.' Jason's voice is smooth in my ear. 'Allow me.'

I do not realize how violently my hands are shaking until I feel Jason's firm fingers steadying my own. He prizes the dagger from my damp palms, nodding for me to step aside.

I do not watch as Jason sinks the blade into the beast's throat but, even with my eyes tightly shut, I cannot escape the bloodshed. I can still see it, still *feel* it, the violent visions burning behind my closed lids. I see the gaping, fresh wound and the wide eyes of a man who knows he is going to die; I feel the heaviness of a lifeless body collapsing on to me, the hot blood staining my skin. I hear my brother crying out my name, desperate, pleading – *Medea . . . Medea . . .*

'Medea?' I glance upwards to see Jason standing before me, his crimson hands glistening. 'Will you lead the prayer to Hecate?'

I nod, my throat as dry as brittle leaves. 'Of course.'

He places a bowl in my hands, the one that has been used to gather the boar's blood. I stare down at the dark, viscous liquid, feeling it warm my palms. My stomach heaves again.

'Hecate, Goddess of the Underworld, I call on you to hear my prayer,' I declare as I tip the blood into the fire. The flames sizzle and spit greedily. Once the bowl has been emptied, I cast my open palms down to the earth. 'Your divine power led us to victory in Colchis. We recognize your generous aid, Great Goddess, and we ask that you accept this sacrifice as a sign of our eternal gratitude.'

Once I have finished, the Argonauts set to work dismembering the beast. The fat and bones will be burnt for Hecate, whilst the meat will be shared amongst the crew.

I watch silently as they carve up the boar, stripping its skin, hacking away at its limbs, slicing lumps of flesh from the bone ...

The nausea finds me once again and this time I do not fight it; I cannot.

I hurry away, collapsing into a knot of shadows to heave up my stomach's few contents. I retch and retch until I have nothing left, until I am empty inside. As hollow as an urn.

Once done, I do not return to the Argonauts. I cannot bear the sight of that flesh being passed around, feasted upon by greasy, hungry lips. So instead, I walk back and forth along the thin slip of shoreline, watching the sea pace restlessly beside me.

I had not realized how blissfully empty my mind had been during our gruesome journey here. Now, a dark part of me longs to be thrown back into those storms, welcoming the distraction of those terrifying waves, letting the fear obliterate all other thoughts from my churning mind.

But perhaps it is foolish to long for such self-destruction.

'So, this is where you wandered off to.' I turn to find Atalanta standing beside me.

'Here, I saved you some.'

She holds out a wooden bowl and I stare at the fat lumps of meat within it.

'I am not hungry.'

'When was the last time you ate?' she asks, unfazed by my hostility. I say nothing. 'You must eat. You need the energy.'

'I am fine.'

'Are you?' The question cuts deeper than Atalanta intended, and she must read this in my reaction, for her face softens. 'Eat, Medea. It will do you good.'

She tries to hand me the bowl again, but I ignore it.

'You weren't at the sacrifice,' I deflect, to which Atalanta offers a teasing grin.

'Wasn't I?'

'Where were you?'

'I was busy.'

'Doing what?'

'Perhaps I'll tell you if you eat.' Her grin widens as she perches herself on a rock, placing the bowl beside her.

I watch silently as she adjusts the bloodied makeshift bandage compressing her shoulder. I know she sustained that wound because of me, because of my own foolishness when I ran from my cover beneath the Colchians' hailstorm of arrows. If she had not been there with her shield, I would have surely been struck down, perhaps never to rise again. And if she had not intervened when she had with my father . . .

I want to thank her for saving my life, but instead I find myself saying, 'You should let me look at that.'

'It's just a scratch,' she shrugs.

'You shouldn't be rowing, you'll keep re-tearing the wound,' I warn, but Atalanta only laughs in response.

'If I stopped rowing, they would never let me hear the end of it.' She jerks her head in the direction of the others. 'They are already convinced I can't keep up with the *big, strong men*.'

I watched Atalanta rowing through the storm and know her pace matched that of any other Argonaut, even with her injury.

'If you are wounded, they would understand. Wouldn't they?' I press, moving to sit beside her. 'They all saw how bravely you fought.'

She clicks her tongue, her smile sharp. 'It doesn't work like that, not for me, anyway.'

'Why not?'

157

'Because I wasn't born with something limp and pathetic dangling between my legs.' She wiggles her little finger at me and laughs again, though the sound is edged with a bitterness. 'I know, I know, it makes no sense. Isn't it baffling how men have managed to fool everyone into thinking they are the smarter sex?'

I open my mouth to reply, but the words evaporate on my tongue as Jason appears beside us. His presence has me bolting to my feet, a childlike eagerness tugging inside me.

'There you are. I was looking for you, Atalanta.' These words cause a stab of jealousy to pierce through my gut. 'Well? Did you do it?'

'I did.' I am not sure if I imagine the sudden tightness in Atalanta's voice.

'Come, then, let us discuss.' Jason jerks his head upshore. His usually bright eyes are shadowed and heavy, his beautiful smile worn down into a tight grimace.

'Medea should hear what I have to say,' Atalanta replies, making no effort to move.

Jason turns to me then, as if suddenly registering my presence, and I love the way his face immediately softens. 'Medea, please forgive my mood. These storms are incredibly vexing. Are you well? Have you eaten?' Before I can reply, he turns back to Atalanta. 'We should not trouble her with this. She has been through enough.'

'She has a right to know,' the huntress rebukes, the edge to her voice undeniable now.

I watch something flicker across Jason's face, but it vanishes too quickly for me to decipher. He folds his arms and turns his face to the raging horizon.

'Very well. Tell us, then, what did Artemis have to say?'
Artemis?
Earlier, when Atalanta caught the sacrificial boar, I overheard the

men trading rumours about her. They said she had been raised by Artemis, after her father abandoned her in a forest as a babe. The goddess, disguised as a she-bear, had found Atalanta and let the babe suckle from her as if she were her own cub, so the stories claimed.

Having seen her in battle, I do not find it hard to believe Atalanta could have been raised by the mighty Goddess of the Hunt herself.

'She confirmed your suspicions, Jason,' Atalanta says, her words weighted by an uncharacteristic solemnity. 'It is not Hecate's wrath we have provoked.'

'Then whose is it?' I interject, glancing between them.

Atalanta sighs, looking as if she is carefully choosing her next words. When she speaks, she addresses me. 'Zeus's, amongst others. They are angered because you took your brother's life and spilt blood within your own bloodline.'

Zeus? The King of the Gods?

I feel the sickness rising inside me again, and I am grateful I have nothing left in my stomach to empty out. I glance to Jason for re-assurance, but his focus is fully on Atalanta.

'So, their concern is with Medea?'

'Not just Medea,' Atalanta cuts back to him, her tone hardening. 'The Gods hold you responsible, too, Jason. For your part in it.'

Jason looks affronted by this, pressing a hand against his chest. '*My* part? What do you mean, *my* part?'

'I am only repeating what the goddess has told me. She warned these storms sent by Poseidon are just a taste of their wrath. You must cleanse yourselves of the murder immediately. *Both* of you.'

'How?' I breathe, a familiar coldness closing over me.

'You must appeal to your aunt; she can absolve you both of Apsyrtus' death.'

'Circe?' I blink.

Beside me, Jason nods eagerly. 'We must go to Aeaea at once.'

Aeaea. The word sparks inside me, inviting a warm flicker of relief. But I can feel something else there, too, a heavy dread that creeps beneath my skin, tightening around my heart.

To ask for Circe's aid means I must first admit to her all I have done . . .

'But how are we to get there?' Jason presses Atalanta, avoiding my eye. 'They say the island is like a phantom, constantly vanishing and reappearing elsewhere.'

'Artemis has told me the course. We are not far, a day's sail at most.' Atalanta glances to the horizon. 'The goddess will grant us safe passage, but that is the only aid she will offer us. We must go now, before she changes her mind.'

From the strain in her voice, I can sense the huntress is uncomfortable asking such favours of her goddess. I wonder what servitude she will have to offer in return. For the Gods never give without taking.

'This is excellent news, Atalanta! We will make a sacrifice to Artemis to give our thanks and set sail at once.' Jason is smiling now, all signs of tension vanishing within that easy curl of his lips. He then moves to me, taking my hands in his, enveloping them within his warm, calloused palms. 'Medea, please, do not look so concerned. All will be well. I promise you.'

I force myself to mirror his smile as Jason lifts my hands to his lips, pressing a soft kiss there. He has not shown such intimacy since we left Colchis, and I want to feel delighted by his tender touch, but something is holding me back.

'I must go and inform the men of our plan,' Jason announces before he disappears.

Once gone, I stare at the empty space where he has been, my hands suddenly feeling so much colder in the absence of his.

160

'I find it strange,' Atalanta mutters to herself, 'that Jason is supposedly favoured by both Hera and Athena, yet he uses *me* as his messenger to the Gods.'

I say nothing, barely hearing her over the realization that continues to nag at me, forcing its way on to my lips.

'Jason didn't know where Aeaea was.'

It is not a question, but Atalanta answers, anyway. 'No. Nobody did.'

'He never mentioned that before.'

She sighs, leaning over to retrieve my untouched food and rising to her feet. 'He has a habit of doing that.'

'What?'

'Bending the truth to his will,' she says, pressing the bowl into my hands. 'Now, eat. You will need the strength if you are to face your aunt.'

18

I can sense Aeaea before I see it.

A power thrums in the air, threading itself through the sea breeze, fresh and effervescent. I feel it buzzing beneath my skin, causing my magic to pace in my veins.

Circe? Is that you?

Beside me, Jason studies my expression, his brow arched in a silent question.

'We are close.' I nod to Atalanta, who has been relaying Artemis' route to Tiphys, the helmsman.

I move to the bow of the ship. Below, the waves are calm and steady, as the Goddess of the Hunt promised they would be. Closing my eyes, I feel my aunt's power calling to me. I imagine my own magic twining with hers in the breeze, like fingers interlacing, holding tight ... but then something snaps and that power in the air recoils hurriedly, as if singed.

I flinch and open my eyes to see it. Aeaea.

The island appears suddenly, its shroud of mist vanishing as if conjured from thin air.

'There, ahead! Look!' the crew exclaim, a new-found adrenaline sparking between them, quickening their pace.

As I stare out at Aeaea, I have the peculiar sense it is staring right back. It feels as though the island has been watching us for a while, debating whether to reveal itself.

A phantom – that was what Jason called it. I can see why.

I feel him move to stand beside me, resting a hand on the small of my back. His touch is light and casual yet still elicits a spark that jolts up my spine, rippling along my bones.

'What a happy reunion it will be,' he says with a smile. 'I can tell you are thrilled, are you not?'

I push away my dread, letting the lie roll smoothly off my tongue. 'Of course.'

His gaze shifts back to Aeaea, and I can see the thoughts turning in his eyes. I wish he would share them with me. There is so much we have left unsaid, words we haven't had the time to voice, or perhaps are unsure how to. I can feel them building up between us, creating a horrible void. If only Jason would lay his mind bare for me, to let me feast upon his every thought, however dark. I want them all.

He reaches out then, as if hearing my silent desire, and grazes his knuckles against my cheek. It's amazing how such a small movement can hush my mind, like vicious flames being extinguished with a single whisper.

When he speaks again, his voice is as soft as a feather, though his eyes are bright and intense. 'I wanted to tell you something before we go ashore. If you will hear it?'

'Yes?' I gulp down the word.

He leans into me, lips brushing against my ear as he murmurs, 'I meant what I said, about taking you as my wife. I would make you my queen, Medea.'

My eyes widen as Jason pulls back, that devastating smile of his greeting my shocked expression.

'Think on it,' he says, before I have a chance to unravel my jumbled thoughts. 'Take your time. Once you are ready, we can discuss.'

*

Aeaea may be Circe's prison, but it is certainly a beautiful one.

As I wade my way to shore, I am captivated by the richness of the island. It is *overflowing* with life; dominated by it. Vibrant plants, shrubs, flora, trees, as far as the eye can see. I have never seen nature so fiercely lavish, so unapologetically wild. It is magnificent.

Nothing was ever allowed to grow freely in my father's courtyards. Anything that tried was cut down. The flowers and trees were pruned so often they became limp and lifeless, forced to create the illusion of perfection my father obsessed over.

But *this*, here. This is how nature is supposed to be.

Defiant. Free.

Jason stands beside me, surveying the shoreline. The sand glitters like powdered gold. Above, a peachy evening sky has draped itself over the island, painting the sea with streaks of fiery orange.

Whilst Jason is distracted, I take a moment to stare at him, my mind still reeling from his offer. I try to picture it, being his wife. His *queen*.

'This is where Circe is exiled?' he asks with a slight frown.

'It is beautiful.'

'Beautiful, yes. But there's nothing here.' He waves a dismissive hand around us. 'Imagine spending a lifetime imprisoned on these shores. You would go mad, would you not?'

His words dampen my wonderment, making me look at the island with a more critical eye. I suppose Jason is right: there is nothing here in terms of civilization – no towns or people or man-made structures. Just pure, untouched nature. But that in itself is a gift, one that bursts with a magic so potent I can taste it sweetening the breeze.

Behind us, the Argonauts are busy hauling the *Argo* on to the shore. I notice the way their eyes scan the island, trying to assess what threat it poses. They have no doubt heard the stories of my aunt, so I do not blame them for being wary. After all, Circe's threat is unknown to them. In battle they are fearless, for they know the parameters of their opponents' abilities, trusting that their strength and skill can best any mortal. But against magic? It is an unfamiliar, indeterminate power to them.

Perhaps that is why they keep their distance from me also.

'Is that her?' Jason asks, causing me to whip round.

Circe storms towards us, pale hair catching in the breeze and tangling around her head like writhing, golden serpents. Her strides are urgent and powerful, fuelled by an intensity that unnerves me, making my pulse strike quicker against my skin.

She stops just short of Jason and me, looking as beautiful as always. Yet her beauty is colder than I remembered it; fiercer somehow. The sharp, knowing smile that once graced her lips is now an angry slash across her face. Those eyes that always glowed with such warmth now spark with an unfamiliar wildness. Her magic feels different, too, crackling around her like a wolf raising its hackles.

Circe stares back at me, assessing my differences as I do hers. Beneath her scrutiny I feel so small, like a child once again, begging for her approval. Her eyes dip to my gown, still stained with my brother's blood.

Our collective silence chokes the air, interrupted only by the lapping waves. When I can bear it no longer, I dare a few steps towards her.

'Circe? It's me.'

Without warning, she grabs me by the wrist and pulls me into her arms. Her embrace is firm and tight, knocking the air from my lungs. Surprise prickles through me as I wrap my arms around her. Circe is not an affectionate person, not physically, anyway. I can count on one hand the number of times we have embraced like this. I try to relish the moment, to take comfort in it. Yet, for some reason, I can only feel the stiffness of her arms, the tightness in her shoulders, all the hard, pointed edges of her body cutting me like glass.

But then it hits me, that familiar smoky scent of hers, and I feel a heavy nostalgia ache through my core.

As if sensing my emotion, Circe pulls away and holds me at arm's length. Her eyes flicker to the Argonauts, then back to me again.

'The Gods are angry with you,' she says in the native Colchian tongue. 'They told me what you have done.'

A wave of guilt rises in my chest, threatening to drag me under the violent tide swelling inside me. But I push the feeling away, forcing my head to remain above those currents.

'I can explain,' I say, matching her chosen dialect.

'Is that why you have come, to ask me to cleanse the blood from your hands?' Her accusatory tone makes the heaviness inside me intensify.

'I came because I wanted to see you.'

Circe's lips quiver almost imperceptibly at that, the only emotion she will let slip in the company of strangers. I open my mouth to say more, but Jason's voice rings out behind me, strong and commanding.

'Great Sorceress Circe, it is an honour to meet you. We have heard great things from your niece, Medea. We come as humble guests seeking shelter on your beautiful island. I hope we are not a burden to you.'

Circe fixes her glare on him as he approaches. The Golden Fleece glows around his shoulders, making his bronzed muscles glisten. Even in just a tunic he is breathtakingly heroic, like a god descended from Olympus. I feel my heart swell as his eyes brush against mine.

'Who is this imbecile?' Circe asks me, her words ugly and cold. 'Why have you brought these men to my shores?'

'This is Jason, son of Aeson, and Prince of Iolcus,' I reply in Greek, keeping my voice level. 'He brought me here, to you.'

Jason takes my hand and I watch Circe's eyes narrow, focusing on our intertwined fingers. Her lips pull back in a slight sneer.

'Your niece saved my life,' Jason says. 'She is a miracle.'

Circe lifts her piercing, golden eyes back to him but says nothing. I have seen her do this countless times before, forcing adversaries to squirm beneath the uncomfortable weight of her silence.

'Jason and I escaped Colchis together. We had an agreement,' I explain, my familiar desperation for her approval straining my words. 'We worked as allies.'

'An agreement?' she repeats, finally flicking her dialect back to Greek. 'What did you get out of this *agreement*, Medea?'

Jason answers for me. 'She helped me obtain the Golden Fleece, and in return I brought her here, to Aeaea. To you.'

'How convenient that this detour to my island benefits you also, Jason, son of Aeson,' she jabs, and I wince at the harshness of her tone. 'It is interesting that in this *agreement* you both had something to gain, yet only *one* of you paid the price.'

Her eyes settle back on mine, heavy with disapproval. There was a time when I would have shattered beneath that look, but now I feel myself hardening against it, my defiance flaring.

'My freedom was worth any price,' I say levelly.

'You think *this* is freedom?' Circe spits, her words dripping with frozen venom. 'You will be forever deemed an outcast, a betrayer, a *murderer.*' She turns to Jason. 'Did you even consider that when you let her destroy her life for you? Or did it simply not matter?'

I recoil, but Jason is quick to rebuke, his voice steady and unfaltering. 'We did what we had to, to survive.'

'Was it survival that drove you? Or your greedy desire for glory?' Circe jerks her head to his fleece, teeth bared.

I have never seen her like this. Circe always wielded her emotions with such deft composure, only ever revealing curated glimpses of her true feelings. But now, it is as if someone has unravelled that calm, collected exterior, stripping it back to reveal a wildness I never knew existed.

'I know your type, Jason. You are a *leech*,' she continues, stepping closer. Behind her, the dying sun blazes, etching her tall frame with a sinister, crimson glow. 'You surround yourself with powerful people, draining them dry of all they are worth to you, and when you are done you simply discard them, toss them away as if they are nothing to you.'

'You do not know him,' I cut in, surprised by the strength in my voice. 'You know nothing of what you speak.'

'No, Medea. *You* are the one who knows nothing. You are a fool for letting him blind you with his hollow charm.' Her severity silences me. She has never spoken to me like this before.

Circe studies my expression, a wisp of something soft and sad catching in her eyes. But it vanishes as she turns back to Jason. 'I want you off my island and far, *far* away from my niece.'

'What?' I gasp. 'You can't—'

'I assure you I can.' She nods, her anger hardening into a cold, steely composure. 'Leave, now, Prince of Iolcus. Do not make me ask again.'

I turn to Jason, watching his mind race, trying to decipher a solution, weighing the threat my aunt poses. I see his hand absently brush against the hilt of his sword. Behind us, I sense the Argonauts mirroring his movement.

Circe sees it, too, her eyes narrowing as she arches a sharp eyebrow. 'Is that how you wish to resolve this matter? How foolish of you.'

She steps forwards, and I can feel her magic rallying with the movement, sharpening in the air with a deadly ferocity like a storm about to unleash itself.

I hear the Argonauts unsheathing their swords.

'*Stop!*' The word rips from my chest as I throw myself in front of Jason. 'You will not harm him. I will not allow it.'

Circe halts immediately, her magic stilling between us.

'You stand against me for *him?*' she asks, her voice lethally quiet.

'I stand against any more bloodshed; enough has been spilt already.' I nod to Jason and his hand falls away from his sword. Turning back to Circe, I continue, 'You will not harm him, nor any member of this crew. We have come here asking for your hospitality. By the divine laws of *xenia*, you must oblige us.'

Circe goes preternaturally still as she stares at me, the coldness in her eyes slowly giving way to something darker, heavier.

It feels like a small eternity before she speaks again.

'I want them gone by morning.' Her voice is unnervingly empty. Behind me, I hear the collective gasp of relief ripple through the crew. 'I will not indulge you with food and shelter. You can find that your-selves. But . . .' She sighs, turning her face to the sunlight bleeding out across the horizon. 'I can offer healing to those who need it. I have a dwelling on the hill; those wounded are welcome there.'

'Thank you,' I say, stepping towards her.

But Circe pulls away instantly, turning on her heel and marching into the forest's thickening shadows.

'How does it feel?'

'I told you; it is just a scratch.'

Atalanta and I are sitting in one of the two spare chambers in Circe's home. It is a simple space, the walls made of mud brick with dark wooden beams reaching across the ceiling. Evening sunlight slants in through small, high-up windows, revealing the bruised sky beyond.

I was surprised, at first, when I saw how small and modest Circe's house was, and even more so when I witnessed the cluttered chaos inside. Wax tablets piled high, half-finished potions scattered across every surface, the only decoration coming from the curious stains and burn marks patterning the floors and walls.

But I like the house, for all its mess. The cosy rooms huddled together make for a welcome change from the empty, echoing halls of my father's palace.

This home has character, has a soul. The palace had none.

Atalanta remains silent as I examine the deep, angry gash slicing across her shoulder. She glances at it then gives a shrug that says, *I've had worse.*

'This is a healing balm,' I say as I lather the salve between my hands. 'It will help with the pain and speed up your recovery process.'

She nods her consent, shifting round to allow me better access to her shoulder.

Being this close to the huntress, I cannot help but admire her muscular body. Before we met, I had assumed such physiques were only obtainable by men, whilst women were to take up as little room as possible. What a foolish notion.

'Yarrow is the primary ingredient,' I tell her as I gently apply the balm. 'The herb is very powerful, even without the aid of my magic.'

'Are you sure your aunt hasn't laced it with some kind of curse?' she grins, seemingly indifferent to the pain.

'I prepared it myself. Circe only supplied me the ingredients to do so.'

There is a shard of bitter disappointment wedged inside my chest. It has been there since we arrived, aching every time I think of my aunt and our disastrous reunion. For how many winters have I been dreaming of that moment? Endless nights spent etching each and every detail in my mind – the love in Circe's smile, the warmth of her hug, the pride in her voice as she welcomed me home. But reality has ripped that dream to shreds.

You are a leech. Circe's words nag ceaselessly at my mind. *Only* one *of you paid the price.*

'You are doing well,' I tell Atalanta to distract myself. 'Meleager howled like a wild animal when I used this balm on his wounds.'

'That's because Meleager is an oversized baby,' she smirks.

'How does that feel?' I motion to her arm.

'Better, actually, much better.' She nods, rolling her shoulder around in small circles. I can feel her eyes lingering on me as I reach for the bandages Circe left out. 'How do *you* feel?'

'I feel fine,' I reply automatically, my voice clipped. 'Lift your arm up.'

'It would be OK . . . if you were *not* fine,' she prompts as she obliges.

I avoid her gaze, focusing instead on weaving the bandage around her shoulder. 'I know.'

'It wasn't your fault . . . your brother's death.' My hands stiffen and falter, a sudden tightness squeezing the air from my lungs. 'You had no choice. He was never going to honour that deal.'

'I had a choice. I chose to kill him.'

I chose to live.

'You saved us, Medea. Remember that.'

'Why are you saying all this?'

'Because your aunt was saying some pretty brutal things. I know that must've been tough to hear.' The softness in her voice catches me off guard. 'And I also know how they will tell this story. It is the same for any woman who defies their place in this world. Jason will be the hero, and you? They'll either make you his adoring, lovesick damsel or they'll make you the villain. Those are the only roles they feel comfortable with us occupying.'

I consider her words as I fasten the binding in place.

When I speak again, my voice is quieter, barely even a whisper. 'What you said before . . . about Jason bending the truth to his will. Are you saying you do not trust him?'

Atalanta sighs as she flicks some dried dirt off her bare knees. 'Look, I will always be indebted to Jason for granting me a place amongst his crew. That is something few men would ever dream of allowing a woman. But that doesn't mean I always have to agree with him or the . . . *methods* he uses to get what he wants.'

'Do you think that's what I am?'

She gives a shrug as she probes her bandage, admiring my handiwork. 'Does it matter now? You both got what you wanted out of your agreement, didn't you? It's done now, it's over.'

Over. The word stings, even though I know she didn't intend it to.

'But . . . he still wishes to make me his bride,' I admit.

Atalanta clicks her tongue, the sound sharp and disapproving. 'You do know "bride" is just another word for "property", don't you?'

'It isn't like that with Jason.'

'It's *always* like that.' She rolls her eyes. 'You've just earned your freedom, Medea. Do you really want to give that up? And what about your life here with your aunt – isn't this what you wanted?'

I avoid her questions, busying myself with washing my hands in the bucket beside me. Blood from Atalanta's wound swirls in the water, curling into dark, crimson plumes. Above me, I hear her sighing.

'Jason is ambitious. It is one of his greatest traits, but also one of his worst.' I glance up to see her watching me, her eyes suddenly intense. 'He is not afraid to step on others and cast them aside to get what he wants. I have seen him do it before.'

'When?'

I note her eyes flicking to the door before she continues, voice lowered. 'You have no doubt heard Herakles was part of our crew when we set sail for Colchis. During our journey from Iolcus, Herakles' companion, Hylas, went missing. He and Herakles had a very *special* bond, if you know what I mean.' I am not sure I do, but I nod, anyway. 'Herakles would not leave his beloved behind and insisted Jason sent out a search party. But Jason refused. We were already behind schedule and Jason made it abundantly clear he would not put his future on hold for anyone, not even the son of Zeus.'

'What happened?'

'We left Herakles behind.' Guilt edges her words. 'Ultimately, I think it worked in Jason's favour. He was always paranoid the men wanted Herakles as their leader instead of him.'

This information settles uncomfortably inside me, and so I rise to my feet, pacing across the room in an attempt to dislodge the feeling. I move to the small table, absently toying with the herbs Circe has left scattered across it. The yarrow's distinctive scent pierces the air, sharp and sweet like fresh pine needles.

'Medea, it is not my place to tell you what to do.' Atalanta's grey eyes follow my restless movements, their intensity pulling my focus back to her. 'I just need you to understand that Jason has a *very* clear vision of his future, and he will cut and carve all those around him to ensure they fit perfectly into it. And those he cannot fit, he will simply cast aside.'

'But what if I *want* to fit into that future?'

She stares at me for a long moment, and I see something flicker across her face. Sadness, perhaps? Or disappointment.

'Just make sure it is *your* decision, Medea. Nobody else's.'

My decision. Such a concept is foreign to me. My whole life has been dictated by others, even down to what gown I wore or what food I could eat.

I watch Atalanta head for the door. Her movements remind me of a mountain lion – sleek and powerful. She pauses at the threshold, bracing a hand on the frame as she turns back to me.

'Thanks.' She motions to her shoulder. 'For the witchy stuff.'

'Thanks for saving my life . . . twice.'

She grins, that playfulness returning to her eyes. 'My pleasure, Princess. But next time . . . try not to run *towards* the hailstorm of arrows. OK?'

19

I cannot sleep.

The darkness feels alive, distracting. As I stare into the gloom, I swear I can feel it leaking like an open wound. It seeps into me, whispering against my bones a language I do not understand but which my body seems to respond to. Magic stirs in my veins, a steady thrumming that begins to build as if the night were feeding into it. It feels like a pressure swelling, a mighty wave preparing to crash right through me.

I must get away from it.

I throw myself out of bed and move to the central room in Circe's home. With shaking hands, I light the hearth and feel a breath of relief as the flames spark to life, soaking the room in an amber glow and chasing back the stalking darkness.

I watch the fire feast off the wood and lean closer to the flames, though their warmth does not thaw the coldness gripping my insides.

Guilt paces at the corners of my mind, just like the shadows around me. It is waiting for my guard to drop, for my resolve to weaken, so it can invade and rip me apart, like vultures circling above a dying beast.

But I cannot let it in. I will not.

Instead, I repeat to myself again and again – *I chose to live.*

I wish Jason were here.

His presence always eases this weight inside me, quietens my mind. Nobody has ever had that same effect before.

He will cut and carve all those around him ...

My conversation with Atalanta nags at me. Yet, with each echo, I feel her words unravelling a little more.

The huntress's warning was intended to drive me away from Jason but, in truth, it has only demonstrated how similar he and I are – two people willing to do whatever it takes for the future we deserve.

And together, look at all we have achieved so far.

What else could we accomplish if I remained by his side?

I wish I could speak with Jason, just the two of us. But, as Circe instructed, he has remained on the beach alongside his crew. Even the wounded are sleeping outside; I believe they are too afraid of my aunt to spend a night beneath her roof. I do not blame them after what they saw.

I told Jason I would stay with him tonight, but he insisted I take the spare bed in Circe's home.

'You need a good night's rest,' he told me with a smile.

A good night's rest. As if that were possible.

Doesn't Jason know the god Hypnos only gifts sleep to the peaceful, the unburdened?

In the stillness, I find my mind reaching into hidden corners, like fingers probing a wound, testing its sting. I think of Chalciope, and the memory of her smile makes my whole body feel impossibly heavy. If only I could explain to her what happened, to make her understand why.

But I killed her brother.

How could she ever understand that? How could I expect her to?

I recoil from the question, my mind retreating to Jason once again.

I would make you my queen.

A glimmer of excitement strikes inside me, faint and fragile yet undeniably sweet. I shield it protectively, like a small flame within a howling storm.

'You are awake.' Circe's voice draws my attention to where she stands in the doorway. Her figure is etched in silvery moonlight, making her hair appear almost white in its ghostly glow.

'I could not sleep,' I admit as she steps forwards.

The night's chill curls in behind her, along with a sharp, uncomfortable tension. I feel it settling uneasily between us as she approaches the wooden table in the centre of the room. Her eyes are distant as she sets down the herbs she has gathered from her little garden out at the back, a small sanctuary of curious plants I have never seen before. I was hoping she would show them to me, teach me their magical properties as she once used to. But she has not offered, and I have not asked.

She has been keeping her distance since our confrontation earlier. Our longest exchange was when she handed me some fresh clothes and told me to burn my blood-soaked gown. The garments she gave me are light yellow, so pale they look almost white. After days spent covered in blood, this colour feels odd against my skin. Wrong, somehow.

'It is time we spoke,' she says.

I feel the knot in my stomach tighten as she comes to sit beside me. Her golden eyes soak in the firelight, the shadows toying with the edges of her face. She looks softer now, more like the aunt I remember. The one I have missed so.

'Hecate came to me,' I say in an attempt to fill the tense silence.

'She told me,' Circe nods. 'What did she say to you?'

'Not a lot. She was vague and somewhat ... irritating. She said she gave me my power out of boredom.'

The faintest smile touches her lips but vanishes before it takes shape. 'That sounds like Hecate.'

'I felt you calling to me,' I say, shifting forwards in my seat. 'When we were approaching Aeaea, I could feel your magic.'

'I felt yours, too.' She nods again, a wariness tightening around her eyes. 'I could feel the stain of Apsyrtus' soul upon it.'

Her words make me flinch.

I remain silent, waiting for Circe to speak again. I watch her sift through her thoughts as she considers what to say. If only I could peel back that beautiful face and see those thoughts for myself, understand what lurks within her.

'Do you know how many times I envisioned killing your father?' she asks suddenly to the flames. I say nothing, unsure how best to respond. 'I always hated him, ever since we were children. That night you and I first met, when I saw what he had done to you, what he had been doing to you, to a *child* . . . I had never wanted to kill him more than in that moment. But I did not, for I knew the consequences.' She stares back at me. 'Consequences you must now face.'

I feel myself sharpening beneath her scrutiny. 'I did what I had to.'

'No, Medea. You did what Jason told you to do. Do not confuse your agency with his manipulation.'

'You do not know him.'

'Of course I know him.' Her voice is underpinned by that wild fury she exposed earlier, a side of her I never knew existed. 'I have encountered numerous men like him. They are all the same.'

'You are wrong. Jason *saved* me.' I clench my hands into tight fists, my own ugly anger suddenly surging up inside me. 'He did not leave me to rot in that prison like *you* did. He would never abandon me like that.'

'Abandon?' Circe bares her teeth at the word. 'You think I chose to be exiled here? To be bound to this wretched island for the rest of my days? To feel my mind slowly unravelling?'

The fire gutters beside us, as if trembling beneath her wrath. I watch the shadows skitter across the floor, my own fury stilling in my veins, bowing to hers.

'I'm sorry,' I murmur, wringing my hands in my lap.

She inhales, turning to the fire. I watch the anger diffuse across her face, replaced by a delicate touch of sadness. I wait for her to respond, but she does not.

'I didn't know you were exiled, not until recently. My father said you left because . . . you grew tired of me.'

Circe closes her eyes for a brief moment, drawing in a slow breath. When she speaks her voice is calmer, softened by a melancholic undercurrent. 'No, Medea, that is not the reason. Not at all. I wanted to come and see you, to explain. But . . . Well, you were locked in your prison, and I was locked up in mine.' She gestures vaguely around the room, a sad smile twitching at her lips.

'I waited for you,' I whisper into the shadows. 'Every day, I waited.'

'Do not think for a second that our separation didn't wound me too, Medea. I have lain awake night after night tormented by thoughts of you alone in that palace . . .' She shakes her head, as if trying to shake those visions from her mind. 'My greatest failure was leaving you under my brother's command . . . and that is why I also bear the weight of Apsyrtus' death.'

'What?' My eyes widen. '*No.* You did nothing . . . nothing wrong.'

'Precisely. I did nothing. I should have been there to guide you. I should have . . .' She trails off, gazing down at her open palms resting in her lap. 'I will absolve you of Apsyrtus' death. I will ensure no curse falls upon you.'

'And Jason?'

Circe sighs. 'If I absolve you, he will also be cleansed.'

I want to say *thank you*, but the words feel weak and feeble in my mouth, not adequate for the monumental gift Circe is giving me. The gift of forgiveness and protection from what further punishment the Gods have prepared for me. Such gratitude cannot be put into words. So, instead, I say nothing.

I want to feel eased, unburdened, but in that space where my relief should be blossoming, all I can feel is disappointment.

Can death really be wiped away so easily?

I sense it then, the darkness shifting around us, the shadows lurking like living, breathing beings. I shudder and shift closer to the fire. Circe notices my reaction, her eyes flickering around the room as if she can sense it, too.

'You can feel it, can't you?' she whispers. 'You can feel its presence.'

'What is it?'

I watch as she leans over and places another log into the hearth, causing the fire to hiss and spit irritably. When she turns back to me, I see a hint of reluctance clouding her expression.

'Death is a terrible burden for anyone to carry,' she begins. 'But when a sorceress takes a life, it is ... different.'

'Different how?'

'Do you remember when I told you of dark magic?'

'You said to master it requires giving something we can never take back?'

She nods. 'Earth magic stems from Gaia, from the life that grows within her – flower, fauna, roots and shrubs. But dark magic is ... different. It stems from the world below, fuelled by death and darkness and all manner of malevolent spirits. Hecate once told me we can channel that power from the Underworld, but to open that doorway, that connection, we must give something in return.'

'What?' I whisper, though I already know the answer before she says it.

'We must give a human soul, Medea.' Circe pauses, allowing the weight of her words to sink in before continuing. 'The death spirits have a channel to reach you now and they will tug on that bond; I am sure you have felt them already. They will wish for you to release them, to feed into your power and let them do your evil bidding. They thrive off destruction and death.'

'Would Hecate allow me to utilize such power?'

'You forget Hecate is a being of the Underworld. These creatures are cut from the same cloth as her. There is goodness in Hecate, however, but the death spirits . . . They are shadows of the most malignant elements of our world.'

I think about the battle in Colchis, about how helpless I felt amidst it all. What could I have done if I had had the death spirits to command then?

'How would . . . how would I invoke them?' I ask, and I feel Circe's gaze cut to me.

'You will not need to cast spells like earth magic. The spirits have their connection to you now and they will come if you summon them . . . but, Medea, *listen* to me.' She leans forwards, her whole body etched with a sharp tension. 'When we practise earth magic we use nature as a mediator, to facilitate our power. But with dark magic you do not have that barrier. The power will flow through you; it will feed off *you*, your mind, your soul. Do you understand what I am saying? You must *not* invoke their power, no matter what. It is not worth the risk.'

As Circe speaks, I slip my focus beyond her to where the darkness shifts, like a hand beckoning. *Come play with us . . .*

'Have you ever done it: killed someone?'

'No. I have never wanted to risk opening that channel.'

'What if I could learn to control it, what if I could—'

'You *cannot*,' she snaps before I can let the idea take shape between us. 'It is too dangerous, Medea. I forbid it. Do you hear me?'

Forbid. The word makes the shadows swell and shift.

I remain silent, weighing Circe's warning in my mind, turning it over this way and that as if I were examining a trinket, trying to decipher its worth.

If Circe had never opened that connection to the Underworld, then how can she be sure of the consequences? All her prior teachings came from her own lived experience, but this is new and unexplored territory. And didn't Circe herself say that magic was 'trial and error'?

'Why did you never tell me about this before?' I ask.

'I considered it. But to be entirely truthful, I was . . . apprehensive.'

'Why?'

She hesitates. The reaction is unnervingly uncharacteristic.

'I believed you might be tempted by the power the darkness promises.'

I am silent as I absorb the unspoken accusation lining her words.

Did Circe really think me capable of *killing* for power?

Is that truly how she sees me?

'Medea.' My name is a heavy sigh, so unlike the way Jason says it. 'Hecate has blessed you with an incredible gift. But your magic has always been . . . volatile. As a child you were wielding spells that should have taken you many winters to master.' Her gaze drifts, loosening into distant memories. 'It was always different for me. It took me a long time. Endless studying, discipline, patience, focus. But for you . . . it came so naturally, so easily. Dangerously so.'

'You think I am dangerous?'

'I think you are powerful, Medea. More than you realize.' She reaches out and takes my hand. 'You just need to ensure that you are always in control of that power.'

I stare down at her slender, perfect fingers against my hideous, tainted claws. Beneath my nails, I swear I can still see the dried flecks of Apsyrtus' blood. I have scrubbed my hands raw and still I can feel it there, staining me. Marking me as a killer. A murderer.

'I had to get out of there,' I whisper, feeling the emotion seeping out of me like a weeping wound. 'I couldn't bear it any longer.'

'I know.' She squeezes my hand tighter. 'You will be safe here, Medea. Once the Argonauts leave, we can resume our lessons. I can also teach you ways of silencing the death spirits. It will take time, though. We will need to be careful.'

My heart constricts in my chest as I think of Jason, sailing away, slipping from my life for ever.

'But Jason ...' The words falter as Circe recoils from me, pulling her hands from mine.

'What of Jason?'

'He wishes to make me his bride.'

'Then you will decline.'

'But—'

'Medea.' She spears me with a glare. 'You will decline the offer. Understood?'

'*But I love him.*' The words escape me in a desperate rush, shocking even myself.

In the silence that follows I feel the realization descend over me; one I had been too afraid to admit to myself – I do love Jason.

Deeply, irrevocably, unbearably.

Circe cuts her hand through the air as if batting away the idea. 'You do not love him, Medea. It is an infatuation, that is all. It will pass.'

'I love him,' I repeat again, my voice hardening. 'And he loves me.'

'He loves what you can *do* for him, like a king might love his gold. But what do gluttonous kings do with that gold? They spend it. Every single coin, until there is nothing left.'

'You do not understand.'

'Believe me, I do, Medea. More than you know.'

Something in her tone catches my attention, that stark thread of pain laced around each word. It causes my indignation to falter inside me.

'What do you mean by that?'

Circe sighs, her eyes darkening, sinking into memories she has never once shared with me. I realize then how little I know of her life outside our lessons, how much she has kept secret from me.

When she finally speaks, I notice her whole body is tensed, as if she were teetering on a precipice, trying to hold herself steady. 'His name was Glaucus. He was a mortal, a sailor by trade. He was handsome and charming in all those dull, obvious ways . . . But there was something about him, or perhaps it was something about the way he made me feel.' She rises from her seat, as if the memories have chased her from it. I watch her walk over to the table and begin busying herself with the herbs she has collected, stacking and restacking them into pointless piles.

She continues without looking up, 'I was indifferent when we first met. He was a pretty face, that was all. But Glaucus slowly wore me down, like waves upon an unyielding cliffside. The man had impressive patience; I'll give him that.' Her smile is a withered, bitter thing on her face. 'Then one day it struck me, that terrible realization that I had fallen *in love* with him. This mortal, who I had merely been using to warm my bed, had suddenly consumed my heart, my mind, my every waking thought. It was like a sickness had invaded me, blinding me to logic and reason, severing my dignity from my

184

body … And so, I did as all lovesick people do, and I confessed my feelings to Glaucus, vowing I would do anything for him, anything at all.' She plucks a flower and crushes it in her clenched fist. 'He asked me to make him a god.'

My breath stills in my lungs. 'Could you do such a thing?'

She nods, unfurling her fingers and staring down at the shrivelled petals in her palm.

'It is a very long and complicated spell, only possible because of the divinity in my veins. Though I had to first ask the Olympians for their blessing. They refused me. But Glaucus was a master with his words. They were his greatest weapon, you see, able to cut deeper than any mortal blade. He kept reminding me of his mortality, how little life he had, how soon he would die, and I would be burdened with spending the rest of my eternity without him. Eventually, I relented and gave him what he wanted.'

Circe finally turns to look at me, though her golden eyes are wholly swallowed by the night. She allows a heavy beat to pass between us.

'What happened … afterwards?'

She shrugs, letting those petals flutter to the ground. 'He got what he wanted and was done with me. He took a new lover shortly after, cast me aside to face the wrath of the Olympians alone. They were furious, of course. Deifying a mortal without their consent? Such crimes are not taken lightly.' She waves a hand around the room. 'And so, here I am.'

'*That* is why you are exiled, because you turned Glaucus into a god?'

'Because I allowed myself to be manipulated by a weak man,' she corrects sharply, though I can sense her fury is marred by the tender edge of humiliation.

She watches me whilst I absorb everything she has admitted.

185

I can hardly comprehend it, the idea that Circe, my brilliant, formidable aunt, could have been fooled by an ordinary, mortal man. In my mind she has always loomed so large, an indomitable force that towered above all else, an idol I have worshipped since the day she walked into my life.

Looking at her now, she has never seemed so . . . *human* to me.

It is like seeing a beautiful statue finally illuminated by the harsh light of day, revealing the small cracks and fissures, those flaws I naively never believed could have existed.

'I am sorry,' I finally say into the silence. 'For what he did.'

'My love for Glaucus made me do horrible, foolish things, Medea. I cannot let that happen to you. I cannot let you make the same mistakes as I did.'

I frown. 'But . . . Jason isn't like that. He wouldn't do that to me.'

'He is *already* doing it to you.' Circe loosens a long sigh, pressing a delicate finger to her temple. 'I know it is difficult to see for yourself. I *understand*, truly. And it's important you know it's not your fault you have fallen into his web. You are a mere fraction of my age, and still I was able to be fooled by such poisonous lies.'

Her words breathe life into the ugly insecurities inside me, allowing those nasty little thoughts the strength to grip hold of my mind, carving out hollow corners where my doubts can mutate.

No. I refuse to let her ruin this, to take this from me. I know what I feel when I am with Jason, I know what I saw burning in his eyes in the Grove of Apollo. It was love.

'*Stop.*' The word has me rising to my feet. 'This is not fair. You cannot try and taint my love for Jason just because you gave yours away to the wrong man.'

'Medea, please listen—'

'No, *you listen*. Jason is not Glaucus. He is a good man; I know he is. I can sense it, in here.' I press a firm hand to my chest. 'Weren't you the one who taught me to trust my instincts?'

Circe's eyes are hollow, her face worn. I have never seen her look like this before. Not quite exhausted, more ... defeated.

'I am not a child any more, Circe,' I press, taking a step towards her. 'You cannot simply tell me what to do and expect me to obey as I once did.'

'You are right, Medea. You are no longer a child. But your heart is still the same. Still lost. Still searching for a purpose. Though, believe me, Jason is not the answer. You will destroy each other.'

'How can you possibly know that?'

'*Because you are broken, Medea.*' The sudden severity of her tone surprises me, causing me to recoil backwards. Circe remains eerily still as she continues, 'And Jason knows it. He will take every damaged piece of you and weaponize it for his own desires, until there is nothing left of you. Can you not see that?'

Broken. The word pierces through me, splintering my soul.

I stare at her for a long moment, my eyes feeling glassy in my head, as if they might roll out of their sockets and shatter across the floor between us.

'You ... think I'm broken?'

Circe says nothing, her silence worse than any response she could have given.

'You are just like all the rest of them. Afraid of me, of what I can do.'

'Was I wrong to have such concerns?' Circe counters, her voice painfully soft. 'Or need I remind you whose blood is on your hands?'

A sharp, overwhelming pain rises inside me, and it feels as if I cannot breathe, cannot even think. My magic surges with it, tearing through me, burning through my insides, so hot I feel as if I might actually catch on fire.

I have to get out. I cannot stay here. I cannot bear to sit here a second longer in this airless room with her cruel, judgemental eyes.

I have to get to Jason.

The one person who does not look at me as a burden, a disease, a stain, an embarrassment, as *broken*.

'I will not let you poison me with your bitterness.' I hurl the words at her as I storm towards the door. 'I will not let you take away the *one thing* in my life I have chosen for myself.'

'I can see where this path leads.' Circe grabs my wrist. I try to rip myself away, but her fingers hold firm, nails digging urgently into my skin. 'Do not go down it, Medea. Please.'

'You cannot force me to live in the shadow of *your* regrets.'

My words seem to jar something inside Circe; I see it settling on her face like dust settles across a defeated battlefield. She recoils, releasing me.

I do not turn back as I walk out into the beckoning night.

Circe's home is positioned upon a steep hill.

In the day, you can see the whole of Aeaea from her doorstep. But tonight, her island slumbers beneath the heavy darkness, all its vibrant details reduced to bulky, blackened shapes.

From where I stand on the hill's crest, I can make out the silver sea wrapping itself around the island, the moon-tipped waves tracing its scoured edges.

Until now, I hadn't realized how *small* Aeaea is. I could walk its entire length in a day, less even. This realization tightens inside my chest, squeezing the air from my lungs. Behind me, I hear Circe calling my name again.

I need to get away.

Breaking into a run, I hasten down the hill's steep edge to where its grassy bank disappears into the undergrowth. When I arrived on this island, I found its wildness inviting, but now it feels as if that wildness is turning against me. Everywhere branches reach like groping hands, tearing at my gown, my skin, my hair, trying to tug me backwards, pull me down. But my pace does not slow. I fight against those claws, forcing my way forwards until I stumble out into a wide, sandy cove.

I do not hesitate as I stride down the shoreline towards the Argonauts' makeshift camp.

Some of them are still awake, sitting round the fire, their faces flickering as they pass around a jug of wine. I notice from the distinct markings on the side of the bottle that it is wine from Colchis.

I can feel the Argonauts' weary eyes on me, but I ignore them as I stalk up to Jason. I stand over him, my breathing ragged. He is mid-conversation with Orpheus but breaks away from the musician to offer me one of his casual smiles.

'Shouldn't you be asleep, Princess?'

'We need to talk,' I say, fighting to keep my voice level.

Before he has a chance to respond, I take off up the beach, ignoring the ripple of snickers from the Argonauts and the enquiring eyes of Atalanta.

The bank slopes upwards into the dense forest. Here, the trees do not claw at me but bow their heads in solemn discussion, their moon-soaked branches whispering against one another like schemers in the night.

I do not check if Jason is following as I pick my way through, letting the darkness guide me. The air is laced with the cloying stench of the earth, as if I can smell what rots within the soil, the death interwoven with life. It makes me think of Apsyrtus.

Are there pieces of him still left in the sea, sunken to a watery grave?

'Medea, slow down,' Jason's voice calls from somewhere behind.

I finally stop at a small clearing to catch my breath, staring at the sky above. The stars glitter like tiny jewels woven into the deep, silky canopy. I remember my mother once telling us that each star was a soul placed by the Gods, a gift of immortalization. Now, whenever I look at the night sky, all I can think of are dead eyes watching me.

Mother. The thought of her makes my chest feel empty.

How did she react when she learnt of her only son's death? Her daughter's betrayal? With Chalciope married off, she has no children left now. She will be alone with my father . . .

The thought makes a slither of sickness ripple through my hollow stomach.

But I push it away, force it down and down and down . . .

I chose to live. I chose to live. I chose to live.

'Medea?' Jason's voice strokes along my neck. 'Medea, look at me.'

Slowly, I turn to face him, my breath catching in my throat at the sight of his beautiful face carved by the moonlight.

'Did you talk to your aunt? Will she absolve us, Princess?'

Princess. I am no princess. Not any more. I stripped that title from myself.

Jason steps towards me. 'Medea? Your aunt, did she agree to it?'

'She did.'

He smiles. 'That is good news, isn't it? Medea . . . what's wrong?'

I lift my gaze to the dead eyes watching from above.

'You didn't know where Aeaea was.' The words escape me as a whisper, catching me by surprise.

I turn back to Jason, watching his brows pinch together in confusion.

'I'm . . . not sure I follow, Princess.'

I fold my arms. This wasn't the conversation I wanted to have with him, not here, not like this. But Circe's accusations have left me feeling exposed, vulnerable. I am like a wounded creature lashing out defensively, biting whatever hand comes its way.

'When you promised you'd take me to Aeaea, you never told me you didn't know where it was,' I clarify.

Jason's smile returns as he shakes his head, golden curls dancing. He then places his hands on his hips and makes an exaggerated point of surveying the forest around us.

'I'm confused. Is this not Aeaea?'

'It is.'

'Well, that's a relief.' He cocks his head, that smile broadening into a grin. 'So, I *did* take you to Aeaea. Yes?'

'Yes.'

'So, all is well, then. Is it not?'

'You *lied* to me.' *Just like everyone else.*

Jason's expression sobers at that, all traces of humour vanishing. 'I never lied to you, Medea.'

'When we made our deal, you never said—'

'When we made our deal, I was prepared to do *whatever it took* to get you here. Perhaps there was some information I withheld, as you did with me. But I never lied to you, not once. And I never would.' His voice is so rich and intense, it is as if I can feel it threading around my heart, fastening itself there. 'I gave you my word, Medea, and I would not have rested until I honoured it. I would have scaled Mount Olympus and demanded the Gods themselves told me where Aeaea was if I had to.'

A small smile twitches at my lips. 'That seems a little dramatic.'

Jason chuckles, his tension easing with the sound. 'Perhaps. But I would have done it ... for you.' He leans in, his voice dropping to a whisper. 'Look around you, Medea. Look where we are ... Did I not honour my word, as I said I would?'

191

As he speaks, I cannot help my eyes from dipping to his lips, remembering the way they felt upon my own. My throat tightens as I nod.

'See, Princess. There's no need to be upset, is there?' He brushes a curl behind my ear, and I instinctively lean into the warmth of his palm.

'Circe wants me to stay here, with her,' I murmur against his skin.

'Is that what you want?'

'I do not know.'

Jason withdraws his hand, turning to the shadows as he considers my words. My face feels cold and incomplete without his touch.

'If it is what you wish, Medea, you should stay here. I only want you to be happy. But ... may I speak truthfully?' He turns back to me, shards of moonlight catching in his eyes. I nod. 'I believe it would be a terrible waste, to go from one prison to another ... This island will never be enough for you. You and I both know that. You are too great for this place. As for Circe ... she treats you like a child, wanting to make your decisions for you, to dictate your future for herself. She came to speak with me earlier – did she tell you that? Of course she didn't.'

'What did she say?'

'She tried to threaten me, to force me to leave in secret without you.'

Something prickles inside me as I absorb his words. Perhaps it is anger, though it feels more painful than that.

'Circe says I must continue my training. She told me ... she believes I am ... That I need fixing.'

Broken. Broken. Broken, the darkness spits as it paces around us.

'Fixing?' Jason frowns, placing his hands on my shoulders. His touch feels reassuringly heavy. 'Medea, do you not see what that witch

192

is doing? She is trying to tear you down, to make you doubt yourself. Do you know why? Because she is *jealous* of your power.'

'I do not think she is jealous.'

'Of course you don't,' he sighs. 'It's because you are so used to letting people take advantage of you.'

'Take advantage?'

'I told her it should be your decision,' he continues, stepping closer so our lips are barely a breath apart. He smells of smoke from the fire, the scent filling my nostrils so that I can almost taste the ash in the back of my throat. 'Medea, if you truly believe this life here, with Circe, is enough for you, I will support your desires. But, if you were to become my wife, my *queen*, I want you to know that I will never let you doubt yourself again. I will never let anyone take advantage of you. I will adore you; I will idolize you; I will *worship* you like a goddess.' With each declaration his lips trail kisses down my cheek to my neck, causing my heart to thunder in my chest, rattling against my ribs as if it were trying to break free of its cage. 'The world will be ours and I will be yours . . . Does that not sound better than spending an eternity on this little patch of nothingness with a jealous old witch?'

He pulls away and I feel my skin tingling in the absence of his touch, as that familiar yearning cracks through my body, letting a liquid fire surge upwards. But beneath that desire, I can feel the darkness shifting. That darkness Circe warned me of. I feel it beckoning a question from the hollow, icy depths of me.

'Why did you . . . make me kill him?'

'Make you?' Jason recoils, as if stung by my accusation. 'Medea, I did not *make* you do anything. We all did what was necessary to ensure we made it out alive. You made your choice, and I will never judge you for that, but you must own your decision.'

He is right. Of course he is.

'I am sorry,' I whisper.

He sighs, pulling me to him and wrapping his strong arms around my waist. I lean into his embrace, not realizing until this moment how desperately I needed to be held.

'Remember, you should not be ashamed of what you did. You had to take his life so you could live your own, so that we could have a future, *together*.'

I study him, the handsome angles of his face, the brightness in his eyes, the easiness of his smile. A man championed by heroes, idolized by all those around him. If someone like Jason could love me, then surely I cannot be as broken as Circe deems me, nor the monster my family believed me to be.

'Medea?'

I kiss him then, throwing my arms around his neck, holding on as if he were the only thing to keep me afloat in the middle of a raging sea.

After a moment of surprise, his body responds to mine, one hand tightening around my waist, the other lifting up into my hair to cradle the back of my head. Our breaths mingle between our kisses, lips urgent and eager, as if we have each been starved of the other for too long.

In my mind, all I can think is: *Don't stop. Don't stop. Don't stop.*

I need him to want me. I need him to keep kissing me, as if each touch of his lips will strip me bare of the girl I once was. That girl who allowed herself to be a prisoner, to be hated, to be used, taken advantage of, beaten and bruised.

Jason begins to tip me backwards, and I realize he is guiding me down on to the ground. I stumble on to my back as he positions himself over me, his chest flush against mine. His kisses have deepened now, and I feel my insides turn molten as his hands begin exploring my body. Beneath me, the sharpness of the forest floor bites against my back, but I do not care.

'Is this OK?' he murmurs against my neck.

'Yes.'

Don't stop. Don't stop. Don't stop.

I do not know exactly where this is leading to, yet my body seems to respond to the motion of his, as if instinct were taking over.

I wrap my arms around him, clawing at his back with a sudden severity that both surprises and delights Jason. He immediately shifts to match my fierceness, all the tenderness and love vanishing. It is as if he were a ravenous animal, and my body the flesh he dines on.

Good.

I do not want him to be gentle.

I want him to hurt her, to destroy that Medea. Rip her from my body. Tear her from my soul.

Do not be tender with her, do not be kind.

She does not deserve it.

At some point he begins nudging my legs apart and forcing my gown upwards around my waist. I ignore the tug of confusion as he pushes himself inside me, trusting my instincts, trusting him . . . then a sudden, sharp pain bolts through my core.

A sound escapes me like a strangled cry, splintering the night. But Jason does not stop. If anything, my cries seem to spur him on, as he drives into me harder, faster, his breath a ragged growl in his throat.

The pain is almost unbearable.

It feels as if he were setting me on fire. I imagine the flames consuming my body, burning me away. That lonely, broken, hated girl.

Burn her. Burn all of her. Turn her to beautiful, irrevocable ash.

And let a new Medea rise from those ashes.

20

I open my eyes to watery sunlight burning through wisps of cloud.

Beside me, Jason dozes, his face smooth and peaceful as he enjoys the deep release of sleep. His hair is tousled, woven with forest debris from our activities the night before. I smile as I pick a leaf from a golden curl, twirling it between my fingers and watching the light illuminate its thin, snaking veins.

I did not sleep well.

Each time I shut my eyes I felt as if I were drowning, being ripped apart by hungry waves. But when I woke and saw Jason sleeping soundly beside me, I felt a calmness descend over me, soothing me back to the edge of my consciousness. Even if only for a little while.

The exhaustion clings to my skull, making the world feel hazy around me. I run a hand through my knotted curls, my eyes heavy in their sockets.

As I watch Jason sleeping, I remember a story Chalciope's wet nurse once told us, about how humans used to walk the earth with two of everything: heads, limbs, organs. But the Gods feared these strange creatures would grow too powerful, so they split them, carving their soul in half in the process. Since then, humans have walked this earth searching for the other half of their soul, themselves.

I dismissed the story when I heard it, whilst Chalciope giggled at the peculiar idea of a two-headed human. But now, I wonder if it is true, if Jason is my other half, the missing piece that could make me whole. Is he the answer to that emptiness I have always felt inside me?

My gaze drifts to the forest around us as I watch dozy insects weave their way through the lush greenery. In the distance, I can hear a chorus of cicadas greet the rising sun, whilst a sweet-smelling breeze skims over the trees.

I know there is a version of myself that could have been happy here. Living a quiet existence beside my aunt, filling our days with magic and nature, relishing Aeaea's solitude. But that Medea would never have met Jason, never allowed her dreams to broaden, never tasted what it feels like to truly *live*. This life would have been enough for her only because she knew of no other.

And I am not that girl. Not any more.

'Why are you watching me sleep?' Jason murmurs, his voice husky.

'Because I like looking at you.'

I prop myself up on my arm and trace a finger over his features, enjoying the simple freedom of being able to touch him as I please. I run an invisible line from his forehead, down between his closed eyes, along the length of his nose, to his full lips that tease into a smile. He playfully bites my fingertip then kisses it, closing his hand around mine.

'Do you love me?' My voice is as delicate as the morning sunlight. I have never felt so vulnerable, so exposed.

'Of course,' Jason says, squinting as he opens his eyes to look at me, his long lashes feathering those perfect, azure irises. He reaches up to cup my face, and I lean into his touch.

'I would do anything for you,' I whisper into his palm, like a prayer. 'Anything you ask of me. I would do it.'

'I know you would, my love.'

My love. Those words fill me with such happiness I think I may burst. I could listen to Jason uttering those two words for an eternity and still I would never grow tired of hearing them.

'What *do* you want?' I probe as I soak in every inch of his effortless beauty, the glint in his eyes, the tilt of his lips, the angle of his nose.

'What do I want?' He toys with the question as he props his head on a bent arm. 'I want to be king of a great land with you as my queen ... and I want sons.'

'Sons?' The idea jolts through me, sharp and unsettling.

'Yes. Lots of them.' That lazy smile widens.

I do not know why I am so surprised; it is perfectly natural Jason would want sons. But I have never envisioned that for myself. I thought no one would want me to bear their children. I have also never thought myself the mothering sort; that was always Chalciope's realm, for she is soft and kind and warm. Even when we were tiny, she used to cradle dolls in her arms, cooing at them in silly voices. It was as if being a mother was as natural to her as breathing. I never played with dolls; I never saw the point. Why tend to a lifeless object made of wood and rags?

A son.

I roll the idea around in my head, then let it settle and slowly take root. I envision a boy with shining golden hair and blue eyes like Jason, smiling and reaching up at me with little, eager hands. Just like Chalciope used to do. I imagine taking the child in my arms, as Jason envelops us in his embrace, kissing us both on the forehead. Our son. Our family.

The vision is so clear and beautiful it makes a lump of emotion rise in my throat.

'I have always longed for a family, after losing mine at such a young age.' Jason's voice breaks through my thoughts.

'I will give you a son.' I twist to face him again, my eyes intent. 'I swear it to you.'

He pulls me down on to him and kisses me. I feel him smiling against my lips as he says, 'My queen.'

I reach up to grab his hair, feeling the kiss deepen as he runs his hands over my hips, that hunger returning to his touch. As Jason moves to strip off my gown, I hold that vision in my head of the little boy laughing in my arms, gazing up at me as Chalciope once did, with love and wonder in his eyes . . .

A son.

My son.

When we return to Jason's crew, they are preparing to depart.

The stretch of shore is a hive of activity as they gather their sparse belongings and secure them aboard the *Argo*. Others are seated around the remnants of the fire, wolfing down their last meal before the long journey ahead.

The horizon is grey and sullen, the hazy sky bleeding into the dark sea; I cannot tell where one ends and the other begins. But at least the waves look calm for now, creeping ashore and painting the air with a salty mist.

'The men are keen to get away,' Jason tells me. 'They do not trust Circe.'

As if his words summoned her, I see my aunt appear, the wind toying with her dark robes as she strides towards us. I watch the men stiffen as she passes, as if frozen in her defiant wake.

When I glance back to Jason, Orpheus is handing him the Golden Fleece. I am not surprised the musician is the Argonaut Jason entrusted to watch over it.

'I can hear her sorrow in the breeze,' Orpheus murmurs to him, nodding towards Circe. 'And the fury that thrums beneath it . . . It is a haunting melody.'

'Be on your guard,' I hear Jason reply as he drapes the fleece across his shoulders.

Circe stops before us, her face like a shaft of winter sun, chillingly beautiful. She looks Jason up and down with blatant disgust. I know her hatred is misplaced, born from the cruelty of another. A cruelty that has been left to fester inside her for the past five winters in isolation.

I feel a sudden swell of sadness for my aunt, but Jason then squeezes my hand, focusing my thoughts.

'You are leaving.' It is not a question.

'We are,' Jason answers, anyway.

She turns her attention to me, her voice as sharp as her glare as she says, 'I suppose you still wish me to absolve you of your crimes.'

'Yes.' I keep my tone level. I will not plead. Not any more.

'Get on your knees.' Jason baulks at her blunt order. Circe registers his response, her lips twitching into a smile. 'What's the matter, Jason? Is your pride too fragile to kneel before a woman?'

I feel my magic begin to simmer in my veins, heated by Circe's irreverence. I pity her bitterness, but that does not mean I accept her erroneous behaviour towards Jason. I glance sideways at him, watching as he considers her words. He looks to Orpheus, who gives a slow nod, and Jason relents, gripping my hand as we lower ourselves to the ground.

Circe stares down at us for a long moment, savouring the sight of Jason kneeling before her. Perhaps she is trying to stoke his anger. I wonder if it is even Jason she sees before her or the man who stole her heart. Glaucus.

Thankfully, Jason does not rise to the bait.

Circe opens her arms wide and the wind intensifies around us, making her gold-spun hair dance in a wild frenzy. The waves begin to swell and churn as the sea becomes restless.

'Medea. Jason.' Circe's voice cuts across the wind. 'I, Circe, sorceress and daughter of Helios, absolve you of your crimes against our bloodline.' She then reaches down and takes one of our hands in each of hers. Her skin feels icy against mine and, as I stare up to meet her eyes, I catch a glimmer of sadness flickering behind the anger.

'May the Gods hear me and know that I absolve you of your offences. I cleanse your hands of the deed,' she continues as a wave surges up to greet us, hungry and impatient. Circe plunges our hands into the water with a sudden force, the coldness biting at our skin. After the briefest moment she lets go, her voice empty as she announces, 'Your hands are clean.'

I glance down at my palms. They still look the same, still *feel* the same. But what else did I expect?

Jason rises and reaches out his hand to me. I take it.

Around us, the Argonauts appear nervous. Even Meleager has a touch of unease pinching between his brows. Only Orpheus looks curious rather than afraid, his eyes widening, lips slightly moving, as if he were imagining what melody could capture this incredible scene before him.

'Thank you, Circe. We are most appreciative of your kindness,' Jason says, bowing his head.

Whilst his eyes are lowered, Circe reaches out and twirls a coil of the Golden Fleece around her finger. She stares at it for a moment, arching an eyebrow.

'All that effort for such a useless thing.' She catches my gaze and I know she can sense it, too, the dull nothingness.

'You are mistaken.' Jason pulls away from her touch. 'This fleece is a gift from the Gods. It promises glory to whomever claims it.'

'If it promises glory, then how did you defeat Aeetes, I wonder?'

Circe's words cause a nervousness to shiver through me as I glance at Jason, watching the indignation flare in his eyes.

'Perhaps Aeetes was never worthy of its glory,' he counters, his tone tightening. 'But I assure you that I am.'

'I suppose time will tell ... Speaking of time, you and your men have used up enough of mine. You must leave my island at once.' She then directs her attention to me. 'If you go with him now, Medea, you will never be welcome here again. Do you understand? You may never return. I can forgive what came before, but I cannot forgive you if you choose to follow this man after what he made you do.' A tension prickles in the air as her words settle inside me. Circe's tone softens, just a fraction, as she whispers, 'I am only trying to protect you.'

Doubt flickers inside me, but then I think of that boy's face. Jason's son. *My* son. I can picture it so clearly – our family, our happiness – and I know this life with Circe will never be enough, for it will forever be eclipsed by this future I see with Jason. A future I will do whatever it takes to protect.

Faintly, I can hear the old Medea screaming at me. But she is gone now. I left her behind in the dirt when I gave myself to Jason.

'Thank you for your hospitality, aunt.' I mirror Jason's calm demeanour. 'It was good to see you again.'

Circe's face tightens. When she replies, her voice is as cold as one of Demeter's unyielding winters. 'Very well.'

She reaches out and places a small leather pouch into my hands. I know without looking that it contains ingredients for spells. Then, to my surprise, she embraces me, her arms firm around my shoulders.

'You will regret this,' she hisses in my ear.

I remain rigid in her embrace, tightening my hand around the pouch. After a moment, Circe draws away and as I hold her gaze, I realize I can still see it in her eyes, that judgement.

'It is time, Medea,' Jason says gently beside me, his hand pressing against my back.

I turn to him and smile slowly. 'Yes, my love.'

Circe's eyes flick between us, then she turns sharply to storm away. As I watch her go, I am certain there is a single, glistening tear staining her cheek.

I will never see her again. The realization hits me, echoing through those empty spaces my aunt has torn open inside me. But then I look to Jason and when he smiles, I feel whole again.

'Take me home,' I whisper.

21

The journey to Iolcus is long and unpleasant.

Now the end of the Argonauts' quest is in sight, their impatience weighs heavily in the air, the collective exhaustion curdling into heated irritation. The men are keen to get back to their homes, their families, to homemade dinners and warm beds.

At least the storms have yielded, the Gods' anger finally appeased.

During our time at sea together, I have learnt some of the crew's names and, more importantly, which of them to avoid. It seems there are many who are still unsure of me, of my intentions with Jason. I have heard their rumours. They believe their leader is bewitched, his mind imprisoned by one of my spells. Others seem convinced I will betray them just as I betrayed my own family.

I do not mind their hostility; I am used to such things. More importantly, Jason does not seem bothered by his crew's opinions of me either. In fact, his attention seems to be elsewhere. I have often seen him staring off into the distance, stroking the fleece around his shoulders. I wonder if Circe's words are playing on his mind.

I know I should tell him what I now know about the fleece, but Jason needs to believe in himself if he is to lead his men safely home. Once we are back in Iolcus, then I shall disclose the truth to him.

'May I join you?' Orpheus' musical voice interrupts my thoughts. He is one of the few Argonauts who will endure my company.

I lean over the edge of the *Argo*, watching the bow slice through the sun-gilded waves. I mostly keep to myself during our long hours at sea. Being too weak to row and too disliked to stir up conversation, I quickly learnt it is best if I stay out of the way.

'Of course.'

Orpheus' long, chestnut hair has been plaited down his back and I watch it flutter in the wind. His eyes, always so quiet and contemplative, trace the water below as if reading a hidden pattern only he can see. When I'm around Orpheus, I always sense he's half lost in the melodies he continually crafts in his mind.

I have recently learnt that Orpheus is an old friend of Jason's. Atalanta told me the musician used his intricate network of bards to ensure word of Jason's quest spread throughout all of Greece, drawing the interest of glory-hungry individuals eager to feed their fame. Without Orpheus, Jason would never have amassed such a formidable crew, so Atalanta claims.

'I wanted to ask you something, if I may?' Orpheus' voice is like a caress, so elegant and gentle; I wonder if anyone has ever denied him a thing in the world. When I nod, he says, 'How does it work – your magic?'

I consider the question as a hissing wave reaches over the stern, a haze of salt spray lightly coating our cheeks.

'I do not mean to pry,' Orpheus continues. 'I am just . . . fascinated by it. By you.'

Not afraid, not disgusted, but *fascinated*.

Orpheus is quiet as he waits for me to reply. I open my mouth, wondering where best to start, when my focus is caught by a curious island in the distance, its mountains glittering as if they were made of pure gold.

'What is that?' I point, and Orpheus follows my gaze.

As we draw closer to the island, those peculiar, glinting peaks begin to shudder and shift, as if drawing breath.

'Could it be?' Orpheus murmurs to himself, leaning forwards.

I blink, trying to wrap my mind around what is happening.

'GET BACK!' Atalanta shouts from behind us, as the mountain appears to sprout a mighty bronzed arm, a boulder between its glittering fingers.

'TURN THE SHIP!' another voice yells as that arm swings towards us.

But it is too late; the boulder has collided with the *Argo*. It crashes through the wooden railing at the back of the ship, the force of it throwing me to the ground as shards of wood scatter across the deck. Pain shoots through my face as my jaw connects with the floor.

'TURN THE SHIP!' Jason echoes the command as Orpheus helps me to my feet.

Around us, the Argonauts strain at the oars, pulling with all their might to steer the ship away from our deadly foe. The *Argo* begins to comply, groaning in protest at the sudden, sharp change in course. She turns slowly, too slowly, whilst the mountain readies itself again. It rises upwards, lifting on to two glittering, metallic legs.

'Talos,' I hear an Argonaut murmur. 'It is the giant Talos! Protector of Crete!'

I might have believed him to be Poseidon himself, if it were not for his body being entirely made of brilliant, dazzling bronze. But before I can take in his terrifying magnificence, Talos hurls another boulder. It arcs through the air and narrowly misses the *Argo*, crashing into the waves beside us, water cascading over our heads.

'Medea.' Jason appears beside me, voice strained with panic. 'Can you send him to sleep?'

'What?'

'Like the dragon! Remember?' he urges, and I feel the pressure of his desperate hope pressing down upon me. 'Command the giant to sleep.'

'It's different, the giant—'

Before I can continue, we are knocked sideways. It is as if the wrath of Talos has somehow bled into the sea, the waves beginning to swell and storm, reaching upwards like frothing, clawing hands, tearing at the stern, making the *Argo* tilt and tremble. Another wave smashes in from the side, knocking down a few of the Argonauts and threatening to suck them into the watery depths below.

'Take cover!' a voice booms as another boulder sails overhead, briefly blocking out the sun. A moment later, I feel Jason's body pressed up against mine, shielding me from the shards of wooden debris.

'Are you hurt?' Jason demands. 'Medea?'

Fear and confusion clog my thoughts as I watch the men fight to regain control of their ship. But then I feel it ... a soothing, night-cloaked hand caressing my thoughts, quietening them. A silken darkness ripples beneath my skin, cool and commanding, beckoning my magic ...

Medea ... the dark voices call. *Let us help you.*

I stare up at the giant. His eyes are like smouldering coals embedded beneath a heavily carved brow. His neck is thick and strained, knotted with bulging, metallic muscles. I see death reflected in the glimmer of his bronzed body and my magic rears up, eager to meet it.

Ahead of me, Atalanta steps up to the stern, nocking an arrow, her calm movements at odds with the boat veering wildly beneath her. I watch her line up Talos' glinting pillar of a throat in her sight. She takes a slow breath, the firm muscles in her shoulders settling, before letting her arrow fly.

She does not miss.

But neither does she hit her mark.

Instead, the arrow merely glances off Talos' metal skin, like a twig brushing the side of a mountain. Setting her jaw, Atalanta rapidly nocks another arrow. The huntress fires again and again, but Talos bats away the arrows like flies and lets out a bone-shuddering roar.

'Medea?'

I turn to Jason, feeling his hope weighing in my name.

In the chaos around me, I hear Circe's warnings: *It will feed off you, your mind, your soul* . . . But what do such things matter if we are all dead? Is that not a worthy sacrifice for our lives, our future? Never again will I allow myself to feel as useless as I did on that Colchian battlefield. I would far rather risk my own soul than let an enemy force it into the afterlife.

No, Talos will not send me to the Underworld.

For I will bring the Underworld to him.

'Medea, get down!'

I hear Jason's cry as I walk towards the stern of the boat where Atalanta stands, still bravely firing her futile arrows. She turns and sees me beside her, a look of raw panic unfurling across her face, her lips twitching as if murmuring a quiet prayer to the Gods. I have never seen her look so afraid.

I motion for her to step aside. After the briefest hesitation, she does so, allowing me to take position at the furthest point on the ship, directly in front of the murderous giant looming before us. He stoops to rip the tip of the mountain beside him.

My magic surges, sparking in my veins, setting every inch of me ablaze, and I realize, in this moment, that the only one who should have something to fear is Talos.

For though his wrath is immense, mine is far mightier.

I open my arms wide, as if in greeting to the terrible giant. Spreading my fingers, I turn my palms down to the sea, to the earth beneath and the depths of the Underworld that lurks within its core. I can sense the darkness thrumming there, the steady, sinister heartbeat beneath our world's existence. It feels like pure, raw *power*. An endless well of it, one I can draw from, I can wield. As I latch on to it, I hear those death spirits howling. They are calling to me, begging to be unleashed.

For darkness calls to darkness.

Power answers to power.

'Spirits of death, in the name of Hecate, I call on thee.'

I fall to my knees as they rip through me, using my body as their channel into the world of the living. Their soul-shattering malevolence chills my very blood, but I steel myself against it, letting that evil set my magic ablaze, harmonizing it with my own, so that I may wield our power as one.

I throw my hands forwards, letting that darkness pour from my soul along with all the anger and hatred and hurt that has clotted inside me throughout my life, hurling this writhing ball of pain and power towards Talos as he hurls his rocks at us.

But I hit harder.

Blackness fills the air, like plumes of smoke seeping from my body. It billows across the waves, turning them to glittering onyx. The sky thickens as those racing shadows begin to take form, pounding feet, gnashing teeth.

The spirits of death have come.

There is a shuddering *thrum* as those spirits hit Talos, singing through his bronzed body, making him stumble backwards. Then, they disappear in a puff of smoke. Talos glances down, unable to understand what just struck him.

A silence settles around me, but my mind is far from quiet.

I sense the death spirits inside Talos' head; through them I can feel the giant's cold, animalistic thoughts. *Protect. Fight. Kill.* His mind is so simple to invade, so easy to destroy.

I give a wordless signal to the spirits, and they begin their attack. They rip Talos' mind apart, severing his thoughts, shredding his sanity into ribbons. *Protect. Fight. Kill.* This chaos is mirrored within my own mind, an insanity that feels like a mighty storm. Only I ride atop those frenzied waves, whilst Talos is drowning in the merciless currents beneath.

The giant stumbles, lifting his hands to gouge at his eyes, an attempt to blind himself from the evil images with which the spirits are plaguing him. He roars in panicked fury, the sound like clanging metal reverberating across the horizon, making the *Argo* tremble beneath my feet.

The spirits smile at his torment, or perhaps it is me smiling – it is difficult to distinguish one from the other in this moment.

Turning, I see the Argonauts watching in silent, motionless shock. Even the sea itself seems to have stilled to watch the spectacle.

I flick a glance to Jason and my smile widens at the awe hanging open from his handsome face.

See what I can do, my love? See what I can do for you. For us.

The death spirits are now spreading throughout Talos' body, carving their way through him. They are on the hunt, searching for a flaw in his impenetrable being that we can utilize to our advantage. It does not take them long to find one. I can sense the death spirits calling to me, drawing my focus low down, to Talos' right ankle. From where I stand at the helm of the *Argo*, I spy a bolt protruding there, a weakness.

Now the spirits are taking hold of a fragment of Talos' thoughts –

kill. They repeat this over in his shattered mind, *kill, kill, kill, kill,* wielding it like a weapon that rips through his entire body, infecting every muscle, every breath, every metallic heartbeat.

Kill, kill, kill ...

Talos howls as he rips that bolt from his ankle, causing thick blood to spill into the sea like molten metal.

'His lifeblood is draining from his body,' Orpheus observes. 'It cannot be possible; Hephaestus himself forged the giant to protect these lands. He was believed to be invincible.'

'Clearly, he is not,' is all I reply.

The death spirits rejoice as the giant dies; they revel in the feeling of his life ebbing from his body as they slowly drag his soul down into the Underworld, claiming it like a reward. I wonder what torment they have in store for Talos within their realm.

The giant's eyes dim to dull lumps of coal as his blood continues to creep thickly across the waves, clogging the sea with glittering gold. It is both hideous and beautiful. In the aftermath of his attack, the quietness of Talos' death seems amplified. The only sound comes from the blood-coated waves lapping at the *Argo*.

I let out a slow breath as I feel the death spirits fading away, draining from my body.

'Medea? *Medea!*'

Someone is shouting my name, but it sounds as if they are screaming underwater. I try to turn but am faintly aware of my body crumpling beneath me, falling against something warm and firm.

Another voice shouts, louder now, more urgent, and that warm weight shifts around my waist, hoisting me upwards.

'Someone help me get her below deck,' I hear Atalanta saying. 'Come on. What's the matter with all of you?'

'What if she curses us?'

'You saw that black smoke . . . it came from *inside* her.'

'She summoned creatures from the Underworld.' I am certain that was Orpheus.

'And it *saved our lives*,' Atalanta snaps. 'Fine. I'll carry her myself.'

'Out of my way! Medea? *Medea!*' Jason. He fills my senses, eclipsing all else around me. 'Give her to me. Medea? Look at me, Medea. Come on, now.'

I try to open my eyes, but my vision blurs and dances. I feel so tired, so very tired . . .

'Something is wrong.'

'Is she dead?'

'*No*. She will be fine. Medea? My love? Open your eyes. Open your eyes for me.'

Beneath the exhaustion that has infected my body, remnants of the spirits' dark power still hum inside me, wrapping themselves around my soul, slipping over my bones. I focus on it, willing that power to seep into my veins, to bleed into my heart and burn away this poisonous weakness.

Let it rejuvenate me, let it consume me.

Let it become *my* power.

'Medea?'

A strong hand cups my cheek and the edges of my vision begin to sharpen into focus. I see Jason staring down at me, golden hair tangled over those bright-blue eyes.

'There you are,' he sighs gently, pressing his forehead to mine. 'You worried us there for a moment. Can you stand?'

I nod as Jason carefully helps me to my feet. Beside us, Atalanta offers a hand to steady me, her grey eyes heavy with concern.

'How are you feeling?' she asks.

'*Powerful.*' My lips curl around the word.

The huntress does not return my smile.

'You were incredible, my love,' Jason enthuses, taking my hand in his. 'I have never seen anything like it.'

Without responding, I tighten my fingers around his hand and pull him to the back of the *Argo*. Ignoring the men's incredulous stares, I lead my lover down into the small storeroom beneath. Once there, I pull Jason roughly towards me, letting the power inside my body mingle with the pleasure of his as the men above steer us back on course, towards Iolcus. Towards my future.

The future I have earned.

The future that no one will ever dare take from me.

22

'I should get back to my men.'

We are entangled on the storeroom floor, the small space cloaked in a clammy warmth laced with the delicate smell of sweat. My head rests on Jason's chest as I listen to the steady rhythm of his heart, knowing that every beat is mine.

Why haven't we utilized the privacy of this storeroom before? I feel there was a reason, yet I cannot place it now. I am too distracted, my body glowing with the aftermath of our lovemaking.

Circe's warning itches inside my mind. *You must not invoke their power, no matter what.* But what does she know of the spirits? She was just afraid of them, and she let that fear stop her from realizing her full potential.

But her cowardice will not hold me back. Not any more.

'Stay a little longer,' I whisper, as I trace the slices of sunlight spilt across his chest.

'Maybe the men are right. Maybe you have bewitched me,' he murmurs, and I can feel the curve of his smile against my skin. 'For I cannot seem to tear myself away from you.'

'Then don't.'

He gives a husky laugh and I savour the sound, letting it seep into my bones.

'You really are a wonder, Medea. What you did to that monster . . .'

He trails off, stroking an idle thumb along my jaw. 'I had gone to Colchis seeking the fleece as my prize, but I believe I have left with an even greater one.'

His words expand inside me, filling all those empty spaces, making me feel *whole*.

'I always thought the Fates hated me,' Jason continues. 'I believed those crones took delight in my suffering. After all I had been through, being born in that prison cell, losing my parents, my brother, my throne . . . But now I know I was wrong. For how could the Fates hate me when they have blessed me with you?'

'They blessed us both.' I smile.

My hand brushes over a thick scar sliced across Jason's right rib-cage, bone-white against his bronzed skin.

'From when I was a boy,' he says, as my fingertips follow the puckered curve of the old wound.

'When your uncle imprisoned you?'

'No, no, this came afterwards. When I was smuggled out of Iolcus, I was taken to Cheiron, who became my tutor. He taught me everything I know.' His eyes soften into distant memories. 'They say he is the greatest teacher who ever lived.'

'What was he like?'

'As grumpy as any centaur,' he chuckles. 'But utterly brilliant.'

'Tell me more.'

'Well, what would you like to know?'

Everything. Every thought, every memory, each individual thread that makes up the beautiful tapestry of who he is. I want it all.

'What is your earliest memory?'

A sadness touches Jason's smile as he says, 'My mother. Her laugh.'

'Will you tell me about her?'

Instead of answering, Jason snaps his head towards the storeroom door, his entire body tensing.

'What is—'

He hushes me immediately, then points to his ear: *Listen.*

That's when I hear it, or rather the *absence* of it . . . of anything. Not a single wisp of sound. Even the waves have fallen completely silent, the sea holding its breath.

Jason quickly pulls on his tunic and makes for the door. I follow behind, slipping my discarded gown back on.

Outside, a creeping mist has descended, folding its eerie embrace around the *Argo*. The haze is so heavy I can barely make out the soundless waves directly ahead of us. The men are alert, scanning the sinister fog, hands poised over their weapons.

Rocks jut out from the mist, clawing fingers piercing through the heavy grey folds. The unnatural silence continues to pace around us, horribly deafening in its emptiness. My magic strikes like flint against my unease, flaring to life in my veins.

Then, finally, I hear a sound . . . a woman singing.

Her melodic voice dances in the stillness like flurries of snowflakes, delicate yet chilling. I cannot see her, but her song echoes around us, bleeding out from the mist.

Brave heroes, we call to thee,
Come seek the safety of our shores.
Heed our words, oh dearest ones,
All you desire shall soon be yours.

I have never heard a voice so beautiful and so disturbing.

Other bodiless voices begin to accompany her, their melodies

216

intertwining effortlessly, weaving a haunting web that laces itself tightly around the *Argo*.

I turn to Jason and see his eyes are glazed, his mouth hanging slightly agape. He looks nothing like himself, as if a mindless stranger has slipped beneath his skin.

'Jason?' He ignores me and walks towards the edge of the *Argo*, towards the calling voices.

Weary travellers, come rest awhile.
Let us fill your bellies, warm your beds.
Lay down your arms, oh sweet beloveds,
And follow our voice inside your heads.

I glance around to see the other Argonauts with similar glassy eyes set against slack faces. Entranced, they abandon their posts and weapons as they lean over the edge of the *Argo*, reaching their hands towards the silent waves below.

'Gods, what are they *doing*?' Atalanta appears beside me. It seems she is the only other person aboard still to have their wits about them.

'Sirens,' I say. 'My aunt told me about them. Their voices lure men to a watery grave. But I will not let them.'

I feel the darkness swell, the death spirits baying, willing me to release them once again. I send a pulse of that power rippling outwards, chasing away the mist, making it hiss and recede. That is when we see them, see *how many* of them surround us, perching on the rocks like hideous shadows of death.

Their bodies are lithe, their mottled flesh the colour of a decaying corpse. Bent, leathery wings fan out behind them, with thin, crimson veins snaking through the taut flesh. But their faces are most terrifying of all – gruesome and gaunt, their pale, sunken eyes utterly soulless. They are like beasts spat from the darkest depths of Tartarus.

The song intensifies, their voices so piercing the lyrics seem to rattle through my very bones.

There is no need to be afraid,
When we possess the secrets of these dark waters.
Let us whisper in your ear which wave
Can carry you to your wives and daughters.

I ready my power, feeling it surge up and up, tearing through me as the ship veers beneath us. Strange, I did not realize the *Argo* was still moving.

I stagger sideways, whilst everyone else remains upright.

'*Stop.*' Atalanta grabs my arm, steadying me.

'What are you doing?' I snarl as she seizes my chin and wipes her hand over my face.

'*Look.*' She holds out her bloodied fingers. 'This is what you are doing to yourself. Do you not see?'

I touch my nose and draw my hand away, staring at the blood coating my fingertips. *My* blood. But it looks different somehow. Darker, much darker.

'You must stop, Medea. Whatever power you're drawing from, it's killing you.'

'Should I let those creatures kill me instead?' I snap back.

Atalanta lets out a frustrated growl. 'We do not have time to argue about this.'

'Then let me handle it.'

'There are *too many of them.* I can't have you collapsing and leaving me to—' A sharp scratching interrupts us, the sound crawling over my skin.

The Sirens have begun scuttling up the side of the *Argo*, their spindly, sharp fingers clawing towards the men who foolishly reach down to greet them. All the while their chilling song continues.

Sweet prey, you're not leaving,
For you our souls catch fire.
Let the claws of our melody seize you.
Your lives are all we desire.

'Your aunt,' Atalanta says, her voice surprisingly calm. 'What else did she tell you about them? Did she say how they can be defeated?'

I try to focus my mind, but the spirits scream at me, begging to be released. They rattle my bones as if they were the bars of their cage.

An old memory suddenly surfaces in my mind, gulping for air. It was one of the first summers Circe spent with me, when she taught me all about mythical creatures.

'She said they can only be defeated by a power that matches their own,' I say as my thoughts click into place. 'Do you not see? Only my power can stop them. I must do this.'

I go to move but Atalanta grabs my arm.

'A power that matches their own,' she repeats under her breath as she scans our enemy. Her eyes widen then, her grip tightening. 'Orpheus! Get Orpheus' lyre!'

'*What?*'

'Trust me, Medea. Please.'

Without waiting for me to respond, she breaks into a run, driving her way through the men. I watch as she struggles against the creatures, who hiss and shriek as she prises their hands off her comrades, knocking them back with fists and elbows. One of them lunges at her,

219

its jagged, rotten teeth opening wide. She grabs it by the throat, its gnashing jaws inches from her face.

'The lyre!' Atalanta shouts again as she wrestles with the snapping beast. '*Medea!*'

I do as she commands, ignoring the night-tipped claws that scratch frantically inside me as I rush to retrieve the instrument.

The musician is leaning over the edge, his gentle face vacant and listless, eyes blank. I pull him backwards, pressing the lyre into his limp hands. His fingers twitch at the familiar feel of the instrument.

Behind me, I hear Atalanta grunting as she finally draws her weapon, slicing it through the Siren. The creature lets out a piercing scream, its thick, black blood spraying across the deck.

The sight of the fallen Siren sends the rest into a wild frenzy. They flood the *Argo* like a hideous wave of ashen flesh and snapping teeth, their focus now set on Atalanta. Even in their attack they continue to sing, their melody mutating into a cacophony of screeches that chills my blood.

I watch as the Sirens swarm towards Atalanta, leaving the Argonauts forgotten in their wake. They move with disturbingly strange mobility, as if their limbs were broken in multiple, unnatural ways.

'Come on, then, you overgrown fish,' she snarls, readjusting her grip on her sword.

'Orpheus, I need you to play.' I tear my gaze away from Atalanta as I instruct him. The musician's face remains utterly vacant, still lost in his strange stupor. 'Orpheus!'

Atalanta lets out a roar as her sword slices through a wall of writhing bodies.

'What are you waiting for, Medea?'

Drawing in a steady breath, I let those fingers of darkness dig into Orpheus' mind, just as I did with Talos. But this time my hold is careful and precise, like a surgeon wielding a scalpel. I feel the Sirens' heavy trance cloaking his thoughts and I focus all my energy on severing their hold without damaging the mind wrapped within. '*Orpheus, I command you to play.*'

A flicker of acknowledgement catches in his eyes as he stares down at the lyre, blinking slowly.

'*Now!*'

Orpheus' fingers begin to strum the lyre, letting a sweet, shaky tune lift into the skies. As the notes swell, he settles into the melody and, with every pluck of his talented fingers, Orpheus seems to rejuvenate himself. The awareness slowly returns to his eyes and he throws his full heart into the song, realizing our lives depend upon it.

His melody harmonizes effortlessly with the Sirens' call and then overwhelms it, unravelling their intoxicating hold.

I turn back to Atalanta, who is now breathing heavily, drenched in blackened blood. The creatures around her have frozen, their hideous faces turned to Orpheus, their own deathly song dying on their lips as they listen.

Orpheus' song intensifies, so beautiful I am almost caught in my own stupor. I feel it rippling through me like a current, calming the darkness roaring in my veins, letting it settle in the depths of my soul.

Around us, the Argonauts stir, shaking their heads as if waking from a strange dream. When they register the horrific creatures surrounding them, they draw their weapons with unsteady hands.

The Sirens swiftly scatter like shadows at dawn, slipping back beneath the waves or taking to the skies.

'I cannot believe that worked,' I say.

'Neither can I,' Atalanta admits, letting out a breathless laugh.

I draw in a breath as my eyes find Jason's across the crowd. He looks utterly bemused, rubbing his face as he attempts to regain his hold on reality.

A loud splash catches our attention as someone shouts, '*Meleager!*'

One of the retreating Sirens has pulled the prince overboard. Before I can even rally my magic, I see Atalanta toss her sword aside and throw herself into the waves.

I rush to the edge of the *Argo* just in time to watch the huntress disappear into the Siren-infested water. Orpheus' song continues to weave around us, though the beauty of his music seems mocking against the horrible scene unfolding.

'Someone needs to go in after her,' I say, feeling a panic tighten in my chest.

'And risk losing a third man?' someone else counters. 'What good would that do?'

'What are you doing?' I feel Jason grab my arm as I hoist myself on to the side of the ship.

'She saved my life. I cannot let her die.'

'Medea, do not be so foolish.' His face tightens along with his grip. I stare down at the churning waves below. 'Can you even swim?'

It does not matter. I will move the sea itself if I must, but I will not let Atalanta die.

'Let me go.'

'*I forbid you.*' These words are whetted by uncharacteristic anger. It makes me falter, the sharpness of his fury, and Jason seems to sense my shock, for his voice quickly softens. 'My love, I cannot risk losing you.'

A shout pulls my focus away. When I turn back to the water I see a flash of auburn hair, like a fire igniting beneath the waves.

My heart lifts as Atalanta bursts through the surface, a spluttering Meleager hooked over her shoulders. Around me, the men snap into action, throwing their comrades a rope to hoist them up.

Once aboard, Atalanta drops Meleager on to the deck with a loud, wet *thud*. The prince rolls on to his side, hacking up a lungful of seawater.

'What happened?' he rasps, his face paler than I have ever seen it.

Atalanta braces her hands on her knees and says, 'Sirens.'

'Trust Meleager to fall to his death chasing after a woman,' one of the Argonauts sniggers.

'You were all about to dive to your deaths, you brainless idiots,' she retorts, turning back to Meleager. 'Are you hurt?'

'Just ... remind me to steer clear of women for a while,' he says with a slight smile. Atalanta lets out a sigh that rolls into a chuckle.

'Only you, my friend, could out-sing a Siren.' Jason claps Orpheus' shoulder and he bows deeply, his fingers never missing a single note. 'We owe you our lives. All of us here – we are indebted to you.'

Beside me, I notice Atalanta's jaw tightening. I open my mouth to interject, but she gives me a slight shake of her head: *Don't bother.*

'Right, men, back to your stations. We need to get out of this cursed stretch of water. Orpheus, whatever you do, do not stop playing.'

As the men disperse, I study Jason's calm face, searching for remnants of that previous anger. My eyes then catch on Meleager as Atalanta helps him to his feet.

'Thank you, huntress,' I hear him mutter quietly, his hand lingering on her arm. For a moment, Atalanta looks as if she might lean into his touch, but then she pulls back and walks away.

The Prince of Calydon watches her go, dejection softening the strong edges of his handsome face. He catches me staring and meets my gaze with a smile, that spark of mischief never far from his eyes, though I can sense something heavy lingering beneath it.

'You love her,' I say to him. The abruptness of my words seems to surprise him, but that smile does not falter.

'Can you blame me, little witch?'

23

The night is alive with music and laughter and wine.

It is the Argonauts' last night together before we arrive at Iolcus' port town tomorrow, marking the end of their quest. Once there, Jason's legendary crew will all go their separate ways, each beckoned by their individual paths of glory carved by the Fates.

We sit around a large fire on the shores of an island unknown to me. The men are passing the last of the wine between them, whilst Orpheus paints the scene with his beautiful music. The looming end has made the collective exhaustion blossom into a jovial, warm atmosphere, as if they are all savouring these last moments as brothers in arms.

There is something else in the air, too, something that glows like a tangible spark between the Argonauts. It is the knowledge that they have just made history. For these men know the adventures of the *Argo* will be sung for generations to come, their names enduring long after they draw their final breaths.

This journey has immortalized them, in memory at least.

I wonder if I will be remembered, too. Though, when I am dead and gone, why should I care if this world sings of me or not?

I remain quiet as I watch the revelry. Since the battle with Talos I have noticed the men growing even warier around me. They are careful to keep their distance, sometimes uttering prayers to the

Gods when they see me walking by. It seems absurd to think they could be afraid of me when I was the one who saved their lives mere days ago.

'Little witch,' Meleager says by way of greeting as he comes to sit beside me. He is one of the few who treat me with any kind of warmth.

Meleager's eyes drift over the bibulous crew as he hands me a jug of communal wine, his smile glowing with flickers of fiery golds and reds. I have never liked wine. My father demonstrated what that poisonous liquid can do to a person, how it can strip you of your dignity. But gestures of goodwill are rare, so I accept Meleager's offer.

'Thank Dionysus we stopped at that port town; there would've been mutiny aboard if the wine had run out,' he says as I gulp down the warm, sour liquid.

'That tastes horrible.' I wince at the tartness coating my tongue, wiping my lips with the back of my hand.

He thunders a laugh as I hand the wine back, watching him take a deep slug. 'It's better than what your people make. You should come to Calydon. Now, *we* know how to make real Greek—'

'They are not my people,' I interrupt, my tone suddenly dulled. 'I am not Colchian. Not any more.'

'I meant no offence, little witch,' Meleager says, holding his hands up in submission. 'Don't turn me into a fish or something, will you? I quite like my body as it is.'

'I think you'd make an adorable mouse,' Atalanta cuts in, plucking the wine from Meleager's hands. I watch his olive-green eyes spark as they always do around the huntress. 'Gods, that truly is horrible.'

'So, if you are not a Colchian, then what do you suppose you are?' Argus grumbles from beside Meleager, his rusty voice grating over the fire.

I open my mouth to respond, but I find my mind empty.

'Oh, throw yourself to the crows, Argus,' Atalanta dismisses him, rolling her eyes.

'It is just a question, huntress.'

'She is to be my queen.' Jason appears, throwing his arm around me. 'Queen of Iolcus.'

'They'll never accept her as their queen,' Argus says under his breath.

'What did you say?' I feel Jason's arm tighten against my waist. Around us, the Argonauts have fallen quiet, surprised by Jason's uncharacteristically cold tone.

'You heard me,' Argus says, seemingly unfazed. 'Your people will never accept a witch as their queen, especially a foreigner who kills her own kin. They are too traditional. Too proud . . . Come on, now, you're a smart man. Surely you have realized that?'

My face burns hot as the fire – with anger or shame, I am not quite sure.

'Do me a favour, dear friend, and keep to your shipbuilding. Leave the politics of my kingdom to me.' There's humour in Jason's response, yet we can all hear the sharpness lingering beneath.

Argus inclines his head in agreement, turning back to his wine, a smug smile at his lips.

'Is this not meant to be a celebration?' Jason says to the gathered hush. 'Orpheus, will you do the honours, please?'

The musician nods and starts up into a faster, upbeat song, each note plucking the tension from the air. Some of the Argonauts begin cheering and clapping, whilst others jump to their feet to dance, their wild shadows scattering across the sandy shore. Someone tugs at Jason's arm and he reluctantly lets them pull him into their drunken, chaotic dancing.

I sit in the shadows as I watch their revelry unfolding, their figures soaked golden in the firelight. It feels as if I am very far away, watching from another world entirely. I try to wrap myself in the warmth of their infectious joy, but Argus' words claw at my thoughts: *Your people will never accept a witch as their queen.* I had not even considered it.

But have I not done enough to prove myself loyal to Jason? Or will they only ever see me as the rumours that stain my name ... A witch ... A traitor ...

A killer.

'You look like you need this.'

I glance up to see Atalanta settling herself down beside me. She hands over a wine jug and I take a long, deep drink.

'Wow, so you *do* need it,' she chuckles as I glug down the foul liquid, letting it burn away my doubts. 'You should ignore what Argus said, you know. He's just a miserable bastard.'

'What if he's right?' I mutter quietly, scratching my nails over the jug's flaking paintwork.

Atalanta leans forwards, bracing her forearms on her thighs, her plaited hair falling over her strong shoulders.

'Ever since he accepted this quest and brought the Argonauts together, the people of Iolcus have adored Jason. He's their hero.' She digs into the sand with her foot, creating deep grooves. 'They will love you because he loves you.'

From across the fire, I see Jason laughing at something Meleager has said. I swallow another mouthful of wine, praying it will douse these ugly concerns rising inside me.

'How's the nose? Any more bleeding?' Atalanta asks. I shake my head. 'You should keep an eye on that. Whatever spells you were using, they clearly weren't good for you.'

'I think Meleager wants you to dance with him,' I deflect. 'He keeps looking at you.'

'That oaf cannot take a hint,' she mutters, amusement catching in her eyes.

'I think he is in love with you.'

She buries her feet further into the sand. 'That's his problem.'

My gaze drifts back to the Prince of Calydon, who is talking animatedly, his muscular frame accentuated by the flickering shadows.

'There are worse suitors.'

Atalanta shrugs. 'I suppose. But he's not really my ... *preference.*'

'What do you mean?'

The corner of Atalanta's mouth curls up into a slight smile but, before she can answer, Meleager barrels over to us, giving a dramatic bow.

'Will you do me the honour?'

Atalanta rolls her eyes at me as she offers Meleager her hand, letting him whip her up and drag her into the fray of wild, dancing bodies. I watch as the Prince of Calydon spins the huntress in dizzying circles, making her laugh and laugh. Beside them, the men have gathered in a tight cluster around Jason, cheering as he glugs down an entire jug of wine. They whoop with delight when he finishes, raising the empty vessel aloft like a mighty prize.

I wish I could join them, but this carefree joy they revel in is distant and foreign to me. My happiness has always come at a price; it has never felt unburdened, as theirs seems to be. I can imagine it, though, the version of myself that would jump to her feet and dance and laugh and sing. She shimmers in my mind, a vision just beyond my grasp. Like Tantalus trapped in the Underworld, forever reaching for that pool of water, its silky surface always dipping just out of reach, mocking the thirst he will never quench.

'Look at that.' A loud voice punctures my thoughts.

I glance over to see the ugly face of Telamon, wearing his usual sneer of disapproval. Beside him sit two other Argonauts who guzzle their wine like starved piglets.

'Meleager actually got the huntress to dance.' Telamon's voice is oily and unpleasant.

'Do you think he'll *finally* get between her legs tonight?' asks one of the others.

'Pfft, not a chance,' the third sniggers.

'One of us better fuck her, or else what was the point of bringing her in the first place?'

'Jason says Artemis will cook us alive if any of us touch her. She likes her favourite mortals *pure*, remember?'

'You believe that tripe? Jason just said that to make sure we all behaved.'

'Either way, Atalanta would never let you near her.'

Telamon shrugs. 'Sometimes it's more fun when they struggle.'

'You really think *you* can take *her*?'

'Gods, no. It would have to be a team effort. What do you say, boys? We could all have a go.'

They laugh at that, and I feel my knuckles popping against my clenched fists. In response, the darkness of the night brushes against me.

I do not think twice as I rise and stride over, enjoying the way their amusement withers instantly at my feet. I stand before them, letting the silence weigh between us, enjoying the way they squirm beneath it.

When I finally speak, my voice is as cold and unyielding as death itself.

'If you *ever* speak of Atalanta that way again, or even *think* about her, I will have your minds infested with a madness so potent your brains will rot inside your skulls and bleed out of your ears. Do you understand me?'

The darkness swells, delighted.

'Jason won't like y-you threatening us,' one of them stutters like a child.

'Well, *I* don't like you threatening my friend.'

Friend. The word has always felt unfamiliar to me and yet it rolls so easily off my tongue.

'You really think Atalanta is your *friend*? How tragic,' Telamon sniggers, the wine clearly fuelling his bravado. 'She's just doing her duty to Jason, isn't that obvious? She'll be rid of you as soon as she gets the chance, witch. Just you wait.'

I harden beneath his cruelty, feeling my magic stirring in response. It feels so different to how it once did, no longer an effervescent glimmer in my veins, but a rich, eddying pool of power spilling from my core like liquid night.

'On second thoughts, perhaps I will leave your brains intact and rot another more *intimate* part of you.' I stare at their laps, quirking an eyebrow. 'How does that sound?'

I smile at their horrified silence before turning to walk away, leaving my unanswered question gripping them like a chokehold.

I excuse myself from the celebrations when the sound of the revelry begins to grate over my skin.

Jason does not question it when I tell him I am going to see what herbs and flowers this small island has to offer. Perhaps if he were sober he would be less inclined to let me wander alone across unfamiliar land, or perhaps he knows whatever threats this island has to offer I can handle myself.

After spending so long confined on a cramped, dirty ship with strangers, it is nice to have some time alone. As I amble along the moon-soaked shore, I take a second to appreciate the silence, realizing that I haven't had a quiet moment to myself since Jason's trials began. But Telamon's words soon chase after me, nipping at my heels, splintering my peaceful solitude.

Was I really so foolish to think of Atalanta as my friend? I didn't know, for I've never had one before, other than Chalciope. But our bond was forced upon her by circumstance, bound by blood she could not change.

Chalciope.

I push her from my thoughts, as I have done since we fled Colchis. Yet the heavy silence feeds my mind, filling it with memories I have been trying to bury within me. I force them away again, focusing instead on Selene's delicate glow. But within the goddess's pale, beautiful face, I see only her. My sister.

I wonder if she knows by now what I have done.

I wonder if she hates me for it.

I would not blame her if she does.

I return to the others sooner than I expected. Their joviality might be annoying, but at least it serves to drown out the thoughts I am not yet ready to face.

When I return, the Argonauts are sitting around the fire, with the brothers I know as Castor and Polydeuces standing before them. The golden twins are identical in every way, but supposedly only one is descended from Zeus. Though the twins will never say who is and who is not. I wonder if either of them truly knows, or if both believe themselves the divine son.

As I silently approach, it appears that Castor and Polydeuces are putting on a play, of sorts. Re-enacting the Argonauts' adventures, with Orpheus accompanying on his lyre.

'The first stop for the courageous Argonauts,' Castor booms, 'was the island of Lemnos, where I believe we *all* had a very good time. Did we not?' His audience responds with cheers and whistles, slapping each other on the back. 'The island was indeed a delightful place, for it was filled with the most beautiful, *frustrated* women. They had killed all the men of Lemnos and now the poor damsels were left with cold, empty beds ...'

I cannot help but be impressed. It is so rare to hear stories of women triumphing over men. Clearly, the women of Lemnos wanted to reclaim that narrative, as well as their land.

'But they needed help *re-populating*!' golden-haired Polydeuces continues, to which the men rumble a dirty cheer. I see Atalanta roll her eyes towards Orpheus, who mirrors the sentiment. 'But one individual did a better job than most.'

'JASON!' someone hollers, and everyone falls apart with laughter.

'I was making *diplomatic* alliances,' I hear Jason saying from where he sits in the middle of the audience.

'Oh, so is "diplomatic alliances" what you call "fucking"?' Meleager challenges, making a filthy gesture.

His question causes a coldness to close in around me. I take a few steps back into the embrace of the concealing darkness, my eyes fixed on Jason.

'Please, men, we have a female in our presence. Let us keep it tasteful,' Jason says as he gestures to Atalanta, who looks unimpressed.

'Of course, of course.' Castor bows. Behind him, Polydeuces has thrown an old rag over his head and is batting his eyelids.

'Oh, Jason!' he coos in a shrill voice, encouraging more laughter from the men.

'Let us just say,' Castor continues, 'that the queen took a very deep interest in our Jason.'

'More like he took a *deep* interest in her,' someone snorts.

'Oh, Jason, you are so handsome and so strong and so ...'

Polydeuces swoons in that high-pitched croon as he pretends to grab between his twin's legs. 'So *big*! Oh my!'

'I know,' Castor says, imitating Jason's smooth voice.

'Take me! Take me now!'

I wince as Polydeuces lies on the floor and spreads his legs wide. But the men only howl like crazed wolves as Castor bends him into vulgar positions. I avert my eyes, but within their gyrating shadows I can see Jason intertwined with the beautiful queen, his lips against her soft skin, her hands clawing at his bronzed body ... I snap my eyes shut, trying to erase the images from my mind.

I was not naive enough to believe Jason had not been with another woman, but the thought that he had lain with someone just weeks before arriving on our shores ... with a beautiful *queen* ... and they all knew, they had all laughed about it. Did they see me the same way, as some royal entertainment for Jason to enjoy on their adventures?

'I am growing bored of Lemnos,' Atalanta interjects, arms folded. 'Can we move this along?'

Castor and Polydeuces quickly transform the scene into more of the Argonauts' adventures, yet I can only partially concentrate. My mind burns with the image of Jason and that queen tangled together.

I consider walking away; I have seen enough. But a self-destructive kind of curiosity roots me to the spot.

I force myself to focus on the twins as they recount a tale about the mighty Herakles fighting a swarm of three-armed giants shortly before he departed their voyage. They then continue with the tale of a boxing match with a king and something about deadly smashing rocks.

'And then we come to Colchis,' Castor announces, the words peeling my thoughts away from taunting visions of Jason's naked body ... the beautiful curves of a foreign queen. 'Where another royal lady took an interest in our beloved Jason.'

Sniggers ripple amongst the crowd and a few men glance around, checking the witch is not playing witness to their little show. I remain motionless on the outskirts of their group, the obedient darkness wrapping itself tightly around my body, obscuring me from view.

'But this was no ordinary lady,' Polydeuces continues, as he throws that dirty cloth around his head again. 'For I am the witch Medea – mistress of potions, destroyer of men!'

'Destroyer of men?' Castor rumbles as a swaggering Jason. 'That sounds like a challenge to me.'

The Argonauts hoot and cheer at that and I even hear Jason chuckling, muttering something to the man sitting beside him.

I remain still as I watch Castor and Polydeuces re-enacting our meeting, Castor playing a valiant, heroic Jason, and Polydeuces a lovesick, swooning version of me. Another Argonaut joins in as a cunning Eros shooting Polydeuces with his burning arrow of love.

Is this really how they see me? After everything I have done for them. Everything I have given, everything I have lost . . . They have reduced me to a simpering stereotype.

I feel an anger begin to stir inside me as two more Argonauts join in, taking the roles of my father and brother. They stumble around like blundering fools, repeatedly tripping over one another to elicit cheap laughs from their audience.

'Jason, I know a spell that will help you defeat the fire-breathing oxen!' Polydeuces squawks, groping towards Castor. 'But you must let me rub those rippling muscles of yours!'

'Rub my muscles?' Castor frowns exaggeratedly. 'Are you sure that's how magic works, Princess?'

'Of course I'm sure! Now take your clothes off!' Polydeuces snaps, to which the Argonauts whistle and hoot delightedly.

Mortification sears through me as I watch Polydeuces run his hands all over Castor, making lewd comments and gestures. My cheeks feel as if the embers of the fire were embedded within them, setting my skin alight. I almost wish it would – so I could simply burn away and disappear.

Polydeuces then reaches for Castor's crotch and exclaims loudly, 'Oh, Jason, we *must* ensure this remains intact!'

'Careful, love, you don't know what your touch is doing to me.' Castor grins, the words sickeningly familiar. 'Or what it makes me want to do to you.'

'Oh, Jason, you can do anything to me! Anything at all!'

This moment. It was supposed to be *ours*, one of trust and vulnerability … but Jason had shared it with his men. Worse than sharing it, he had reduced the moment into a taunting anecdote, a punchline.

The channel to the Underworld pulls taut inside me like a question being asked – *do you wish to summon us?* I try to ignore it, but my magic jolts in eager response, like a wild horse pulling against its reins.

Atalanta is saying something to Polydeuces, though I cannot hear her. Nor can I focus as the performance continues. All I can hear is the laughter. That horrible, ugly laughter. It rattles through my bones. Suffocates my mind.

I cannot bear it any longer.

I storm forwards, darkness peeling from my skin as I materialize at the centre of the crowd. The fire shivers and cows in my presence, sending shadows skittering like demons escaping into the night. The men fall silent around me.

They watch me with careful eyes, the humour leached from their faces. I notice some of them reaching for their weapons.

235

'My love, there you are.' Jason rises to his feet, unfazed. He is all smiles, all sweetness. 'I am glad you are here. I did not want you to miss out on the fun.'

'I saw,' I seethe.

'What's the matter?' He reaches for my hand, but I snatch it away. 'Medea?'

The darkness inside me tugs again, firmer this time . . . I could do it . . . I could unleash it . . . I could tear at their minds as their laughter tears at mine.

'Come now, my love . . .'

I walk away, the coldness of the night enveloping me so seamlessly it is as if I had always belonged there.

I expected Jason to come sooner than he does.

It feels like hours as I stand at the edge of the shore, staring up at the stars, those dead eyes watching.

'Medea.' His voice breaks the silence.

He is standing beside me, his face turned to the sky, the faint glow of the moon illuminating his eyes. I can tell he is drunk.

'Why did you wander off?' The slight slur in his voice confirms my assumptions.

I have never seen Jason drunk before and I note how it transforms him into a version of himself I do not know, his face shapeless and unfamiliar.

'I did not care for the . . . spectacle,' I say, crossing my arms tightly around myself.

'You should not deny the men their fun.' The shadows around him shift as he shrugs. 'They have had a difficult journey; it helps them to laugh about these things. Can you not allow them that?'

'Allow them to laugh at *me*?' I feel him tense at the edge in my voice.

'Nobody was laughing *at* you, my love. We were enjoying the memories of our voyage together, as comrades.'

'I am not part of your crew,' I counter, digging my fingers into my ribs. 'I am not your *comrade*, nor theirs.'

'No, but you will soon be my wife. My queen.' He unravels my folded arms and pulls me towards him. His breath smells sour.

'What about your other queen?' I feel something ugly knot in my stomach as I say it. 'The Queen of Lemnos?'

'Hypsipyle?' I hate the sound of the queen's name on his tongue. 'What did you hear of her?'

'I heard enough.'

'Gods, Medea. Really?' Jason pulls away. He has never said my name like that before, laced with annoyance. 'When did you become so paranoid? You are sounding like your father, you know.'

I feel a familiar hardness closing over me, my defences rising. 'Did you fuck her, too, then?'

Even whilst drunk and draped in Nyx's shadows, I can still see his eyes narrow at my vulgar language.

'You have been spending too long with foul-mouthed men,' he comments, though his voice lacks its usual, easy humour. 'A queen does not speak like that.'

'You did not answer my question.'

'What does it matter?' He lets out a wine-soaked sigh, running a hand through his hair. 'I have not questioned you on your past, have I? So why can you not offer me the same courtesy?'

I want to point out that there is nothing in my past worth noting, but the words lodge in my throat. I wrap my arms around myself again, digging my nails in deeper at my sides, feeling them bite against my skin. I know they will leave little crescent marks there, physical remnants of the invisible pain.

'Medea, there's really no need to be upset,' he sighs.

'You told them things we shared in *private*, Jason.' The words come out weaker than I intended, laced in a trembling whisper.

'What did you expect? I *had* to tell them what transpired between us, or else they would never have trusted you. Their lives depended on our alliance; I could not keep it from them.'

'But they were *mocking* me—'

'Let me understand this, Medea,' he interrupts. 'My men cannot make harmless jokes, yet *you* are allowed to openly threaten them. Is that it?'

I stiffen beneath the sharpness of his question. *Of course*, Telamon went running to Jason at his first opportunity. Spineless mutt.

'My actions weren't without reason. They were saying things about Atalanta. Horrible things.'

'So?'

'So, I told them to stop.'

'No, Medea, you *threatened* them,' Jason snaps back at me, throwing his arms wide.

'But the things they were saying—'

'They *do not matter*. Do you know why, Medea?' He pushes in closer, swallowing up my space. 'Because your loyalties do not lie with Atalanta. They are supposed to lie with *me*.'

'I *am* loyal to you.'

'You know, you've really showed your immaturity tonight,' he mutters into the darkness.

I wince as his words lodge inside me, pressing against old wounds and causing my anger to fade into a dull, heavy ache.

'Please don't say that, Jason,' I whisper.

'My love.' I am relieved to hear his voice soften as he turns back to me. He braces his hands on my shoulders, tilting his face down so he looks me straight in the eye. 'It does not matter what came before us. All that is in the *past*, and all I care about is the future. *You* are my future. Can you not understand that?'

His words are everything I want to hear, and I will them to smooth over the crooked pain inside me, and yet . . . I can still feel that raw humiliation pulsing in the pit of my stomach, like a dying heartbeat.

'Come now, my love. Won't you give me a smile?'

'I do not want to be laughed at like that. Never again.' I feel my vulnerability opening to him like a flower reaching for sunlight.

He plants a kiss on my mouth, the movement sloppy, his teeth clacking against mine. He then presses his mouth to my ear, whispering gently, 'You look beautiful in the moonlight.'

I want to feel pleased that he desires me so deeply even after all he said, yet I cannot help but think about how quickly he has dismissed my feelings in favour of his own lust.

Before the thought can fully take shape, he kisses me again. I stand stiffly as his lips trail along my neck, waiting for the desire to stir inside me, but it does not come. All I can hear is the echoing laughter of the Argonauts, laced with Jason's words: *You are sounding like your father.*

'I want you,' he murmurs, beginning to paw at my gown. 'I want to taste you.'

'I am not in the mood, Jason.' I turn away from him.

'Really?' He pulls back, staring at me beneath lowered brows. 'You are going to be like this? All because of some harmless fun.'

I can feel it then, that familiar self-loathing I thought I had stripped from my body. Clearly, I haven't. Remnants of the old Medea still linger within me, still fight for breath.

But I cannot let her.

I need to suffocate her. Shut her out.

I need her *gone* so that I can be the woman worthy of Jason's love. The woman deserving of happiness.

I reach out for Jason and he pulls me to him, pressing his lips against mine. I lock my arms around his neck as he half tumbles us to the floor, hastily pushing up my gown, his hands clumsy with drunken greed.

I clutch for the threads of desire inside me, trying to tug them to life, willing them to pull me into that burning bliss. But I cannot escape the yawning numbness from closing its jaws around me as Jason shifts on top of me, his wine-soaked breaths ragged against my neck.

As he works against me, I am only faintly aware of the pain. I pull again on those threads of desire, my grip firmer now, yet still there is no response. It is like tugging the reins on a dead horse.

But I do not want Jason to stop, because I could not bear to see the disappointment in his eyes if I asked him to.

I stare blankly up at the stars, those dead souls trapped in the endless darkness, whilst Jason satisfies himself with my body. In the night-kissed stillness I swear I can hear the echo of their laughter. Taunting me.

But I push the idea away, constricting my mind, allowing space for just a single thought. One that I repeat to myself over and over, like a silent prayer – *I am worthy of this love.*

I am worthy of this love.

24

The Argonauts are welcomed like gods.

The people of Iolcus swarm the harbour, desperate to catch a glimpse of the victorious heroes. They swell and crash against one another like the waves we battled through, filling the dry morning air with a feverish urgency.

As we disembark, Jason holds the Golden Fleece aloft and the crowd erupts, their roars so loud they vibrate through the ground, rattling up into my chest. He then turns back to me and presses his lips to my ear.

'Smile, my love. These are your people, now.'

We walk in a long procession towards Pelias' palace with Jason at the front, the fleece held high above his head like a golden beacon. Crowds line every street, bursting from every corner. I even spy groups of gangly-legged children clambering on rooftops to try to get a better view of us.

Small trinkets and flowers are thrown at our feet as we walk. All around us hands grope blindly outwards, desperate to touch the Argonauts, to have the chance to feel their greatness beneath their fingertips, perhaps hoping a small piece might rub off on them.

The atmosphere is unlike anything I have experienced. Of course, I have attended public ceremonies before, but nothing compares to this level of fanatical ecstasy. The people are acting as if the

Olympians themselves have just graced their shores. Are the Greeks always so excitable?

As I look past the frenzied faces, however, I am struck by how similar Iolcus is to Colchis. Of course, there are differences – the people's slightly darker skin, for example, and their looser, plainer clothes. The buildings are noticeably smaller, less ornate, and the land itself feels drier, the ground dusty and cracked underfoot. Yet, despite this, the bones of this land appear much the same to me. I suppose I should have expected this. After all, when Helios gifted my father Colchis to rule, I know he intentionally sculpted his new kingdom with the influences of his Grecian upbringing.

Ahead of me, Jason basks in his people's adoration, flourishing beneath it. He throws waves and kisses, reaching back to shake hands and clasp shoulders. He is a natural at this, able to indulge his people without being caught up in their currents, navigating through the hordes as he continues to press forwards.

As I watch those desperate hands grasping for him, I imagine each one snatching a piece of Jason for themselves, secreting it away from me. Until now, I had not considered what it would be like to share his love and attention with so many.

I walk a few paces behind Jason with the Argonauts positioned on either side of me. This protective formation is not by coincidence. Jason has decided it is safer this way, to keep me separated from the people, until he has had the chance to formally announce me as their queen. Though, every now and then, my wall of protection fractures slightly and I find myself locking eyes with nearby onlookers. I note the way their faces seem to sharpen with recognition, their smiles vanishing.

'*There she is,*' they whisper. '*The witch of Colchis.*'

I tell myself I am imagining the hostility in their voices and focus my attention on Jason, on the palace looming ahead, and the arid, unrelenting heat scratching at my skin.

'Does Jason have a plan?' I hear Castor mutter. 'Or does he truly believe Pelias will simply hand over his throne?'

'He says his uncle swore an oath to the Gods,' Polydeuces replies as he accepts a flower from a small child, giving it a theatrical sniff.

'This is the same uncle who killed Jason's father and imprisoned his family, right?'

'Right.'

'*Right.*'

They share a look I try to ignore.

I am all too familiar with what little worth a king's word can hold. But if Jason believes in his uncle's integrity, then I know I should, too.

To my relief, the crowd breaks away once we reach the palace. The giant edifice looms proudly before us, its vibrantly painted pillars baking beneath the afternoon sun. As we approach, the colossal columns seem to tower forwards, as if inspecting us.

As I stare up at the palace, it feels unsettlingly familiar.

'You should wait outside,' Jason instructs the Argonauts, raising his voice against the din of the crowd behind us. 'Keep watch of Pelias' guards. If I need you, I will send a signal.'

But the Argonauts do not appear to be listening, their attention wandering to the numerous food stalls and tavernas beckoning in the distance. As I look around, I realize some have already disappeared, caught up in the excitement of the streets, or perhaps lured away by their doting fans.

I glance back to Jason, watching a frown crease between his brows. It is clear his hold over the Argonauts is slipping. Their quest has come to an end, and with it Jason's power over them.

'Did you hear me?' Jason presses, receiving a few half-hearted nods in reply. 'Medea, you will come with me.'

'Is it not safer for Medea to wait here, with us?' Atalanta interjects.

'No.' Jason's voice has a slight edge to it. 'It is *safer* for Medea to remain by her future husband's side.'

'Safer for who?' Atalanta mutters under her breath, at which Meleager lets out a rumbling chuckle.

If Jason hears, he pretends not to. Instead, he turns on his heel and strides into the palace, the fleece set triumphantly around his shoulders. I move to follow him, but someone tugs me backwards. Turning, I find the huntress's grey eyes on mine, her fingers laced around my wrist.

'Remember, you are to be his wife, not his weapon,' she says, her voice as firm as her grip.

'I know that.'

'I know *you* do. But does he?'

The atmosphere inside the palace is eerie.

The space is dimly lit, the windows blocked up. I expect to see slaves flitting about their daily tasks, but everywhere appears empty, the grand rooms gaping like gutted, gilded corpses.

After all the commotion outside, the stillness inside the palace is deafening.

'Is it usually like this?' I ask Jason, my voice splintering the thick silence.

He shakes his head. 'Not at all.'

'Where is everyone?'

'I heard rumours Pelias' health has deteriorated since I left for Colchis. He has always suffered from ailments; I believe it divine punishment for what he did to my family . . . Perhaps he does not want anyone to see just how weak he has become.' He scans the desolate passageway. 'The throne room is just ahead.'

We press onwards, Jason's strides slow and deliberate, each one fuelled with calm purpose. It is the walk of a victor, the walk of a king. In this light the fleece appears even brighter, making Jason look like a god amongst mere mortals.

Beside him, I mirror his poise, his pride, though the light of the fleece seems to recoil from me, chased by the shadows that follow in my wake, pressing in close, whispering against my skin.

At the end of the passageway the space opens outwards, and my eyes lock on to the throne before us and the traitor sitting upon it. Pelias. Jason's uncle.

The man who took everything from him.

In my mind I had fashioned Pelias in the mould of my father, tall and cruel and ugly. But as we approach the dais, I am surprised to see the man who sits before us is . . . *old*. His wrinkled skin looks as thin as a butterfly's wings, his hair so fine I can see his spotted scalp dappled beneath it. I glance to Jason to see if he mirrors my surprise, but his face remains impassive.

We stop before the throne. Neither of us bows.

As I stare at Pelias, I feel the tension inside me subside a little. Someone has swathed his shrivelled body in expensive robes to try to give him the illusion of stature, but all it has done is emphasize how small and frail he looks, the thick material swallowing him up like a child trying on their father's clothes.

Behind the king, four women stand in the shadows. Their faces are obscured by pale veils, their hands clasped in front of them. If it weren't for the slight rise and fall of their breathing, they could be mistaken for marble statues. I assume they are Pelias' beloved daughters;

the ones Jason has told me about. Apparently, they utterly adore their father, their devotion so unwavering they have all refused to marry so they may remain by Pelias' side.

I cannot fathom such a desire.

After a lengthy silence, Pelias finally clears his throat to speak. When he does, his voice is painfully thin against the gathered hush.

'My dear nephew. Welcome home.'

'Thank you, uncle. It is good to see you.'

'And welcome to you as well, Medea.' Pelias swivels his eyes to me, and I notice they are the exact same shade as Jason's. Though his are set in a bed of thick, greying wrinkles, they still hold a bright alertness. 'I had heard word Jason was returning with a bride.'

'A queen,' I correct, my lips tilting sharply upwards. Beside me, I can feel Jason mirroring my smile.

Pelias says nothing, though I note the way his gnarled, knotted hands tighten against the carved arms of his throne.

'I must ask, are you well, uncle? You are looking a little . . . pale.' Jason's words are cut with a sardonic edge.

'Thank you for your concern.' If his voice were stronger, I might have believed Pelias' tone to be defensive. 'But I can assure you I am in good health.'

Jason allows a beat to pass, the silence pointed like an accusatory finger. *Lies.*

'Very well. Then I shall begin.' He takes a defiant step forwards, clearing his throat. 'Last harvest, I stood before this very throne and claimed my right to sit upon it, a right bestowed upon me by my father. You, Pelias, assured me this throne would be mine to claim *if* I retrieved the famed Golden Fleece to prove my worth. And so I did exactly as you asked, gathering the mightiest crew this world has ever seen. Heroes from across Greece rallied behind me, including

Herakles, the son of Zeus himself. They had all heard of my quest and believed my cause worthy.'

Jason's voice lifts as he continues, 'I led the Argonauts on a journey so ambitious it will be sung of for generations. You cannot even fathom the foes we faced, the hardships we endured, the battles we won. All for this.' He holds his prize out before him. 'The Golden Fleece. As promised.'

Another beat of silence follows as Jason awaits his congratulations.

'And where are your famed comrades now?'

Jason's jaw tightens at Pelias' bland reply, but he keeps his voice even as he says, 'They are waiting outside. But believe me, uncle, they will not wait for long. They have had a long and difficult journey, and they wish to indulge in what our beautiful city has to offer.'

There is no denying the threat behind Jason's words, though Pelias remains unfazed.

'As have you, nephew. You must be exhausted.' He smiles thinly.

'I am. I would like very much to sit down and rest my legs, but I believe you are in my seat.' Jason eyes the throne as he runs an absent hand through the curls of the Golden Fleece. He then shifts his gaze to our silent spectators. 'Would one of my lovely cousins like to help him up?'

Behind Pelias, his daughters remain motionless save for the tallest, who twitches, causing her veil to quiver, the material rippling like liquid starlight.

'Consider how you address your king.' Pelias' voice hardens. It seems Jason's insolence has injected some life back into the old man's bones.

'Perhaps you have become confused in your ... *delicate* state. So, allow me to put it plainly for you. I have retrieved the fleece and proven my worth. So now the throne is rightfully mine, as we agreed.'

Pelias leans forwards and I am not sure if the creaking noise comes from the throne or his frail bones.

'We agreed, Jason, that if you returned with the fleece, you would become my *heir*. You shall become king once I am ready to pass the title on.'

Jason stiffens, his voice lowering as he says, 'You claimed no such condition before.'

'Did you really think I would simply hand over my throne, boy? After all I did to secure it?' Pelias leans back, a rasping laugh rattling through his lungs. The sound of it grates over my nerves.

'We had an agreement. You swore an oath to the Gods.'

'I swore to declare you as my heir, yes. Have a little patience, nephew. The throne will be yours, in time.'

In time. The words hang limp and lifeless in the air, as meaningless as every other vow I have heard a king make. Pelias has no intention of giving Jason his throne; he clearly never did.

As I glare up at the king I feel my power ripple through me, those midnight waves lapping against my soul, slow and soothing.

Pelias is so weak, so easy to destroy . . .

I push the thought from my mind instantly.

'Give it here, then.' Pelias reaches out a hand. 'Our agreement was that you bring *me* the fleece, no? Unless you no longer wish to honour your side of the bargain.'

'It is not I who is dishonouring our agreement,' Jason counters, his tone hardening just a fraction, but enough to make the room feel airless.

From the fringes of my vision, I can see armed guards materializing, their hands hovering over the hilts of their swords. Jason's own grip tightens on the fleece, his jaw locked with a cold resolution.

My tether to the Underworld pulls taut, sensing the danger around us.

'Hand it over, Jason.' Pelias' voice, though withered, holds a threatening edge.

The seconds slip away, each one feeling heavier than the last. The guards take a decisive step closer – a silent warning for Jason to obey their king.

In the silence, I can see it unfolding in my mind – a small nod from Pelias and the palace guards will rush forwards, swarming Jason. He will call to the Argonauts for aid, but none will come. Jason will not yield, though, even when abandoned by his crew. For he will never again allow himself to be taken prisoner in this palace. He would rather choose death.

I envision Jason thrashing out wildly with his sword, making a valiant effort against the hordes of palace guards. But it will not be enough. There will be too many of them and he will be too tired and weak after our long voyage. I will be there fighting beside him, of course, my power ripping down every man who stands against my love. But all it will take is one quick blade to his gut or a slice to his throat and Jason will fall, the fleece slipping from his shoulders as he collapses.

I flinch from the image in my mind, of Jason gasping in a pool of his own lifeblood.

'My love.' I turn to him now, my voice puncturing the tension that chokes the room. 'Please, allow me.'

I reach for the fleece and Jason's grip instinctively tightens around it. His eyes blaze so fiercely I can hear the unspoken question hissing through his glare: *What are you doing?*

Trust me, Jason, I silently beg, sending a pulse of my power towards him, mollifying his outrage. *Please. This is the only way.*

After a long moment, he finally relents, the fleece sagging in his hands as if embodying his dejection. As I take it from him, I cannot help but notice once again how dull and useless it feels beneath my fingertips.

'It seems your future wife has better manners than you, Jason,'

Pelias says as I approach the throne. His smile is a thin slash across his weathered face. 'Clearly the Colchians are not as barbaric as people say. Thank you, Medea.'

'It is my honour,' I say as I place the fleece at his feet.

Pelias stares down at it and I can see an intense hunger reflected in those eyes, revealing a glimpse of the covetous, ruthless king that lies within his decrepit body.

He leans forwards then and reaches down for the fleece. His movements are slow, his hand trembling as his snarled fingers strain inches away from the golden curls. I watch him struggle, making no effort to help him.

A shadow flutters beside me and I glance up to see one of his daughters bending down to retrieve the fleece. She places it delicately on her father's lap and then cups his cheek with her slender, pale hand. The movement is fleeting yet filled with such love.

I find it strange to witness this adoration between a father and daughter.

'Thank you, Alcestis,' I hear him mutter.

Before she turns to leave, his daughter looks up at me and I can just make out the shadowy outline of her face behind her veil. I sense her stare piercing through the rippling material and the fear that burns within it. But there's something else there, too, a dark kind of curiosity that pulls her towards me like a moth being drunkenly drawn towards a flame. I nod to her, and she flinches in response, before scurrying back to her sisters.

'If I am to be your heir, then what of your son?' Jason demands.

'Acastus is overseas at present, but I will explain to him upon his return.'

Jason lowers his gaze to the fleece on Pelias' lap. He swallows thickly before arranging his face into a strained smile.

His next words are forced through gritted teeth. 'Understood, uncle. I apologize for any . . . hostilities on my part. As I said, we have had a long, difficult journey and are in desperate need of rest and a hot meal, if you would be so kind as to oblige?'

'Of course.' Pelias waves a thin hand, and two slaves appear as if the gesture moulded them from the shadows. 'Escort our guests to their chamber, will you? And tell our cook to prepare food and wine, lots of it. We must celebrate the happy news of your impending marriage, must we not?'

Jason nods without looking at me.

The men exchange further small talk, but the words are hollow. They are like foes circling on a battlefield, biding their precious time, waiting to strike as soon as the other's guard falters.

'If there is anything you need, do not hesitate to ask,' Pelias tells us as he leans back in his chair, placing his hands over the fleece. 'And please, make yourselves at home. After all, we are family, are we not?'

25

Pelias' palace has the same soulless feel to it as my father's did.

A labyrinth of passageways, lofty ceilings and vast chambers. Endless, meaningless space, choked with garish decor in a lazy attempt to convey power.

My mind flickers to Circe's home. That tiny, chaotic little haven lost on the edge of the world. I had not realized until now how much I liked it, how homely it felt to me.

Not that it will ever be my home.

Nor will I ever see it again.

I push the thought away as we enter our chamber. The room is not as grandiose as those in Colchis, but it feels like the luxury of Mount Olympus compared to the conditions on the *Argo* and the nights spent sleeping out on the hard ground.

A sigh of relief escapes me, my limbs begging to collapse on the fur pelts piled beside us. I wonder what it will be like to finally lie with Jason in a proper bed, to feel the brush of our bare skin against those soft furs . . .

'*I should have known.*'

A crash splinters my thoughts as a wide circular bowl clatters at my feet, spilling apples across the floor. I lift my gaze to Jason, watching his broad shoulders heave as he sucks in heavy, uneven breaths. His eyes are the darkest I have ever seen them, like storm clouds rolling over a summer sky.

'My love—'

'*Don't,*' he growls at me, kicking the table the discarded bowl had been placed upon. I flinch as it topples over, clanging against the floor. 'I should have known that wretch would have *lied.*' His face twists with a fury so raw he is almost unrecognizable.

I sit down on the bed as he turns his face away from me, bracing his hands against the far wall. I keep my eyes set on the strong contours of his back, watching them quiver with the rage undulating beneath his skin. He punches the wall and I feel every muscle inside me coiling tightly.

'And *you.*' He turns on me. 'Why did you hand him the fleece? What were you *thinking?*'

'The fleece is useless,' I say.

'*What?*'

A tense stillness settles between us as I hold Jason's blistering glare.

'The fleece is useless,' I repeat, my fists clenched in my lap. 'Did you really think I would willingly give Pelias the gift of eternal glory?'

Jason's scowl darkens. 'What do you mean? How do you know?'

'Hecate told me, and Circe confirmed it with her comment on Aeaea.'

'They could be lying.'

'They are not.' I shake my head. 'I cannot feel it, Jason.'

'Feel what?'

'Its power. If it were there, I would feel something.'

He considers this for a moment. 'How long have you known?'

'Hecate told me the morning of your trials.'

He rubs his jaw, his anger dispersing into stunned confusion. He shakes his head as he adjusts to the weight of this realization settling over him. 'All this time?'

'I should have told you sooner,' I admit. 'But I was not sure if

Hecate's words were true, not until I held the fleece for myself. And I feared you would lose belief in yourself without it . . . but do you realize what this means, Jason? It means your glory is your own. Your victories were not because of some divine object; they were because of *you*.' I watch as he mulls over my words, his anger receding.

'The fleece is useless,' he repeats to himself.

'Are you . . . angry with me? For not telling you sooner?'

'Angry?' He turns to me and, to my surprise, a giant smile cracks across his face, chasing away any remnants of that vicious temper. 'Medea, do you not see? This is brilliant! Pelias now believes himself undefeatable. He no longer sees me as a threat, which will buy us time to secure the throne.'

I stare at his bloodied knuckles, my mind replaying the way the fury had consumed his entire body so quickly, disfiguring that beautiful face. It is as if the image has burnt itself into my eyes. I cannot unsee it.

It reminds me of my father.

I wish it would not.

Jason regards his knuckles, then gives a shaky chuckle as he runs his hands through his hair. 'It seems I lost my manners there for a moment. I apologize. I must be overtired from the journey . . . Medea, my love, why are you looking at me like that? You're shaking. Here, come here. Come on, now.' He strides over to the bed, cutting the distance in a few easy steps, and sits down beside me. I lean stiffly into his open arms. 'Why are you so frightened? What is the matter? My love, do not make me feel more wretched than I already do. Please, do not think less of me. I could not bear it if you did.'

'I do not,' I say, gazing up at him. 'I could never think less of you.'

'It is just that seeing that man brings out the worst in me. When I think of what he took from me, what he did to my family . . .' He falls silent, letting the unspoken words gather in the shadows.

254

I think of his mother and brother, locked away in that prison cell, left to rot. If someone had done such a thing to Chalciope, there is no telling the severity of the punishment I would have unleashed upon them.

'I understand,' I say, cupping his fallen face.

'Perhaps I am a fool for thinking Pelias would be true to his word.'

'You are not a fool. You are a man who believes in honour, and there are too few of you in this world.' He looks at me and I savour the way he smiles at my words, the light I bring back into his eyes. He plants a gentle kiss into my palm. 'So, you are truly not angry with me?'

'I could never be angry with you, Medea. In truth, I never cared for the fleece. It was only ever a means to reclaim my throne.' He smiles. 'And I will have that throne. No matter what. My mother and brother died so that I could live, so that I could avenge my father. What use would their sacrifice be if I failed now?'

'You will be king,' I assure him. 'Pelias is dying; you saw the condition he is in. The throne will be yours soon enough.'

'He will not claim me as his heir.' His eyes suddenly darken. 'He has already shown he is a man of no honour. As soon as his son, Acastus, returns, he will find a way to dispose of me.'

'But it is *you* the people want; you saw them out there. Can you and Acastus not come to an agreement? Perhaps he will honour your uncle's word?'

'Medea, I will not wait around to be slighted again . . .' He trails off and gives a deep sigh, turning his face away from my touch. 'I thought you would understand. Perhaps I was foolish for thinking that, too.'

'I do understand,' I assert, gripping his hand. 'I do.'

'Then will you help me claim what is rightfully mine?' He tilts his face back, his eyes sliding down to our intertwined hands.

'Of course.' I nod as he kisses our locked fingers. 'But what of the Argonauts – could they not help also? Pelias' army is no match for them, surely?'

'I cannot take the throne by slaying Iolcus' own soldiers. The people will not take kindly to a king who killed their sons, brothers, fathers. Besides, even if I *wanted* to, I do not believe the Argonauts would risk their lives for me again. You saw how they were today; they believe their work is done.' He shakes his head as he begins to make small circles on my palm, his touch so tender it's almost teasing. 'We need to be smarter than that. Cleverer. More ... *magical.*' He adds the last word with a knowing grin.

'Magical,' I repeat, watching his finger trace along my skin, leaving a trail of sparks in its wake.

'I was thinking ... you could cast one of your little spells.'

'Perhaps ... I could.'

'Will you?' His face tilts closer to mine and I can see the dark intent flickering in the depths of his gaze. 'For me?'

I feel the darkness creeping inside me, that channel slithering open, the death spirits' hunger crowding in my mind. But the feeling is dampened by Atalanta's voice.

You are to be his wife, not his weapon.

'What if the people turn against me for using my magic against their king?'

'If we are discreet, how will they ever know it was you?'

'I suppose you are right ...'

'Of course I am. Do you not see? Pelias believes he is undefeatable now he holds the fleece. His guard will be completely down, thanks to you ... You are so very clever, my love.' He leans in and kisses my collarbone, his lips igniting a pulse of pleasure beneath my skin. He then trails his mouth along my neck, causing me to tilt my head backwards. 'Come now, Medea,' he whispers between kisses. 'Did you not say you would do anything for me? Anything at all?'

'Yes . . . but—'

'But?' He pulls away slightly. 'Do you not want me to be a king? And you my queen?'

I want to tell him I have never cared for such titles, but the words seem to lodge in my throat as he stares at me with those bright eyes.

'I want to be your wife,' I manage.

'And you will be, my love . . . once I am king.' He closes his hands around mine in my lap. 'We cannot give up now, Medea. We must keep fighting for us, for our future.'

That vision blossoms once again in my mind – the little boy in my arms, Jason laughing beside us. A perfect, shimmering drop of happiness permeating my every thought. I hold it carefully in my mind, as if cradling it with invisible hands, keeping it safe. Our future. Our perfect, beautiful future.

I will fight for it.

I will do whatever it takes.

'Perhaps if we ask for a private audience with Pelias tomorrow . . .'

'We?' Jason pulls back. 'Medea, you must realize I cannot be here when it happens.'

'But—'

'I cannot risk any blame falling upon my name. I must be innocent in this; it is imperative I keep the people on my side in order to secure the throne. Do you understand that?'

Do I understand it? Is it fair that my hands must be bloodied so that his can remain clean? He says he needs the people on his side, but what of me? What if their hatred falls upon my shoulders?

Jason takes my hands in his again, pressing his lips to my fingers. 'Please, Medea. Trust me in this, as I trusted you in Colchis.'

'I do trust you.'

His eyes flicker up to mine. 'So, you will do it?'

My mind turns over those words and the unspoken question lingering within them – *you will kill him?*

With each passing second, I feel the shadows pressing in closer, eager to hear my answer. Their darkness is a whisper in my soul; they are impatient, hungry. Though sometimes it is difficult to know where their desire ends and mine begins . . .

Because I do *want* Pelias to suffer, as he made Jason suffer.

He killed Jason's father, left his mother and brother to die in a prison cell and would have let Jason face the same fate if he had not escaped. And, after all that, he still has the audacity to deny Jason his rightful throne, even after he returned with the Golden Fleece to prove his worth.

For that, Pelias must die.

He deserves this punishment, and I have always believed in punishment.

'I will do it,' I say, my voice burning with quiet conviction. 'Whatever you ask of me. I will do it.'

Jason smiles and kisses me deeply, whispering into our shared breath, 'My queen.'

The next morning, Jason rises early.

'I need to gather the Argonauts, or whatever is left of them after a night of indulging in the city,' he tells me as he dresses.

'Will you ask them to remain in Iolcus until your throne is secured?'

'That's my intention. Though they'll need some convincing . . . I'll have to dazzle them with my charm.' He grins at me with a wink. 'It will also be good for me to show my face to the people. To remind them of their beloved hero. If the people are on my side, it will be an easier transition to power.'

His face is so bright, his eyes practically glowing, burning away any remnants of his fury from the night before. It makes me wonder if I imagined the severity of his anger; perhaps my mind has exaggerated the memory, blurring it with ugly nightmares from my past. Yet his cut, bruised knuckles tell me otherwise.

'Could I go with you?' I sit up in bed, watching Jason buckle his robes at either shoulder.

His smile softens. 'I would love for the people to meet their future queen . . . but I need you to stay here and work out our little plan.'

'What about poison?' I ask quietly, causing Jason's eyes to flicker sharply to the door. 'The man is so frail it would not take much to—'

'Medea,' he cuts me off, raising a hand to silence me. He sits down on the bed, taking my hands in his. 'There could be eyes and ears everywhere here.'

'But what do you think?' I lower my voice to just a breath.

Jason considers my words for a moment then leans in and murmurs, 'Poison is too obvious, too predictable. Fingers would be pointed at us before his body even went cold. We would need the evidence that points to another suspect, to avoid any contention to me claiming the throne.' He makes a gentle swooping motion across the air with our intertwined fingers. 'We will guide the blade, but it needs to look as if it were in another's hand. Do you understand?'

I carefully turn his words over in my mind, feeling an idea take root.

'What if he were to do it?'

'Who do you mean?' Jason frowns.

'What if Pelias were to wield the blade himself?'

26

'Tell me, Medea, why should I trust you?'

I am in Pelias' personal quarters, compromising three interconnecting chambers, each of which opens out into a private central courtyard. The space is surprisingly understated for a king. Sparse furniture sits forgotten in the corners of the room, coated in a thin layer of dust. Painted statues have been left to crack and peel, revealing the white marble beneath. Everything looks tired and worn, as if Pelias' condition has permeated his surroundings.

My attention has been fixed on the far wall, where a fresco depicts Zeus's mighty defeat of the Titans. Despite the ancient story it tells, this painting is ironically the only thing in the room that doesn't appear timeworn. The scene has been crafted with exquisite detail, the artist using bold splashes of colour that stand out with an oddly beautiful violence.

In front of this, Pelias sits in a large, ornate chair, akin to the one in his throne room. His face is turned to the courtyard, where the sky is dull and dreary, a canopy of grey draining all vibrancy from the world outside.

'You say you can cure me,' Pelias continues in that thin voice of his. 'So, tell me, then, why I should believe this claim?'

I draw in a breath, noting the faint smell of saffron woven into the air.

'Not just cure, my King. I can rejuvenate your body, your mind. Make you young again.' I offer a polite, disarming smile, one Chalciope would have given if she were here. Though hers would be genuine, as all her smiles are.

Chalciope. The thought of her makes my mind stumble, snagging on memories rooted deep inside me. What would she think of my plan, my treacherous plotting to take a life? Would she understand?

No, of course not, and how could I ever expect her to?

As my sadness wells up, I feel something cold and smooth pulse through me, rippling from my core. A night-kissed shadow that shrouds my senses, smothering the pain like a soft hand closing over a mouth, choking it of air.

I draw in another steady breath, welcoming the numbness. Its emptiness is far easier to navigate than the tumultuous storm of my emotions. But in that empty space where the pain had been, I feel something else beginning to stir. Gentle, seductive whispers echoing down the channel.

The death spirits call to me.

For they know what I am planning.

'You truly possess such abilities?' Pelias inclines his head, the wrinkles around his mouth deepening as he frowns.

'My powers were gifted to me by Hecate herself.'

I could kill him right now.

With a single command I could let the death spirits feast upon his weakened body. I could tie his mind into madness, have him slash his own throat with the dagger I have seen stashed in his robes.

But there are guards everywhere and they know I requested an audience with their king. So if Pelias were suddenly to take his own life whilst we were alone . . .

No. I must be smarter than that.

'I do not expect you to trust me, my King,' I continue. 'But I can prove to you that I speak the truth. Please, allow me to show you the spell. Then you can decide if you require my aid.'

Pelias shifts beneath the layers of animal furs that have been piled atop him despite the morning's humidity.

He draws in a rattling breath before speaking. 'And why, Medea, would you extend my life when my death would ensure Jason's right to my throne?'

'Because I know true power when I see it.'

'Is that so?' I can feel his ego flaring, stoked by my words.

Men are so predictable.

'Power calls to power, and I sense greatness in you, Pelias.' He remains silent as he considers my words. 'Why else would I have given you the fleece?'

'What of your husband-to-be?'

'I answer only to Hecate, and she has never set me on the wrong path.'

'So, you claim the goddess has told you to assist me?' I nod, my eyes never leaving his. 'Why would she do such a thing?'

'It is not our place to question the will of the Gods,' I counter.

Pelias rubs a crooked finger over his chin, and I see the cogs of his mind turning. He clearly doesn't find it hard to believe I'd realign my loyalties so quickly. After all, I am the foreign princess who betrayed her entire family for a stranger.

It is clear, also, that Pelias does not trust me; he has no reason to. But his guard is down, as I knew it would be. With the fleece in his power, he thinks himself invincible. Just as my father did.

What fools these kings are.

'You are a curious creature,' he murmurs.

'I prefer the term "sorceress".' I smile.

We are interrupted by a sudden patter of urgent feet, followed by a squawking voice. 'What is *she* doing *alone* with you, Father?'

Pelias' daughters file into the room. With their veils removed, I can now see their faces. The older two are near identical, their faces dominated by large, deep-brown eyes set slightly too far apart, throwing their features out of balance in a strangely appealing way. The only difference between them is that the taller sister – Alcestis, I believe – has her long chestnut curls unbound and the other's tresses are plaited into a tight coronet around her head.

'Who allowed this?' It is the one with the plaited hair who speaks, her voice laced with a cold fury.

Behind them, the two younger sisters follow.

A cold dread rises in my chest. They were not supposed to be here; this was not part of my plan.

Perhaps, though, I could use this to my advantage.

Pelias dotes on his daughters, and if they love him as fiercely as Jason claims, they will no doubt support my offer to cure his ailments. I wonder what it must feel like, to be loved by a parent like that. It must be a unique kind of bond . . . the kind I could make use of.

But Pelias' death would ruin them, especially if they believed themselves complicit in the act. These girls are too weak to carry that kind of burden on their fragile souls.

'Medea claims she can cure me,' I hear him telling his daughters, a note of scepticism weighing down his words.

'Can you really?' Alcestis asks me. She was the one who studied me in the throne room. I can feel that curiosity now, like a delicate tendril pulling away from the neat, orderly tapestry of her thoughts. All I need to do is tug on that loose thread and let the rest begin to unravel . . .

But am I really prepared to do this?

Pelias is deserving of this fate, but his daughters are innocent. Their only crime is standing in the way of my and Jason's happiness.

Am I prepared to ruin their future to secure my own?

I believe I know the answer before I am even willing to admit it.

Though, if I have learnt one thing in my life, it is that *nobody* will hand you your happiness. For happiness is not a gift to be given freely but a prize to be claimed.

And I am ready to take what I am owed.

'Can you?' the princess presses.

'Yes.' I nod. 'I can.'

'She lies, Alcestis,' her sister hisses. 'How can we trust that witch?'

'Compose yourself, Pelopia,' the king warns.

'I know of a rejuvenation spell that will not only heal the king, but breathe new life into his body,' I say, my voice commanding the space.

It is technically true: I know such a spell exists. I have just never done one before ... nor will I today.

'Why would we believe a barbarian? A murderer?' Pelopia snarls.

Murderer. The word makes the shadows swell around us, stalking closer.

It would be so easy ... to release those spirits from the Underworld again, to let them feed off these girls' minds, to drive them insane like Talos ...

No. They are not my victims, and I am not a mindless killer.

Though would they prefer death over what I am about to make them witness?

'I can show you,' I say, turning my attention back to Pelias. 'If you will allow me, I can demonstrate the spell ... But first we must go somewhere you can guarantee privacy. I will only allow those worthy to witness my gifts.'

Pelias glances to his daughters, an unspoken conversation passing between them.

'Very well.' He nods. Only Alcestis smiles.

Foolish girl, the darkness purrs.

I slit the ram's throat quickly and cleanly.

No need for any theatrics.

The sisters still flinch, recoiling when the blood spills on to the kitchen floor. This was the location Pelias chose, his palace kitchens, a space he assured me would guarantee privacy and the equipment required to perform my spell.

The youngest ones cannot watch the creature die. The way they grab their older sisters' hands tugs at memories of when my father made us watch him beat the slaves and Chalciope would hold on to me for comfort. Those memories are so visceral it is as if I can feel her hand in mine, her fragile body leaning into me . . .

Chalciope will never seek comfort from me again. Nor should she.

As I stare down at the blood coating my fingers, I feel my body cracking open, allowing my mind to detach and slip out into the air. Hovering just above my head, I watch myself cradling the dying creature. Though it is no longer the ram in my arms, but my brother. He cries against my chest, begging for me to stop, but I do not . . . I cannot . . .

The darkness smiles around me. The whispering of the spirits intensifies.

They are ready for another kill. Another soul.

'I do not understand,' Pelias rasps. The fleece is draped protectively around his shoulders. 'How does killing the beast help?'

His voice grounds me back in my body. I rub my chin with my hand, realizing the blood has now smeared across my face. I do not bother wiping it off.

'Death and life walk hand in hand,' I tell him. 'Are we ready to begin?'

I loosen my leash on the spirits gathered around me just an inch, so their invisible fingertips can reach out towards my audience. I can feel them tugging for more, eager to be fully unleashed. But I fasten my control on them, like chained hounds.

You answer to me, I remind them.

As they spill from the Underworld through me, I can feel our power mingling and wrapping itself around the room. The feeling is intoxicating.

Circe feared this kind of magic, but she did not know what glorious power the Underworld could feed us. Such beautiful, endless power.

Around us, the darkness seems to close inwards, the shadows thickening as the spirits grow impatient. I let those shadows seep into my audience, wrapping them around their thoughts. It is not a violent intrusion like with Talos, but rather a gentle caress, painting images I have carefully chosen for them.

They gasp as their eyes lie to them, feeding them visions the death spirits have planted. They see the dead ram writhing, brilliant sparks of light shining from its skin. The younger sisters cower, but the older ones are transfixed. Even Pelias looks awed by the visions blinding his eyes.

I feel the darkness jerking against my hold, defiant, restless. The death spirits want *more*. It takes almost all my strength to hold them back, to stop them from shredding their fragile minds.

No, I hiss silently.

They obey, but I can feel their bloodlust so potently as if it were my own.

Whilst Pelias and his daughters are distracted by the visions, I drag the dead creature from the room by its hind legs. It is no easy feat and I silently curse the time I am wasting. If only Jason were here, he could have lifted the ram from the room with minimal effort.

Once done, I retrieve the young ram I stowed away earlier from Pelias' personal stock. As the creature sniffs at the blood on the floor, I let the visions loosen, pulling back on the reins of the darkness clogging my audience's minds. The spirits rebel at first, not yet satisfied, but eventually they settle in the shadows around us. Waiting.

I feel a familiar warmth dripping from my nose and quickly wipe the blood away.

Pelias and his daughters blink slowly, as if surfacing from a strange dream. They then stare at the ram standing before them – young, healthy and very much alive.

'Do you see?' I ask, as they gawp.

'She did it. She *rejuvenated* the beast, she made it young again!' Alcestis gasps, excitement catching inside her.

'So, you are saying our father must *kill* himself in order for you to heal him?' her sister Pelopia frowns at me, though there is a slight tremble of awe in her voice.

'As I said, death and life walk hand in hand. A rejuvenation spell must begin with death.' The lie rolls easily off my tongue. 'If Pelias takes the knife to his throat, I will ensure he comes back a strong, youthful man.'

'He is so young,' Alcestis breathes, crouching down to stare at the ram. She strokes under his chin with a gentleness I have rarely seen people offer to animals.

'As you will be, Pelias,' I tell him.

He watches the ram for a long moment, the shadows exaggerating the sallowness of his skin. When he speaks, he sounds tired. 'I will admit I am impressed by your gifts, Medea. But I will not be placing my life in your hands. I have heard enough talk of you and your homeland to know it would be an unwise decision.'

'You trust rumours over the truth you see before you?'

'I trust in my instincts,' he counters, though his fragile voice makes the statement lack conviction. 'It is against the will of the Gods to extend the lifespan given to us by the Fates. I will be grateful and enjoy the time I have left.'

'You have mere days,' I warn, stepping towards him. 'Do you realize that?'

'Father.' Alcestis turns to him. 'Please consider what she is offering. Remember, you have the fleece's protection.'

'And you must remember your place, daughter,' he warns her, irritation edging his words. He turns back to me. 'You will not frighten me into using your magic, Medea. I allowed your little demonstration and I have made my decision.'

I nod, feigning indifference as panicked desperation knots inside my chest. 'Very well. If you do not wish for my help, that is your mistake.'

I know I will not get this chance alone with Pelias again and I cannot return to Jason a failure, cannot bear the thought of seeing the disappointment weighing in his eyes.

My gaze drifts to where Alcestis still crouches, transfixed by the ram. I notice she has been toying with the dagger, the one I discarded. The blade is still slick with the creature's blood.

She glances up to me and I can see it in her eyes, as if I am watching her future play out within them. I know what she is considering. I know what she is willing to do. She loves her father so much; she would kill for him.

As I would kill for Jason.

Such blinding, unwavering love.

She is there, on that same precipice I have found myself upon. All it would take is one little push . . .

'It is a pity,' I say, as I watch the tears roll down her pretty, glistening cheeks. 'I could have given you so many more beautiful summers with your father.'

She rises slowly, her eyes still set firmly on mine. Around us, the darkness crawls closer, the spirits practically vibrating with their violent eagerness.

One tiny push . . .

'Treasure this time,' I say softly. 'He has so little left.'

Alcestis moves quicker than I expected, driving the dagger into her father's heart. Pelias gasps, his eyes wide as he stares at his daughter, the tears continuing to stream down her face.

'I am sorry, Father,' she whispers. 'But I cannot lose you. Not yet.'

Heart-shattering grief begins to take hold of Alcestis, her hands trembling so violently she might drop the blade. But Pelopia closes her hand over her sister's, holding the dagger firmly in place. They stare at one another for a long moment. Then the younger ones move to do the same, so that all four sisters now plunge the dagger deeper into their father's heart.

'I'm so sorry,' they weep.

The betrayal in Pelias' face nearly breaks them, but the daughters hold firm as the light ebbs from his eyes.

Mercifully, the king dies quickly, his body too weak to fight.

As he succumbs to the hand of death closing over him, I feel the darkness around me rejoicing, firing in my veins. Then, all at once, that taut cord goes slack as the death spirits retreat, leaving a hollow space inside me.

In their absence my whole body feels numb, as lifeless as Pelias' corpse now lying on the floor.

269

Perhaps a piece of me died with him.

Perhaps I am already dead, my soul fed to those spirits.

'Now, do it. Bring him back. Do it *now*,' Alcestis demands, sobs ripping through her body as she turns to me. 'Please, bring him back.'

'Do it,' Pelopia orders, her face calm, though I can see the guilt already festering beneath her skin.

'Please,' the younger sisters cry quietly, kneeling over their father.

The silence takes a breath around us, as the heavy presence of death settles in the room. I stare at the girls' hands, all covered in their father's blood. It is a stain they will never be able to wash away . . .

'I am sorry,' I say, holding Alcestis' red, swollen eyes with mine. 'But I cannot.'

'*What?*' Pelopia rounds on me, holding out the dagger. 'You bring him back now or else I'll—'

'Do what?' I ask calmly. 'I do not think the new king would appreciate you threatening his future queen.'

'*You are not the future queen*,' Pelopia snarls, baring her teeth like a cornered wild animal. She points the dagger towards me, though her hands begin to tremble violently.

'Your father is dead. Jason is his chosen heir and I his future wife.' My smile feels cold around my lips.

'No, no, no.' Alcestis covers her face, sobs sawing through her chest. 'Do not do this, please, Gods. You can have the throne, have whatever you want . . . please just let him live. Do not let him die. Do not do this.'

'You tricked us!' Pelopia seethes, panic hardening her face.

'Father, no, no . . . please . . . Gods, please, spare him. I beg of you.' Alcestis falls to her knees, cradling her father's body, rocking his limp corpse back and forth, the blood pooling around her skirts, soaking the useless Golden Fleece. 'I did not mean to. I did not mean to. Forgive me . . .'

The sight makes the emptiness inside me sink deeper, and suddenly I am not watching Alcestis at all, but rather see myself cradling Apsyrtus' body, his blood blooming against my chest as I sob and sob and sob . . .

I did not mean to . . .

As the wailing sisters embrace their dead father, Pelopia storms towards me. Her eyes blaze with a hatred so vicious I imagine it scorching my skin, leaving a permanent mark.

'You are a vile, soulless creature. You will not get away with this. I will tell all of Iolcus what you have done, I will—' She stops abruptly, making a gagging sound as the words seem to lodge in her throat. Behind Pelopia, her sisters' sobbing pleas have fallen quiet too, and I watch them try to scream but no sound escapes.

The death spirits have stolen their voices, silencing them so they may never communicate what they have witnessed here.

'I am sorry it had to be this way,' I say to Pelopia as she claws helplessly at her throat, choking on her silence. 'But I will never let anyone take my future from me.'

27

'Stop fussing!'

'I am *not* fussing!'

Atalanta's and Meleager's voices tumble in from the adjoining room, their banter warming my new chamber. The queen's chamber.

'Yes, you are. You are like a child.'

'These fancy clothes make my balls chafe.'

'That was a mental image I really did *not* need, Meleager.'

'Don't act like you haven't thought about them before, huntress.'

'Yes, you're right . . . I have thought a lot about how *satisfying* it would be to jam my foot into them.'

'Orpheus, do you hear that? The huntress thinks about my balls!'

'You two are as bad as each other.' A melodic voice seeps through their playfulness.

'For the love of Zeus,' I hear Atalanta sighing. 'Oh, Medea.'

I stand in the doorway, shrouded by thick drapery. I cringe as my presence unleashes a palpable tension, leaching all humour and warmth from the air. I seem to have that effect on any room I walk into now. Is that what queens are meant to do? I do not know. Though I am not queen yet, not until Jason and I officially marry. He promises me that will be soon, but there are other pressing matters to attend to first.

It has only been three days since Pelias died, but it has all felt like a strange blur, as if I were detached from time itself, watching from a liminal place that nobody else can reach.

After the princesses had driven the dagger into Pelias' heart, I alerted the guards, who arrived on the scene with Jason. They were dumbfounded by the sight of the silenced, bloodied girls hunched over their father's corpse, Pelopia still gripping the dagger. Jason wasted no time taking control of the situation, barking out swift, firm instructions, his voice strong and commanding. The voice of a king. The guards were so bemused they seemed unable to do anything but obey his command, whether they thought it right or not. But blind obedience is second nature to them; they answer to authority and Jason wields his without hesitation.

Jason has claimed it was the Gods who drove the princesses mad, as punishment for Pelias not honouring his oath and giving him the throne. It is a plausible lie – the Gods are often prone to such cruel acts – though I do not yet know if the people believe it.

Over the past few days Jason has held funeral games in honour of his uncle. He said the atmosphere in Iolcus was sombre, and he hoped the games might lift the people's spirits and ease his transition into power. Unsurprisingly, the Argonauts – those who remained here – have dominated the competition. Even Atalanta was allowed to compete, winning a wrestling match. So I am told . . . I have not been feeling well enough to attend.

It was a blessing, really, for I wanted to be left alone.

'Hello.' I nod to them, taking a moment to register their appearances.

I have never seen them in formal dress. Orpheus is wrapped in swathes of deep green that flow from one shoulder and ripple down his body. The musician suits the lavish design, whereas Meleager beside him looks almost comical, his giant, muscular frame practically ripping out of his crimson robes.

'I was . . . having difficulty with the buckle,' I say, motioning to the brooch at my right shoulder.

'Here, let me help.' Atalanta approaches me, her expression guarded.

Her robes are golden, like watery sunlight, and though I know she is uncomfortable in them, she looks like a floating goddess. Her hands close over mine as she helps with the clasp; her skin is warm and smells earthy, rich, like a thriving forest. Her auburn hair is loose, and it is the first time I have ever seen it not tied back in fierce plaits. I take a moment to admire the coppery coils spilling around her shoulders.

She looks worthy of being a queen.

'Are you feeling better?' she asks.

I nod as she secures the brooch. 'You look . . . beautiful.'

'I feel foolish,' she confides. 'I do not know how you wear these gowns all the time . . . There's so much . . . *material*. What happens if you want to run? To fight?' Her words are amicable, but I notice she is having difficulty meeting my eyes.

'There will be no fighting today,' Orpheus chides gently. 'We need to be on our best behaviour for Jason's address to his people.'

'All hail the new king,' she murmurs, her lips twitching into a grimace. 'There you go.'

She steps back and I glance down at my robe, a deep crushed purple with gold detailing. It reminds me of a gown my mother would wear.

'Meleager, what in Gaia's name are you doing?' Orpheus groans.

Atalanta and I turn to see Meleager ripping the top of his robes and tying them around his waist, baring his broad torso. My eyes cannot help but slip over his sculpted body, marking his strong chest dusted with dark curls and his tightly carved stomach muscles. Beside

274

me, it seems Atalanta is taking note, too. I watch her throat bob as she quickly averts her eyes.

'There. Much better,' he grins.

'Are you not a prince, Meleager? Should you not be used to this attire?' Orpheus rolls his eyes, though there is humour there, too. Even when he is pretending to be annoyed, his voice sounds as beautiful as any melody.

'Why do you think I took any chance I could to get away from my princely duties?' Meleager smirks, placing his hands on his hips.

'I think it suits you,' I offer.

Meleager's eyes touch mine, but there is none of the usual mischievous warmth in them.

'Thank you,' he says, the words heavy and awkward.

Meleager thinks me a monster now. Not because of Pelias' death; he and all the other Argonauts hated the king for not being true to his word. It is because of whom I forced to wield the weapon, whose innocent hands I covered in blood.

Jason once told me Meleager has many sisters whom he utterly adores, so I suppose his resentment makes sense. But it hurts more than it should, to feel this coldness from him. I did not realize before how much I cherished Meleager's friendliness. Now, he can barely look at me.

'Is it true?' he blurts, as if he cannot hold the question in any longer. I feel Atalanta and Orpheus stiffening. 'That Pelias' daughters are being kept in the palace cells? The same ones Jason's family were held in.'

'They killed the king; their imprisonment is mandatory until Jason decides what to do with them.' My voice is steady.

Meleager's face hardens and he looks momentarily lost for words, perhaps for the first time in his life. Then he finally says, 'The king was dying. Could you not have waited a few months, weeks even, to get what you wanted? Were you so desperate to become queen?'

He thinks I did this for *me*, so that *I* could become queen?

'You know nothing of what I want,' I say, my voice deathly quiet.

A silence stretches dangerously thin around us as I feel a tendril of violence unfurling in my soul. The Prince of Calydon may be strong, but his might is nothing against the kind of power I can wield.

He could break my body, but I'd break his mind first.

'We should depart. We do not want to keep the new king waiting,' Orpheus interjects, his voice severing the bloody desire inside me.

I turn away from Meleager, an acidic shame pooling in my stomach.

'You go.' Atalanta waves them off. 'I will follow shortly.'

Meleager strides furiously from the room. Behind him, Orpheus trails like a calming shadow, his eyes lingering on me. There is a sadness cradled in his gaze, tinged with a slight concern. When he looks at me, it feels as if he were staring at a caged beast, one he pities but would never dare release himself. He sighs as he disappears after Meleager.

Once they are gone, I feel the weight of Atalanta's full attention on me. We have not been alone since Pelias' death.

I move across the room, my gown whispering along the stone floors. This room feels suffocating, all the gilded furniture and garishly painted decor. What I would give to be outside, amongst nature, feeling the magic that breathes from Gaia's lungs ... Earth magic. It feels so much cleaner, so much purer than what I can feel pulsing through me now.

'Do not take Meleager's words to heart,' Atalanta says gently.

'I will not.' I shrug as I walk over to where Jason has laid out jewellery for me. The pieces glitter like fallen stars scattered across the table. I pick one at random and turn it over in my hands. It is shaped like a flower, with large, fat jewels fanning out, forming each petal.

'He has been in a foul mood all morning,' Atalanta continues. 'He received word from his father about a giant boar raising havoc in his homeland.'

'A boar?'

'A punishment sent from Artemis, so they say . . . A few of us are going with Meleager to hunt it.' She walks over to stand beside me, picking up one of the jewels and staring at it with disgust. 'Of course, Jason is not. He is *far* too busy with his own interests.'

'It is a delicate time for Iolcus,' I say. 'Jason needs to be here, with his people.'

She tosses the jewel down as if it were any ordinary rock. 'We leave tomorrow.'

'Tomorrow?' The word catches in my throat, my fingers fumbling over the glittering rings. Something heavy sinks in my stomach, but my face remains impassive.

She'll be rid of you as soon as she gets the chance.

Telamon was right; of course he was. Atalanta's kindness towards me has only ever stemmed from her duty to Jason. She is indebted to him; she told me so herself.

I try to ignore the heavy disappointment aching in my chest as I fidget with a golden bracelet, my fingers clumsy under the weight of Atalanta's scrutiny.

'So, Jason is announcing the wedding today,' she says to fill the silence. 'Why now, I wonder, after he has kept you locked away for the past three days . . .'

'He has not kept me locked away,' I retort. 'We both decided the news should be announced after Pelias' funeral.'

'Like you both decided to kill him?' The question is so direct, so brazen, it causes my thoughts to stumble and falter. For a moment, all I can do is stare at her.

Nobody has dared utter such an accusation. Not even Jason and I have discussed what I did. I tried to on the night of Pelias' death, but Jason simply replied, 'The princesses killed the king. There is nothing more to say.'

We have not spoken of it since.

'I do not know what you mean,' I finally manage.

'Yes, you do.'

I set the bracelet down with too much force, the *snap* of its impact betraying my composure.

'The king was killed by his daughters,' I reply, smoothing my voice into bored indifference.

'You do not expect me to believe that, do you?'

'Believe what you wish.' I shrug. 'I do not care.'

I reach for another bracelet, but Atalanta's hand shoots out and grabs my wrist, wrenching me around so I am forced to look at her. I hold her stern gaze, those grey, stormy eyes sifting through her thoughts. I hate the judgement burning within them; the same judgement I saw in Meleager's glare, in Circe's . . .

Before I can stop myself, I hear myself whispering, 'We did what we had to.'

'Like when Jason made you kill your brother?' Her words are like talons scraping over my insides, making my chest constrict.

'Jason did not *make* me do anything.' I pull my wrist free from her grasp.

'I saw him place the dagger in your hand, Medea,' she says, her voice quiet yet fierce. 'Jason was going to let Apsyrtus take you. He forced you to decide between your life and your brother's. Do you even realize how cruel that was?'

I shake my head. 'You do not understand.'

'Don't I?' She steps closer and we glare at one another for a long moment, our faces barely a breath away. That familiar anger begins to thrum in my veins once again. I open my mouth, but she cuts across me with a whisper. 'Come with me.'

Her words catch me off guard, rendering me silent.

Come with me. It is not a request; it is a plea.

'Tomorrow, when I leave for Calydon, come with me,' she clarifies, slower this time, firmer.

'Why?' is all I can think to ask.

'Because I can see what he is doing to you,' she says, the words puncturing something deep inside me. 'And I fear what will happen if you stay with him.'

I shake my head, pulling away from her. 'My loyalty is with Jason.'

'And are his loyalties with you?'

'*Do not,*' I hiss, the darkness swelling around us, extinguishing nearly all the light from the room so that only Atalanta's glowing eyes remain. 'Do not speak of him like that.'

I could destroy her with a single thought.

She would not stand a chance against me.

'Do you not see?' Atalanta motions to the darkness writhing around us like a living, breathing beast. 'He brings out the worst in you, Medea . . . and he knows it, he *encourages* it.'

'No. You are wrong. Jason sees me for who I am. He sees my worth, my *power*.'

'He sees you as a weapon.' Atalanta remains calm, her voice infuriatingly steady. 'He does not deserve you, Medea. He never has. He will—'

'*Stop*. Do *not* speak ill of him.' My power pulses outwards, rippling over her skin. It is a warning. An unspoken promise of violence.

Atalanta ignores it, stepping towards me again. 'Or what, Medea? Will you hurt me? *Kill* me? Is that really who you are? Is that who Jason has made you become—'

The darkness lashes outwards, closing around Atalanta's throat, silencing her poisonous words as it did with Pelias' daughters.

'I will never let *anyone* take Jason away from me,' I vow as I watch her choking on my power. I can see the veins in her neck straining as she fights for words, for breath.

Raw fear fills her eyes; the sight of it spears through my fury, shattering it instantly.

I release Atalanta and watch her stagger towards the table, bracing her hands against it. She bows her head as she composes herself, shoulders heaving with the motion of her unsteady breaths.

Guilt swells in the hollow spaces my rage has left.

'Atalanta, I—'

She turns sharply, her eyes heavy and cold. They are no longer the eyes of a friend.

My words wither beneath her glare, and I can do nothing but watch as Atalanta stalks towards the door. At the threshold she stops herself, hands flexing and tightening into fists at her side.

She does not turn as she says, 'One day you will see him for what he is, Medea. I just pray it is not too late.'

28

I stare out at the people of Iolcus.

And they stare back.

A sea of faces, each distinct, and yet there is a thread of sadness woven between them, tainting each with the same grey sombreness.

The change in the crowd is jarring. All that joy and excitement that greeted us mere days ago has been leached from their faces, crushed beneath the weight of their sorrow. What remains now is the bitter residue of their grief, tinged by something a little sharper.

They are still mourning their beloved king. Had Jason known Pelias was adored so? If he is troubled by the collective sombreness, he does not show it.

'My people, I feel your pain.' Jason's voice carries easily through the crowd, rich and warm like a comforting embrace. 'I, too, am deeply saddened by my uncle's tragic death.'

We stand on a raised dais before the crowd. Behind me, I can feel the shadow of the palace pressing heavily upon my shoulders.

Jason is looking resplendent in his finery, the Golden Fleece fixed proudly around his shoulders, setting him ablaze. I don't know how he managed to get all of Pelias' blood out of it. I keep staring at those tight curls, expecting to catch an accusatory crimson droplet.

'Pelias was a good man, a beloved father and king,' Jason continues, his voice so strong, so sure. How easily these lies roll off his tongue.

'As you all know, Pelias wanted me to prove my worthiness as his heir, as any diligent king would. And so I took the greatest crew in history to reclaim the Golden Fleece from the barbaric lands of Colchis.'

Barbaric. The word scrapes over my skin. I glance at Jason. His eyes are so bright and clear; he is always so alive when he is in front of an audience.

He runs a hand through the glimmering curls of the fleece as he continues, 'I succeeded in my task and Pelias pronounced me his rightful heir. And so now I stand before you, my dear people, as your new king. I assure you I shall follow in my uncle's footsteps and be a ruler worthy of this great land.'

There is a ripple of murmurs and a smattering of weak applause. A subdued response. I know this is not what Jason expected, but he hides his disappointment with one of his dazzling smiles. My own smile feels stiff around my lips as my gaze drifts over those sombre, guarded faces. Their eyes touch mine – cold, judging – and I realize they are not looking at Jason at all . . .

They are staring at me. All of them.

Noticing this, Jason turns to me with his hand out, palm upright. 'Allow me to introduce you to this beautiful, incredible, peerless woman,' he says, and I feel a warmth spread through me as I take his hand, my tension burning away as I look into his loving face. He guides me forwards as he announces, 'I introduce to you my future wife and your queen.'

'*Witch!*' A voice rips through the crowd.

I glance at Jason, whose smile is unfaltering. My eyes then dart to where Atalanta, Meleager and Orpheus stand at the fringe of the crowd. They are scanning the audience with cautious focus. Beside them, the palace guards do the same, trying to locate the source of the outburst. But the crowd has fallen still.

'We shall be married the day after tomorrow,' Jason continues, the joy in his voice now sounding a little more forced. 'I wish for all of Iolcus to join in the festivities, for this is indeed a time for celebration and—'

'Where are the princesses?' The question pierces Jason's address, momentarily silencing him.

He clears his throat and replies, 'My cousins are being dealt with for their crime.'

'Lies! He lies!' A new voice carves through the crowd, slitting open the tension and spilling the collective rage into the air.

'She did it!'

'Betrayer!'

'It was her!'

'The witch!'

'Killer!'

'Murderer!'

The crowd swells, fuelled by the indignation these words ignite inside them. They begin to push and shove, churning like a furious sea. Jason tries to speak, but their vehement jeers and boos drown him out.

As I stare across their hateful faces, Argus' words whisper in my mind: *Your people will never accept a witch as their queen ...*

I notice Jason's hand has gone limp in mine. I glance at him, watching the bemusement hang from his handsome features. He is utterly stunned, as if he had never once considered this could happen, as if he only ever expected his people to love me as he did.

Their heckling hits me like physical blows. *Witch, murderer, barbarian, bitch, traitor, whore ... She did it, she did it, she did it ...* Each word cuts me, rattling my very bones. My mind echoes their taunts, so loud I cannot think, cannot focus.

'Please, my good people, listen to me—' Jason's futile words are gobbled up by their jeers, which have grown louder now the guards have stepped in. They push the crowd away from the dais, but their forcefulness only feeds into the people's rage.

My skin feels cold and damp, my mouth dry. I glance to Jason, my lifeline, but something in his demeanour has changed. Those beautiful blue eyes have gone distant, as a realization settles across his face, hardening his features. He stares at me, but there is none of his usual warmth or love in his gaze. It is as if all those hateful words have stripped me bare and Jason is now seeing me for what I truly am, and he does not like who stands before him.

I open my mouth to say something when a voice slices through the mayhem, *'JASON!'*

The crowd falls eerily quiet. The crush of bodies peels obediently backwards, bowing their heads as a figure walks towards us. He is tall and narrow and unnervingly familiar.

Pelias?

How can it be? The dead king risen from the grave, striding towards us with a new-found youth injected into him, as if the spell I pretended to cast had manifested itself into reality.

'Acastus.' Jason nods his head in greeting.

'Jason.' He bites out his name like a curse.

'Hello, cousin.' Jason's voice is calm and collected, yet I can sense the razor-sharp edge to his words. 'I did not expect you to return so quickly. I had heard word you were travelling distant lands. I am sorry you missed your father's funeral.'

Acastus stops before the dais. He is so much like his father it is unnerving. 'Save your poisonous civility, cousin. You fooled my father into believing he could trust you, but you shall not fool me.'

Before us, the silenced crowd watches the exchange with wide, hungry eyes. Even the guards have edged away, looking torn as they glance between Jason and Acastus.

'You are upset; I can understand that. It is difficult to lose a loved one.' Jason nods gravely. I notice he has shifted his stance, so he stands a little taller, puffing his chest out. 'Your sisters—'

'My sisters are innocent,' Acastus snarls through gritted teeth. 'They would never harm a single hair on my father's head; all of Iolcus knows that. Just as they know *she* is the one to blame.' He jabs a finger at me as he says this, and the crowd lets out a cry of agreement. Jason opens his mouth to counter, but Acastus continues, 'The witch of Colchis who betrayed her family and *butchered* her own brother to ensure her escape. We have all heard of her evil powers, conjuring creatures of the Underworld to do her foul bidding.'

'You are mistaken.' I hear a slight crack in Jason's voice as the crowd eats his words alive, their jeers echoing Acastus' sentiment.

'My father's blood is on *her* hands. *She* is to blame. You are either as depraved as she is, Jason, or you are under one of her evil spells.'

The fury of the crowd seeps into me, their hatred tugging on that connection to the Underworld, pulling it so taut it feels as if it might actually snap. I feel the death spirits hissing as they crawl up that cord, feeding off the crowd's fear and anger and hate, so much hate . . . Reams and reams of it . . . It swells inside me until I can barely contain it any more . . .

Let us out, it purrs, *let us show them what you really are . . .*

Through the chaos I hear Acastus shouting, 'So, which is it, Jason? Tell us. Are you really to stand beside this soulless monster?'

'*Enough!*' The word explodes from me, a blast of power pulsing outwards.

Their fury has flooded into me and now I unleash it back upon them, allowing the darkness to spill from my soul in great curling wafts. It blankets the sky, swallowing the city.

The crowd is silent. Terrified.

'Do you see?' Acastus bellows, though a shiver of fear betrays his voice. 'Do you see the magic she wields? She is a demon from the depths of Tartarus.'

'*Silence.*' I step forwards, a tendril of darkness spearing Acastus, closing around his throat, strangling those hateful words.

He scrabbles at the spirit's invisible claws sinking into his neck. Around him, the crowd has begun to retreat, terrified of the shadows pressing in around them.

I watch Acastus struggle for breath, watch the panic set into his eyes.

'Medea, *stop*!' Jason grabs my shoulders, forcing me to look at him. The motion rips my focus from Acastus, dropping my hold so he crumples to his knees, gasping for breath. 'Enough.'

'I am doing this for you,' I say, confused by the anger burning across Jason's face.

'You are making everything *worse.*'

'I will make them obey you,' I tell him. 'I will make them bow, I will—'

'Medea, *stop it.*' He shakes me, fingers digging into my skin. 'I want my people to love me, not fear me. Can you not understand that?'

'But . . . they will never love me.'

Jason lowers his gaze, his shoulders drooping as the realization drags him downwards.

He knows I am right.

'Jason, let me—'

'Go inside, Medea,' he orders.

'But—'

'Inside. *Now.*' His voice sounds unrecognizable, speaking to me like a master might bark at his slave. 'Do not make me ask again.'

I stare at him for a long moment, feeling crushed beneath the weight of that hideous disappointment. Struggling for breath, I glance back towards the crowd, to those cowering, frightened people. *Innocent* people I had intended to harm.

My eyes focus on Atalanta. She is standing near Acastus with her bow drawn, though her arrow is not aimed at him but ... *me.* The threat, the enemy.

What am I doing?

What have I done?

Fastening my control on the darkness, I force it to retreat, wrenching that bond to the Underworld. I use every ounce of my strength to will it to respond to my command.

You must leave ...

You must stop this ...

It feels as if I am ripping a piece of myself apart. The strain of it makes my head feel light, my thoughts loose and scrambled, left to tumble wildly around inside my skull ... but through the chaos, there is something nagging inside me, something demanding to be known. I try to focus, but my head is throbbing, causing sparks to bloom across my vision.

'Medea.' My name is a warning in Jason's mouth. I hate the sound of it.

I try to step towards him but stagger slightly. Instinctively, I touch a hand to my stomach. As soon as my fingers make contact, a vision cuts through my confusion.

A vision of the future ...

Our future ...

I can see it ... see us ... see *him.*

And he is just as I imagined he would be.

'Medea, stop.' Jason is gripping my arms now, though I am only faintly aware of his touch. 'Stop it, *now*.'

'I ...'

The vision burns before my eyes then vanishes, like a flame being blown out. The darkness envelops me before I hit the floor.

I rouse to crackling flames and warm sheets.

My mind feels heavy in my skull, my thoughts clogged. I shift upwards in bed, realizing I am in one of the palace guest chambers. It is night outside and a figure sits beside my bed, his golden head resting in his hands. *Jason*. He looks dejected, as if the gathered shadows are weighing down his whole body.

Thoughts tug at the seams of my memories, unravelling the haziness knotting in my mind. Closing my eyes, I can see the events unfold – the crowd jeering, Acastus taunting, my darkness unleashing itself on all those innocent people. Shame fills me, fresh and raw.

I touch a hand to my stomach, feeling that vision stir again, along with something else.

'Medea?' Jason breathes, and I realize he is now staring at me. His eyes are heavy, face drawn. He looks like a ghost of himself.

'What happened?'

'You collapsed,' he says, voice thick. 'I had the doctor check you over. He said you are fine.'

'I did not mean to worry you.'

'I know,' he says, though his eyes remain bleak. He lowers his gaze.

'What happened ... after?' He seems reluctant to speak. 'Jason?'

His voice is just a whisper. 'Acastus challenged me to a duel for the throne.'

'A duel?'

'I lost.'

I sit upright at his words, my mind sharpening through the haze of my slumber.

How could Jason lose? He never loses . . .

'Are you hurt?'

'The people are with him.' Jason continues as if I had not spoken. His voice is knotted with emotion, his hand tightening around mine. 'They blame us for Pelias' death.'

I shake my head. 'But you have claimed the throne; you are king now. Surely he is too late?'

'Do you not hear me, Medea?' he snaps. There is a raw, painful edge to his anger. 'I lost. I *failed*. I shamed myself in front of all of Iolcus.'

He pulls away from me, rests his elbows on his knees and cradles his head in his hands. Along the wall, the shadow of his strong, curved back flickers like a beast transforming.

'Jason . . .'

'Everything has been for this throne. *Everything*. It is all I have wanted, all I lived for since I was a child. It is what my mother died for.' His fingers curl to claws against his face as he shakes his head violently. 'I was so close.' He lifts his head up, his eyes glistening with tears.

I have never seen him cry before. The sight makes my heart ache.

'But Pelias named you as his heir; you have the fleece.'

'Do you not understand?' His voice hardens as he stands up and begins pacing. 'Even if I had won the duel, the people do not *want* me. They think me guilty. They think I am a traitor because of what *you* did to Pelias, to his *darling* daughters . . . and your outburst earlier did not help the matter. What in Hades' name were you thinking, Medea? Acting out like that, nearly killing Acastus in front of his own people. Are you mad?'

I slip out of bed and approach him, reaching out a hand to steady his relentless pacing.

'I did what you asked me to do,' I say carefully.

'I never asked you to do that.' He shakes his head at me as he continues stalking back and forth across the room.

'But . . . you asked me to kill Pelias. It was your—'

'*I did not ask you to kill him.*' His words slice across mine, strangled with rage. 'I asked you to make me king.'

I stare at Jason, feeling the excuses wither inside me under the weight of his anger.

'It is my fault,' he continues. 'I expected too much from you. I should have known better. I should never have got you involved.'

His words are like a blow to the gut, so visceral it makes me wince.

'Is there nothing we can do?' I whisper, wrapping my arms around myself. 'What of the Argonauts? Atalanta, Meleager . . .'

'They have already left for Calydon.'

They have *left*. How long have I been unconscious? I feel a twinge of pain at the thought of Atalanta leaving without me, but I know such a thought is foolish. I would never have gone with her. Nor would she have wanted me to, not any more.

'What if we—'

'It is too late.' Jason turns his face to the fire, the shadows contorting his features. 'Acastus called the duel in the name of the Gods. It would be impious not to accept his victory . . . It is over, Medea. The throne rightfully belongs to him now.'

'But we can take it back. Use me, Jason, use my power, I could—'

'*Enough*, Medea. You cannot solve all your problems with bloodshed.' The accusation stings. I watch silently as Jason braces his hand against the wall beside him, bowing his head. 'Acastus has exiled us. We must leave Iolcus tomorrow or face death.'

'Exiled?'

'It is over. All of it.'

All of it. The words terrify me. He could not mean *us*, could he?

'Jason . . .' I step towards him, reaching out a tentative hand.

'I am a failure,' he mutters to himself, silent tears dripping down his cheeks. I have never seen him look so broken. 'What is the point of living any more?'

'Jason, do not speak like that.' I place my hand on his arm. 'Please.'

'You do not understand.' He drags his hands over his face, eyes red and glistening. 'How could you? You willingly betrayed your own people. Sometimes I think you enjoy it, being hated. That is why you encourage it.'

I swallow down the pain of his words as I whisper, 'That is not fair.'

'Do you even realize the consequences of your little tantrum? You turned them all against me. You *ruined* everything.'

My patience snaps like a tether, letting my words fly at him. 'If I am truly so terrible, then why are you still here? You could have left with the others; you had your perfect chance to abandon me. Yet here you stand, Jason. *Why?* Or did you remain merely to tell me how much you despise me?'

Jason is still for a long moment, and I watch the anger shatter across his face, replaced by a grief so sharp I can feel it piercing through my chest.

'Despise you? How can you say that?' he whispers, voice cracking. 'You are all I have left, Medea.'

To my shock, Jason falls to his knees before me, gripping my hands. The tears come thick and fast as the next words burst from him. 'Medea, please do not look at me like that. *Please*, I beg of you. I cannot lose you also. You are all I have.'

'No, Jason, not all,' I whisper, taking his hand and pressing it against my stomach. My voice is strained with emotion as I continue, 'You asked what the point is, Jason? This. This is the point.'

'What?' He stares up at me with wet, sparkling eyes.

'Your child.'

'H-how . . . how do you know?'

'I had a vision, before I collapsed. I saw him . . . our son . . .' I reach down carefully and tuck a curl behind his ear. 'He is beautiful, Jason. Just like you.'

'A son? Are you certain?' The words are so delicate, so raw, it makes my heart ache.

'I am.' I nod as he presses his forehead against my stomach. 'This is proof it is not over; a gift from the Gods. One dream has ended, but another has just begun . . . This can be a new beginning, *our* new beginning.'

'My son.'

'Your son.' I smile as the vision glows in my mind.

'He . . . he will be the child of an exile,' Jason says, rising to his feet.

'He will be the child of a great man.' I take his face between my palms, forcing him to look me in the eyes. 'You are the man who led the Argonauts to victory, who battled across the world and claimed the Golden Fleece, who defeated the Colchian armies.'

'What does any of that mean if I cannot be king?' His face drops in my hands. 'It was all for nothing.'

'It was *not* for nothing. You have built a legacy, Jason, one that will live on for generations, far beyond that of Acastus or Pelias. You will be remembered by history; they will not.'

'Yet he sits on the throne and not I.'

'You can still sit on a throne, Jason. Iolcus is not the only land you could rule.' Something in Jason's eyes seems to spark at that and so

I stoke those flames further. 'When I asked you what you wanted, do you remember what you said? You said you wished to be king of a great land. That is still possible. Iolcus is not your only option.'

He leans forwards to press his forehead against mine, resting his hand over my stomach. I can feel the heat of his tears against my face as I stare up into his shimmering eyes.

'You really believe I can still be a king?' he whispers as I nod.

'If that is what you wish.'

'I could rule a greater kingdom than Iolcus,' he muses to himself. 'I could plant my father's legacy in a new land and make our son the heir to a far mightier kingdom.'

'You could.'

'But where could we go?' He pulls away, a smile warming his lips, though his eyes remain heavy. 'Where could we conquer?'

'Anywhere. Anywhere you wish. It does not matter. So long as we are together ... you and I ... and our son. That is all that matters. *This* is all that matters.'

He kisses me gently, whispering against my lips, 'Our son.'

'Our son,' I murmur back.

'I will be a king, Medea,' he vows to me.

'You will. But, Jason ...' I pull back for a moment, studying his face. 'I will do everything in my power to give you what you want but ... I think ... I should not use my magic whilst I am with child ... I do not think it is safe.'

Somewhere inside me, I hear the death spirits roaring with frustration, agitating the magic in my veins. I must close them off, drive them out. It won't be easy, this I know, but I will do whatever it takes for him. For my son.

'I understand.' Jason takes my hands. 'And I forgive you, Medea. For all that you did.'

I frown at his words. I do not recall apologizing, nor asking for Jason's forgiveness.

'I love you,' he says, before these thoughts can fully take shape.

I allow Jason to pull me into him, locking his arms around my waist. As he holds me, I feel my vision glow before us, so bright and beautiful, outshining the darkness shadowing our path.

'I love you, too,' I whisper back.

TEN YEARS
LATER

29

I am watched constantly here.

Murmurs echo every step; whispers punctuate each breath. I can hear them in the walls, in the shadows. Everywhere those judging eyes follow me.

Ten winters and I have never been left in peace.

They are watching me now, the gaggle of women gathered outside our home. It seems Corinthian wives have nothing better to do than waste their days gossiping. Instead of weaving at their looms, they weave with their mouths, spinning ridiculous stories laced with ugly threads of hate and fear. They pretend they are going about their daily chores, but really they just come here to watch, plotting new strands to knot into their tapestry of lies. Odious little stories of the foreigner who lives amongst them. The witch. The murderess.

I am to blame for all their suffering.

Ever since we settled in Corinth, I have been deemed the catalyst for the city's misfortunes. If a child falls ill, or crops die, or a sickness spreads – I am to blame. They spin these senseless lies like spider's webs that coat the city, delicate in their substance but managing to knot into every dark corner, clogging the very air until every citizen is choking on their lies, swallowing it down as fact.

It does not matter that I have not practised my magic in a long while; too long. For in their eyes, I will only ever be their villain.

297

I tried to speak with them once. I simply wanted to talk some sense into them, yet somehow someone ended up screaming. I can't remember who. It could have been me. Either way, Jason advises me not to leave the house any more.

So, I stand guard instead.

I watch those women watching me, eyes upon eyes upon eyes. I could stand here for hours, draped in the shadow of the entry pillars to our home. I would stand here for days if I had to, a tireless look-out. After all, it is my duty to protect my house, my home, my sons.

Because that is what a good mother would do.

I am here now, in the day's dying light, eyeing the women whilst they swell and shift like a bubbling current outside our home.

Within their gossiping I can hear other voices, too, though they are quieter than they once were, but always there, always waiting . . .

For so long I have tried to sever my connection to that darkness below, but the bond endures.

A scream pulls me from my focused duty.

At first, I am not sure if the screaming is in my head, but then I hear the slapping of sandals against floor and see Pheres, my young-est, stumbling through the hallway. He runs past me and throws himself into the slave Myrto's arms. I hear the sobs rattle from his small chest as he buries his red face into her skirts.

I tell myself it does not hurt, to see him seek comfort from another.

'Now, what's all this about, then, little master?' Myrto asks him in her soothing voice.

There is an effortless warmth about Myrto. I find it unnerving how easily this lovingness comes to someone who has spent her whole life being owned as a piece of property. Should she not be filled with bitterness? How can someone treated so poorly be so full of kind-ness? Perhaps it is an act. But if so, my sons are surely fooled by it.

They adore Myrto and it is not hard to see why. She is the sort of person who was meant to be a mother, honey-sweet and soft around her edges. Chalciope would adore her.

Unsurprisingly, I do not think Myrto likes me very much. Or perhaps I am projecting my own thoughts on to her; these days I find it hard to distinguish between the reality before me and the one that lives inside my head, mutating in the darkness I am forced to swallow down like poison.

What happens when death spirits have nowhere to go, have nothing to satiate them?

Perhaps they start feeding off their prison walls.

'Come now, little master, what is it?' Myrto coos to Pheres.

'Why are you crying?' I ask as I approach.

Against Myrto's gentle lilt, my voice sounds like jagged flint, a spark away from fire.

Pheres looks up at me with his sparkling blue eyes, the eyes of his father. They are swollen with tears as he sniffs, his plump cheeks red from crying. I want to hold him, to comfort him with soft words and warm touches. But I do not.

It is better this way – I know that.

Even so, I find myself thinking of my own mother and all the times she turned from me . . . But this isn't like that; *I* am not like that. For her detachment was a punishment, forged by hate and ignorance. Whereas this distance I keep from my sons is a necessary *sacrifice*. I am doing what any good mother would do.

I am keeping my children safe.

'Pheres?' I prompt again.

Instead of replying, he points to the courtyard before his face disappears again into Myrto's drab skirts.

I walk out into the small, open-air space at the centre of our home.

It is harvest season once again, a time when shadows stretch long like yawns and Nyx grows hungry, emerging earlier and earlier to feast off Helios' light. A delicate chill sharpens the air, making the world feel fresh and awake.

I find Pheres' older brother hunched over something, his narrow back facing me and golden curls spilling over his shoulders.

'Mermerus?' I call to him, but he does not look up. 'Why is your brother upset?'

As I draw closer, I see a large dead rat lying belly up on the ground, its little scrawny feet twisted inwards. In his hand Mermerus holds a stick, which he uses to prise open the gash across the rat's belly. The creature's organs spill out from the wound, a feast for the flies and maggots.

I stare at the lesion for a long moment, the gash curving upwards like a smile. The organs, slippery and glistening in the light, make me think of my brother ... Of how his throat felt as my knife sank into him. The feel of his life leaving his body.

The spirits like those memories; I can feel that starved darkness grinning. Yet somewhere beneath it there is a dull ache, stiff and painful, like a fractured bone that never properly healed.

Behind me, I hear Pheres scream again as Mermerus jams the stick in deeper.

'Why are you doing that?' I ask him.

'Because I want to see what's inside,' he replies, looking up at me.

His eyes are blue, like his father's. But whilst Jason's are the blue of a summer sky, Mermerus' are that of winter – icy and bright.

Those eyes have always unnerved me, even when he was a babe.

When I look at Mermerus I have always sensed something ancient lurking within him, something eerily familiar ... Sometimes it feels as if I am looking at my own reflection. But like a reflection atop water, I can feel him fracture and scatter whenever I try to reach for him, try to hold that likeness in my hand.

In truth, I believe Mermerus has hated me since birth. He refused to feed from my breast as a babe, as if he couldn't bear being close to me even then.

I watch him drive the stick in deeper, piercing those small organs.

'Mother!' Mermerus whines as I snatch the stick from him.

'Stop it.' My voice trembles with a quiet rage that seems to startle him. I am so quick to anger these days, the spirits so eager to stoke those flames. It is exhausting. 'You are scaring your brother.'

'It is not my fault he is a coward,' he sniffs.

I am about to respond when I hear a distant cackle from the Corinthian women outside. The sound grates across my every nerve, causing my hand to tighten around the stick like the hilt of a sword. After so long, I should have become immune to their foolishness, but it has only worsened.

I have thought time and time again about releasing the death spirits on their hateful little minds . . . It would silence all the voices, all the whispering, all the laughter . . .

But a good mother does not go around obliterating the delicate minds of her neighbours, does she?

'Mistress, what should I do about the mess?' Myrto asks me as I return to our entryway.

I ignore her and press myself into the shadow of the pillars, watching those women as they laugh and scheme and lie. I imagine transforming them into a flock of squawking hens and the thought almost makes me laugh.

Squinting, I watch as the women begin to peel backwards, allowing a broad figure to pass. The women's hostility melts like ice beneath the baking sun. They coo and croon as Jason saunters through them, flashing that smooth, confident smile he gives away so freely.

The smile I used to think was reserved only for me.

These days Jason dresses for a different kind of battle, one of politics and power. This fight requires him to wear richly dyed robes that whisper luxury and wealth. An illusion we are trying to cling to with the edges of our worn fingernails.

Even without the weapons and the armies, the battles he now faces still have monsters to slay. The elite members of Corinthian society are a deadly foe, backstabbing and avaricious. It has taken Jason many winters to be accepted into their fold, despite having the favour of their beloved King Creon.

From the heaviness in his eyes, I can tell today he has lost another fight.

I hold my breath as I watch him approach; his features that have chiselled with age, his body a little softer now he no longer spends his days on the battlefield, yet still undeniably strong. When I see him like this, walking towards me, gilded in sunlight, I remember the day I first saw him on the steps of Colchis. I had been so young then, so clueless of the world. Yet, in that moment, I had known that our fates were woven from the same thread. His future was mine and mine was his.

Would I have acted differently if I had known it would lead here? I smother the thought instantly, snapping its neck before it can take a single breath.

The women of Corinth ogle Jason. He is still deemed a valiant hero in their eyes – yet his victories were born from the same bloodshed that makes me a villain.

'Medea.' Jason's face hardens as he regards me. 'For Hera's sake, why are you just standing there? Have you prepared the house as I asked?'

He strides past me with a brush of cold air, leaving his smiles and warmth outside in the dirt. I loosen the breath I had been holding, turning to follow him inside.

'Those women are out there again,' I say, as I trail him into the courtyard. 'They are out there nearly every day.'

'Pheres, what happened?' He stoops to crouch before our son, who is still sobbing as Myrto clears away the remnants of the butchered rat.

'I made him cry,' Mermerus states.

Jason rises. 'Were you alone with them?'

'Does it matter if I was?' I counter, hating the unspoken accusation laced within his question.

He only sighs in response, his face gathering into a sullen look I have come to know so well.

'Mermerus killed a rat,' Pheres whimpers.

'I did not kill it.' Mermerus rolls his eyes. 'It was already dead.'

'Is that so?' Jason's eyebrows knit together as he surveys the mess Myrto silently carries away.

'It upset Pheres because he is a coward,' Mermerus says with a coldness that seems so out of place for a child.

Perhaps it is the familiarity in his iciness that makes me snap, 'Do not speak of your brother like that.'

'Leave the boy alone; it is not his fault his brother is sensitive,' Jason dismisses me, patting Mermerus on the arm.

'He should be kinder to his brother.'

'Really, Medea?' Jason flashes me a look. 'You do not actually believe you are in any position to give sibling advice, do you?'

My face burns with a sudden blaze of shame. As Jason walks away, I become painfully aware of my sons staring at me, soaking in my red-stained cheeks.

'Go and play, boys. *Now*,' I instruct, before turning to follow their father. 'Jason, you cannot say such things in front of the children.'

'One of these days they will hear the rumours for themselves, Medea.' He shakes his head. 'Would you rather they hear them from a stranger or from us?'

'They are not ready to know yet.'

He does not respond but gives a dismissive shrug as he carries on walking. I fall into step beside him as Pheres trails behind, tugging on Jason's gown.

'Papa.'

'We would not have to worry about rumours if it weren't for those women,' I continue.

'Papa?'

'And?' The word is a frustrated sigh.

'They are always out there; they are always watching me, watching *us*.'

'Medea, I do not have time for this.'

'But—'

'*Papa!*'

'*Silence.*'

Pheres flinches at the severity in his father's tone as he snaps his head round. The tremble of his little body shivers through my mind, tugging at threads of buried memories. A flash of Chalciope's frightened eyes as we listened to our father's anger reverberating through the walls, accompanied by the sombre undercurrent of our mother's sobs.

'Do not speak to him like that,' I snap back.

Jason stares at me for a long moment. He looks bored by my anger, his eyes hooded and weary.

'Is Papa angry at me?' Pheres whimpers as Jason disappears down the hall.

'No.' I shake my head. 'He is just tired, that is all. Just very tired.'

Pheres stares up at me with wide, shining eyes. Jason's mood has rattled him. Chalciope flickers again in my mind like a stream of sunlight reaching through heavy clouds . . . If she were here, she would bundle him into her arms, smother him with the warmth and affection that always came so effortlessly to her. That is the kind of mother my sons want, the kind of mother they deserve.

But that supposed instinctive motherly affection has grown crooked inside me, like a plant that has been starved of light and water, left to grow gnarled and twisted. I know I love my sons, yet I find it hard to articulate that love into anything tangible for them to hold on to. I do not know what is wrong with me.

Perhaps I was never meant to be a mother.

In the shadows I sense Mermerus lurking, his face unreadable as he stares into the space where his father has just been.

'Go find Myrto and tell her to prepare you for bed,' I instruct, my hands frozen at my side. I try to ignore the disappointment in Pheres' eyes at my dismissal.

Mermerus walks over and gently takes his brother's hand. His eyes regard me, sharpening with an unspoken accusation. I try to ignore it. Push it down, suffocate it like all the other demons that lurk within me.

I have become something of an expert at this.

I find Jason in our entertaining quarters.

It is our most lavish room, though the ornate furniture and glittering adornments seem mocked by the near-constant emptiness of the space. The dishes are usually draped in a thin layer of dust, dulling the golden details we paid for so dearly. Yet today they gleam with the rare promise of good company.

I stand in the doorway for a moment, watching Jason assess the food laid out by our cook. He takes an olive and pops it into his mouth, chewing distractedly.

Over time, I have learnt that Jason's love is like the harvest seasons. It swings between days of feast and famine. Sometimes, his love fills me so deeply and completely I think I may burst. Far more often, I am left with nothing but a coldness that rattles through me, stealing across the empty plains where his love had grown rich and wild mere days before. There seems to be a skill to this treatment, an art form, like a jailer toying with his prisoner. Jason starves me on the edge of breaking, inching me so close to that brink ... and then, all at once, his love returns, overwhelming in its intensity, and somehow burning away all the doubts and anger that the loneliness has conjured.

Recently, Jason's days of famine have grown longer, colder, to the point where he will barely even look at me. I must be due a feast soon, for I can feel myself nearing that brink. I do not know what will happen if I tip over it. Jason has never let me. But sometimes, during quiet moments, I catch myself wondering what lies on the other side.

'What is it?' His voice is gruff as he catches me lurking in the doorway.

'I want to talk about the women outside.'

'Had we not finished this discussion?' Jason pinches the bridge of his nose – an indication of his exasperation, I have come to learn.

'They will *not* leave us alone, Jason,' I press, stepping closer. 'I have endured ten winters of this, of them always being out there, talking about us, whispering, spreading their lies.'

'What lies?' He whirls around, his tired eyes swallowing the light. 'That you betrayed your homeland? That you are a witch? A murderer? Where are the lies in that, Medea? Please, show me.'

'That is not fair.'

306

'Not fair.' He laughs at the sentiment, then covers his face with both hands, dragging his skin down as he expels a rush of air. 'Medea, please be reasonable. Tonight is incredibly important for me. I do not have time for this.'

'But—'

'*Medea.*' He slams a hand on to the table, causing the wood to shudder. I feel myself stiffen, the words dying in my throat. 'Please, just go and make yourself look presentable for our guests.'

As I stare at Jason, a heaviness settles inside me. I barely recognize him these days. That charming, brilliant prince has been swallowed up by this sullen, irritable stranger who now haunts our home.

A ghost of the man he was.

This is not how I pictured our life together, our marriage . . . It was supposed to be different; *we* were supposed to be different. Happy. I *saw* it.

But my vision only ever showed me a glimpse of the future, a sliver of happiness that has already passed. Was that all it was ever meant to be: a brief breath in the middle of a lifetime of . . . *this*?

As I silently turn to leave, I am certain I can hear the Corinthian women still laughing outside, causing my blood to simmer.

Violence breeds violence, Circe whispers in my mind like a promise.

30

I have not seen Jason this happy in years.

He sits on the reclining chair beside his guest, Aegeus, his face split into a smile that lights up the whole room. How I have missed it.

Aegeus is resplendent in his royal finery. Of the King of Athens, I expected little else. His robes are deep mauve with intricate detailing along the edges. At his right shoulder, the material is clasped by a brooch in the shape of an owl, shards of coloured glass making up the owl's feathered chest, whilst glittering emeralds are the eyes.

Aegeus is older, though his face still clings to the remnants of his handsome youth. His skin is bronzed and creased in the corners, his starlight-coloured hair swept back over his head like a flowing wave. His lips are wide, and when he smiles it reveals a slight scar over his top lip.

Jason was elated to learn Aegeus was visiting the King of Corinth and wanted an audience with us. It turns out the Athenian king was an admirer of the Argonauts. As for Jason, a man who is perpetually trying to gain his footing in Corinth's social hierarchy, what better ally is there to make than the king of one of the most powerful cities in Greece?

Sitting next to me is Aegeus' wife, Meta. She is distractingly beautiful: a soft, round face with gentle features and a full, sensuous mouth that works in tandem with her rich, earthy eyes. Her skin is dark, with chestnut hair that falls past her shoulders and swishes when she laughs.

It is not customary for women to join men for their socializing, nor is it for men to bring wives on their travels. But Aegeus, with his mischievous, burnt-cinnamon eyes, had insisted he has always enjoyed the company of women, as well as having 'something pretty to look at'. He had also disclosed to Jason his hopes of producing an heir soon, and that he did not want his travels to delay the couple's dedicated efforts.

I could tell Jason did not want me at dinner, but he obliged nonetheless, playing the gracious host – a role I know he has sorely missed.

Behind Jason, the Golden Fleece hangs on the wall. A rare appearance. These days, its glimmering coat seems more mocking than beautiful, a reminder of promises unfulfilled.

'Tell me more about Herakles,' Aegeus is saying around a mouthful of wine. 'Is he really as strong as they say he is?'

'Stronger.' Jason grins, loving every second he can relive of his famed voyage. But it is both a gift and a curse, his glorious past, for it burns so brightly that it has cast the rest of his life into shadow. Nothing will ever live up to that voyage, not for Jason. I believe he knows this, too, and it eats away at him. Though he would never admit it.

'And Meleager? What was the beloved Prince of Calydon really like?'

Jason's face darkens, as it always does whenever Meleager is mentioned. He offers a sombre smile as he says, 'Meleager was like a brother to me. I am sure he is now stirring up mischief in the Fields of Elysium.'

Meleager died not long after he left Iolcus.

When we heard the news, I found it hard to wrap my head around. Meleager had been so full of life, it seemed impossible that death could ever touch him.

But of course, no mortal can escape the inevitable.

After Meleager and his crew had slain the boar that was terrorizing Calydon, the prince had rewarded Atalanta with the beast's hide. Knowing his fondness for her, I do not find this difficult to believe. But Meleager's family did not approve of bestowing such a valiant gift on a woman and a battle soon broke out with his uncles. Meleager, unsurprisingly, defeated them all. It was his mother who killed him in the end, in an act of revenge for her brothers. Knowing the man that Meleager was, I believe he would have let her do it rather than raise a hand against his mother.

'And Atalanta?' Aegeus presses. 'I must admit, I was surprised you allowed a woman amongst your crew.'

'If you met her, you would understand,' Jason chuckles.

As I think of the huntress, I remember the betrayal in her eyes when I used my magic against her. My chest twinges at the memory.

I have only heard morsels from Jason about her movements beyond Calydon. Apparently, the huntress reunited with her birth father, the one who abandoned her as a babe. The man tried to utilize her fame to his advantage, wishing to marry her off. But Atalanta vowed only to marry a man who could beat her in a footrace. Last Jason heard, the huntress remains unwed.

'What tales you have, Jason,' Aegeus says, slapping a hand on his shoulder and drawing my attention back into the room. 'Now, you must tell me of Aeetes' dragon.'

My dragon.

'A dragon?' Meta gasps beside me.

'Yes, my lady.' Jason grins at her, and I can feel the charm oozing off him like the glow of the fleece behind him. Each as useless as the other.

Meta blushes under the insufferable weight of Jason's allure. I imagine I looked just the same when I was younger – clueless and dazzled, like a moth drawn to Jason's flame, burning its own wings amidst its drunken rapture.

'I pray to Zeus you never have to encounter such a beast, for they are fiercely foul-tempered,' Jason continues with a wink, prompting a laugh from Meta.

'So how did you slay the creature?' Aegeus presses.

'We did not slay him.' My words cut across the room, slitting open the easy, warm atmosphere. They are the first words I have spoken all night.

I know I should have remained quiet; speaking is not worth the potential headache of aggravating Jason. But the wine seems to have loosened my tongue.

'Then how did you overcome it?' Aegeus' eyes catch mine and I see the roguish spark within them, the vibrant youth to which he still clings.

'Medea charmed the beast,' Jason says. I flick my gaze to where he sits opposite me, his eyes glowing over the rim of his cup as he sips his wine.

'Is that so, Medea?' The king grins at me, though I only incline my head in response before draining my own cup. 'Fascinating. Tell me also, Jason, how were you untouched by the oxen's flames? I have tried to rack my brain on how you pulled that off.'

'That was Medea as well,' Jason says, his voice level, though I can see the irritation sharpening his smile.

'Well, well, quite the remarkable wife you have here.'

'Quite.' He nods, still holding my gaze across the room. I can feel the familiar, unspoken tension thickening in the air between us, stretching and pacing like a beast awoken from its brief nap.

Jason is annoyed; he hates it when I outshine the glory of his past. To him, I am not the princess who acquired the Golden Fleece for him and saved his life, but rather the witch who had him banished from Iolcus. To him, I am a disappointment, one that seems to have grown with time.

'You are marvellous, truly!' Meta reaches over and grabs my hand, pulling my focus away from Jason.

I stare at her slender fingers wrapped around mine, confused by the intimacy of her touch. It sparks old memories of my sister, ones I have tried hard to forget.

Meta seems to sense my stiffness as she clears her throat and withdraws her hand, folding it into her lap with a polite smile.

'So, Jason,' Aegeus says as he helps himself to another plate of food. 'Why did you choose to settle in Corinth?'

'I ask myself the same question every day.' Aegeus laughs politely at his response, but I watch as Jason's smile tightens. 'I was acquainted with the king here, Creon. I sent word to him that I was seeking asylum after my . . . exile.' The word is like a bad taste in his mouth. 'Creon was kind enough to accept me into his lands.'

'No doubt the people were thrilled to have the hero of the Argonauts amongst them.'

'"Thrilled" is not the word I would use.'

'The people were not welcoming?'

'They do not like having a witch amongst them,' Jason says, as he rises to refill Aegeus' wine.

'Thank you . . . But surely they can see the benefit of having a woman with your talents amongst their people?' Aegeus directs this question to me. If we were not in the company of our other halves, I would assume that spark in his eyes held another meaning.

'It seems Medea's reputation troubles them,' Jason says, filling Meta's cup next. 'And really, can you blame them? My wife does not have the . . . cleanest of pasts, as I am sure you know.'

I feel my body straighten at his words, as if a bolt of fire had cut through me.

'Could you not show them your talents, Medea – perhaps a little demonstration of what you have to offer?' Aegeus asks, seemingly oblivious to the tension in the room.

'I do not practise my magic any more,' I explain, as Jason moves to stand beside me.

The warmth of his body burns against my shoulders and neck as he leans over to refill my cup. It is the closest our skin has been in many moons, and I feel something deep and aching stir to life inside me.

Gods, I need that feast . . .

'Medea stopped practising magic whilst she was pregnant with our first son,' Jason explains, pulling away and causing that swell of desire to snap. 'Afterwards, we felt it best if she continued abstaining from her little tricks for a time.'

Little tricks.

'You see, nobody wants to associate themselves with a witch. Even a man married to one,' Jason continues, laughing as he settles back into his seat. 'Perhaps I should have known, considering I was exiled from my homeland for the same reason. But, then again, what was I to do? Medea was pregnant, after all, and I am an honourable man.'

My glare singes from my sockets.

'Were we not exiled because you lost in combat against your cousin?' I counter, my voice lethally calm. I turn my attention to Aegeus. 'I was unconscious at the time. It was, in fact, the only time Jason was left to face his foe alone. Quite the coincidence.'

Jason's face hardens. 'That is enough, Medea.'

'I apologize.' I nod, taking a slow sip of wine. 'It's been so long since I've had company, it seems I've forgotten how to conduct myself. I suppose that is what happens when you are kept shut away like a shameful little secret.'

'I think it is time the ladies retire,' Jason cuts across me. Aegeus nods and waves his hand to his wife, though his eyes remain on mine, that grin curling wider around his lips.

'Thank you for the dinner.' Meta bows her head. 'Medea, would you kindly show me to my chamber?'

'Do you trust your wife alone with a witch?' I ask Aegeus, taking satisfaction in Jason's silent outrage at my brazenness.

'Of course, my dear.' Aegeus nods as he runs a possessive hand over Meta's backside. 'You should know, Medea, I am not afraid of powerful women. In fact, I am *very* fond of them.'

There is no denying the shamelessly seductive curl of his words. I glance at Jason, who is glaring at us, though he swallows back whatever retort is knotting in his throat. Of course, he cannot say anything, Aegeus is a king, and what is Jason?

'Come,' I say to Meta. 'Let us leave the men to discuss.'

As I exit the room, I can feel Jason's eyes cutting into my skin. Admittedly, I enjoy the sensation of his attention on me, even if it is fuelled by hatred.

It is better than being ignored.

'You have two sons?' Meta asks me as we walk to the guest chamber.

She looks nervous, twisting her fingers together as if to distract herself. She has no doubt heard the rumours. Everyone has.

'Yes.'

'How lovely.'

We say nothing as we draw to a natural stop in the passageway fringing the courtyard. Meta places a hand on the columns, her fingers toying with the vines that snake upwards like dark veins. I had planned to tend to the garden in our home; I had wanted to cultivate a beautiful orchard. But time somehow slipped away from me, and it has now become a wild mess of weeds and flowers tangled angrily together.

I think I prefer it this way, though. It reminds me of Aeaea.

I watch Meta tilt her head up to Selene. Tonight, the goddess's large, pitted face shines with an ethereal amber glow. As I observe Meta, I see a sadness welling in her eyes, her hands falling still at her sides.

'What is it like?' she asks quietly. 'To create life?'

'Would you like the truth, or the answer my husband prefers I tell?'

'The truth.' Her eyes close slightly. 'Always the truth.'

'Mermerus, my eldest – his birth was . . . complicated. In creating life, I almost lost my own.' I move to lean my back against the column, my eyes lifting to the sky as the memories seep through me. I only remember hazy glimmers of it now, wisps of pain that echo in my dreams, spinning together violent nightmares of bloodied hands and Jason's fearful, ashen face.

Beside me, Meta is silent, waiting for me to continue.

'We had just settled in Corinth, but we had been here long enough for the rumours of my past to spread . . . Only one doctor in town agreed to deliver Mermerus; the rest refused on account of who I am. Or, perhaps more accurately, *what* I am.' Meta inhales a careful breath, her eyes lowering to the ground. 'This doctor had barely reached manhood. His inexperience was painfully obvious.'

His pimpled face flickers in my mind, that awkward sprout of hair on his chin and frightened spark in his eyes. 'She is older than I expected': that is what he had said to Jason when he arrived. I suppose he was right. I was eighteen at the time.

315

'I remember the doctor's hands shaking as he prepared,' I continue, a little unsure why I am sharing this with a stranger. Perhaps it is the wine. Or perhaps I have been more starved of company than I realized. 'In that moment I saw my life hanging between his trembling fingers. I believed I was going to die.'

'But you did not.'

I nod, my eyes distant. 'I knew that I could not. So, I did not.'

Even when oblivion beckoned, I held on to the light, to that vision of my son and Jason. I held on to the future I had earned, the happiness I had fought and sacrificed so much for. I would not let anyone take it from me. Not even death.

'I suppose I have quite an idealized view. But I still imagine it is incredible, to give birth.'

I stare her dead in the eye. 'I would rather face battle three times over than suffer childbirth again.'

I study Meta's reaction, noting the heavy sadness etched into her beautiful features. I realize I have shattered a part of her that she has always held sacred and special in her heart. I have ruined the beautiful illusion of motherhood. But I do not feel guilty. The ugly truth is better than a beautiful lie.

'Was it different with your youngest?'

'His birth was easier, but . . .' I pause, feeling the confession crawling up inside me, refusing to be swallowed down. 'I loved Pheres from the moment he was born and yet . . . afterwards, it felt as if a piece of me had died. I am not sure what piece; I am not even sure I know the shape of it. I just knew, after that moment, it was gone. There was a hole inside me, and the more I tried to ignore it or fill it, the more it grew.' I draw in a slow, steadying breath. 'I thought a child would make me feel full, complete. But nobody told me they could make you feel this kind of emptiness. Nobody talks about these things . . .

Perhaps there is something wrong with me. There must be, mustn't there? For what kind of mother feels that after her child is born?'

I stare at Meta, waiting for a reassurance I know she can never give me. The Queen of Athens remains silent, allowing my words to hang in the air between us.

'I am sorry . . . it is the wine. I should not speak of such things.'

'We women spend far too much of our lives not speaking of the things we should,' she says quietly. 'I think your honesty is brave.'

Brave. I let the word settle over me, soaking it in.

'Aegeus cannot have children,' Meta confides. 'He is unable to.'

I stare at her and see a slight relief lift in her eyes, as if she had been holding on to this painful secret for a long time, as if she, too, had never had anyone to share it with.

'How can you be sure?'

'Because he has bedded every eligible woman in Greece.' She gives a bitter snort. 'Not a single one has fallen pregnant by his seed. Even so, he insists we continue trying. I believe he is in denial.'

I think of Aegeus' unapologetic flirtatiousness tonight; how it must feel for Meta to watch her husband behave like that. Jason might not be perfect, but at least he has never let me question his faithfulness. Or perhaps that is because I have never let my mind wander that far.

'I'm sorry,' I finally say when I realize Meta is waiting for me to speak. An apology seems pointless, but I feel it is what she wants to hear. After all, she will never get one from her husband.

'It is not the infidelity that upsets me. It is natural for men to seek their . . . indulgences. I just wish he could give me a child. All my life, all I have ever wanted was to be a mother. Was it like that for you?'

'No.' The abruptness of my answer makes Meta tense. 'I never even considered it before Jason.'

'Why not?'

'I never thought it would be very fair.'

'Fair?'

'If I had a child . . . they might become like me.'

'Medea.' I hate the way she says my name, that sickening pity laced in her sigh.

'You have heard the rumours, have you not?'

My directness seems to catch her off guard, but she answers levelly, 'I do not take much note of hearsay.'

'Perhaps you should.'

She stares at me for a long moment, her eyes heavy and intense, as if she were trying to decipher something written across my face.

'Your rooms are just down here.' I motion down the hallway, unable to meet her probing gaze any longer. 'You should have everything you require—'

I stop as I feel her hand slip into mine, just as it did at dinner. I stare down at her fingers wrapped around mine, feeling my heart constrict as she squeezes tighter.

'Thank you,' she says gently. 'For speaking with me; for your honesty.'

I only nod in response, unable to tear my attention away from her hand in mine. I think of my sons and of all the times I have restrained myself from holding their hands because I feared tainting them with my touch. I think of Chalciope, too, and of how I will never get the chance to hold her hand again, how she would not want me to even if I could.

'And Medea, what I told you . . . about Aegeus . . . it is not something he wishes anyone to know. I could get into a lot of trouble . . .' She trails off, chewing her lip nervously.

'I understand.'

She smiles and squeezes my hand a final time before turning to walk away.

318

In the wake of her presence, I am met with the familiar loneliness. It was different in Colchis. Back then I saw my loneliness as a companion of mine, one I told myself I preferred over the company of my hateful family. One I wrapped myself in protectively to hide from the world around me.

But here, this loneliness is the kind that eats you alive.

31

In my dreams I see my brother.

I see him drowning in the sea, dragged under by Poseidon's raging waves. I stretch my hand out to him, straining every inch of my body so I can grab hold and free him from those vengeful currents. He reaches for me, desperate, panicked, his eyes pleading, *Save me*. But as soon as we touch, his fingers turn to claws, ripping at me, dragging me under the waves in an attempt to keep himself afloat.

I try to scream, and my mouth fills with water. But then I realize it is not water at all ... but blood. Thick, hot, syrupy blood clotting in my throat. The metallic taste makes my stomach heave. I try to spit it out, to gasp for breath, but it is everywhere, seeping into every inch of me. All I can see are Apsyrtus' dead eyes as he watches me drowning, a sinister smile curled around his rotten lips.

You are a disease.

I wake in the middle of our courtyard, the stars above watching me.

Something feels odd. The house around me seems slightly out of place, as if the familiar edges have been worn away and drawn anew. Then I hear a noise, small voices whispering ...

I find myself outside my sons' chamber, creeping forwards, peering in ...

They're crouched on the balls of their feet, their small backs facing me. Mermerus has a stick in his hand and he's poking something ...

'What are you doing?' My voice sounds warped and unfamiliar.

'I wanted to see what was inside,' he says without turning.

A body lies beneath them, carved up so I cannot tell who it is. The limbs have been severed, the chest slit open so the entrails spill across the floor, glinting hideously.

'Stop it!' I scream, running forwards to drag them away.

'I wanted to see what was inside,' Mermerus repeats as I wrench him backwards. His entire body is covered in blood, but his face is so calm, so cold . . . It is a face I recognize.

My face.

'Will you show us, Mama?' Pheres asks beside him, his skin also stained crimson. His eyes are vacant, his smile cruel. 'Show us what's inside?'

From the corners of the room, I feel the death spirits closing in and scream at them, 'No, no, *no!*'

I wake with a jolt, still screaming, my sheets damp and tangled round me like grasping hands.

Sitting upright, I take slow breaths as I familiarize myself with my chamber. I focus on the dying hearth, its light pulsing like a fading heartbeat.

I slip from my bed, knowing if I close my eyes the nightmares will find me once again. They always do. And if it is not Apsyrtus' rotting corpse that greets me, it will be the screaming faces of Pelias' daughters.

You are a vile, soulless creature . . .

But the worst is when I see my sons. That vision of them covered in blood haunts even my waking hours . . . I cannot rid myself of it, the sight of their innocent skin stained so horribly.

I wish sleep were not a necessity. I loathe letting myself fall victim to my unconscious mind. It is a dangerous place to wander unfettered.

It is far safer being awake, where I can guard my consciousness, keeping those memories and fears at bay.

The death spirits enjoy my nightmares. I can sense their delight when I wake screaming. They glimmer inside me like a flame I cannot extinguish, a flame I once lit willingly.

From down the hall I hear a crash followed by scrambling feet. Pulling on my discarded gown, I follow the noise to our smaller guest chamber, the one Jason favours over our own.

Inside, the space is strewn with Jason's clothes, the table at the centre of the room crowded with empty jugs of wine and a plate of half-eaten food. I tell Myrto not to clean in here, in the hopes that the mess will drive Jason back into our shared bed. But it seems he would rather sleep in filth than beside his own wife.

I watch Jason struggle to undress, the hearth etching the strong contours of his back. My mind dips to the first night we met, when I stole to his room and promised to aid him in obtaining the fleece. I was so young, so desperate, so drunk on my love for this stranger.

It consumed me; *he* consumed me.

And I let him.

'You do not wish to sleep beside your wife?' I ask from the doorway.

He turns to me, the movement slow and ungainly, his gaze loose. He is drunk.

'I did not want to wake you.' It's an excuse I have heard many times before.

He sits down on the bed, letting out a sigh as he attempts to unlace his sandals. His fingers fumble with the intricately laced design – the new style in Corinth, so Jason says.

'Let me.' I kneel before him and he draws his hands away, eyes glassy. For a moment I think he will stop me, but he says nothing.

I loop my fingers through the thin leather strips criss-crossed over his shins, gently freeing them layer by layer.

I work slowly, savouring the contact, the feel of Jason's body so close to mine. When I look up, I catch him watching me, his eyes swallowed by shadows.

We both know we are struggling – with the life we live, this love we share. We've known for a long time, though we do not speak of it. Admittedly, I've always feared that giving voice to our problems would somehow grant them the power to shatter us completely. Yet, I now realize ignoring our pain has only granted it the space to grow and fester.

'Thank you,' Jason murmurs as I finally pull off his sandals.

Something has shifted and softened within him, but his eyes still look distant, plagued by thoughts he will never share with me. I am not sure when it all started to change; it was so gradual at first, I believed I was imagining him pulling away. And then, one day, he was too far for me to reach. Even during those rare times when he suffocates me with sudden bursts of love, I have still felt it between us, this distance.

'The dinner with Aegeus went well,' I say.

'He seemed more interested in you than me,' Jason grumbles, a sour look staining his face. 'He did not stop asking about you after you left.'

I move my hands up his legs, settling them on his thighs. I begin to trace idle circles there, my touch gentle, yearning. If I can just re-kindle that flame between us, if I can coax that fire to life again . . .

'You know I am yours,' I say. When Jason does not respond, I lower my voice to a husky whisper. 'Will you . . . come to my bed? It has been so long since you have slept beside me.'

Around us, the silence holds its breath in anticipation.

323

'Medea.' My name is a heavy sigh and I feel my disappointment rise with Jason as he stands, brushing off my touch. 'I have had a long day.'

'That is what you always say.' I get to my feet to follow him across the room, but he will not meet my gaze. 'Why do you refuse me?'

'I am not in the mood for this.'

'Why?' I press, the insecurities I have buried for so long cracking open inside me. 'Why can you not even bear to touch your own wife?'

'Do you think I *want* to touch you after how you acted at dinner?' The words escape him in a heated snarl. 'You embarrassed yourself tonight, Medea, and you embarrassed *me*.'

'Aegeus did not seem to think so.'

Jason gives a humourless laugh as he goes to pour himself another cup of wine. 'And there it is.'

'What does that mean?'

'I saw the way you were looking at him, Medea.' He shakes his head, knocking back the wine before refilling it again. 'He only wants to fuck you because he hopes a witch's cunt will cure his sterility.'

Before I can quieten my rage, I slap the wine from his hands. The cup clatters across the floor, dark liquid spilling beneath our feet like blood. Jason stares at it for a moment, his body stilled. Then, in one fluid movement, he braces his forearm against my chest, slamming me against the wall.

I let out a hiss of air as he crushes against me. We stare at each other for a long, hateful moment, and I wonder if he might hit me. I imagine what the force of his fist would feel like, envisioning the pain blossoming across my face. I wonder if it would feel the same as when my father hit me. Or would Jason's fists hurt more because I have only ever known his touch as tender? Or would the passion and pain blur and curdle into some kind of strange pleasure?

324

As if reading my perverse thoughts, he pulls away. I am not sure if the sinking feeling in my chest is disappointment or relief.

When he speaks, his voice is ragged. 'You are never to disrespect your husband like that again. Do you understand me?'

'What husband?' I goad, seeking his hands on me again. Even if his touch is tainted by hate, it is something. A way to punctuate the emptiness he has carved into my life, into my soul. 'You are never here; you will barely even look at me, let alone share a bed. You are more a stranger than a husband to me. And I have been trying, Jason. For ten winters I have done nothing but play the dutiful wife. But you keep pulling further away. What am I to do? *Tell me.*'

For a moment, I hold his eyes with mine, feeling the memory of him fill my mind like an embrace. Then I watch as those eyes drop to the floor, dragged by the weight of whatever thoughts torment him.

'Why is this life not enough for you?' The question hitches in my throat.

A pregnant silence fills the room, ripping open the misery rotting between us. As I stare at Jason, I can feel him drifting further and further away from me.

It wasn't supposed to be like this.

We were supposed to be *happy.*

After everything I have done, everything I sacrificed ... if I lost Jason now, then it would all have been for nothing. I would have destroyed myself for *nothing.*

And what of our sons? How could I let them lose their father?

'Come back to me.' I step towards him, daring to place a tentative hand on his chest. 'Please, Jason.'

'Medea, stop.'

'Come back to me,' I repeat, firmer now, cradling my hands on either side of his face. That beautiful face that makes me feel both impossibly full and utterly empty. 'Jason, please. Come—'

'*Stop.*' He grabs my wrists and shoves me backwards, hard enough that my head cracks against the wall, causing a white light to burst across my vision.

'Papa?'

In the doorway, Pheres whimpers, clutching his brother's hand. Beside him, Mermerus' eyes travel from my face to Jason's hands wrapped around my wrists, dissecting the scene with an eerie impassivity.

Jason drops me, smoothing his hair back as he strides over to them.

'What are you doing awake at this hour, boys?'

'Pheres had another nightmare,' Mermerus says, his eyes still flicking between us. 'The same one he always does.'

'What nightmare?' Jason's voice softens. I rest my throbbing skull back, my palms flat against the wall.

Pheres gives a little whimper, so Mermerus answers for him, 'He dreams he is being turned into a monster.'

My body stills as my nightmare visits me once again, closing its cold hand around my mind . . .

No. Stop.

'Pheres, you were born to be the *hero* of your story, not the monster.' Jason kneels before them, resting a hand on both their shoulders. His eyes are so tender, so loving. He looks at nobody the way he looks at his sons. It is both beautiful and painful to witness.

'You are always safe with me, you always will be,' he continues as he pulls them into his arms, closing his eyes as he soaks them in, letting their warmth steady him. 'Come now, my boys, let me see you to bed.'

As they walk away, I feel Mermerus' eyes lingering on me – that reflection in the water, shifting and rippling. Watching, always watching. And somewhere, in my mind, the voices of my past whisper again . . .

Violence breeds violence.

Darkness calls to darkness.

'Does Hypnos elude you as well?'

I stiffen as I hear Aegeus' silken voice caress the night. He comes to stand beside me in the courtyard, his hands laced behind his back. He is quite short, for a man, yet his presence still fills the space.

'He is a fickle god,' he continues, offering a smile.

I nod, hoping my silence indicates my wish to be alone. After my argument with Jason, I can think of nothing worse than making idle small talk. But instead, Aegeus goes and sits on the stone seat at the edge of the courtyard, stretching his legs out and tapping the empty space beside him.

'Do you not find your sleeping arrangements suitable?' I ask as I sit down, folding my hands neatly in my lap.

'Of course, your hospitality has been most generous.' Aegeus nods. 'But sleep has never come easily to me, even as a child.'

'Sleep is for the unburdened,' I say, tilting my head up to the dark sky.

'And what burdens you, Medea?' He leans in then, so close I can smell the richness of his perfume, notes of flowers and spice. I watch the corner of his mouth coil into a conspiratorial smile.

'A king does not wish to hear the ramblings of a bored wife,' I deflect blankly.

'Medea, *you* are anything but boring.' As he speaks, he reaches out and trails a finger the length of my thigh, causing a shudder to ripple across my skin. 'In fact, I think you might be the most remarkable woman I have ever met.'

'How disappointing for you.'

He barks out a laugh, then surprises me by asking, 'Have you heard much news from Colchis?'

My body is quick to suffocate the emotions rising inside me. It is like muscle memory now.

'I know that my father was overthrown by his brother, if that is what you are asking.'

'And what do you think of that?' he probes.

'Colchis is nothing to me now. So, I do not think much of it at all.'

His only response is a curious smile. Afterwards, we sit in silence, and I am painfully aware of his hand now resting on my thigh, his palm warm and heavy. I consider pushing him away, but I know I cannot offend him with such a rejection. And perhaps a small part of me is enjoying his attention, feeling the heat of his attraction seeping into my skin. It has been so long since I have had this, I had forgotten how intoxicating it feels to be desired. *Wanted*.

'I am just trying to understand it,' Aegeus murmurs, rubbing small, teasing circles against my thigh with his thumb. Even with the material of my gown blocking his flesh from mine, it still feels far too intimate. Only a king would dare touch a man's wife in his own home like this. His sense of entitlement is slightly nauseating, yet still I do not brush him off.

'Understand what?'

'Why him?' His question causes a knot to form in the pit of my stomach. 'Why Jason?' he clarifies, not even bothering to lower his voice. I cannot decide if the self-assurance of this man is impressive or infuriating. 'He is handsome, of course, an undeniable charmer, but surely a woman such as yourself desires a lover of equal power. Or have I misread you?'

I remain silent. Even if I knew how to respond to such a question, I wouldn't share such vulnerable truths with the likes of Aegeus.

'He united and led the Argonauts, which is obviously an impressive feat,' he continues, as if musing out loud; his thumb still moves against my thigh. 'But I know Jason's secret.'

'His secret?' I echo, forcing my tone to remain neutral.

'He is an unexceptional man who hides behind exceptional people . . . Come now, Medea, anyone with a brain knows it was the Argonauts who got Jason to Colchis, and it was you who secured him the fleece. You said it yourself; the only time Jason was left to his own devices was when he lost to Acastus.' I am stunned into silence, yet Aegeus must read something in my expression because his smile widens. 'Am I wrong?'

He isn't, not entirely. Jason has always been an expert at wielding people to his advantage, utilizing their talents to shield his own flaws. I once believed this demonstrated great leadership, but these days I am not so sure. It seems there's a lot of my past I look at differently now, viewing memories from angles I never knew existed. Often, I find I do not like what I see.

And yet, I refuse to accept Jason is *unexceptional*. This word is an insult to him and to *me*. Does Aegeus really believe I would sacrifice everything for an unexceptional man?

'If you find my husband so disappointing, then why come here?' I counter.

'I think you know why, Medea.' Aegeus stares at me, the heat in his gaze causing his unspoken meaning to catch alight between us. 'I wanted to see if you were as remarkable as they say you are . . . I must tell you, I am a little disappointed.'

'Disappointed?' I frown.

'There's no denying you are incredible, Medea. I am merely

329

disappointed that you have allowed Jason to reduce you to, well . . . this.' He gives a vague wave towards me with his free hand. 'What was it you called yourself? Jason's "shameful little secret".'

'I must apologize for my behaviour at dinner. I was not feeling well.'

'Do you not see, Medea?' Aegeus continues as if I had not spoken. 'You could be so much *more* than Jason allows you to be. He stifles you.'

He begins to lean in closer, and I feel my whole body go rigid as his hand slips further up my thigh to settle on my hip. A sensual hunger glows in his eyes as they flicker to my lips.

My thoughts suddenly dip to Meta, to the sadness in her eyes when she asked about my sons.

My sons. Their faces catch in my mind, eclipsing all other thoughts.

'It is late. I should retire to my chambers,' I say abruptly.

Aegeus lets out a low hum as he leans back, finally pulling his hand away. My skin feels eerily cold in the absence of his touch.

'It is a pity. We could have made quite the pair, Medea,' he muses, smoothing a hand over his grey-speckled beard. 'Though I must admit, I do admire your loyalty to Jason, even after his arrangements to take a new wife.'

The words pierce me deep in my core, letting a cold sickness spill out into my stomach, into my veins. Just three little words, but they carry enough weight to risk ripping apart my entire existence.

A new wife.

No. It cannot be.

Aegeus tilts his head as he studies my reaction. 'Oh, my dear, I thought you already knew? Jason has been announcing it to his associates . . .' He clicks his tongue, and the sound makes me flinch. 'Well, my mistake. I am sure he was planning on informing you soon.'

'I . . . have to go.' I rise to my feet, my body feeling as though it were crumbling in on itself. If I stand here for a moment longer, I believe I will turn to dust.

'I shall retire as well. I have a long journey tomorrow.' Aegeus stands. 'Goodnight, Medea. It was a *pleasure* chatting with you.'

He leans in and kisses my cheek, the touch fleeting yet sensual.

I am silent as he turns to walk away, watching as his guards peel themselves from the shadows behind us. I did not even notice they were there. He nods his head before disappearing down the passageway to our other guest chamber.

Once alone, I feel his words expanding in the silence, feeding off my emptiness as they swell and swell – *a new wife*.

No. *No.*

It cannot be. Jason would not do that to me.

He would not dare.

32

I do not rise from my bed the next morning.

I do not want to face Aegeus' mocking smile, nor Jason's cold indifference. Nor can I even bear the thought of Meta's kind, concerned face.

I want to be left alone whilst I suffocate beneath my overcrowded thoughts.

A new wife.

Things may be strained between Jason and me, but that does not mean he would seek another, not after everything we have been through. What Jason and I have faced, what we have sacrificed for one another – that binds us deeper than marriage.

And what of our sons? He would never abandon them.

He could not.

I stare at nothing whilst my mind twists back and forth. After a while, exhaustion finds me and my thoughts grow thick and sluggish, sticking to the corners of my mind in ugly clumps, weighing me down until a headache begins to take over.

'Mama, will you come and play with us?' Pheres asks from the doorway to my chamber.

'Not today.' I dismiss him from where I am cocooned in my bed.

I can sense his disappointment without even looking at him, yet I do not have the energy to feel guilty about it.

I keep my eyes closed, waiting to hear the quiet patter of feet as he walks away.

'Are you OK, Mama?' A small, damp hand cups my cheek.

I open my eyes to see Pheres staring at me with those summer-blue eyes: Jason's eyes. I close my hand over his, feeling a delicate warmth flicker within me.

'I am fine.' I nod to him, forcing a smile. His hand feels so small in mine, so fragile. 'Did you have any more nightmares last night?'

He shakes his head.

'Papa said he would chase the monsters away,' he tells me. 'Like he did to protect the Argonauts.'

'Papa didn't chase the monster away,' Mermerus' voice comes from the doorway, and I shift myself up in bed to look at him. 'Mama did that.'

I stiffen at his words. Beside me, Pheres withdraws his hand as he breathes, 'Mama?'

'Because she is a witch.'

Witch. I have never told him that before. I did not even know he knew the word.

'I heard the king say it,' Mermerus says to my stunned expression. 'Is it true?'

I wait to see that ugly glimmer of fear, but they both just look … curious. Pheres takes my hand again, staring at my fingers with a new-found interest, as if they are unlike anything he has seen before.

'Do you know what that means?' I ask.

Mermerus steps into the room, his voice steady as he says, 'It means you are very powerful.'

Very powerful. I feel the words knot in my throat.

'Is that right, Mama?' he prompts with a slight frown.

'Yes, you are right.'

'Will you show us?' Pheres squeaks, his whole body vibrating with excitement as he grips my hand tighter.

I have kept my magic from them for so long. I believed it was the right thing to do, to keep them distanced from all of it, from all of *me*.

Jason has warned me that if I tell our sons of my magic, I must be willing to tell them everything. But he knows I would never be ready to do that. How could I be? For I know that once my sons learn the truth, all of it, they will look at me like all the others, with fear, with disgust. I cannot bear to think of it.

But I am so tired of it . . . this shame, this self-loathing, this horrible distance I have forced between my sons and me. I am so tired of it all.

'Please.' Mermerus surprises me with the softness in his voice. 'Will you show us?'

'Yes.' I nod slowly. 'I . . . would like that very much.'

'Mistress, are you sure this is wise?' Myrto asks as I walk out into the courtyard. She has been watching over my sons whilst I prepared the concoction now clutched between my hands.

At first, I feared I may have forgotten how, but this is a knowledge that is engrained in my very being, woven between every bone and muscle, carved into my very soul.

It was invigorating, to feel that spark flickering inside me once more and have my senses flooded with the rich tang of earth magic. I felt like a weathered voyager finally returning home, stepping through that familiar doorway and being struck by all those wonderfully nostalgic sensations.

It was like a piece of myself had been returned to me. A piece I had not realized how incomplete I was without, until now.

'Master Jason said there should be no magic in this house; he insisted. And the children—'

'I will decide what is best for my children. Leave us.'

She dares a step closer. 'Master Jason said you should not be alone with them.'

'Is Jason here?' I challenge. 'No. Then you answer to me, and I am dismissing you. So, go. Now.'

She holds my gaze, silent accusations burning in her eyes. Finally, she relents, and I watch her throw a tortured, lingering look towards my sons before disappearing.

'Pheres, Mermerus,' I call to them, and they scurry over from where they are playing together.

I kneel and place the small bronze bowl in my lap. My sons plop themselves down in front of me, crossing their legs and sitting up with eagerly straight backs.

'What was it you heard King Aegeus call me?'

I feel more awake now, more alive, as if my sons' curiosity is fuelling my spirit, luring it from its suffocating lethargy. I stare at their wide, inquisitive eyes and think what a beautiful, fragile gift it is, to have their attention like this. So fully, so completely.

I cannot remember the last time we were alone together.

'A witch,' Mermerus says. His emotions are more guarded than his little brother's, yet I can sense his curiosity sparking quietly behind his eyes.

'I prefer the term "sorceress".' I smile as memories of Circe flicker in my mind, that day when she walked into my life and ignited something inside me – a passion, a purpose.

'Do you know what magic is?' They shake their heads. Of course, they do not. Jason does not allow us even to talk of such things. 'Magic is a gift from Hecate. Do you know who Hecate is?'

'A goddess!' Pheres exclaims, clutching his crossed ankles and rocking back and forth. 'From the Underworld!'

'You have a gift from the Gods?' Mermerus' eyes narrow. Beside his animated little brother, his stillness seems amplified.

'Magic is a gift from Hecate, but it can also be found right here, in this very garden.'

Pheres glances around us, as if he expects some tangible creature to lumber out from the shadows and greet him.

'Here, let me show you.' I place the bowl down and rise to my feet, motioning for them to follow.

I walk towards the flowerbeds fringing our courtyard, scanning my gaze across the angry tangle of wild flora. When we first settled here, Jason was in one of his good moods. I remember he took me into the empty, lifeless courtyard and told me it was now my 'kingdom to rule', encouraging me to plant and nurture whatever my heart desired. At first I was invigorated by the chance to connect with the magic of nature once again, though I was not practising magic myself. It was comforting to hear it whispering between the growing buds, to feel it thrumming in the soil beneath my fingertips. But the feel of it always stirred that darker power inside me, and those soothing whispers soon became demanding hisses. *Use us ... Release us ...*

As time passed, my attentiveness for the courtyard waned just as Jason's did for me. But the plants continued to flourish despite their deprivation, learning to adapt and thrive on their own.

'Can you hear that?' I ask my sons. 'Listen closely.'

Pheres closes his eyes, scrunching up his face with exaggerated concentration. Beside him, Mermerus stares at the cluttered flower-beds, his expression unreadable as usual.

After a moment, Pheres whines, 'I can't hear anything.'

'It's OK.' I offer him a smile. 'I couldn't hear magic at your age, either.'

'*Hear* magic?' Mermerus' brows knit together.

336

I nod. 'It calls to me. The magic of Gaia, of the earth. It calls to my own magic.'

I run my hand over the flowerbeds, pausing as my fingers caress a purple-petalled flower. The *heliotrope*. My mind reaches back to that evening with Phrixus, when he twirled the flower between his fingers whilst I explained its magical origin. That memory seems like a life-time ago now, that version of myself so distant and unfamiliar I often wonder how we could possibly be the same person.

'Shall I show you the spell now?'

I follow the harsh call of a cicada, spying the insect on the trunk of a little olive tree. Bending down, I close my hands around it and walk back to the centre of the courtyard. I can feel the little creature buzzing against my skin as I kneel back down. My sons trail behind me, Pheres vibrating with excitement, mirroring the insect tickling between my palms.

'Look.' I show them, parting my thumbs slightly to allow them a small peek. Pheres squeals. 'Mermerus, when I tell you, I want you to pour the contents of that bowl between my hands. Can you do that?'

He nods as I carefully set the cicada down on the ground with my hands cupped in a dome shape over it. I signal to Mermerus and he retrieves the bowl, poising it over my hands. His face is drawn in solemn concentration as he watches me, awaiting his signal.

Parting my fingers, I create a small opening as I nod to Mermerus again. Without hesitation, he begins to pour the contents into the small cage I have created.

Once the bowl is empty, I seal my hands to stop the doused cicada from escaping, muttering the familiar incantation under my breath. I concentrate on the feeling that sparks inside me, the one that used to come as naturally as breathing. But it is so long since I have used my magic, it feels feeble and fragile, like trying to use a limb that has been left to wither and waste away.

I focus my mind, sharpening my senses, pleading with Hecate.

Goddess, I know I have neglected you ...

But, please, answer me ...

I wish to show my sons your gift ...

The death spirits answer instead.

They begin to close in, coaxed by the stirring of power they sense inside me. I feel that cord between us grow taut as they inch closer, eager to breathe life into my magic, to bleed their malicious power into my own. That ripple of darkness caresses my mind, but I force it away, deafening myself to their seductive call. I will not let them taint this moment.

This power is *mine* to wield. Not theirs.

A sweat breaks out across my brow, my body already drained from the strain of holding the spirits at bay whilst attempting to summon my own magic. In my head, I hear Mermerus' voice: *It means you are very powerful.*

When did I allow myself to forget that?

My magic surges with this thought, the sharp thrill of it cutting through my veins, causing my hands to tingle with its effervescent power. I smile at the familiar feeling, that tang in my nostrils. It is like being met with a beloved old friend, one I have missed more than I allowed myself to realize.

I look up at my sons, marking their wide, curious eyes.

'Look,' I whisper, as I remove my hands.

The cicada is nowhere to be seen. Instead, a small bird emerges, stretching its tawny-feathered wings. It springs into the air, fluttering upwards in confused, haphazard circles as the cicada comes to terms with its new form. Then the bird swoops down to my sons, twirling around their heads, causing Pheres to shriek with delight.

I soak in their reaction, the way their eyes glow and their mouths hang slightly agape. They are not afraid, nor disgusted by my magic at all, but rather they are *captivated* by it. Their fascination is so bright and pure, it makes a protectiveness flare inside me. I want them always to look at the world like this, with fearless curiosity, and I pray they only ever see the beauty it has to offer them.

I smile as the bird lands on Mermerus' finger. He seems mesmerized by the creature, his eyes following its jittery, sharp movements. He then shifts his gaze to mine, a look of genuine awe softening his face.

'Will you show me how?' he asks quietly.

'You want to learn magic?' Nobody has ever asked me such a thing before.

I can see it, see myself teaching him. Hecate will bless him with this gift . . . this curse. I see him excelling as I once did, embracing the power within him. But I can see the darkness, too; it will call to him, luring my son as it once lured me. I see those death spirits feasting off his innocence, savouring every strip of his soul as they rip it apart . . .

'Are you OK, Mama?' Mermerus asks, studying my expression and the pain I have exposed there.

In my mind, I can hear the death spirits laughing at my vision, revelling in my torment.

'I am fine.' I nod with a stiff smile, though I cannot meet his gaze any more.

'Will you show me how you do it? The magic?' he presses.

'Please show us, Mama,' Pheres enthuses, reaching for my hand.

'Not now.' I flinch from his touch, trying to ignore the rejection in his eyes. 'Your father would not approve.'

Mermerus frowns, his eyes following the bird now soaring high above our home. 'Because he is to be a prince?'

'Who told you that?'

'I heard him say to the King of Athens. He said he will become the Prince of Corinth when he . . .' Mermerus hesitates, drawing back from me.

'When he *what?*' I push, my voice an empty void, sucking all the joy from the air.

'When he marries the princess!' Pheres interjects with oblivious excitement.

A new wife.

No, not just a wife . . . a *princess?* Just as I was, once, before I stripped that title from myself, along with every other title I lost for Jason – princess, daughter, sister, niece, friend . . . all so that I may be called his wife.

And now Jason plans to take that from me as well?

'Mama, if Father becomes a prince, what will that make us?' Mermerus' eyes, so wise beyond their years, study my reaction, seeing more than they should, more than I wish to reveal. 'Does it mean Father will leave us?'

'*Leave us?*' Pheres whimpers, then hiccups a small sob. 'Papa will leave us?'

'No, he will not.' I kneel so I am at their eye level. 'Your father will not leave us; do you hear me? Not now. Not ever.'

Mermerus' frown deepens. 'How do you know?'

'Because I will not allow it.'

'Do you mean it?' Pheres sniffs, eyes shining. 'Do you swear it?'

I nod, an icy determination settling in my veins.

'I swear it.'

33

When Jason returns home, Nyx has crept over the house.

I am waiting for him in our guest chamber, perched on the bed, staring at nothing. The hearth is unlit, allowing an attentive coldness to sharpen the air. Above, silvery moonlight reaches through the windows, tripping over the heavy shadows.

'Medea.' Jason regards me as he enters, his figure just a dark silhouette in the doorway. 'What are you doing awake?'

'I was waiting for you.'

My mind feels clear, alert, perhaps for the first time in months, as if I have finally awoken from a heavy stupor.

Jason watches me now, a slight awkwardness stiffening the air around him. He then moves over to the hearth, perhaps to give himself something to do, something to focus on other than the accusing stillness.

'It is freezing in here,' he murmurs.

I say nothing. As I watch him coax a fire to life, I remember the sight of him being engulfed in the oxen's flames. He would have been nothing but ash and dirt by now if it were not for me.

Jason sighs as he stares into the hearth. He tosses another log on to the flames, causing the fire to hiss and spit angrily. As I watch his movements, I can feel the heaviness of my love for him, like a weight tied to my soul. When did this love start feeling more like a curse I carry than a blessing I cherish?

'Where are the boys?' he asks with his back to me.

'Asleep.' My voice is detached as I continue, 'I showed them today.'

'Showed them what?' Jason rubs his hands together then turns his palms to the fire to warm them. He sounds disinterested, as if his mind has wandered elsewhere. To another woman, perhaps.

'My magic.'

He turns to me then. 'Why would you do that?'

'Why would I not?' My voice remains calm. 'It was a harmless transformation spell. They found it amusing.'

In my mind, I cradle the memory of my sons from this afternoon, the way they welcomed my power with such delighted awe.

Their father had done so, too, once, a long time ago.

'Medea, we have discussed this.' Jason sighs. 'If you tell them about your magic, you must be willing to tell them about *all* of it.'

'What if I am willing?'

Jason swallows a humourless laugh. 'You really want our children to know what you have done? To learn who their mother truly is?'

It means you are very powerful. Mermerus' words glow inside me like a fire that is catching, spreading.

'Would that be so terrible?' I counter evenly.

He opens his mouth to argue, but then he shuts it again, shaking his head as if defeated.

'I am too tired for this,' is all he says.

A silence follows and within its depths I can almost taste his guilt souring the air. I think I know where that guilt stems from and what deceit decays beneath it . . . But I am still not willing to accept it, not until I hear the words from him, from those traitorous lips.

'I heard a peculiar thing yesterday,' I say, my voice steady, though I can feel my heartbeat quickening. A nervous adrenaline fizzes in my veins, making it difficult to keep still. 'I heard you were taking another wife.'

'*What?*'

My head tilts to one side, studying the way Jason's eyes betray his panic.

'I told you the gossip here is terrible,' I say with a shrug, keeping my hands laced in my lap to stop them from shaking. 'I know it is just a lie, of course. Because I know you would never do such a thing. Not to me.'

We stare at each other for a long moment, the charged silence punctuated only by the popping of the fire. This scene feels like a perverse replica of the night we met, when the space between us felt so full of possibility. Ten winters on and Jason feels like a stranger once again, and I am still a trapped girl longing to be needed by him.

How pathetic, the darkness in me purrs.

'Tell me it's not true.' I rise to my feet, stepping towards him.

He is quiet, still. Then his eyes lower to the ground and, in that single motion, I have my answer.

He has betrayed me.

'Creon wishes me to marry his daughter.'

'Creon. The king.' It is not a question, but Jason still nods.

When he finds my eyes again, I see a cold resolution has settled within them. 'I have agreed to the marriage.'

'But you are already married.'

'Creon will nullify our marriage. He has the power to do so.'

His words suck the air from the room, crushing the breath in my lungs. The floor tilts beneath me as I touch a hand to my head, trying to focus my thoughts through the swell of pain raging inside me.

Traitor, traitor, traitor ... the darkness sings, that cord to the Underworld pulling taut. The connection aches, like a withered limb sparking to life.

'Medea . . .' Jason steps towards me, reaching out his hand. 'Please try to understand, this is for your own good—'

'*My own good?*' I hiss, pulling away from his touch.

'This marriage will benefit all of us.' He nods earnestly. 'The people of Corinth do not want a witch living amongst them any more. There is unrest brewing and I fear the consequences it might bring . . . But as a prince of this land, I will have the power and influence to protect you and our sons. I can ensure you are cared for and kept safe.'

'Whilst you warm another woman's bed?' I spit.

'Medea, please calm down. Let us discuss this rationally.'

'If my safety is of such concern, then why do we not leave? Go elsewhere and start anew?'

'How many times have we been over this, Medea? The world knows what you did. Do you think anywhere will welcome you? Do you think anywhere will *want* you?' He reaches for my hand again, his palms rough and calloused against mine. 'This way I can protect you and our sons. Please, Medea, try to think of what is best for them.'

'You think abandoning us for some whore is what is *best* for our sons?'

Jason's face hardens. He drops my hands and I ball them into fists to steady their furious shaking.

'There is no point discussing this when you are being hysterical. We should wait until you have calmed down and are in a more reasonable mood.'

He moves over to the table and begins to pour himself a cup of wine. He sighs, sounding wearied, as if the act of destroying my life is an inconvenience for him.

A rush of dark rage swells inside me. I lunge to snatch the jug from him, but Jason catches my wrist before I can do so, holding it firmly between us.

'*How could you?*' I hiss. Jason's grip tightens around my wrist as my fingers strain like talons unsheathing. 'How could you do this to me?'

'I am doing this *for you*, Medea. So that I can protect our family—'

'*Do not.*' I rip my hand free from his grasp. 'Do not insult me by pretending this has *anything* to do with us, Jason. This is only about your pathetic obsession with power, with being idolized by all those around you. Why does the approval of others matter to you so much?'

'I will not have this discussion when you are acting like a child.'

'After everything I have done for you. After everything I sacrificed.'

'After everything *you* sacrificed?' He slams his wine on to the table, a flash of anger cracking through him. The shadows from the hearth exaggerate the fury twisting across his face, turning his scowl into something monstrous. 'What of *me*, Medea? What about all that *I* lost because of what *you* did?'

'I did those things for you, because *you* asked me to.' I hate the way my voice breaks as I say it.

'Really? You are going to twist the truth like that?' He gives an empty laugh, folding his arms. 'Do you not remember coming to my chamber that night I arrived in Colchis? You were so eager to betray your family, so desperate to spread your legs for me, for a foreign stranger you had shared all of five words with.'

I turn away from him then, the anger clotting in my throat, choking my words back. There is so much I want to say and yet I find myself staring wordlessly at the ground, the fury pounding in my temples, making my vision swim.

'*You* betrayed your family, Medea,' Jason continues, his words hitting like a physical blow. '*You* killed your brother, and *you* orchestrated Pelias' death. Stop trying to put that blame on to me and take some responsibility for once in your life.'

Around us, the shadows seem to take a quiet breath in anticipation, skulking closer.

I turn back to Jason slowly, my eyes orbs of fire and ice. 'I do not deny the things I have done; I never have. But do not forget that *I* was the darkness that allowed *you* to shine. Without me, you would be *nothing*. Without me, you would be a corpse rotting in Colchian soil. I did *everything* for you, Jason—'

'Not everything,' he snaps, a vein in his neck pulsing. 'You said you would make me king, and look at me now. Look at us.'

I stare at him for a long moment.

'Is that really all that matters to you? A hollow title?' He glances away, letting his silence sour the air between us. 'Why, Jason? Why is this life not enough for you?'

'*How could it be?*' His eyes then slide to mine, gleaming with a quiet fury. 'How could this be enough, Medea? I am meant to be the *king* of my homeland, ruler of my people. Instead, my pathetic cousin sits on *my* throne, whilst I spend my days grovelling at the feet of lesser men. Do you know how demeaning that is? Do you know how every day I have to swallow my pride before I step out that door?' He is close to me now, so close I can see the red veins sparking in the whites of his eyes. 'And still, even when I grovel, even when I beg, I am treated as an outcast because of what *you* did.'

'What *we* did.' My voice is a blade wrapped in darkness. I hope Jason can feel the sting of it.

'I want you to leave.' He turns away, but I reach out and grab his arm.

'Is this really the man you have become?'

When he replies, his voice is a ragged whisper. 'This is the man you made me.'

The words crush me, swift and brutal.

346

I let go of his arm and he moves to the bed to sit down, laying his head in his hands. As I watch him, I think how defeated he looks, how different from the charming prince who swaggered into my father's palace all that time ago, so full of that dazzling confidence I was inexplicably drawn to. Now he seems like a mere shadow of his former self, ravaged by the weight of his own expectations. The life he envisioned has slipped away from him and Jason has been trying to hold on to that illusion with all his might, digging his fingers in deeper and deeper, causing the reality around him to crack and break.

And so now he seeks to build a new life with another.

I press my hand over my stomach and lean back against the nearest wall, feeling a sickness so deep it is as if it is churning through my bones. I have known pain before, but this . . . I cannot even begin to comprehend the shape of it, the feel of it.

I would rather feel nothing at all.

'If you do this, it means it will have been for nothing,' I say, my voice fracturing the swollen silence. 'All of it.'

All that death, destruction, betrayal . . . It felt a worthy sacrifice when it was for love. But if there is no love left, then how can I rationalize it? How can I justify all the horrific things I have done if they were for nothing? How can I live with them?

Jason sounds defeated as he whispers, 'It was already for nothing, don't you see?'

'What of our sons? Are they *nothing* to you also?'

'That is not what I meant. Do not put words into my mouth,' he snaps without looking up.

In this moment, I hate him.

I hate him for not thinking this life is enough. I hate him for betraying our beautiful sons. I hate him for pretending the blood we spilt does not stain both our hands. I hate him for infecting me with this love I have carried for so long – I wish I could remove it, sever it from me like an infected limb. Anything that would free me from this endless torment.

But without Jason, what else is there for me? What life exists beyond him?

I have nothing. I have no one. Because I destroyed my life so thoroughly for him, so completely.

But I will not let him destroy the lives of our sons.

I will fight for them, for our family. Even if Jason will not.

'Glauce.' I draw the syllables out slowly, as if tasting them on my tongue. 'That is the princess's name, is it not?'

'Yes.'

I draw in a breath as Pheres' voice fills my mind.

Do you swear?

I swear it.

After a long moment, I approach him, hooking my index finger under his chin and lifting his head up to mine.

'This girl, Glauce – what would she do for your love?'

'Medea,' he sighs, 'this is not about love.'

He pulls away but I grab his face, forcing him to look at me. In those azure depths I am certain I see a flicker of something, like a shadow shifting beneath a beautiful, endless sea.

'What would she do?' I press, my voice as steady and soft as midnight darkness. 'Would she sacrifice everything for you? Would she betray all she knows? Destroy her own name, her own self? Would she *kill* for you, Jason?' His eyes gleam in the dimness. 'I would do all of that, without question. You know I would. You have seen me do it and you know I would do it again.'

'Medea.' My name is a broken plea on his lips. But I can see something loosening inside him, so I press the knife in deeper, twisting it.

'No one will ever love you like I do, Jason.' My hand around his face melts into a caress. He does not pull away. 'There isn't a soul on this earth I would not destroy for you. For us. Not even the Gods could stand in the way of my love for you.'

'You should not speak of such things.' His voice is thin, cracking. I can feel his resolve crack with it, splinters of doubt ricocheting through him.

'I do not care.'

'I am marrying her, Medea.'

'She will never be enough for you.' I run my hands through his hair, gripping those golden curls, pulling slightly so his head tips back. 'She will never deserve you.'

'*Stop it.*'

He grabs my wrists, pulling my hands from his head. The movement is not gentle, yet there is an electricity to his touch, shooting through my skin like a bolt of Zeus's lightning. I know he feels it, too; I can see it in the way his gaze flickers to my lips, heat pooling in his eyes, setting them ablaze. His desire. It is still there, rooted within his very core.

It always will be there, as will mine.

For we *belong* to one another.

'Stop,' he says again, voice fainter now.

'Make me,' I breathe.

His eyes meet mine and something silent and powerful passes between us, a connection beyond the realm of words and logic. It is a kind of madness, toxic and all-consuming, but dangerously sweet in its ability to undo us both.

He suddenly pulls me down on to him, the movement rough and graceless as our lips meet with an unforgiving ferocity.

We do not kiss as lovers, for they kiss with a soft, considerate tenderness. The meeting of our lips is fuelled by an aggression swollen with unsatiated anger, as if our fight has moved to new plains, and now our bodies are the battlefield.

Jason throws me down on to the bed and manoeuvres himself over me. He pulls at my hair and claws at my skin. An animalistic cry rips from me, one that he echoes, his mouth opening wide as I bite my teeth down on his lower lip, hard enough to taste blood.

A guttural growl escapes Jason as he pulls back, his thighs remaining on either side of my hips, holding me in place. He probes his lips carefully, drawing his hand away and inspecting the blood smeared across his fingertips, his expression unreadable. Slowly, I take his wrist and pull his hand to me, holding his gaze as I lick the blood clean from his fingers. I can taste him on my tongue, every beautiful, treacherous inch of him.

I watch as the look in Jason's eyes swells into something more primal. He moves to kiss me again but, without warning, I clamp my legs around his waist and knock him sideways, hoisting myself on top and pinning him to the bed with a hand to his throat. Our eyes meet and I can feel his pulse quicken beneath my fingertips, thick and fast.

As I stare down at him, I can feel his entire body blazing with those wild flames of desire. He smiles, his lips still bloodied.

I release him and he throws his hand up, knotting a fist into my hair as he pulls me to him. He kisses me and I can taste the hate and love and anger and passion curdling between our lips. It is as if the edges of our emotions have vanished, causing them to bleed into one another, creating a confusing cacophony of feelings that crash together along with our bodies.

Inside my head, the words hiss like water scattered across a raging fire – *I will not let go. I will not lose him.* How could I, when our fates are already irrevocably bound, the cords intertwined like nooses around our necks.

'I love you,' I whisper against his flesh.

He does not reply, except for a stifled moan. But he does not need to.

I know he does.

He must love me.

Because if this is not love, then what else is it?

34

I wake to an empty bed.

A morning chill whispers in the air, amplifying the emptiness of the room, the familiar hollowness Jason carves out of me whenever he disappears. But I tell myself not to worry as I search the house. I tell myself all is well as his absence swells like a pressure inside my skull, causing a headache to blossom with sickening ferocity.

Everything is fine.

Jason will be back soon; I know he will.

I wrap my arms around myself, the flesh Jason held and kissed and enjoyed just hours ago. It is as if I can still feel the remnants of him on my skin, his familiar scent, the lingering burn of his lips. The mark of his love, his anger.

He must have gone to see the king.

He will have gone to Creon to decline his foolish marriage offer. For Jason has seen sense now, seen reason. He has come back to me, to where he belongs. Where he has always belonged.

This stumble in the road has been painful for us both, but perhaps it was what we needed to shake us from the stupor we had fallen into. To remind us of what truly matters.

When Jason returns, we shall leave this wretched place. We will take our sons far away; we will start a new, fresh life.

And we will be happy. Deliriously happy.

Because we deserve to be. Because my vision promised we would be. Because we have fought too hard not to be.

I stop outside Pheres and Mermerus' chamber. They are still asleep, draped in drowsy shadows. Their faces so peaceful, contrasting with their small bodies splayed across their beds.

I lean against the door and stare at them, letting the doubt inside my mind ebb away with the rhythm of their breathing.

For so long I have kept my distance from them, in fear of infecting their innocence, staining their souls. But as I gaze at them now, I can only see their light. Their sweet, shining goodness. It is their father's light, and the light of the love they were born from – so bright and fierce it will burn away any residue of my darkness.

And I will nurture that light, with everything that I have.

I would swallow every drop of misery on this earth so that they may never know the stain of its touch, so they may never be forced to turn to such extremes as I did. I want them always to see their lives as a gift, a beautiful, joyous gift that *I* gave them.

They will be proof that the loathed, murderous witch of Colchis can put goodness into this world. And if I can create this goodness inside me, give life to it, then surely I cannot be as evil as the world deems me. Perhaps, when my sons grow into proud young men, people will finally see that. Perhaps they will finally understand.

I wish Chalciope could meet them.

This thought clangs inside my head, catching me off guard. It is accompanied by a vision of my sister embracing my sons, grinning up at me with pride as she moves to take my hand in hers.

A sadness wells in my chest as that impossible vision withers away, chased by the morning light spilling into the room.

For the past decade I have longed to reach out to my sister, spending countless sleepless nights carefully constructing what I would say, how I would explain . . . but I never have, and I know I never will.

For I do not deserve a place in her life, not any more.

'Mistress?' Myrto appears in the doorway, her voice soft so as not to wake the children. She looks pale. 'There is a visitor. He says he has a message from the king.'

I ignore the knot of dread in my stomach as I leave my sons sleeping.

The king's herald stands in our central courtyard, inspecting the flowerbeds. I watch him pluck a flower and turn it over in his hands to examine it.

'Saffron,' I say as I approach him. 'You can make quite the powerful love potion from that flower. Though its effects are rather fleeting.'

The young man drops the flower instantly. I watch it fall to the ground, its beauty plucked and discarded.

'My lady.' His lips split into a tight smile that does not reach his eyes.

'If you are here to see my husband, I must inform you—'

'I am here for you, my lady.' A slight twitch of his fingers betrays his composure. He is nervous, scared even. 'I have a message from the king.'

'Very well.'

'Creon, the honourable King of Corinth, decrees that you, Medea, and your sons, Mermerus and Pheres, are hereby permanently exiled from his kingdom with immediate effect.'

'Exiled?' I bite down on the word, teeth grinding over its bitter, familiar taste.

'For the threat you pose to the king and his daughter.'

I step closer, watching his eyes flicker to the doorway, mapping his escape route, as if I were some crazed animal preparing to strike.

'What "threat"?' The question is as sharp as the morning chill cutting through the house.

The herald is visibly quaking. 'The king has spoken.'

'Well, you can tell *your king*—'

'Medea.' Jason's voice invites a rush of cool relief to slit through my rage.

I turn to see him striding into the courtyard, wearing the same clothes I stripped from him hours ago.

'Husband, please tell this man he is talking nonsense.'

He stops before me, eyes settling on mine. I feel my relief snagging on the sombreness of his expression, the coldness in his gaze.

'You may go, thank you.' He dismisses the herald, who needs no further encouragement. He flees like a deer might flee a wolf, with wild, panicked urgency.

'What is going on?'

Jason draws in a steady breath. 'I tried to stop it, Medea. Truly, I did. I went to Creon this morning to plead your case, but his mind was already set.'

'To exile us.'

'Yes . . . You must understand, you have brought this upon yourself, Medea. You are too much of a threat to the princess. Creon cannot allow you to remain here.'

'I see.'

He stares at me for a long moment, seeming bemused by my calmness. When he speaks again, his voice is tentative. 'Do you understand what I am saying, Medea? You must leave Corinth immediately.'

I move to the statue of Hera at the centre of our courtyard, staring at the paint flaking around her calm eyes, revealing the blank white marble beneath. I scratch away some of the loose flecks, taking the moment to steady my thoughts.

'I understand.'

'You . . . understand?' he repeats, seeming unconvinced.

'You know I have wanted to leave here for a long time, and now we have a reason to. We can take the boys and begin our new life, a new start. This will be good for us, Jason. This is what we needed.'

A silence follows. I turn back to Jason, but he is staring past me, to the passageway that leads to our sons' chamber, where they continue to sleep, blissfully unaware.

'I am not leaving, Medea.' His voice is gentle. 'I told you, I am marrying her.'

I feel my heartbeat thicken inside my chest and the world slows with it, the seconds coiling around my body, dragging me downwards. I feel as if I cannot move, cannot even think, as if I am being paralysed by time itself.

'But . . . last night—'

'We should not have allowed ourselves to get carried away like that.' Jason brushes his fingertips absently over his slightly swollen bottom lip. 'It was irresponsible of us.'

'But you . . . we . . . made love.' I hate how pathetic the words sound in my mouth. They are the words of a girl, not a woman. I can tell Jason thinks so, too, from the way he looks at me, with a nauseating pity in his eyes.

'You think a night of intimacy can fix what is broken between us, Medea?' His voice sounds distant, drowned out by the anger clawing its way up inside me, fuelled by pain. I think I hear him laugh, but I cannot be sure. 'Please tell me you are not still so naive?'

My mind snaps back into focus as I feel his question stab through my gut.

'Do not do this, Jason.' My voice is surprisingly steady.

'It is already done.'

The words cut me open, allowing my pain to spill out into the space between us. But that pain is quick to harden into something else, something ugly and wild.

I feel the darkness rearing inside me as I storm towards him, the death spirits howling like starved beasts. Jason holds his ground, does not so much as flinch. He has never been afraid of me. I once thought that a gift, but perhaps now I see it for what it is – he has never truly understood my power, never truly respected it.

He has never truly respected *me*.

'You said you were doing this to protect us,' I hiss inches from his face. 'And now we are to be banished?'

'You brought this on yourself, Medea.' His eyes reflect the sun-beams reaching overhead, but there is no warmth in them. They are as cold and cruel as a clear winter sky, watching the world shrivel and die beneath it.

'This is *my fault*?' I snarl. 'What have I done except rot away in this house, this tomb, for the past decade?'

'You know what you are like.' His words drip with sickening con-descension. 'You said it yourself last night – you would kill for me. How is Creon to trust a vengeful, murdering witch?'

'I never said I would harm the girl.'

'Do you think anyone would believe that?' Jason moves past me. As he walks away, his voice is stiff with formalities. 'I convinced Creon to allow you until sundown to prepare for your departure. I can send some slaves to assist with preparations. You are to be gone by daybreak.'

'*What of your sons?*' I move in front of him, blocking his path. A sudden breeze makes my unbound hair whip around me, snak-ing wildly across my neck and face. 'You would banish them, too? Let them starve on the streets as exiles? Who will take them in as the bastard children of a foreigner witch? You said it yourself: all of Greece knows what I did. They will *die* without you, Jason. Do you really wish to kill your own sons?'

He winces at my words, a wisp of sadness catching in his eyes, and something heavier – guilt, perhaps.

'We need time for things to settle. Once Glauce and I are wed, I will talk to Creon and see if he will allow us to take the boys in, have them work in the palace.'

'Work? As what – *slaves* to your new whore?'

'Do *not* speak of Glauce like that,' he snaps, the ferocity of his defensiveness wounding me. 'She is innocent in this.'

'So was I, Jason. And look what you did to me.'

He ignores me as he continues, 'You know it would be best for our sons to remain with me.'

'And take them from their mother?' I seethe. 'How is that what is best for them?'

'Medea.' Jason throws a piercing look at me. 'Do you really wish me to list all the ways you are unfit to be their mother?'

'How dare you—' I cut myself off as I see our sons watching us from the fringe of the courtyard. Pheres drowsily rubs the sleep from his eyes, whilst Mermerus' gaze flickers between us, his expression unreadable.

'My boys.' Jason goes to them, a hint of emotion finally cracking in his voice, causing the words to tremble.

I watch him kneel before them, placing a large hand on the back of their necks. Pheres stares up at him with such love, such adoration, it makes me feel sick. Mermerus' expression is more guarded.

'Tell them. Tell them of your betrayal.'

'I have to go now,' Jason says, ignoring me.

'Why, Papa?' Mermerus demands.

'Because . . . I must.' He lowers his gaze to the floor, unable to look his own children in the eye. 'But know that I love you. So very much. You know that, don't you?'

'Yes, Papa,' they say in unison.

'Look after each other,' he tells them, voice catching as he rises. 'We will be reunited again soon. I promise.'

'*Jason*,' I hiss, following him as he moves towards the entryway.

'Medea, please, for our sons' sake, just . . . go quietly. Do not make a scene, do not cause more harm than you already have.'

'And if I will not go quietly?' The unspoken threat tightens the air around us, but Jason's face remains composed.

'I will do whatever I must to protect my bride.'

I draw in a sharp breath, wishing I still commanded the composure I had as a child when I refused to give my father the satisfaction of my pain. But Jason's words bruise so much deeper than my father's fists ever did.

'You will ruin the girl.' My eyes and throat feel as if they were on fire, burning with the rush of emotions eating me alive. 'You will ruin her as you ruined me.'

'Medea.' He laces my name with such ugly, entitled pity. 'Enough.'

With that, he strides out into the street. In the distance, I see the gaggle of Corinthian women watching like vultures, eyes greedy, feeding off the spectacle unfolding before them.

'You will regret this, Jason,' I call after him.

He turns back to me, raising his brows as if unimpressed, letting my threat fall flatly at his feet. Behind him, I can hear the women tittering.

'Come now, Medea, let us not part as enemies.' Jason tilts his head to one side, his eyes glittering with an arrogance I had once mistaken for charm. 'We are too grown up for that, are we not?'

In this moment, I want to hurt him.

I want to cut that smile from his face and wear it as my own, so he may see how hideous it is. And then I will pluck those dazzling eyes from his skull and watch them turn dull and useless in my palms. My desire is so visceral I can feel my hands twitching at my side, like claws unsheathing, ready to strike.

Jason saunters away, nodding politely to the crowd of women.

As I watch him go, I feel a strange numbness descend over me. A hollow nothingness. I cannot even feel the breeze in my hair, nor the sun against my skin. It is eerily peaceful, this moment of emptiness, as I watch Jason walk out of my life.

I feel it then . . . the illusion I have shrouded myself in for the past decade. It splinters inside me then shatters completely. Shards of reality cascade through my entire body, slicing me open, letting me bleed out the poison Jason has filled me with. A poison I once welcomed into my heart, mistaking it for love.

But this was not love. It was never love.

It was some kind of toxic dependency, one born and cultivated in the most vulnerable corners of my bruised heart. And Jason knew; he knew exactly which words to say, which strings to pluck, how to shape my loneliness, my naivety, my sadness into what suited him. Into a weapon he could wield. A monster he could command.

He used me . . .

And I let him.

I became the darkness so he could shine.

And now . . . he abandons me, casting me aside like a soldier discards a blunted sword. He goes to find a new victim, a person he can leech from, filling his gluttonous desire for power and adoration.

It is all so clear to me now. How have I been so blinded for so long? Even when the truth was staring at me so plainly.

He loves what you can do for him, like a king might love his gold . . .

You will give Jason everything ... every inch of you, every shred of your pathetic soul ...

It will never be enough for him ...

You will never be enough ...

He sees you as a weapon ...

You will destroy each other ...

Through the suffocating torrent of my emotions, I can hear the death spirits howling again, fed by the hateful pain coursing through me. They call for vengeance, for retribution ...

And I will answer their call.

For Jason must pay.

Anger fills the space Jason leaves.

I feel it slicing through my insides, igniting every thought with its incinerating touch. It is the kind of anger that consumes completely and irrevocably; its sole purpose is to destroy, to burn.

Good. Let it burn, all of it. This life. This world.

And let Jason burn with it.

As I walk back inside, my strides are fuelled by the fury thumping through my veins. My hatred is like a bottomless cup, pouring into my soul, overflowing.

Hecate. My mind reaches outwards. *My Goddess. Forgive me for neglecting you. Forgive me.*

I call to you now.

Bring me your power ...

Bring me your darkness ...

'Mama?' The small voice splinters my thoughts.

I am kneeling on the floor of my chamber, barely aware of how I even got here. My hands are braced on the ground, fingers arched like talons. From the doorway, my sons watch me, their faces wide with confusion. They are a ray of light piercing through the fog of my rage.

'Is Papa coming back?' Mermerus asks me, his voice so small.

'No.' The word trembles.

Pheres lets out a noise that swells into a sob. Even Mermerus' eyes begin to shine, though he rubs the tears away furiously.

I know I should reach for them, embrace them, comfort them . . . but how can I when I have no love to offer them? I can only feel the hate inside me, smothering all else. I have nothing to offer them, nothing to give them . . .

'Mama.' Pheres' small, sticky hand slips into mine; his blue eyes sparkle. His father's eyes . . . I cannot look at them.

These poor boys, born from two vile creatures. A man so selfish, shallow and cruel he uses emotions to twist all those around him to his own will. A woman so starved of light she brings darkness wherever she goes.

They do not deserve this. Any of this.

And I do not deserve them.

Neither does Jason.

'I need to be left alone,' I croak, as a wave of sadness steadies my anger. 'Please.'

They do not move, but continue standing there, staring at me, their tearful eyes watching, accusing.

You did this to us, those eyes say, *you ruined us.*

You ruin everything.

You are a disease.

Your violence breeds violence.

You did this.

You vile, soulless creature.

You. You. You.

362

'*Get out!*' I scream, and I feel their small bodies jolt as they scramble away, their sobs resonating off the walls.

I have failed them.

No, not I . . .

Jason.

A fresh wave of anger ignites inside me, bringing with it that violent desire . . . I want to hurt him, but not with weapons and fists . . . No. That is not enough, for that pain is only skin-deep, only temporary.

I want to ruin Jason.

As he has ruined me, ruined our sons . . .

He believes I am expendable, something he can use and toss aside, but I shall show Jason that his life is *mine*. I handed him his victories, fed him his glory. I breathed life into his fame and secured his name in history. I built him up, allowing him to step on my neck to reach such dizzying heights . . .

And I can take it all away.

I can tear him back down into the dirt where he belongs.

It is the punishment he deserves, and I have always believed in punishment. My father made sure of that.

Around me, I feel the darkness's smile widen.

35

Poseidon guards the palace of Corinth.

A statue looming so large, I have to crane my neck to see the full might of him. He stands ready for battle, twisting his body to summon all his earth-shuddering power before hurling his famed trident.

The statue perfectly captures a moment of coiled tension before a devastating storm. A fitting scene, one that almost makes me smile. Almost.

The day has worn away, allowing Nyx to bruise the sky into shades of purple and blue, streaked with remnants of fading gold. Poseidon's statue glows in this dying light, and I regard him silently as I walk past, feeling his dead eyes on me.

I wonder what the Gods will think of my actions today. Will my wrath invoke theirs?

I realize, as I approach the steps to the looming palace above, that I no longer care.

This is the path I have chosen and there can be no turning back. I am already too far gone. For I started down this route long ago, the day I drove that knife into my brother's throat. Since then, I have been free-falling into this oblivion.

The death spirits knew . . . They knew my path could only ever lead here, to more violence, more death. That is why they waited in the shadows, so patiently, so loyally.

My only allies.

Inside me, that tether to the Underworld quivers with dark anticipation, sending smoky ripples through my blood, feeding the violent desire.

'You! Stop,' a guard barks, clocking me immediately. Behind him, his comrades bristle with an outrage underlined by fear. 'You cannot be here, witch.'

I let a whisper of my power pulse outwards, wrapping around their fragile little minds. They slump to the floor like sagging bags of vegetables, their bodies thick and awkward from the slumber that has paralysed them.

'I will show myself in,' I say as I walk past, my gown caressing their crumpled bodies.

The entryway to the palace is large and ornate, the uniform pillars holding aloft a colossal triangular pediment depicting Poseidon on a mighty golden chariot, led by his famed white horses. The scene is expertly detailed, brought to life with splashes of blues, greens and sun-baked reds. The sculptor has even taken the time to paint the whites of Poseidon's rageful eyes, giving his masterpiece a sinister yet effective touch.

Before me, the palace yawns outwards, marble floors glinting. I see a slave on her knees, scrubbing with red-raw hands. Her face constricts with fear as she regards me and the fallen guards slumped in my wake.

'Princess Glauce. Where is she?' I ask, my voice level, polite even.

The slave is silent, frozen by her fear. Her lips quiver but no sound escapes. In her hand the soiled rag drips, marking my seconds she is wasting.

Drip. Drip. Drip.

I do not have time for this.

'If you tell me, I will not have to turn you into a mouse.' My smile is one cut from ice and nightmares.

365

'In the west wing,' she splutters, her voice stilted with an accent I do not recognize. 'The furthest room, facing the sea.'

'Thank you.' A thread of darkness coils around her sweet, innocent mind. Her body crumples as I tug her down into a peaceful sleep. She looked like she needed the rest.

Gliding through these hallways feels like second nature to me. The design is different, more artistic, stylized – but the bones of the building remain the same, bones I spent my childhood learning how to slip between.

As I approach the girl's room, my mind suddenly reaches to my sons, to their tearful faces when I shouted at them this morning. They will be waiting for me at home, confused and perhaps afraid.

They do not understand, of course not. They are too young, too innocent.

But I am doing this for them, for *us*. I am doing what any good mother would do.

How many times did my mother witness my father's cruelty and look the other way? She never fought for me. Never even tried.

I will not be like her.

Because nobody hurts my children without paying the consequences.

'Who are you?' The shrill voice cuts through my thoughts as I find myself inside the princess's chamber.

I take a moment to observe the space, the small bed tucked in the corner of the room, beside which sits a table with jewellery scattered across it. A large, colourful tapestry hangs along the far wall, the woven threads illuminated by a small hearth. The tapestry depicts Aphrodite watching over her son Eros, who fires his arrows of passion towards unsuspecting mortals.

So, she is a romantic.

'Who are you?' the girl repeats.

My eyes shift to hers and for a moment I am silenced.

She is so young. Her face still holds the softness of childhood, an endearing plumpness that gathers around her cheeks and jaw. She has a smattering of freckles across her face, as if some playful god had flicked paint over her at birth. Her nose is small and upturned, her top lip barely covering her two front teeth.

Glauce's face is framed by mousy-brown hair, that falls in soft waves down to her shoulders. Her eyes are blue like Jason's, and they shine with the excitement of those youthful souls that have not yet been weathered by the world.

Innocent – that is what Jason called her. The word causes something to curdle inside me.

Does Jason find it alluring, her *purity*? Is it a nice change from his tainted wife? Perhaps he takes a sick pleasure in corrupting such innocence. Well, Jason, I think it time I wield that poison for myself, to demonstrate to Glauce what it truly feels like to be infected by your love.

Let her witness how painful it is. How cruel.

And may you, Jason, witness the consequences of it.

'Are you her?' the girl asks, a spark of fear in her eyes. 'The witch?'

'I am,' I say, watching the panic disperse through her, stiffening every inch of her small body. She is at least a head shorter than me.

'Who let you in?' she demands, though her voice lacks authority. Something about her nervousness makes Chalciope flicker in my mind, but I force the thought away as quickly as it surfaces.

I cannot think of her. Not now. For if I mark a single similarity between Glauce and my sister, I know it will risk splintering my resolve, and I cannot allow that.

'The guards,' I reply, keeping my eyes on hers. I am blocking the doorway, her only escape.

367

'You should not be here.'

'Why?' I tilt my head.

'Because you are *exiled*!' Her voice hovers on the edge of a whine. She looks as if she might cry.

'I am to leave in the morning,' I counter. 'I did not mean to upset you by coming here, Princess, I merely wanted to wish you all the best on your union with my husband.'

My choice of words makes her flinch.

'He is no longer your husband,' she says, her small hands balling into fists at her sides.

I find her anger amusing. It is so juvenile, so untried – not like the ancient rage inside me that has spent an entire decade taking root, growing into every inch of my body.

'I know you shall make Jason very happy,' I continue, testing a step towards her. She holds her ground. 'You are so young, so beautiful.'

'Why are you saying this? Why are you here?' She has a look in her eye like she might bolt for the door, or perhaps scream.

I cannot allow either of those things.

'I want to thank you,' I say, my lips curling into a smile I hope she believes is genuine. 'Jason and I were miserable together. You have taken him off my hands, you see. You have set me free.'

She says nothing, her eyes tight with suspicion.

'You look unsettled,' I continue. 'I'm guessing you have heard the rumours about me. The women of Corinth are terrible gossips.'

'I'm well aware.' She nods. My silence encourages her to continue. 'They have spun so many lies about my mother. Claiming she is riddled with jealousy and will dispose of any beautiful woman who comes near my father . . .' She waves her hand in the air to demonstrate the ridiculousness of these accusations.

'Rumours are such nasty little things.'

'They are.' She studies me, her expression still guarded, yet her body begins to loosen. Just a fraction. 'So, you and Jason . . . You were truly unhappy together?'

'Terribly.' I smile. 'Though it was not his fault. We are just . . . incompatible.'

'Incompatible,' she repeats, considering it.

A silence settles between us; within it I can feel the seconds falling away. It will not be long before the sleeping guards are discovered.

I am running out of time.

'I will be a good wife to Jason,' she tells me.

Did I sound this naive when I declared my loyalty to Jason the day I met him?

I glance at the package in my hands, feeling a hint of guilt break through my anger, sparking along that dark, adamant wall. But the death spirits swiftly respond, pooling into those fractures.

Do not fail now. You have come so far.

Glauce steps closer, clutching her golden gown in her fists. 'I am sorry . . . about your sons.'

'My sons?' I feel my smile slipping.

'I know Jason loves them dearly. He tried to convince my father to let them stay here, with us, but, well . . .' She sighs gently. 'The king can be a stubborn man. But I think he will warm to the idea.'

I stare at her. 'You would . . . take my children?'

'I believe it is the right thing to do. Exile is no place for children, do you not agree?'

Is my husband not enough that she wishes to rob me of my sons as well?

Will she and Jason rejoice in stripping me of the only piece of happiness I have left in this world?

'This must be difficult for you,' Glauce says gently, as if she could comprehend a fraction of what I have been through. 'But we must trust in the future the Fates have woven for us, must we not? That is what Jason says.' She twirls a lock of hair between her fingers. 'He told me he used to believe the Fates hated him, for all the suffering he was forced to endure in his childhood. But now he realizes they cannot hate him, for they blessed him with our union. That is what he said to me. Is that not the sweetest thing you have ever heard?'

How could the Fates hate me when they have blessed me with you?

'So sweet.' My smile is saccharine.

'You must not hate him, Medea. There is too much hate in this world,' Glauce enthuses, her blue eyes so full of love, so blind to logic. 'Jason is a good man and a patient one.'

'Patient?' My eyebrow quirks at the word.

Glauce's cheeks redden. 'Well . . . I only meant that he waited for me . . . for my . . .' She trails off, fingers fumbling together. 'But you knew, did you not? Jason said you had agreed to part ways when my . . . *bleeding started.*' She whispers these words. 'Though, admittedly, I did not believe Jason would be so patient. Three winters is a long time to wait.'

I stiffen as her words settle over me. Three winters.

Jason had been planning this treachery for *three winters.*

Something in my expression must rattle Glauce, for she takes a step back. Her lips loosen as her anxiety swells. 'Please don't be upset, Medea. I know exile wasn't part of your agreement with Jason, but he only wants to protect me. You must understand, it wasn't an easy decision for him . . . He did not look himself this morning when he came to speak with my father. I have never seen him so *broken.* I believe this whole situation has really taken its toll on poor Jason.'

I frown. 'Jason *told* Creon to exile me?'

Glauce chews her lip, visibly flustered. 'He insisted . . . f-for my safety.'

And there it is. The final piece of Jason's betrayal.

I feel it snap into place inside me as my anger surges up to greet it, obliterating all in its path.

How dare he . . .

'Perhaps I have said too much.' A flicker of fear dances across Glauce's face.

'No, not at all.' The words taste bitter in my mouth as I swallow my rage. I then hold out the package in my hands, smoothing my lips into a wide smile. 'Please, I wanted to give you this wedding present, a peace offering.'

She eyes it suspiciously, but I can see a curiosity fizzing beneath that uncertainty.

'I am grateful, Medea, but I must warn you, I have no power to undo your exile—'

'This is not a bribe, Princess. It is a gift. Nothing more. In Colchis we always give gifts to brides before their wedding day.'

'I am not sure—'

'It is a gown,' I continue, inching a step forwards. 'I made it myself. They say Colchian women are experts at the loom, you know. We have all kinds of luxurious materials, too. Have you ever worn silk?'

'Silk?' Her eyes widen.

'Yes. It feels exquisite to touch.' I pause, lowering the package in my hands. 'I can see you do not want it. Foolish me, I should have known a princess such as yourself already has plenty of beautiful gowns. Forgive me. I shall leave you be . . .'

I turn to go, adrenaline burning in my veins. I take one slow step towards the door . . . Another . . .

'Wait!' Her voice halts me. Around us, the shadows mirror my smile. 'I suppose I could take a look at it, your gift. It would be rude not to.'

'Thank you, Princess.' I bow slightly as I hand the package to her.

She holds it in her small hands for a moment, testing the weight of it. I imagine those hands touching Jason, running through his golden hair, clinging to his muscular body. I imagine them embracing my children, showing them the affection I was never able to.

My heartbeat thuds in my chest as she unwraps the dress, letting the crimson material ripple to the floor. It is the dress I wore the day I betrayed my family, the day I killed Apsyrtus. I have mended it since then, sewed up the snags from our violent escape, scrubbed clean my brother's blood. I even added some silver embellishments, which now twinkle attractively in the firelight.

'Red was my father's favourite colour,' I say.

'It is . . . beautiful.' Glauce's eyes pore over the rich fabric.

'Perhaps you should try it on, so I can ensure it fits—'

'*GLAUCE!*'

A thunderous voice crashes into the room, causing the fire to shiver and shrink. I feel the weight of his shadow fall across me as I turn to greet him.

Creon. The King of Corinth.

He is a colossal man. Nearly the size of Meleager, but instead of his sculpted chest and stomach, a swollen, bulky gut hangs from his giant frame. His eyes are a dark, rich brown with a touch of green around his pupils. Beneath his tangled, greying beard I can see his vicious snarl.

'Get away from her, witch!' He strides towards me, grabbing my arm. His touch reminds me of my father.

'Father!' Glauce protests. 'She was doing me no harm!'

He ignores his daughter, hauling me from the room, his giant hand spanning the length of my upper arm.

'I apologize if my presence has offended you, Creon,' I say calmly, as he throws me out into the hallway. Armed guards line the corridor.

I regard them with a nod, taking a moment to pat down the creases in my dress, flicking an invisible fleck of dust off my shoulder.

Around us, the darkness vibrates with anticipation.

'You assaulted my guards.' The lines in Creon's face deepen, spittle gathering in the corners of his mouth.

'I assure you, I have no idea what you mean.'

'You entered my palace without my permission,' he continues, jabbing a meaty finger into my face.

'I wished to deliver the princess a wedding gift.'

'You stay away from her, do you understand?' He steps towards me again, but I hold my ground.

'Of course.'

'You are testing my patience. I could have you slaughtered for trespassing.' The threat is a guttural growl. 'Leave, immediately. Leave my palace, leave my kingdom. Take your bastard sons and go. If I see your face again, I will have you executed. Do you understand me?'

'Perfectly.' I stare at him for a moment, tilting my head to the side. 'Glauce is lovely, by the way. It is a shame Jason dragged her into all this.'

'Do not speak of my daughter again. You are not worthy of her name on your tongue.'

My smile hardens. 'Where is Jason?'

He scoffs a cold laugh. 'He is not here and, even if he were, the man would not want you near him. He is done with you, witch, and believe me, he has been waiting a *long time* for this day.'

His words intend to wound me, but I do not feel them.

'Jason isn't here? That's a shame – he will miss it.'

Creon looks unnerved by my impassivity.

'Miss what?' He bites out the question.

Before I can answer, a blood-curdling wail rips through the palace.

Seconds later, Glauce stumbles into the hall, hands covering her face as she screams unceasingly.

She is wearing the crimson dress.

'Make it stop!' she shrieks, her voice raw with agony. 'Gods! Make it stop!'

The dress is eating her alive.

The poison I wove into its threads is now burrowing into Glauce's skin, spreading through her like a fire catching light. Her flesh begins to bubble up in hideous, swollen welts, disfiguring her pretty little body and face. Then those welts begin to pop, the remnants sizzling and burning away her skin. It smells foul.

The princess screams, writhing in violent agony. She tries to rip off the dress with panicked hands, but her flesh begins to pull away in large chunks beneath her fingers. When Glauce realizes, she tries to scream again, but the sound is wet and gargled. She is choking on her dissolving organs. The poison has worked its way inside her.

If only Jason were here to see this.

To witness the effect of his cursed love.

The princess falls at my feet, grabbing at my skirts with ruined hands. Her lips are moving but the strangled pleas are no longer forming into words. As I stare down at the girl, a bubble of bloodied spit gurgles from her mouth.

Inside me, I feel the death spirits rejoicing, basking in her pain. They are so loud I barely hear Creon's cry as he falls to his knees.

'*Help her!*' he begs me. 'Please, Gods, I will give you anything, just make it stop! *Please!*'

'I cannot,' I say, as Glauce's grip loosens. Her face begins to sink inwards as her melting body caves in on itself.

Creon then does something foolish, but predictable.

He tries to strip the dress from his daughter, but as soon as he touches the material, the fiery poison seeps into his own fingers, spreading through his mighty body in mere seconds, devouring his flesh as it goes.

The king howls like an animal, writhing in agony whilst his men look on, paralysed by their horror, weapons slack in their hands.

I watch the poison strip Creon's flesh from the bone. But, even now, he still reaches for Glauce, still tries to save his beloved daughter with the last of his dying breath.

I wonder what it would feel like, to be loved like that.

I thought I knew once.

Some of the guards finally remember their duty, rushing forwards to help their king. They are met with a similar fate. The ravenous poison consumes all it touches. A nasty, destructive spell. A magic so dark it would make even Hades himself blanche.

It is impressive what can be achieved by combining the different mediums of magic. I have not tried such a thing before. The poison lacing Glauce's dress is a simple concoction derived from earth magic, which I then infused with my dark power to weaponize it.

A clatter of swords and spears rings out and I turn to see the remaining guards running for their lives. Their cries mingle with those of my victims, creating a haunting cacophony of shrieks that resonate off the palace walls.

I am left alone in the passageway with the dying. The smell of burnt meat fills the air. It is a slow death. A cruel one.

I wait to feel something – satisfaction, remorse, closure, victory, repulsion, anything. But there is nothing. Nothing at all. Just an emptiness that has neither beginning nor end.

I had hoped Jason would be here. I wanted him to see the devastation he has caused, to feel their lives staining his hands, to let the guilt butcher his soul.

Glauce could have lived a long, happy life. The girl deserved to. She was sweet and innocent and kind ... But Jason had to tangle the child in our mess, had to ruin her life with his own selfish deceit.

She did not deserve to die, Jason.

Her blood is on your hands.

That guilt is yours to bear for evermore.

When the bodies have finally stopped writhing, I murmur a few words under my breath. Within seconds, the dress ignites in a blaze of crimson flames that crawl up the walls, infesting the bones of the palace just as the poison infected those of its king and princess.

I exit the burning palace cloaked in darkness. Outside, people are already gathering. I glide past them, unseen, as they watch the thick smoke fold into the twilight sky, blocking the last of the day's light.

The screaming begins then. It reminds me of the screams I heard when my father flogged his slaves, but now it is I who inflicts that pain.

Now it is I who holds the power.

36

My sons are waiting for me when I return home.

They stand in the doorway, their faces bright with wonder as they watch the fire raging in the distance. From here, the palace is just a crimson smudge against a canopy of darkness.

Soon the people will realize who did this. Soon they will come for me.

'Mama!' Pheres rushes forwards when he sees me, looping his small arms around my legs.

'Come inside now, quickly.'

'Why is the palace on fire?' Mermerus asks, touching my dress as I usher them inside.

I ignore the question. 'Where are your things? Did Myrto pack them as I asked?'

'She saw the flames and went to help,' Mermerus says and I curse under my breath.

'Where are we going, Mama?'

'Away from here,' I reply dismissively as I move into the kitchen to retrieve the goods I stored earlier.

'But where?' Pheres presses.

I do not know.

I had been so focused on my revenge that I had planned for little else. But now that rage has burnt away, a cold uncertainty left in its wake. Where can we go now? Who can help us? Who would take us in?

'Mama?'

'We're going somewhere far away.'

'Where is that, Mama?'

I do not know – those four words taunt me as I stride through the house, gathering whatever belongings I can carry. My sons trail behind, chasing me with questions I cannot answer.

'Where is Papa?'

'Why are we leaving?'

'Are we coming back?'

'Will Papa be coming with us?'

'What is this?' This question snags my attention and I finally look down to see Mermerus touching my gown. When he pulls his hands away, they are stained crimson. The blood glints in his small palms.

Glauce's blood . . . Creon's blood . . . All over his hands.

For a moment I cannot breathe.

All I can do is stare at my son, his hands covered in the blood I have spilt, his skin marked with the stain of my crimes. Beside him, Pheres looks down to see his clothes are the same violent shade of red from where he embraced me moments ago.

My boys. My sweet, innocent boys, covered in my sins, my *darkness* . . .

Something deep inside me gives way, like an earthquake sparking through stone, causing it to splinter and crack. Through that fissure I feel a wave of emotion burst, surging up and up, choking me, overwhelming me – it is a paralysing concoction of pain and guilt and anger and shame. It is almost too much to bear; I can feel it tearing me apart from the inside.

I fall to my knees, gasping for air.

'What is wrong?' Mermerus asks beside me.

'I don't like it – make it go away, Mama.' Pheres sounds scared now as he tries to wipe the blood off, but it is too late. It is all over him. It is *everywhere*.

As I stare at them, I feel a sharp pain split open my head. I press my palms into my eyes as a vision burns violently before my eyes, just as it did the day in Iolcus when I discovered I was pregnant with Mermerus. But this vision is nothing like that joyous, shining image; this is a nightmare, one forged from the depths of Tartarus itself.

I see my sons, still covered in blood, but now as grown men. Handsome and vibrant but . . . tormented. I can taste their pain like ash in my mouth. As my eyes lock with theirs, I see myself within them. My bond to the Underworld has shackled itself to them, and I can feel the death spirits feeding off their innocence like hungry, restless beasts. Destroying their souls, turning them into the same monster their mother has become.

For I am a monster. Am I not? The kind that preys on young, innocent girls and doting fathers.

The kind that kills their own flesh and blood.

I had the chance for peace, and I chose revenge. I had the chance for light, and I chose darkness. Because the monster inside me craves it. It is the same monster that lurks inside my father, only mine is stronger, fed by the death spirits I welcomed into my soul. And now, this darkness has been embedded within my sons.

I did not want this. I did not want any of this.

I did not mean to . . .

I believed Jason's light could counteract it, but now I know he possesses no such virtues. If I am the darkness, then Jason is the obstacle that causes those ugly shadows to be cast.

You are just as rotten as me, Jason.

I thought we could put goodness into the world, but violence only breeds violence, and we have dealt our fair share, have we not?

I believed I could take my sons away from all this, that once I'd made Jason pay, we could leave this land behind, leave it all behind, then we could be happy, be free. I believed the same in Colchis. That once I was rid of my father, I would be rid of the monster. But that creature followed me still, and it will follow me now because I cannot run from this, and neither can my sons. It has them in its claws now.

The seeds have already been sown.

And it will only grow and grow and grow.

Consume and consume and consume.

Destroy and destroy and destroy.

I cannot bear it.

I cannot bear to watch them become like me.

They do not deserve that torment. That cruel future.

But ...

I could still save them from it.

I could ensure the darkness never reaches them.

'Are we leaving, Mama?' Pheres whispers.

'No,' I say, my voice calm, becoming as soft as the night around us. 'No, it is too late. We are too late.'

We are standing in the courtyard, Selene's curved moon smiling down on us. I turn my gaze up to her, feeling her delicate light caress my cheeks as a cold serenity descends over me.

My sons watch me with those wide, blue eyes. Their father's eyes.

I can still be a good mother. The mother they deserve.

I owe it to them.

'It is time for bed, boys.' I take their hands in mine, so small, so trusting. 'It is time to sleep.'

37

The house is quiet as a tomb when Jason arrives.

I hear his footsteps fracturing the peaceful stillness, his strides quick and agitated.

'*MEDEA!*' He shouts my name like a soldier cries to his enemy in battle. A bloody promise ringing through each syllable. '*MEDEA!*'

'Jason.' I walk out into the passageway.

He stands on the other side of the courtyard. He is bathed in moonlight, pale beams that reach from overhead, carving twisted shadows that look like bodies strewn across the ground between us.

Jason stares at me for a moment. His body is still except for the rise and fall of his chest as he settles his breathing. There is ash in his hair and black traces of it smudged across his skin.

'You killed her,' he breathes, as if only just comprehending the magnitude of that statement. '*You killed her.*'

He breaks into a stride, slicing the distance between us into a few furious paces. I hold my ground, watching his face contort.

'She was just an innocent girl,' he spits.

'She was.' I nod. He stops just in front of me, so close I can smell the sweat beading along his forehead. 'What's the matter, Jason? You used to love it when I killed for you.'

'You are a monster, Medea. You have no soul, no heart,' he spits, and I wipe the residue slowly from my cheek.

'You are right, and why is that?' I smile up at him, continuing before he can respond, 'Because I gave those things to you. I gave *all of me* to you. I loved you, Jason, so deeply, so painfully.' He turns away but I move in front of him, forcing him to look at me. 'But do you know what is stronger than a lover's love? Their *hate*.'

He closes his hand around my throat, shoving me against the nearest wall, the impact sending a jolt of pain through my spine. 'I am tired of listening to your poison. You have ruined *everything*. You have destroyed me, destroyed my life.'

'As you destroyed mine,' I reply calmly. 'And what a beautiful mess we have made of each other, husband.'

He presses his hand tighter, constricting my airway. Dark blotches begin to bloom across my vision and, for a moment, I think he might actually do it. He might kill me. But then something cracks across his face and his grip slackens. He goes to pull his hand away but I catch his wrist, holding it firm.

'Go on,' I goad. 'Why not finish what you started?'

'*No.*' He rips his hand away furiously. 'This is what you want. You want me to become as depraved as you are ... but I am not like you, Medea. I am no murderer.' He runs shaky fingers through his curls, eyes wide and panicked. Drawing in a slow breath, his voice steadies as he says, 'Besides, I would not want to deprive the people of Corinth of their justice. They are on their way now. They plan to slaughter you for what you did. They want to make you suffer as you made Glauce suffer.'

'Did you come to warn me? How thoughtful of you.'

'I came to take our sons away from here,' he snarls. 'They are innocent in this. They should not suffer for your crimes.'

'So now you care for them?'

'I have *always* cared for them.'

382

'Even when you *told* Creon to banish us?' He flinches at that, taking a step backwards. 'Oh yes, Jason, I know about that. I know everything.'

'*Medea*. We do not have time for this. Tell me, where are they? Where are my sons?'

A pause, just a brief one, as the darkness gathers its breath around us. Eager. Waiting.

'Safe.' I smile. 'Our sons are safe now.'

'What … what do you mean?' The question catches in Jason's throat as he studies the shift in my countenance, his anger dissolving into something more real. 'I want to see them, now. Take me to my sons. *Let me see them.*'

A part of me does not want to. He does not deserve it and I know he will not understand.

'Let me see them.' He steps closer to me, his words cut with a silent threat.

I do not reply but instead flicker my eyes towards the boys' chamber. Without further encouragement, Jason tears into the room, a ragged breath loosening from his chest. I follow behind him slowly. I know I do not need to rush, for I know he cannot harm them now.

Nobody can harm them now.

Not even me.

Our sons lie in their bed, nestled together. Pheres' head rests on his brother's narrow chest. I have tucked the blankets up around them to keep the chill away; I want them to be warm, comfortable.

They are so peaceful.

So perfect.

There is a quietness inside my head as I stare at them, a stillness I have never felt before. It is like a sigh of relief in my soul.

Jason mirrors the sound, sighing as he watches them sleeping. He then rubs his face with his hands, as if to dispel whatever dread had been rising within him. After a moment, he approaches their bed, placing a hand on Mermerus' small cheek.

'It is time for us to go, sons,' he whispers, shaking them gently. 'You need to come with me now.'

They do not move.

They will not wake.

'Pheres? Mermerus?' He shakes them a little harder, watching their heads loll like a child's lifeless toys.

'It was my gift to them,' I say from behind, as I walk to stand at the foot of their bed. The darkness swirls around me like wisps of smoke. I watch that panic begin to rise in Jason once again as the realization sets into his bones. He is now grabbing their faces, shouting their names.

'No, no, no.' A sob escapes him as he seizes the empty cup beside their bed.

'Hemlock,' I confirm. 'Well, my own version of it. Adapted so that there is no pain, no suffering. Just a gentle drift off into sleep. I had prepared it in case my plan at the palace went awry. But this is a much more worthy purpose for it.'

'*How could you?*' He chokes on the words as if gagging on his own pain.

'How could I?' I frown, moving to sit on the bed beside them. I stroke a gentle hand down Pheres' cheek, then Mermerus'. My beautiful sons, forever safe in their innocence. Forever perfect. 'I have done what any mother would do: I have protected them. I have set them free. They are safe now.'

'I took another bride, so you took their *lives*?' Jason has crumpled to his knees now, head bowed against the bed.

'No,' I say firmly, as I continue to stroke their faces. 'This was not for *you*, Jason. It was for them.'

An anguished cry rips from Jason's chest as he rocks on the floor; I can only make out the words 'my boys' in between his gulping sobs.

I knew he would act like this, for a man as selfish as he could never understand.

Jason would never destroy his soul to protect another's.

He would have let our boys live and suffer, just so he would not feel alone. He would have encouraged that darkness inside them, taken advantage of it. Just as he did with me.

Only a true, selfless parent could make this necessary sacrifice.

And so, in this act of mercy, I have finally done it. I have become the mother my sons always deserved.

I hope they see that from where they watch in the world beyond.

'Are you going to kill me now?' Jason asks, his voice muffled by his hands still covering his face.

'Kill you?' I roll my eyes at him. Typical Jason, always thinking of himself. 'I don't want to *kill* you, Jason. I just want you to suffer.'

I reach down and brush a curl from his forehead, the waves of his anguish soothing me. Jason flinches from my touch, his red, swollen eyes widening as he stares up at me. For the first time ever, a genuine, raw fear consumes his face, and I smile down at it in greeting.

'*Witch! Witch! Witch!*'

I hear the distant rumble of the Corinthian mob as it approaches our house. The bloodthirsty chanting fills the night with a new kind of darkness.

They have come to kill me. To claim my life for the ones I took.

But my life is not theirs to take.

'I have to go now, Jason,' I say, moving to lift my boys.

'Where are you going with them? Do not take them away.

Please, Medea. Please let me bury them. Let me have that. I beg of you.'

'You do not deserve the honour of burying them, Jason. You lost that privilege when you left them to exile,' I say coolly as I hoist their small, slack bodies into my arms. They are heavier than I expected.

But I have always been stronger than I realized.

Jason is quiet as I walk carefully to the entryway of our home, my sons slumped over my shoulders in their eternal, peaceful slumber.

Outside, the sky is hazy. The palace continues to burn in the distance, dark smoke curling upwards in thick, sinister plumes. The smell of it hangs heavy in the air. I pause and look up, seeing ash dance on the breeze like beautiful, smouldering snowflakes.

Down the street, the mob approaches, a pulsing river whose currents churn with a violent, ugly rage. Weapons glint alongside the torches they hold aloft, their chant echoing their thunderous steps . . .

'*Witch! Witch! Witch!*'

A chariot is waiting for me, the one I prepared earlier. It buzzes with a quiet power, the traces of my spell glimmering around its edges. I bundle the boys inside, ensuring they remain wrapped tight and warm in their blankets.

I do not want them to feel the cold.

'Medea.' Jason's voice comes from behind, stronger now. 'You will not take them from me.'

I turn to him, regarding the sword in his hand. His previous fear has burnt away, revealing a fresh layer of fury, bolstered by the rage of the crowd marching towards us.

'I thought you believed you were better than this, Jason?' My eyes flick to the blade, then up to the sky.

With each passing second the pulsing mob grows closer, their thirst for my blood burning as fiercely as their beloved king's palace.

'That was before you killed my sons, you soulless monster.' He re-affirms his grip on the hilt, stepping closer. 'You have taken *everything* from me, Medea. You have ruined me.'

'You have ruined yourself,' I reply, bored by his self-serving misery. 'You suffocated yourself with your sense of entitlement, thinking you are owed so much by this world when you give so little in return.'

He lunges, grabbing my hair and wrenching me around to face the crowd. The mob swarms us, crashing and swelling like a wave over a rock. They are mostly men, but amongst them I can see those crones, the ones who gathered outside my house every day, their faces illuminated by the torches held in their hands.

Someone reaches out to grab me, but Jason forces them back.

'Hold! Hold!' he commands. 'You want justice for your king and princess. I understand that, my good people.' The crowd bellows in response, weapons clattering. Jason was always an excellent performer. 'But the witch's life is mine to claim, in payment for ruining my own. She has tainted me with her darkness since the beginning, cursing me with the Gods' wrath when she killed her own brother. Then forcing me into exile when she killed my poor uncle. Now, she has murdered my future wife and *butchered* our sons. All in the name of vengeance, all because I wished to be rid of her poisonous ways.'

The people gasp as Jason points his sword to where our boys lie in the chariot. Their horror does not faze me, for they could never understand my sacrifice.

'Her life is mine to take. Please allow me that.' The crowd roars its approval, as Jason turns his gaze to me. His eyes glow in the torch-light, little crimson stars dancing in his irises. 'On your knees.'

I flicker my eyes to the sky, watching the ash flutter down in lazy circles.

'*On your knees,*' he snarls again. 'Or do you wish to die standing?'

I smile at Jason, and this disconcerts him. He was expecting me to cry, to grovel for my life like his snivelling victim, and, as I soak in his reaction, I realize something.

This man does not know me at all.

He never did.

Jason draws his sword back, readying to swing, to remove my head from my neck. I hold his gaze; his blazing eyes are lined with silver as he fights back furious tears. For a moment, I think he might falter, but then I watch the resolution settle across his face.

There is a moment of quiet and the world stills; it is as if the Gods have paused time itself to watch.

'This is for our sons,' I hear Jason saying, as he prepares for the final blow.

'Do you want to know what I find most amusing?' I continue before he can respond, 'Even after all that has come to pass, you still underestimate me.'

The night sky is ripped open with a blaze of crimson and gold.

Jason glances upwards to see a mighty form swoop over the crowd, causing a rush of air that threatens to knock the people from their feet. Giant wings stretch across the sky, blocking out Selene's calm face.

The vast form banks and glides overhead again, before landing with bone-shuddering force atop our home. The creature lifts its head and lets out a mighty shriek, one that would make Mount Olympus itself tremble.

He is still as magnificent as the day I created him.

Amyntas.

The dragon. *My* dragon.

He releases a stream of fire from his mouth, the world bursting to life with violent streaks of colour. Around me, the crowd flees, scattered by their fear. They are shouting, screaming, drowning in their panic. Some attempt to fire arrows, but they ricochet off Amyntas' glittering scales.

I watch his giant talons pierce the walls, causing our home to crumble beneath his mighty weight as he clambers down to the ground. It has been ten winters since I saw him last, when I stood before him and commanded him to sleep outside the Grove of Apollo.

'It cannot be . . .' Jason murmurs, his sword lowered.

'I called to him for aid, and he answered.' I stride forwards. 'It is good to see you again.'

Amyntas bows his head, amber eyes aglow. Before him, Jason looks so small, so fragile. He raises his sword and an answering hiss erupts from the dragon's throat, causing Jason to drop the weapon instantly.

I then make quick work of attaching the chariot to Amyntas, who grumbles a little in protest. The reins were designed for a creature far smaller, but they will do for now.

'Go on, then,' Jason spits when I am done. 'End it. Kill me. What do I have left to live for?'

I turn to him, feeling Amyntas swelling behind me like a nightmarish shadow.

'Kill you?' I tut. 'I have already told you, Jason, I do not want you to die. I want you to *suffer*. And, as that suffering eats you alive, day after day after day, I want you to think only of me.'

He does not reply. I do not need him to.

I do not need anything from him.

I never did.

I place a hand on his shoulder, patting gently. 'Come now, Jason, let us not part as enemies. We are too grown up for that, are we not?'

He opens his mouth, but a low grumble from Amyntas silences whatever hateful retort had crawled up his throat.

I offer a smile, as patronizing as all the ones he ever offered me, before stepping on to the chariot. Without hesitation, Amyntas takes flight. The chariot, enchanted with my magic, stays hovering upright whilst Amyntas beats his wings, launching into the moon-soaked sky.

Beneath me, I watch as Jason grows smaller and smaller, shrinking away until he is just an insignificant mark on the world below, and then disappears.

38

I bury my sons on an unremarkable hill in an unfamiliar land.

The hill overlooks a quiet valley lined with rivers that wind across the grassy plains. On the horizon, dawn kisses the sky awake, her rosy fingers painting the view with streaks of soft pink and honey gold.

The burial is quick and efficient. I cannot allow my mind to linger, cannot allow self-centred emotions to seep through my resolve. To feel sadness over their deaths would be selfish.

Their graves make me think of my brother, or rather, his body, those pieces of him swallowed by ravenous waves. I regret letting Jason throw his body into the water more than I regret killing him. Apsyrtus was cruel, but even he did not deserve such degrading treatment.

I hope they retrieved the remnants of his body. I hope my mother and father were able to bury him properly, and he was able to find peace in the eternal resting place beyond.

And what of Glauce and Creon? Will the people of Corinth manage to perform burial rites with their ashes? Or will their souls be trapped on the shores of the river Styx for evermore? I vowed their lives were Jason's burden to bear, but why do I feel this heaviness inside me at the thought of their perpetual limbo?

Or is this heaviness just the weight of a body that no longer harbours a soul?

My gaze lifts to the rambling valley below. The quietness unsettles me. It is too peaceful, too calm, and that feels wrong after all that has happened.

I have just ripped my life apart with my bare hands, and yet the world remains unchanged.

The silence mocks me.

So, I scream at it.

I scream at the world.

I scream at my father for making me feel worthless and at my mother for never fighting for me.

I scream at Chalciope for leaving and at Circe for letting me go.

I scream at Apsyrtus for hating me and at Hecate for burdening me with this curse.

I scream at Jason for making me destroy myself for him, and at the girl who let him.

I scream for the love I thought I'd lost, but never had.

I scream for my sons who deserved none of this, and at the pain I cannot bear to feel.

I scream and scream, letting that wounded fury rip from my throat, from my soul. I scream until my skin feels as if it were on fire and my cheeks are wet. I scream until my whole body aches.

And then, silence once more.

In the echo of my screams, I feel my anger pulse like a dying heartbeat, growing quieter with each thickening *thud*. I can sense the other emotions lingering beneath it, vultures waiting for that heartbeat to still, so they can flock upon its corpse, ripping me apart with their guilt-tipped claws.

But guilt is for the weak, for those too cowardly to stand by their actions.

And I am done being weak.

There are things I regret, of course. Wasting so much of my life with Jason, letting him crush me down into his pathetic, subservient wife.

But I do not regret making him suffer.

He deserved every inch of his pain.

Beside me, Amyntas lets out a warm, shuddering breath that is peppered with embers and ash. His eyes regard the graves of my sons and, as I gaze up at his magnificent form, I wonder which remnants of the man he was still live within his beating heart, if any at all.

'Thank you,' I say to him, my voice ragged. 'For coming to my aid.'

I know it was not his choice to help me. He is bound to me by powers stronger than free will, so when I silently reached out to him through the darkness of the night, he had no choice but to answer my call. Amyntas' eyes shift to mine, his pupils like shards of obsidian cutting through those glowing amber irises. I cannot tell if it is hate or amity in his gaze, or perhaps something else entirely.

'I can reunite you with your previous form if you wish it. I could make you human again.' He blinks slowly, as if considering my words. Then he raises his mighty head, unfurling those glorious wings, the span of which dominates the hill we stand on. The morning light illuminates the veins snaking across the stretch of leathery skin, the talons at the tips gilded with dawn's rose-gold touch.

He is truly beautiful.

'I suppose a lion would not wish to turn back into a mouse,' I say with a nod. Amyntas bows his head, perhaps in agreement.

A gentle wind picks up then and he begins to shift his stance, heavy, taloned feet thundering towards the edge of the hill. I know he wants to leave, to follow whatever calls to him on that breeze.

'I still wish to give you a gift, to show my gratitude,' I say, causing him to still. 'I wish to free you from your bond to me; I wish to release you. You no longer serve me.'

There is a slight pause as Amyntas absorbs my words, feeling that bond inside him unravelling. Then he beats his wings, slicing through the air as he shoots upwards. I watch him soar higher and higher, cutting across the sky as it slowly rouses from its slumber.

My eyes hold on to him until he is just a smudge in the distance, until the heavy stillness sets in around me once again and I am left alone with my sons.

My boys.

I hope they understand the gift I gave them, the gift of eternal innocence, of souls unburdened. I will explain this to them when I see them in the beyond, when we are reunited. One day.

But not now.

I do not fear death – how could I when I am so familiar with its face? But to end my life now would mean Jason has won. It would mean he succeeded in destroying me. He would like that; I know he would. I can imagine him gloating at the idea that he drove the infamous Medea to her grave. He would claim it as a victory.

And I cannot allow that.

Even if I find no pleasure in this life any more, I will live just to spite him, and I will take satisfaction in that.

And I will not just live, I will *thrive*. I will claim that power Jason never could. I will go to Athens, to Aegeus, and I will take up his offer. I will become his queen, not because I care about such meaningless titles but because I know it will torment Jason, and that brings me a deep, delicious sense of comfort.

I smile as a wave of rich, smoky darkness rises from my core, whispering against the embers of my fury, stoking it to life. In my veins, my magic answers, surging upwards, the power burning in my blood, making my fingers itch.

Atalanta once told me the world would make me the villain of this story, but she was wrong.

The world tried to make me the victim, so I became its villain.

When I was with Jason, I wanted to destroy every inch of myself so I could start anew. I was ashamed of who I was, a shame that was planted by my parents and cultivated by all those around me. I swallowed down the lies the world told me: that my power was something to fear, to hate. I believed myself worthless and that belief drove me to seek validation from whomever I could grasp hold of, as if their love would prove I was enough.

But I have always been enough.

And I no longer wish to destroy what I am to create a version of myself this world will accept.

I will embrace it all. Every ugly, monstrous part of me. I accept you.

I let my power seep through me now, allowing it to consume every inch, even those small, forgotten corners I once tried to keep out of reach. I have no use for them any more.

Consume me. Completely. Irrevocably.

Let us become one.

'Medea.' I hear Hecate's bodiless voice weave into the breeze, bleeding into my mind like a gentle caress against my thoughts. I turn to see her standing beside me. One of her faces stares down at my sons' graves, another gazes out over the valley and the third is looking straight at me. Around us, the last remnants of the night press inwards, shadows clinging to her ethereal form like a dark gown. I feel the space between us thrum with her cold power. 'This was the path you chose.'

'It was.' My voice sounds different – stronger, perhaps.

'And you believe it the right one?' Her voice has its usual indecipherable tone.

'It was the only path.'

All three heads turn to the graves and I am certain I can see something whisper in those depthless eyes, but the emotion is too quick to place.

'And now?'

'Now I choose to live for myself.'

Hecate tilts her head to one side, surveying me carefully. Her face is so serene, like the glassy surface of a still lake, masking whatever creature lurks beneath. 'And what if the Gods do not agree? They are angry with you for what you did to Jason, to your sons.'

'Jason deserved what came to him.'

'But your sons?'

My gaze flickers over to their graves, the anger stumbling slightly in my veins. 'I saw their future, I saw what they would become . . . and so I freed them of that, of what the Fates had planned. I saved them.'

'And still . . .' Hecate's voice is smooth as ice. 'You killed your own flesh and blood. That is a crime the Gods cannot let go unpunished; you know that, Medea. If you wish to live, you must earn their forgiveness.'

'How?'

Hecate is silent for so long I begin to wonder if she will ever answer me. As I wait, I feel the resolution hardening inside me like a silent promise – this will not be my end.

I will storm the Gods and shake the very universe if I must.

But my story will not end here.

'Zeus requires a favour,' Hecate finally says. 'If you appease him, he says he shall pardon your crimes.'

I watch the sun rise higher in the sky, gilding the world in a new dawn.

'Whatever you ask of me, I will do it.'

FIVE YEARS
LATER

39

Chalciope

Colchis is a graveyard of memories.

As I stand in the courtyard, visions of my childhood whisper around me like ghosts reaching from the depths of my mind, causing a chill to pebble over my skin.

I think of my mother, the feel of her slender fingers combing through my curls, hearing fragments of that familiar tune she would hum. I always tried to harmonize with her, though I would inevitably end up singing the wrong melody, making her laugh. I loved it when my mother laughed; it was such a pretty sound. It made me feel special when I heard it, like glimpsing a rare, beautiful creature only few have ever seen.

Within the passageways I can see my father pacing, that quiet fury clinging to him like an extra layer of heavy clothing. Wherever he went he would leave a trail of unease in his wake. I cannot remember a time when I was not terrified of him. That fear permeates every corner of my childhood.

Here, in the courtyard, I see Apsyrtus practising with his wooden sword. He was always a talented fighter. My memories of him dance within the ripples of heat rising from the ground. I remember his face shining with such confidence, such delight, as he showed off the new techniques he had learnt. I cherish those moments when my brother would soften for me, revealing the kind soul trapped within his nasty exterior. *Look after Medea, please.* Those were the last words I ever spoke to him. The thought makes my chest tighten.

Medea. I see her most of all. That quiet, contemplative face haunting every shadow I pass.

I can feel my sister's presence so potently it's as if she's standing beside me, squeezing my hand for reassurance, just like she used to. Medea could always tell when I was upset, even if I tried to hide behind my bravest face.

A faint memory glows in my mind from when we were children and I was pestering Medea to play with me, as I often did. In my attempts to capture her attention, I accidentally knocked over a vase. I can still picture those pieces shattering across the floor just as my fear shattered inside me, cutting through every nerve. Medea was there in an instant, trying to sweep up the mess whilst I just cried, useless tears slipping down my cheeks. Medea even sliced her palm open in her hurry, causing blood to mingle with the debris. She did not complain; she did not even wince.

Our father was furious, of course. Even now I can feel that icy terror sluicing in my veins as he demanded, 'Who did this?'

'I did,' Medea confessed. I stared at her, mouth agape, guilt-tinged relief washing through me.

Medea had bruises on her chest and ribs for weeks afterwards, though she would not accept my gratitude. She would not even speak of it.

That was the sister I knew, fiercely protective of those she loved. Granted, she could be distant and cold and a little intimidating, but I always believed there was a light in Medea, even if my sister could not see it herself.

How wrong I was.

For surely there can be only darkness inside someone capable of such evil. Someone capable of killing and dismembering her *own brother*, not to mention those vicious rumours that have circulated since . . .

Two dead kings . . .

A slaughtered princess . . .

Medea's *own children* . . .

I have prayed, with every inch of my being, that these rumours are not true, that my sister is not capable of such depravity. Killing our brother was undeniably iniquitous, an act for which I will never forgive her. And yet, in truth, I can imagine how the events that un-folded could have led Medea to believe that violent conclusion was her only option.

But this? Her *sons*?

I cannot fathom it, do not want to. The thought of harming a single hair on my own sons' heads makes me feel sick. It goes against every single instinct inside me.

'Chalciope?' I look up to see Phrixus standing beside me, a hand resting on the small of my back. His touch is gentle yet reassuring. 'Are you all right?'

I nod, gazing out across the familiar courtyard. 'Is it time?'

The question makes him stiffen. 'You do not have to do this, dearest one. We can leave now if you wish it. If you have changed your mind—'

'No.' I squeeze his hand, more for his reassurance than my own. 'I must do this.'

'What if she . . .' He swallows, his fingers tightening around mine. 'What if she tries to hurt you?'

'She will not.'

'How can you know that?'

I say nothing, for in truth, I do not.

All I know is that I have to do this.

Phrixus stares at me as his question hangs unanswered between us. I can see the familiar thoughts swirling in his mind. It is an argument we have visited countless times, before and during our journey here. But my mind is made up; it was made up the day I heard Medea had returned to Colchis.

Nothing, not even the Gods, could stop me from seeing my sister again.

'I have to see for myself,' I whisper, my voice quivering with determination. 'I must see the monster she has become. Only then can I finally let her go.'

Phrixus' eyes are heavy as he nods. 'I know.'

He pulls me to him, and I sigh into that safe space between his arms. The shape of Phrixus is so familiar I could trace every curve and edge of him by heart.

I rest my head against his chest, my tension easing a little.

'I know this must be terribly difficult, after all she has done to you,' he murmurs against my hair.

Difficult. The word can scarcely encapsulate the exhausting emotions that have been battling inside my mind for so many winters. All that anger and fear and ugly, consuming *bitterness*. But perhaps worse than that was this ache of nostalgia that weighs inside me whenever I think of Medea, and that horrible sense of loss that has defined so much of my adult life.

Today, though, I will put an end to it. Like cutting cloth down from a loom, I will sever those messy, loose threads inside me and find the closure I have been longing for. The closure I deserve.

'Princess.' A slave appears beside us, bowing low. 'The queen will see you now.'

It sounds strange, hearing it aloud.

My sister, Medea.

The Queen of Colchis.

I stand outside the doorway, my hands twisting in front of me.

'Darling, I—'

'Phrixus, please.' I turn to him. 'I am doing this.'

'I wish there was something I could say to change your mind,' he murmurs, eyes heavy with the weight of his fear.

I kiss his cheek. 'I know.'

'If she tries to hurt you—'

'Phrixus.' The way I say his name quietens him, and he loosens a tight breath. My hands slip into his; they feel clammy and warm. 'Trust me. It will be OK. You can wait outside if you wish—'

'No,' he cuts across me. 'I am staying by your side. Always.'

'Come in.' We both flinch as a smooth voice filters from beyond the doorway.

Drawing in a careful breath, I walk inside, Phrixus close beside me.

The room is one I am certain I have never been in before, as this was my father's wing of the palace. Though it is hard to tell, for the space looks entirely different. Gone are the gilded ornaments, lavish decor and crimson drapery my father favoured. Instead, mismatched furniture litters the room, decorations dotted around: vases, plants, bowls, little statues of goddesses. Along the walls thick tapestries hang, overlapping for lack of space. It is like a child has been given free rein to decorate as they please, choosing one of everything possible. It gives the room an odd sense of character, despite feeling like the visual manifestation of a headache.

Is this a glance into Medea's mind?

'Sister. Phrixus.' That voice again, as soft and dark as Nyx's embrace.

It comes from the far corner of the room, where a figure sits draped in heavy shadows. As I draw closer, a hanging light splutters to life, making Phrixus flinch. This torchlight soaks the room in a warm, golden glow, allowing me finally to see the woman sitting before us.

The witch of Colchis and, now, its queen.

Medea looks exactly how I remember and yet, somehow, entirely different. Or rather, her features are the same, her moonlight skin and long onyx hair, that sharp, prominent nose and those intensely dark eyes.

Yet the way she presents herself has transformed.

The sister I knew always seemed unsettled, restless, despite her contemplative exterior. When I was younger, I imagined there was a creature pacing inside Medea, desperate to claw its way out. It frightened me a little, though I also felt sorry for the thing locked away inside my sister, desperate to be free.

I saw glimpses of the creature when Medea let her control slip. Like that horrible night when I was promised to Phrixus. Though I always believed Medea's anger was never directed at others – not even at our father, though the Gods knew he deserved it. It felt to me as if Medea was always directing her anger inwards, as though she was ripping herself apart to try to understand who she truly was underneath, or perhaps trying to fight whatever lurked inside.

But the woman who sits before me now is something else entirely. She seems relaxed, serene almost, as if she is finally at peace with herself, with whatever lives within her.

And she oozes *power*. Pure, unapologetic power.

It radiates from her, pulsing like a heartbeat that I can *feel* against my skin. A dark, silky touch brushing against me, as if assessing my threat. I shudder from the electric feel of it, both terrifying and intoxicating. Flicking a glance to Phrixus, I can tell he can feel it, too.

Medea sits on a simple, faded chair, though in the shadow of her power it might as well be a magnificent throne. Her face is calm, her eyes as dark and depthless as a midnight forest, full of horrifying possibilities.

There is something else about her, something deeply discomforting that I cannot place my finger on . . . then I realize.

Medea doesn't *feel* human any more.

Her presence feels like that of divine beings, of the Gods. Medea's lips cut upwards into something reminiscent of a smile, as if reading my thoughts.

See, she is no longer your sister, I tell myself, waiting for that feeling to come, the closure I so desperately long for. But, as I stare at Medea, all I can feel is a potent knot of emotions thickening in my throat.

I cough, trying to dislodge it.

'H-hello.' I finally find my voice, though it sounds small and delicate in Medea's presence, like a moth's wings fluttering against a flame. 'Thank you for hosting us.'

'It has been a long time.' Medea's voice seems to caress the darkness around us, causing the shadows to crawl closer. 'Please, sit.'

Phrixus shoots me a glance as I lower myself into the chair opposite my sister.

I clear my throat again, that knot persisting. Once I am certain I can speak without my voice cracking, I say, 'You seem . . . different.'

The words feel clunky and foolish as soon as they leave my lips.

'Do I?' Medea's own lips twitch.

I draw in a steadying breath. The room smells rich and smoky, punctuated by strange spices I cannot name. I wonder, warily, if Medea has been preparing her potions in here.

'Wine?' she asks, as if reading my thoughts once again.

I reluctantly accept the cup she offers.

'No.' Phrixus' voice sounds rough as he holds up a hand. He then bites out the next words through clenched teeth: '*Thank you.*'

Medea's eyes glow with cold amusement as she draws a cup to her lips and drinks, her gaze cutting between the two of us. A silence settles, and it seems as if Medea is waiting for me to speak, but I do not know where to start. There is so much I wanted to say, so many things I planned to ask. But now, I cannot seem to find the words. It is as if Medea's presence has completely eclipsed my mind.

As I stare at my sister, I feel a sudden, overwhelming urge to reach out and embrace her. But I force that impulse away, focusing instead on Medea's hands, reminding myself whose blood stains them.

'Is Father . . .' I trail off, not sure how to finish the question.

'I have not killed him, if that is what you are wondering.' Is that amusement rippling in Medea's voice? 'He is alive. Mostly.'

Mostly. The word makes me shiver.

'He's resting now, but you can see him later, if you would like,' she continues.

'I would . . . thank you.'

Another silence constricts the air around us, though Medea seems perfectly at ease within it. She sips her wine idly, her attention flicking back to Phrixus.

'You have many questions,' she says. 'Ask them.'

Tell me you didn't do it. The words ache in my throat. *Tell me they are all horrible lies. Please, sister.*

'Last we heard you were Queen of Athens.' I am relieved to hear Phrixus speak, his tone calm. 'And now you are Queen of Colchis.'

'Indeed. I was not a fan of the weather in Athens.' Phrixus stares at her, a frown darkening his brow. Medea lets out a husky laugh, the sound like rich, curling smoke. 'That was a joke, Phrixus. Do not look so sombre. Yes, I was Queen of Athens, for a little while.'

'But how did you manage that after—'

'After all I have done?' Medea finishes for him. 'Because not all men fear power, Phrixus. Some men actually admire it. Aegeus is one such man.'

'But the King of Athens was already married.'

'He was.' She nods slowly at him, eyes sparking. 'Meta was better off without him, believe me. And I offered Aegeus something nobody else could . . . an heir.'

'You . . . had another son?' I cannot stop the question from tumbling out.

A nervousness curls in my stomach at the thought of Medea's other children, those horrific rumours I have tortured myself with night after night. How I wish I could unhear them. But words can be a cruel curse – once they lodge inside you, it is near impossible to be rid of them.

'I did.' Medea's eyes slip back to mine.

Another silence follows and within it I can feel the silent accusations lurking. Can Medea sense them, too?

'C-congratulations,' I manage.

'Thank you.' Medea's eyes are steady, calm. So different from how I remember them. 'Obviously, things did not ultimately go to plan. It was that boy Theseus' fault, the one who came to the palace claiming to be Aegeus' heir. Of course, that was impossible, considering Aegeus' *condition*, but he was a persuasive individual. Irritating, too. His claim to the throne was a minor issue, but then he began making Aegeus doubt the legitimacy of our child and, well . . .' Her smile is a dangerous thing. 'I could not allow that. I tried to handle the situation, but Aegeus was not pleased with my . . . methods.'

Her eyes glint with unspoken violence, as if daring us to probe further.

Phrixus takes the bait. 'Did you . . . kill the boy? Theseus?'

'I tried to.' Her expression is eerily indifferent. She swirls the wine in her cup, the dark liquid nearing the edge but never spilling. 'After Aegeus banished me from Athens, I considered my options. Admittedly, I had limited choices. But I knew my son was the legitimate heir to Colchis, and why should he not be?'

The accusation is written in Phrixus' glare: *Because you killed the rightful one.*

'And Perses?' I prompt, thinking of our uncle who had stolen the throne from our father.

'He was a weak, pathetic man. It took no time removing our uncle from the throne.' Medea shrugs. 'The people, however ... They have been a little trickier to persuade. They remember my betrayal from before and their trust has been ... shaky. Fortunately, Perses was an awful king, so they were pleased to be rid of him.'

'*How?*' The word rips from Phrixus in a sharp breath, causing me to stiffen. 'How can the Gods let you continually get away with this behaviour? All the bloodshed? All the *death?*'

Medea goes very still then, and the tangible presence of her power seems to thicken, as if its pulse were clotting in the air. A chill scrapes over my skin, like night-kissed talons, making me tremble all over.

Perhaps coming here was a terrible idea after all ...

'The Gods and I have an understanding,' is all Medea says.

'What does that mean?' Phrixus presses and I reach out to touch his shaking fists. *Enough, husband.*

'The Gods *were* angry at me.' Medea nods, watching Phrixus' hands slowly relax beneath my fingers. 'I granted Zeus a favour. His son Herakles had got himself into a touch of trouble with Hera. He wanted me to ... tidy the mess.'

A favour? I can hardly fathom it, how a mortal could have anything worth bartering with the *King of the Gods.*

At our bemused expressions, Medea continues, 'Hera had driven Herakles mad, on account of him being the illegitimate child of one of Zeus's many lovers. Of course, Zeus could not openly denounce his wife's punishment, so he asked me to . . . handle things. Now, *inflicting* madness is tricky magic, but reversing it? That is a simple spell. You just need a single plant: hellebore. Have you heard of it?'

Phrixus and I stare blankly at Medea.

'Clearly not.' She clicks her tongue. 'You haven't touched your wine, sister.'

'She is not thirsty,' Phrixus cuts in.

'Does your husband always speak for you? Or has being a wife made you forget how to use your own tongue?'

'N-no.' I shake my head, wishing it sounded more convincing.

'Someone once told me "wife" is just another word for "property". Is that what my sister is to you, Phrixus? A possession?' Medea's voice is smooth, yet I can sense the silent threat cutting through her question.

Beside me, I hear Phrixus swallow, a bead of sweat slipping down his temple as he debates how best to respond.

Before he has a chance, Medea rises to her feet, making us both flinch.

'Father is awake,' she announces. How she knows this, I cannot understand. 'Would you like to see him?'

It feels strange to walk the familiar palace halls beside Medea.

How many times as a child did I long for this, to be able to stroll beside my sister without fear of reprimand? I allow my mind to wander, imagining we are children once again, stealing a secret moment together. I even feel that urge to glance over my shoulder to check nobody is watching, waiting to scold us. But then I feel that pulse of Medea's power tugging at the illusion, letting it unravel at our feet.

I steal a glance at my sister, wondering if any remnants of the Medea I knew still exist within her.

If they do, I certainly cannot see them.

'I have to warn you.' That silky, dark voice still unnerves me. It sounds too calm, too calculated. 'Father is not as you will have remembered him. He is quite unwell.'

'Is it the same sickness that took Mother?'

Our mother died a few winters past. I was not able to say goodbye, nor help send her soul to the world beyond. When my uncle took the throne, he forbade me from stepping foot on Colchian soil, afraid I would claim his title for my sons.

I hate the idea of my mother dying alone, with only my father beside her. It is something that has always haunted me and perhaps always will.

And whose fault is that? The question flares in my mind. If Medea had not betrayed our family, Colchis would never have been weakened enough for our uncle to attack.

'No. Father's sickness is of the mind.' She slips a sideways look at me, reading the doubts crowding my thoughts. Behind us, Phrixus follows silently. 'It is not a curse by my hand, if that is what you are wondering. It is merely a natural result of old age, when the mind can no longer keep up with the world around it. Unlike Circe, the divinity in father's veins did not grant him the gift of immortality.'

No wonder Father always hated Aunt Circe. It must have tormented his ego to know his powerful sister would live on whilst he one day would waste away into nothingness.

Medea turns down a passageway that leads off towards the guest chambers. Her steps are so smooth and assured; there is a confidence to her gait I have never seen before.

As we walk in silence, I find my gaze wandering, searching for Medea's son, the one she mentioned earlier. It is odd that I have not seen him yet. *Is the child safe?* I hate that my mind could leap to such horrific assumptions about Medea, yet perhaps more painful is the knowledge that my fears are valid.

There is no sign of the boy. I only catch clusters of slaves who disperse when they see Medea approaching, their eyes wide with fear. Medea seems not to notice the effect she has on them, or perhaps she is just used to it.

We come to a doorway where two armed guards stand watch. Their expressions are impassive as Medea enters. I follow close behind, whilst Phrixus gives me a nod and lingers in the hall.

The room is wrapped in a blanket of sticky heat, lit by a roaring fire despite the humid day. There is a sweet, cinnamon-laced scent coming from an incense burner. I watch thin tendrils of smoke dance lazily upwards from the smouldering dish, coating the air with a hazy sheen.

A large bed has been placed beside the fire, stacked with furs. At first I think the bed is empty, but as I draw closer, I see a small, withered figure lying within it.

My father.

I know it is him, though my mind has trouble comprehending the fact.

The figure that lies before me now is a mere shadow of the man I knew. For a long moment all I can do is stare at him, adjusting to how horribly old he looks. How fragile. The man whom I spent my entire childhood fearing, who has haunted my memories all my life . . . has been reduced to this.

'Did he eat?' I hear Medea asking someone.

'No, my Queen.' I had not even noticed the other person in the room. 'I'm afraid his condition has deteriorated.'

'Thank you, doctor.' Medea nods, moving to sit on the stool beside our father's bed. I watch as the doctor packs up his things and leaves, offering me a polite bow of his head before doing so.

'Father, you must eat something,' Medea murmurs, her tone firm yet not unkind.

As I draw closer, I see his eyes rolling behind his closed lids as he fights the lethargy laced into his bones. His skin is so sallow and gaunt, he looks as if he were already on his way to the eternal world below.

My eyes shift to Medea, who has a bowl of soup cupped in her hands. She holds it to his thin lips and urges again, 'Eat.'

Our father lifts his head a little, though he barely has the strength to swallow a mouthful. I watch, fascinated by Medea's gentle patience. What I am witnessing before me seems almost unbelievable, more unbelievable than when I heard Medea had conjured a dragon. I never thought I would see my father so weak and frail, but to see Medea tending to him like this . . .

My gaze drops to his gnarled hands, the blue veins snaking beneath his thin skin. Those hands I have seen beat my mother, my sister. I was lucky he rarely laid those hands on me, but watching my father hurt those I loved was a far deeper kind of pain.

How can Medea stand to be around him, to tend to him so? A shameful part of me wonders why she has not ended him like all the others. The Gods know he would deserve it.

'You have a visitor, Father,' Medea tells him when he starts turning away from the soup. Some of it has slipped down his chin, pooling in the wrinkles at his neck. It is unsettling to see him so pitiful. 'Look, Father, Chalciope is here. Your daughter.'

'Hello,' I say weakly.

Our father's eyes open a fraction, though his vision seems glazed.

He glances around the room, lips trembling. Medea goes to wipe the soup from the creases in his neck.

'Where ...' His voice is so terribly thin. 'Where is Apsyrtus?'

Apsyrtus. The name makes my heart constrict.

'He is not here,' Medea replies.

'Iydia, where is our son?'

'He is not here,' she repeats, seeming unfazed by being called our mother's name.

Our father appears to grow distressed by his own confusion, trying to sit up though he is too weak to lift himself. He keeps repeating over and over, '*Where is my son?*'

I feel tears burning my eyes as I glance away, unable to watch.

'Apsyrtus will visit later.' The lie rolls smoothly from Medea's tongue. 'You must rest now.'

'I will see him? I will see my son?'

'Yes, Father.' Medea turns to me, watching as the tears spill down my cheeks. 'You will see your son soon.'

And I realize, then, that perhaps her words are not a lie after all.

'He is dying.'

'Yes.'

We are sitting out in the courtyard. Medea has her hands folded neatly in her lap, her face tilted up to the sun. Beside her I am rigid, staring at nothing, unable to shake the sight of our father's withered face from my mind.

Phrixus is loitering somewhere in the shade, keeping a respectful distance to allow us a moment alone.

'I hated seeing him that way ... despite everything,' I admit.

'You should have seen the condition he was in when I found him. Our uncle had him rotting in a prison cell.'

'Why do you do it? Care for him, I mean.' I glance sideways at Medea, whose eyes are closed, her pale face glowing in the afternoon light. 'You know he does not deserve your compassion.'

'I would not call it compassion.' She meets my gaze.

'What would you call it?'

'Satisfaction.' Medea smiles with an eerie vacancy, the word skittering uneasily over my skin. 'I am sorry it upset you to see him.'

I lower my eyes, discomforted by the intensity of Medea's full attention, the weight of it. 'Does he ask for ... Apsyrtus often?'

Apsyrtus. It feels strange saying his name aloud, especially to Medea. I cannot remember the last time I did so.

'Every day.'

We are silent for a long moment. As I look out across the courtyard, I see those memories of our brother flickering between the columns. I wonder what kind of man he would have grown to be. Would he have given in to his cruelness or would Apsyrtus have been strong enough to embrace the goodness I knew existed inside him? I will never get to know.

Medea has taken that from me.

Yet, try as I might to revive my resentment, I cannot seem to muster it. Instead, I am met with a heavy wave of sadness, one that has no real beginning or end, just an endless, swirling current inside me.

'I heard news today,' Medea says, her tone light, conversational almost. 'Jason is dead. He hanged himself from the rafters of the *Argo*. Imagine that.'

I stiffen, unsure how to react. Medea's face remains blank.

'I ... I am sorry.'

'Sorry? Why, did you string him up yourself?' She quirks an eyebrow, her eyes glowing with a dark amusement.

I feel flustered as I grope for the right words. 'No, but . . . he was once your husband . . . I just thought, perhaps—'

'He is nothing to me, Chalciope. Not any more. His death means nothing.' Her words are empty, flat, yet something shifts within Medea's eyes, betraying that cold composure.

I open my mouth to probe further, when a loud squeal has me jolting out of my skin. A small boy totters across the courtyard, stumbling excitedly into Medea's waiting arms. He gives another squeal of delight as she lifts him into her lap and he breaks into a bubble of laughter.

'Medus, there you are.' Medea embraces the boy, a sudden softness descending over her, though her power seems to swell, like a she-wolf's hackles rising, defending her cub.

For a moment, all I can do is stare at them.

It is so beautiful to see Medea like this, with such warmth to her, and the boy seems totally at ease in his mother's arms, smiling up at her with radiant joy. And yet, I cannot silence the question burning inside me: *Is this child safe?*

'Medus, this is your aunt, Chalciope.' Medea turns to me. 'Chalciope, this is Medus.'

The boy's skin is pale, with curling, ebony hair that flops over two large, deep-brown eyes.

'He looks just like you,' I smile. Medea says nothing to this as she sets Medus down on the ground.

We watch the boy scramble over to where the wet nurse crouches, holding a toy that seems to fascinate him. His innocent delight is a breath of fresh air within these walls that hold so many dark memories.

'He seems . . . happy,' I murmur.

'I did not think such a thing possible.'

415

'What do you mean?'

Medea is quiet for a moment. When she speaks her voice is different, gentler perhaps, but only by a fraction. 'I feared he would . . . become like me. I am not ashamed of my power, not any more. But neither would I ever wish it upon another . . . As such, I had not planned to bear Aegeus a child – not naturally, anyway. I had been plotting ways around it when I discovered I was pregnant with Medus. I planned to terminate the pregnancy before Aegeus would ever have known. It seemed like the kindest thing to do for the child.'

I stifle a gasp at her words and the bluntness with which she can discuss such a thing. But something in Medea's face makes me ask, 'What changed your mind?'

'I saw a vision,' she says, her eyes still intensely focused on her son, as if she were afraid to look away in case he might vanish altogether. 'Of Medus as king of a great land. I saw his happiness, his virtue, and I knew, in that moment, that I was capable of it.'

'Of what?'

'Creating goodness in this world.'

The words pierce deep inside me, and I feel a surprising sting of tears in my eyes. I blink them away as I turn to watch Medus playing in the grass, hiccupping an excitable laugh as a butterfly flurries around him.

I want to tell Medea she has always been capable of goodness, but the words lodge in my throat.

A tear escapes down my cheek and I dash it away.

'It was different, before,' Medea adds, ever so quietly.

Before. With her other children . . . those poor boys.

What really happened to them? And what part did Medea play in it?

As if sensing the direction of my thoughts, Medea says, 'I know why you are here.' I feel my body coiling inwards. My eyes flick to hers, though her attention is fixed on Medus. 'You want an explanation. You want me to say something that will make you feel better about what I did, that will help you understand. You want a reason not to hate me, because you hate having to hate me.'

My mouth falls open. I cannot think what to reply, but what else is there to say? Medea has been brutally accurate, voicing the words I had not even had the strength to admit to myself.

Her voice remains hollow as she continues, 'I am sorry to disappoint you, sister, but I cannot give you what you seek. I will not excuse what I have done, nor do I care for your forgiveness. There are many salacious rumours about me, but you should know that whatever you have heard is likely based in truth. I have done things many will deem evil, perhaps rightly so.'

The words feel choked as I whisper, 'But . . . don't you regret it?'

It is more a plea than a question.

'Regret it,' Medea repeats, her voice vacant. Just empty syllables between us. 'Which part?'

This strikes me like a physical blow.

Which part? For there is so much of Medea's life she *could* regret, perhaps all of it. As I stare at my sister, I consider how much she has endured, all that hate, cruelty, manipulation, abuse, rejection . . . When you fill a person with such ugly things, is it surprising that they would unleash it all back on the world? Medea chose the path of hate because nobody had ever shown her another route.

That ache in my chest intensifies as I say, 'I am sorry I left you here alone.'

'I do not want your pity.' Medea's voice is clipped, dismissive.

'It is not pity, but I . . . I believe if I had been here, perhaps I could have—'

'Chalciope, nothing could have stopped what I did, which path I chose.' A smile touches her lips and Medea's power seems to dampen like the air before a storm. 'That girl was too lost to see reason. She could not be saved.'

I can sense it then, the great tide beneath the calm surface Medea has learnt to master so perfectly. It is still there, still churning away. How does she do it, how does Medea hold all that inside her and not sink beneath it? Perhaps she already has. Perhaps that is why I recognize so little of my sister, because the pieces I once knew and loved have long since drowned within this torment, leaving only the harshest, coldest parts to weather that storm.

'I mourned for you,' I whisper, my voice thick with the tears burning in my throat. 'When I found out . . . all that had happened . . . it was like you had died along with Apsyrtus.'

'Maybe I did.' Medea nods, her tone still empty.

I stare at her, willing my sister to react, to be upset, angry, defensive, to convey *something* human. Anything.

'I was *so angry* at you. I still am,' I say, the tears streaming down my cheeks now, hot and urgent. The emotions spill from me like poison from a wound, one I have left too long to fester. 'I loved you, Medea. I loved you more than I have ever loved anyone. But you kept giving me reasons to *hate* you, you kept forcing me away and I just . . .' Medea watches me as I shake my head, the words tangling inside me. A sob rips through my chest. 'Do you know how *exhausting* it is, hating someone you love? It is like a poison, and I am so *tired of it*. I cannot do it any more. I do not want to, even if I know I should.'

Without thinking, I reach out and clasp Medea's hand. She flinches from my touch, her face hardening. Around us, I feel her power sharpen like a blade.

'I do not want your forgiveness,' Medea says, her voice lethally quiet.

I try to ignore that frightening swell of her power as I say, 'I am not giving it.'

My sister stares down at our hands, her entire body tensing as if every inch of her were focusing on that tiny point of human contact.

'Then what are you doing?' she asks, voice faint.

'I am just . . . being here.'

Medea's expression remains unreadable, but her *eyes* . . . They are like lightning striking across a midnight sea, darkness and light crashing together with devastating power.

I squeeze her hand and, for a moment, I think Medea is going to squeeze back. I feel my chest swelling in anticipation, so eager to feel Medea reach across that void between us, to see a glimpse of the sister I lost long ago, to sense the goodness I pray still lingers within her. The goodness I am desperate to hold on to so I can justify all this painful, confusing love I still feel for her.

But all Medea says is, 'You are too late.'

There is no accusation in her tone, no bitterness or even sadness. It is just a statement of fact. She then gently pulls her hand away, turning her attention back to where Medus plays happily.

As I watch Medea, I can feel her drifting further and further away, being ripped from my grasp by the storm that rages inside her, the one she has weathered alone for so long. That storm that the entire world left Medea to drown within. Even when she was screaming for help, nobody reached out a hand. They just threw her to those monsters that fed off her struggles, dragging her down deeper into her torment.

I cannot imagine what that must have been like, nor do I want to . . . to envision being in a place so dark one would turn to such unthinkable violence. It does not excuse what Medea has done; I know nothing could ever do that. And perhaps, for this reason, I should walk away, should finally sever those cords. Perhaps a wiser person would, a better person . . .

But then I remember those bruises on Medea's body, when she took all those beatings so I would not have to. She accepted our father's cruelty so I might be shielded from it, breaking herself so I might remain whole . . . and I let her. Does that not make me partly to blame?

I cannot walk away from her again.

I will not.

As I gaze at my sister now, I vow to keep holding out my hand within that storm. Perhaps Medea does not deserve forgiveness, but she deserves this at least . . . to have one person who will not turn away, who will not give up on her.

I will keep reaching out my hand because I know that no one else ever did, ever dared. And perhaps Medea is right, perhaps I am too late . . . but I will still try.

And I will continue to believe, to hope, that one day my sister might reach back.

Acknowledgements

Ever since I first read Euripides' *Medea* in school, I have been completely captivated by the fascinating, formidable Witch of Colchis. If I could go back to that moment and tell that awkward, frizzy-haired schoolgirl that she would one day be retelling her own version of Medea's myth, I think her first question would have been *'how did you manage that!?'* The answer, I would tell her, is with the support of all the incredible people I am fortunate enough to have around me.

I want to firstly thank Jemima for making all this possible and for being my ultimate dream agent. From our very first email exchange you have been nothing short of fantastic, bringing boundless enthusiasm and passion, as well as your unwavering support and guidance throughout this incredible journey. Thank you for taking a chance on me and for believing in this story and helping bring the best out of it. I feel so very lucky to have you fighting in my corner. Thanks also to everyone at David Higham Associates for all their dedicated work behind the scenes. It is a true honour to be represented by such a brilliant agency.

Thank you to my editor, Lara. As soon as we met, I knew our visions for *Medea* were perfectly aligned and that you loved her character for all the same reasons as I did, flaws and all. I am deeply grateful for your diligent efforts in shaping this book and strengthening Medea's voice. Your meticulous attention to detail and insightful

421

suggestions have been truly invaluable, and I am so incredibly proud of what we've achieved together. Additionally, I want to say a huge thank you to the whole team at Transworld – words cannot describe how proud I am to have my book championed by such a talented, passionate and hard-working group of people.

Thank you to my US editor, MJ, for your continued support and infectious enthusiasm. I am honoured that *Medea* has found her US home with you and the inspiring team at Sourcebooks, and I feel truly empowered to be working with the country's largest women-owned publisher.

Thank you to my friend, Jess, for being the superbly sinister voice of my sirens! How would I have lured men to their death without your incredible poetic talents? As well as your skill with words, thank you also for being an excellent listener. It seems like only last week we were rambling around London whilst I nattered on and on about all my hopes and dreams and ideas. I hope everyone is lucky enough to have a friend as supportive as you.

To my sister, Holly, thank you for teaching me what it means to be a strong woman in every sense of the word. I'm so lucky to have grown up with a big sister like you to look up to and cheer me on. You have always set the bar so high (yet so humbly), inspiring me to push myself further year after year. Also, I will never stop thanking you for telling me to study Classics! Somehow you just knew I would fall in love with the subject and, as usual, you were a hundred per cent right.

Thank you to my wonderful husband, Peter, the first person to read this book and my most brutally honest critic (I mean that in the best way possible). When I told you I wanted to take this giant, scary leap and quit my career to focus on my dream, you never once doubted my decision, but instead took my hand and proudly leapt with me. I am forever grateful I get to share my life with someone who believes in me so completely and who will keep pushing me to dream bigger and aim higher. I love you, always.

Thank you to my parents, Gilly and Simon, to whom I owe everything. There have been many highs and lows throughout this journey, and you have both been there for every single one of them, always just a phone call away whenever I needed you. I truly mean it when I say none of this would have been possible without your endless love, encouragement and support. If I were to list all the reasons I am grateful to you both, we would need a whole extra book! So, I will keep it simple and just say this – thank you for not only believing in me, but for teaching me how to always believe in myself. You are the best parents anyone could ever ask for.

To all the amazing women in my life whom I have the honour of calling my friends and family, thank you for continuing to enrich and inspire me. There's a piece of you in every strong woman I write.

Finally, to my readers, those who have been here since my very first, frightening steps into the world of publishing with my novel *Medusa*, those who've joined us along the way, and all the new readers whom I've yet to meet – thank you, thank you, thank you. By holding this book in your hands and reading these words, you are breathing life into a dream and helping shape it into a reality. I am so grateful for the lovely community I have found through my writing and the amazing support that has come with it. I hope I can continue telling you stories for many, many years to come.

About the Author

Having secured a first-class honours degree in Classical Literature and Civilisation at the University of Birmingham, Rosie Hewlett has studied Greek mythology in depth and is passionate about unearthing strong female voices within the classical world.

Her self-published debut novel, *Medusa*, won the Rubery Book of the Year award in 2021.

rosiehewlett.author
rosie_hewlett